100 Reasons to Celebrate

We invite you to join us in celebrating Mills & Boon's centenary. Gerald Mills and Charles Boon founded Mills & Boon Limited in 1908 and opened offices in London's Covent Garden. Since then, Mills & Boon has become a hallmark for romantic fiction, recognised around the world.

We're proud of our 100 years of publishing excellence, which wouldn't have been achieved without the loyalty and enthusiasm of our authors and readers.

Thank you!

Each month throughout the year there will be something new and exciting to mark the centenary, so watch for your favourite authors, captivating new stories, special limited edition collections...and more!

Christmas really was magic.

Imogen had seen it in her training when she'd worked a shift on the children's ward—seen how, no matter how dire, everyone pulled together and made the impossible work on that day. She had seen it in her own family a few short years ago, and she was seeing it now with his.

Angus, with only an hour's sleep to his name, was trying to work out what parcel Santa had left for whom—because he'd been sure when he'd wrapped them that he'd remember! He was smiling and holding it together, and just doing his very best for the two little people who mattered most.

Imogen was blinking at her rather big pile of presents. A big pile she truly hadn't been expecting.

'From me,' Angus said gruffly, as she pulled back the wrapper on a vast silk bedspread. 'I figured if I can't be with you…'

And it was so nice…too nice. And a whole world away from the time when she'd have to cuddle up to this instead of him.

Imogen crumpled. And she truly didn't know if she was crying because she'd miss him, or crying because right now she missed her little boy, or crying because one time in her life she had had the *crème de la crème* of *everything* lined up and at her service, raring to go, she was in absolutely no position to take what was on offer.

ONE MAGICAL CHRISTMAS

AND

EMERGENCY AT BAYSIDE

Carol Marinelli

MILLS & BOON®
Pure reading pleasure™

First published in Great Britain 2008
Harlequin Mills & Boon Limited,
Eton House, 18-24 Paradise Road, Richmond, Surrey TW9 1SR

ISBN: 978 0 263 86364 2

Set in Times Roman 10½ on 13½ pt.
03-1208-89626

Printed and bound in Spain
by Litografia Rosés S.A., Barcelona

CONTENTS

For Bob and Glynn

Love you lots

xxx

ONE MAGICAL CHRISTMAS

CHAPTER ONE

'HI THERE! I'm Imogen.'

Accident and Emergency Consultant Angus Maitlin looked up from orders he was hastily writing as, wearing a smile and not a trace of unease, the woman walked towards him.

'Sorry?' Handing his orders to his intern, Angus frowned at the unfamiliar face.

'Heather said I should come introduce myself to you,' she patiently explained, and Angus picked out an Australian accent. 'I've been sent down from Maternity to help with the emergency you're expecting in…'

She watched him glance at her ID badge.

'You're a midwife?'

'And an RN.' Imogen added, without elaborating. Something told her that this good-looking package of testosterone really wasn't in the mood to listen!

'Have you worked here before?' His hands gestured to the frantic Resuscitation area. The five beds were full and one was being cleared for a burn victim trapped in a car on a busy London motorway. 'Do you know the layout?'

'Not yet,' she said, looking around her. 'I've only been in the country two days. Still, I'm sure—'

She didn't have a chance to finish so she just stood there as he stalked off, no doubt to complain to the nursing unit manager. Well, let him complain, Imogen thought—she didn't want to be here and he clearly didn't want her here either! With a bit of luck she'd be sent back to Maternity.

'Heather!' Angus barked, not yet out of Imogen's earshot. 'When I said that I urgently needed more help in Resus I didn't mean you to send in a midwife!'

Angus rarely lost his temper but he was close to it now. The department was full, Resus was full, and his request for more staff had been met by this rather large, grinning woman in a white agency nurse's uniform who had only just set foot in the country!

'I'll come and help if need be,' Heather responded calmly. 'But the nursing co-ordinator did tell me that not only is Imogen a midwife, she's also advanced emergency and ICU trained. Though,' she added sweetly, 'I do have a grad nurse in the observation ward. I can swap her over if you think that would be more—'

'I'll manage,' Angus cut it in curtly, and then changed his mind, closing his eyes for a second and running a hand through his dark blond hair. 'I'm sorry, Heather—I didn't think to ask about her qualifications. It's just when she said that she'd only just arrived here…'

He glanced over to where Imogen stood where he'd rudely left her, and gave a small wince of apology. He expected to receive a rather pained, martyred look back—it would have been what he deserved—only, clearly amused, she merely shrugged and smiled. The strangest thing of all was, given the morning he was having, Angus actually found himself smiling back.

'I'm sure people suffer from burns in Australia!' Heather's sarcasm soon wiped it from his face, though.

'I get it, OK?' He reached for his water bottle at the nurses' station and took a long drink. The patient they were expecting was still being extricated from the car and there was plenty he could be doing in that time, but from the brief description of the horrific injuries that would soon present, Angus guessed a minute to centre himself was probably going to be time well spent.

'Is everything OK, Angus?' Heather Barker also had plenty she could be getting on with but, used to priorities shifting quickly in this busy London accident and emergency department, she took a moment to deal with the latest category one to present. Angus Maitlin, the usually completely together consultant, the utter lynchpin of the department, seemed for once to not be faring so well.

Not that he said it.

Not that he ever said it.

Impossibly busy, he was usually infinitely calm and dependable. Not only did Angus help run the accident and emergency department, he was also married to a successful model, a proud father to two young children *and* had, in the past few years, become something of a TV celebrity. Angus had been asked, by the local television station, to give his medical opinion on post-traumatic stress syndrome. His deep, serious voice, his undeniable good looks, combined with just the right dash of humour, had proved an instant hit, and the cameras, along with the audience, had adored him. Which meant he had been asked back again, and now Angus Maitlin was regularly called on to deliver his particular brand of medicine on a current affairs show. Yet somehow his celebrity status hadn't changed him a jot—Angus still had his priorities well in place—his family first, the emergency department a very close second, or, when the situation demanded, Emergency first, family second, and then, somehow, everything else got slotted in.

Just not today.

Not for the past couple of months, actually.

'Angus?' When he ignored her question Heather rephrased it. 'Is there a problem?'

'Of course not.'

'Anything that you might want to talk about?'

'I'm fine.'

Sitting on a stool, muscular, yet long limbed and elegant, his thick fringe flopping over jade eyes, his immaculately cut suit straining just a touch to contain wide shoulders as he drank some water, Angus Maitlin looked better than fine—the absolute picture of relaxed health, in fact—only everyone in the department knew better.

'It's not like you to snap at the nurses.'

'I'll apologise to Imogen. I really am fine, things are just busy.'

'It's not just Imogen…' He could tell Heather was uncomfortable with this discussion and he was too. 'I've had a couple of grumbles from staff recently. And we always are busy—especially at this time of year.'

They were. It was a week before Christmas and London was alive. The streets were filled with panicked shoppers, parties, cold weather, ice, families travelling, people meeting. Combine all that with alcohol in abundance and December was always going to be a busy time—only it had never usually fazed him.

'What's going on, Angus?' Heather pushed. 'You just haven't been yourself lately. Look, I know it's not a great time to talk now, but once we get the place settled…or we can catch up for coffee after the shift…'

'Really, I'm fine.' Angus said firmly. Heather was the last person he wanted privy to his problems. Oh, she meant well and everything, but some things were just… private. 'I hate burns, and this one sounds bad.' He gave her a tight smile, picked up the phone when it trilled and spoke to Ambulance Control. Then took another quick drink of water and stood up from his stool. 'They've just got the victim out of the car—ETA twelve minutes…'

For someone who hadn't been shown around, Imogen *had* done a great job of setting up. Burn packs were opened on a trolley, sterile drapes were waiting, and despite his rather abrupt walk out earlier she gave him a roll-of-the-eye smile as Angus returned.

'Couldn't get rid of me, then?'

'Believe me, I tried!' Angus joked, surprisingly refreshed by her humour.

'Given that we're going to be spending the next few

hours together, I'd better introduce myself properly—I'm Imogen Lake.'

'Angus…' he offered back, 'Angus Maitlin—I'm one of the consultants here. Look, I'm sorry if I was curt with you earlier.'

'That's OK.'

'No, it's not…' He was washing his hands, but he looked over at her as he spoke. 'I completely jumped the gun—when you said that you'd been pulled from the maternity ward, that you were a midwife, I thought the nursing co-ordinator had messed up.'

'They often do!' She was smiling even more readily now—his rather snooty English accent along with his genuine apology making it very easy to do so.

'You weren't in the middle of a delivery or anything?' Angus asked, wincing just a touch as she nodded.

'And I was enjoying it too.' Imogen added, just to make him feel worse. 'So what do we know about the patient?'

'The victim coming in was the driver of a motor vehicle heading onto the M25.' Angus told her the little he could. 'According to Ambulance Control, the car lost control at the junction, hit the sign and exploded on impact, a fire truck witnessed the whole thing and the crew were straight onto it, putting out the fire as quickly as they could…'

'Is the patient male or female?' Imogen asked.

'We don't know yet.'

'OK.' It was her only response to the grim answer—that the victim's gender hadn't been immediately identified was just another indication of the direness of the situation.

Imogen truly didn't want to be here.

She had spent the last hour in a darkened delivery room, coaching Jamila Kapur through the final first stages of labour and into the second stage. Jamila had just been ready to start pushing when Imogen had been called to the phone.

When the nurse co-ordinator had rung and asked if she'd help out in Emergency, Imogen had immediately said no and not just because she didn't want to go down there. Continuity of care with labouring mums was important to Imogen, and just as she wouldn't have walked out on Mrs Kapur if she had been at that stage of labour when her shift ended, in the same way she hadn't wanted to walk out on her then.

Then the co-ordinator had rung again, reading off her qualifications as if Imogen mightn't be aware that she had them! Telling her that her skills would be better deployed in Emergency and that was where they were sending her.

Her first shift, in a different hospital, in a different country and an agency nurse to boot, she really wasn't in any position to argue.

Imogen felt as if she'd been pulled from the womb herself—hauled from where she had been comfortable and happy then plunged into the bright lights of the busy department, to be greeted by unfamiliar faces, chaos and noise. But—as Imogen always did—she just took a deep breath and decided to get on with it.

It wasn't the patient's fault that she didn't want to be here!

'Where are the gowns?' She answered her own question, pulling two packs down from the rack on the wall. She handed one to Angus before putting on her own, her ample figure disappearing under a mass of shapeless paper, and Angus felt more than a pang of guilt at complaining about her earlier. She seemed completely undaunted by what was coming in, and by all accounts it would be horrific, yet from the organised way she'd set up for the patient, from the qualifications he now knew she had, her unruffled manner wasn't because of ignorance—she was clearly a very experienced nurse.

'The anaesthetist should be here.' Angus glanced at his watch. 'You paged him?'

'Twice.'

On cue he arrived and Imogen handed him a gown too as Angus gave the information they had.

Her fine red hair was already scraped neatly back in a ponytail, but she popped on a paper hat, as Angus did the same, to maintain a sterile field as far as possible and minimise the risk of infection.

The wait was interminable and Angus glanced at his watch, the delay in arrival possibly meaning that the patient had died en route. 'What the hell's keeping—?' His voice stopped abruptly, the short blast of the siren warning of the imminent arrival.

Even though it was still only nine a.m. the sky was so heavy with rain it was practically dark outside. The blue light of the ambulance flashed through the high windows, and Angus gave Imogen a grim smile as they waited those few seconds more. This time, however, her freckled face didn't return it, blonde eyelashes blinking on pale blue eyes as instead she took in a deep breath then let it out as the paramedics' footsteps got louder as they sped their patient towards Resus.

'I hate burns!' Imogen said, catching Angus still looking at her.

It was the only indication, Angus realised, that she was actually nervous.

CHAPTER TWO

IT WAS organised chaos.

The type where everyone worked to save a life—and not just in the emergency department but in so many unseen areas of the hospital. Porters running with vital samples up to Pathology, who in turn raced to give baseline bloods and do an urgent cross-match—as the radiographer came quickly around to take an urgent portable chest film.

The patient's name was Maria. That was all the information they had so far. Her bag carrying all the details that would have identified her had been lost in the furnace of the car. But in a brief moment of consciousness as they had extricated her from the car she had given her name.

The paramedics were dripping wet—a combination of rain, sweat and the dousing of the car, and smelt of petrol and smoke. Their faces were black with soot and dust from the fire. Two of the firefighters were being triaged outside, one with minor burns and one with smoke inhalation.

By every eye-witness account that had been given, Maria should have been dead.

'Core temperature?' Angus snapped as he viewed the young woman in front of him.

'Thirty-four point eight,' Imogen responded.

And it seemed bizarre that someone who had been severely burnt might be suffering from hypothermia, but the dousing, the exposure, the injuries just compounded everything. The thermostat in Resus was turned up, the staff dripping with sweat in the stifling warmth as the patient's burnt body shivered.

'She put up her hands…' Angus was swiftly examining her, and the little bit of hope that had flared in Imogen as they'd wheeled her in was quashed. The beautiful face that she'd first glimpsed was, apart from the palms of her hands and some area on her forearms and buttocks, the only area of her body that wasn't severely burnt.

'TBSA, greater than 85 per cent.' Angus called, and Imogen wrote it down. The total body surface area that had suffered burns was horrific and for now intense Resuscitation would continue. Maria would be treated as any trauma victim, airway, breathing and circulation the first priority, and they would be assessed and controlled before a more comprehensive examination would occur, but things didn't look good. Even though the depth of the burns still needed to be assessed, with every observation, with every revelation the outcome for Maria was becoming more and more dire.

'There was one more victim at the scene—deceased,' the paramedic added quietly. 'No ID.'

'They were in the car together?' Angus checked. 'Is the deceased male or female?' The paramedic gave a tight shake of his head. 'We don't know at this stage. Adult,' he added, which couldn't really be described as consolation, but when the paramedic spoke next, Angus conceded, it was perhaps a small one. 'The child car seat in the rear of the vehicle was empty.'

There were many reasons that no one liked burns—the rapidity, the severity and the potential for appalling injuries, the sheer devastation to the victim's life, the long road ahead, both physically and mentally if they made it through. It took a very special breed of staff indeed to work on a burns unit, and most emergency staff were grateful that they only dealt with this type of injury relatively occasionally and for a short time only.

The golden hour—the hour most critical in determining the outcome for the patient—was utilised to the full for Maria. Despite her appalling injuries, as the fluids were poured in and oxygen delivered, she began to moan.

From the firefighters' accounts and the police officers' initial assessment, the skid marks on the road indicated Maria had struggled desperately to regain control of the car. When it had crashed the nature of her injuries suggested that she had put up her hands instinctively to shield her face, and in doing so she had protected her airway too. Still, she was being closely monitored by the anaesthetist, delivering high-concentration humidified oxygen as well as generous amounts of morphine, ready to intubate earlier rather than later if her airway declined. The paramedics had managed to insert one IV at the scene, but it was insufficient for the volume of fluids required and further access proved impossible. Instead, Angus delivered the vital fluids she desperately needed via intra-osseous infusion. This was a quick procedure, which needed strength to execute and involved puncturing the bone and delivering the fluids straight into the bone marrow. As Angus did that, Imogen, with great difficulty, inserted a catheter, and watched with mounting unease as Maria's urine output dropped down to zero.

'Can we roll her again?' Angus ordered, and with Heather's help Imogen gently held Maria on her side as Angus, assisted now by a fellow emergency consultant, examined her.

'It's OK, Maria…' Through it all Imogen spoke to her patient, focussing on her face, actually trying not to look at anything else. 'The doctors are just taking a look at you.'

As Maria groaned, Angus nodded and gestured impatiently, telling them they could roll her back. This time neither Heather nor Imogen took any offence at his brusque manner.

'Can I leave you for five minutes?' Heather pulled off her gloves and cursed the ringing phone on the wall and the doctor calling her from the other side of the curtain. 'Press the emergency bell if you need anything at all.'

Now that the patient was relatively more stable, another RN was floating between two patients and assisting where she could, but, for the most part, Imogen was nursing Maria one on one.

Angus now confirmed that most of the burns were full thickness—the most severe kind. It took everything Imogen had to deliver a smile as for the first time and just for a second Maria's eyes briefly opened.

Imogen lowered her head nearer to the patient's. 'It's OK, Maria, you're in hospital, we're looking after you.' It was all she got to say before Maria's eyes closed again.

He'd apologise to Imogen again.

Talking on the telephone to a burns specialist at another major London hospital, and taking a quick swig of water as he did so, Angus looked over and saw Imogen pause for a second to lower her head and talk to the unconscious patient again. She'd done this every couple of minutes or so since Maria had arrived in the department and Angus knew it would be helping as much as the morphine if Maria could hear her.

Angus was proud of the team he had helped build at this hospital, considered them absolutely the best, and yet there was no one who could have done better than Imogen had this morning. Through it all she had been quietly efficient. Everything he had needed had been handed to him and not once had she flinched in assisting Angus in a procedure so vile that even an intern, who had asked to observe had at one point had to walk out.

A vile procedure in a vile, vile morning.

When the burns consultant, Declan Jones, arrived Angus ushered him over to the far wall to discuss the patient privately in greater depth. The stench in the warm room matched the loathsome diagnosis that Angus was just so reluctant to come to.

'I respect your opinion, Declan…' As Imogen walked over to the huddle she could hear the restraint in his voice. 'More than respect it—you know that …'

'She's talking,' Imogen said.

'Is she orientated?' Angus asked, swallowing down a sudden wave of bile.

'Fully. She's Italian, but her English is very good, though she has a strong accent. She's struggling obviously, but she's conscious now. She's confirmed that her surname is Vanaldi. Her husband Rico was the passenger in the car.' He watched those blonde eyelashes blink a couple of times before she continued. 'She has a son called Guido, he's fifteen months old and at day care…'

Till this point information had trickled in in dribs and drabs. The police had managed to ID the vehicle and registration, which had given them an address. They had then been and spoken with neighbours and were now on their way to the day-care centre her child was attending.

'That matches what the police said,' Angus nodded. 'Are there any other relatives we can call?'

'She said not.'

'There must be someone!' Angus insisted, because there just had to be. Maria was a young woman, for goodness' sake, with a child, and she'd just lost her husband. She couldn't be expected to face this alone. 'She needs someone with her.'

'I'll ask her again.'

'Is there any urine output yet?' Angus called as she walked off, his jaw clenching closed when she shook her head.

'Still zero.'

Usually it was good news that the patient was talking. For a patient so ill to now be alert and orientated, in practically every other scenario it would be reason to cheer, but not today.

Maria Vanaldi had awoken probably to be told that she would inevitably die—her calamitous injuries simply incompatible with life.

And it was Angus who would have to be the one to tell her.

'Is there anyone else I can discuss this with?' It was always exquisitely difficult, questioning a colleague, one who actually specialised in the field and whose expertise Angus had called on, but etiquette couldn't really come into it and Declan understood that.

'I'll give you some names.' He let out a sigh. 'Though I've already called two of them. I'm sorry, Angus.'

'There's an older brother,' Imogen stated as a policeman came over, clearly just as drained from it all as the rest of them, and his news wasn't any more cheering.

'We've contacted the day-care centre, they're open till six tonight. The husband's the only other point of contact on their forms.'

'Bring the child to Emergency,' Angus interrupted. 'She'll want to see him and hopefully we'll have some relatives arriving soon.' He turned to Imogen. 'You say that she's got a brother?'

'He's her only relative.' Imogen gave a troubled nod. 'But he's in Italy and Maria doesn't know his phone number. She says it's on her mobile, which is in the car…'

'Can I talk to her?' the police officer asked. 'We can enter the house and go through her phone book or whatever to try and locate the contact number for him, but it would make it quicker if she could tell us where to look.'

Angus shook his head. 'I'll talk to her.'

He approached the bed and smiled into two petrified eyes. 'Hi, Maria, I'm Angus, I'm the doctor looking after you.'

'Guido!'

'Your son?' Angus said. 'He's being taken care of.'

'He's at day care.' In the few minutes since he'd left her side, Maria's degree of consciousness had improved, but even generous amounts of morphine couldn't dim her anguish as adrenaline kicked in and her mind raced to recapture her world. 'He will not know! They will not know…'

'We know where he is,' Angus said gently. 'The police have contacted the day-care centre and are bringing him in here. You'll be able to see him soon.'

'He's not well…' She was choking on her tears, each word a supreme effort. 'He has a cold—I should have kept him at home…'

If only she had, Imogen thought, then checked herself. It was a futile exercise, one patients went through over and over when they or their loved ones landed in Emergency. The recriminations and the reprimands, going over and over the endless, meaningless decisions that had brought them to that point and wishing different choices had been made. As Angus caught her eye for a moment, she knew he was going through it too—if only. If only she had left him at home, or left later, or earlier, or stopped for a chat, or not stopped…

It truly was pointless.

'You couldn't have known,' he said firmly. 'You couldn't have foreseen this. This was not your fault.'

'I wasn't speeding…' And Imogen watched as Maria thought things through. 'Rico?' Her eyes fled from Angus's to Imogen. 'How is Rico?'

'Who's Rico?'

'My husband.'

'Was he in the car with you?' Angus checked, because he had to.

'How is he?'

And then came the difficult bit, where he had to tell this young woman that there had been another fatality in the car. It was hard when the identity hadn't been confirmed, hard because there was absolutely no point in giving her false hope, and he delivered the brutal news as gently as he could, watching as her shocked, muddled brain attempted to decipher it then chose not to accept it.

'No.' Her denial was followed swiftly by anger, her Italian accent more pronounced, her eyes accusing. 'You've got it wrong. It might not be him.'

'Someone needs to be here for you.' Angus said, choosing not to push it. 'Imogen said you have a brother in Italy. Are there any family or friends closer?'

'Only Elijah.'

'What about Rico's family?'

'No!'

'OK.' She was getting distressed, alarms bleeping

everywhere, and he hadn't even told her the hardest part. 'The police are near your house, they can break in and get your brother's phone number. Do you know where it would be?'

'No…' She closed her eyes, swallowed really hard and then gave an answer that only a woman could understand. 'By the phone—but it's a mess.'

'Is it in a phone book?'

'The place is a mess.' Angus frowned just a fraction. People's bizarre responses never ceased to amaze him. Here she was lying in the Resuscitation bay, her husband was dead and she was worried that the house was a mess.

'You should see my place,' Imogen said as she watched Angus's expression, her calm voice reassuring the woman. 'I can promise you that they've seen worse. In fact, I can promise you that they won't even notice the mess. They won't even bat an eyelid.'

It had taken him a moment to get it, but he realised then that it was easier for Maria to focus on the pointless for a moment.

'It's a mess…' The morphine was taking over now, or maybe Maria just didn't care any more as she closed her eyes.

Despite the closed eyes, still Imogen chatted easily to her and Angus could see they had already built up a rapport, which Maria was going to need. 'Just tell me where the number is—his name's Elijah. What's his surname?'

'My surname…' Maria answered.

'Have you got a lot of pain still?' Imogen checked, turning up the morphine pump as soon as Maria nodded wearily. 'We'll keep turning it up till we get on top of it.'

Sometimes, Angus thought to himself, you had to face up to facts. As he desperately did the rounds on the telephone, calling as many people as he knew to ask for a second opinion or for some objective advice, Angus realised that, despite extenuating circumstances, despite supreme effort, despite so much potential and no matter how much he didn't want it to be so, Maria's life would soon fail.

'Her lactate levels alone will kill her.' Imogen met him at the soft-drink machine in the corridor. Heather had taken over for five minutes, giving Imogen a chance to dash to the loo and to get a quick drink. 'You haven't got any change for the machine?' he asked as he ran his hand through his hair.

Imogen emptied her pockets, handing over some coins, and he popped them into the machine, too distracted to ask what she wanted and she too distracted to care. He punched in the same number twice and they gulped icy, fizzy, sweet orange which proved a great choice, sitting in a relatives' interview room for a couple of minutes, before heading back into hell.

'Would you want to know?' Angus looked over to Imogen. 'I want to give her hope—I mean, we'll follow the burns protocol, she'll go up to ICU, but…'

'They moved here from Italy two years ago apparently.' Imogen didn't immediately answer his question. 'The neighbours told the police that they kept themselves pretty much to themselves. They found the brother's number too…' Her voice trailed off as she thought about it, really thought about it, and Angus waited. 'Yes,' she said after the longest time. 'I'd want to know, I'd want to use whatever time I had to make arrangements for my son.'

'Me, too.' He rubbed his hand over his forehead and Imogen could see his agony, could see the compassion behind the rather brusque facade, and knew that this was tearing him up too.

'A little bit of hope is OK, though,' she added.

'There's going to be no Christmas miracle here.'

'I know.' Imogen nodded. 'But Maria's not me and she's not you and if she doesn't want to know…'

'I'll play it by ear.' He stood up, turned to go and then paused. 'Thanks, by the way.' They both knew he wasn't thanking her for the drink. 'I'll go and ring the brother,' Angus said, grateful that she didn't wish him luck, grateful that she just nodded. 'God, I hope he speaks English.'

'I'll send someone to get you if there's anything urgent.'

'Thanks.'

Ringing relatives was never easy and Elijah Vanaldi proved more difficult than most. Hanging up the phone, Angus dragged his hand through his thick mop of hair and held onto it, resting his head in his hand for the longest time, trying to summon the strength to face the *most* difficult part of this vile day: to tell the beautiful, vibrant woman herself that her life would soon be over—that not only had her son lost his father but that, in a matter of, at best, hours, he would lose his mother too.

He flicked off the do-not-disturb light and almost instantaneously someone knocked at the door to his office. Imogen's face was grim as she stepped into the unfamiliar terrain and Angus wondered whether or not it would even be necessary to tell Maria now.

'She knows…' Swallowing hard, Imogen's pale blue eyes met his. 'She knows that she's dying.'

'You told her?' Angus barked, his voice gruff. It was *his* job to do that, and as much as he was dreading it he wanted to ensure that it was done right, but as Imogen shook her head, he regretted his harsh tone.

'Of course I didn't tell her—I'm not a complete idiot!'

And just because they were both snapping and snarling, they knew that there was no need for either of them to say sorry. In the short but painfully long time they'd worked together, they'd already built up a rapport.

'Maria worked it out for herself,' Imogen explained, and he watched as she chewed nervously on her bottom lip for a moment before continuing. 'She said "I'm going to die, aren't I?" And I didn't tell her she was wrong, I simply told her that I'd come and get you to talk to her. I'm just letting you know that she's already pretty much aware…'

'Thank you for telling me.' He gave a weary smile. 'You've been amazing this morning.'

'Not bad for a foreigner?' Imogen gave her own weary smile back, just letting him know that she'd heard all of his earlier complaint to Heather.

'Yes, not bad.' Angus smiled. 'I guess we might have to keep you.'

'How was the brother?' Imogen asked, and neither smiled now.

'Brusque, disbelieving, angry...take your pick. He's on his way.'

'That's good...' Imogen found herself frowning, and couldn't quite work out why. Angus Maitlin had every right to look grim. As gruelling as Emergency was at times, this morning took the cake. Yet she could see the purple stains of insomnia under his eyes, the swallow of nervousness over his perfect Windsor knot, remembered the short fuse he had greeted her with, and knew there had to be more, knew, because she'd been there herself. 'Gus could talk to her...'

'Gus?'

'The other consultant.'

'I know who Gus is,' Angus snapped. 'Don't worry, I can be nice when I remember. Look...' He stopped himself then and forced a half-smile. 'It's just with it being Christmas and everything, my wife's the same age...'

'I know.' Imogen nodded her understanding, but a smudge of a frown remained, not for her patient but for him.

'Come on.' Angus stood up. 'Let's get this over with.'

As they reached the nurses' station, quietly discussing the best way to go about it, Angus became aware that Imogen had more insight into Maria's personality than he did and absorbed her words carefully.

'She's going to be terrified for her little boy, for Guido and his future. I guess the main thing I'd want to hear is that—'

'Angus.' Heather's interruption halted Imogen's train of thought. 'Gemma's on the phone for you.'

'Tell her I'll call her back.'

'She says that it's urgent.'

'It always is with Gemma,' Angus snapped, and Imogen knew that he just wanted to get the unpleasant task of speaking with Maria over with. 'Tell her I'll ring her back when I can.'

'She says that it's to do with the kids.'

'What's the problem, Gemma?'

Imogen frowned as with a hiss of irritation Angus took the telephone. Of course Angus was busy, and of course he didn't want interruptions, but if it had been Brad ringing to say there was something urgent going on with Heath, Imogen would have been tripping over her feet to get to the phone—no matter how busy she was at work.

'What do you mean—you sacked Ainslie?'

Imogen's glance caught Heather's, and they both shared a slightly wide-eyed look.

'The nanny!' Heather mouthed for Imogen's benefit.

'Oh!'

'The morning I'm having and you ring to tell me you've sacked the nanny. I couldn't give a damn if you've got a photo shoot tomorrow, Gemma.' Pinching the bridge of his nose with his finger and thumb, Angus closed his eyes. 'Frankly, I couldn't have cared less if Ainslie *was* stealing the odd thing—she was the best thing to happen to the kids and to get rid of her one week before Christmas…' He went to hang up then changed his mind. 'No, Gemma, you sort it out for once!'

He aimed the receiver in the general direction of the phone but missed spectacularly, then as he strode towards the Resuscitation area he stopped, dragged in a huge breath and leant against the wall for a moment. Imogen was glad he did, glad he took a moment to compose himself before he went in to see Maria—she deserved calm and his full attention.

'Sorry about that.'

'No problem.' Imogen smiled, because it wasn't. Oh, she didn't have a nanny, of course, but had Brad rung her with something so trivial, she'd have no doubt put on a similar show herself.

'It's just sometimes…' He stopped himself then, just as she had so many times in another lifetime. And even if she had only just met him, even if they were from opposite sides of the globe and even though he was stunning looking and she was rather, well, plain, Imogen knew that they had one thing in common: both of them had had to work, to function, to keep on keeping on through the rocky part of a failing marriage—even if Angus wasn't ready to admit it.

'Impossible?' she offered, watching his eyes jerk to hers, seeing that flash of surprise that someone might just possibly understand. 'Brad used to ring me all the time with some perceived drama, or I'd be ringing him with one of my own…'

'Brad's your husband?'

'Brad's my ex-husband.'

'Oh!' He pulled away from the wall then, clearly deciding that she didn't understand at all, that the flash of recognition that he'd thought he'd seen actually didn't apply to him in the slightest.

'It isn't actually a *perceived* drama,' he said tartly. 'Gemma was right to ring, she just caught me at a bad time.'

'Sure.'

'Really,' he insisted. 'Gemma and I are fine. It just wasn't the best time to call, that's all.'

'Good.'

He was about to insist again that nothing was wrong, but Imogen decided it wasn't her business anyway, the fleeting moment of connection long since gone. It was time now to get on with the unpleasant task in hand—and it was Imogen who concluded the conversation.

'Let's go and speak with Maria.'

CHAPTER THREE

IMOGEN HAD nursed since the age of eighteen, and now at thirty-two years of age and with most of her experience in either Intensive Care or Emergency, she had seen more than her fair share of tragedy and dealt with many unbearably sad situations. Most stayed with her enough to be recalled when required, some would stay with her for ever—and some, like Maria, would actually change her.

Despite his cool greeting and sometimes brusque demeanour, still Imogen had liked Angus. She had worked in Emergency long enough to form a very rapid opinion, and generally she was spot on.

And now, listening to him confirm Maria's darkest fears, Imogen knew that she was right. Understood even why he wanted to be the one to tell her. Lacing compassion with authority, he led her through the news, tender yet firm he let her find her own route, which was, for Maria, to face the truth. When many others would have left, Angus stayed, reiterating when needed and sometimes just quiet as Maria had to grieve for her own short life too. Yet somehow she rallied, maternal instinct kicking in, knowing that in the little time that remained she had to make plans for her son.

'I have to speak to my brother.' Her blue eyes were urgent. 'I cannot die before I speak with him.'

'He said the same thing,' Angus said gently. 'He's flying in.'

'I need to speak to him about Guido—about what must happen to him.'

'I'll also get Social Services to come and speak to you—' Angus started, but Maria was having none of it.

'I just want Elijah.'

'Do you have a will, a lawyer?' Angus asked, but Maria simply wouldn't go there. Her brother was the only one she would consider talking to, the only person she wanted now apart from her son.

'Your brother's on his way,' Angus said.

'How long does a flight take from Rome to London?' Imogen asked.

'About three hours,' Angus answered, but there was also getting to the airport, booking a flight and realistically they were looking more at five or six hours, and no one was sure Maria had that.

'I think I want to see Guido.' Maria screwed up her eyes with the agony of it. 'But I'm worried that I'll scare him…'

'Your face is fine,' Imogen said softly. 'I'll give it a wash and we'll make sure everything else is covered. I'll turn down all the machines so that they don't alarm him.'

'I won't be able to hold him,' Maria croaked.

'I'll hold him for you,' Imogen said. 'I'll put his face right next to yours and you can feel him and smell him…'

'I don't want to start crying. I don't know if I want him to see me like this.'

'OK,' Imogen soothed. 'You let me know.'

'How's her pain?' Angus checked a little while later. Maria was calmer, lying with her eyes closed but not sleeping as Imogen sat quietly by her side.

'I'm OK.' She opened her eyes to let Angus know she wasn't sleeping. 'Any word from my brother?'

'Not yet.'

'Then I'll wait.'

'Don't try and be brave,' Imogen said. 'We can keep increasing your morphine, make you more comfortable…'

'No more till Elijah is here—I want to be conscious when my brother comes.'

Imogen had long since learnt that people were people, women still women even in the most dire of times—even when they were dying. Friends and just a bit of a smile were always needed. Suddenly Maria was asking for her face to be washed and if she could be tidied up a bit—as she emotionally prepared herself to see her son. A healthy dose of morphine combined with a good measure of denial meant that Maria managed a little chat as Imogen gently tended to her.

'I forgot to bring my make-up.' It took a second to realise that Maria had managed a joke and they shared a smile. 'I am never without it.'

'I've got some lipstick,' Imogen offered, 'if you want to use it.'

'Thank you. You know, I thought I was imagining things when I saw Angus.'

'I thought I was, too, when I came on duty,' Imogen grinned, glad to be Maria's friend today, glad that for a little while more Maria could be Maria. 'Bloody gorgeous, isn't he?'

'He's on the television, too.' Maria said, her eyes almost crossed as she tried to focus.

'Angus?' Imogen frowned.

'A lot—he's a TV doctor or something.'

'I'll have to remember to set my DVD to record him.' Imogen winked. 'A little memento to take back to Australia. Hey…' Imogen frowned for the first time at her patient. 'How come your eyeliner's still on?'

'It's a tattoo!' Maria coughed as she tried to laugh.

'Wow!' Imogen was genuinely impressed. 'I've always wanted to get my eyelashes dyed—I've just never got around to it.'

'Do it!' Maria said, managing to focus her eyes on Imogen. 'Go and do it!'

'I will.'

'Have a proper break.' Heather was insistent. 'I'll go in and stay with her. I want you to go and have a coffee and a sandwich and catch your breath for a little while. You, too!' Heather added to Angus.

There really was no point being a martyr—Imogen had learnt that long ago. Sure, there were times when ten minutes for a quick drink and a sit-down *were* impossible to find, but today Imogen knew that a quick refuel would help not just the doctor and nurse but the patient too. Maria was being reviewed by the anaesthetist now, the team ensuring that everything possible was being done to keep Maria pain free and to respect her wishes to remain conscious for as long as possible until her brother arrived.

Peeling off the dirty gowns and paper hats, it was a relief to be out of them. Imogen was aware she must look a sight, her red hair damp with sweat and stuck to her head. Looking at Angus, there was no doubt that she too had a nice big crease around her forehead where her hat had been, only her uniform, she was sure, wasn't quite as fresh looking as his crisp shirt.

And though she had joked with Maria about it, now that she was alone with him, away from the horrors, for the first time Imogen *really* noticed how gorgeous he was.

His beautifully cut hair had recovered from the cap just a little better than hers, and as she walked behind him to the staffroom she saw how it tapered into his neck, saw the wide set of his shoulders and caught a whiff of his gorgeous scent as he held the door open and they walked inside. He was so tall and broad he actually made Imogen feel slender as she stood beside him and loaded four slices of bread into the toaster and he made two quick coffees. He had nice hands too, Imogen thought, noticing how he stirred sugar into her coffee. But seeing his wedding band glint, she chose not to go there.

Wouldn't do to others what had been done to her—not that a man as divine as Angus Maitlin would even deign her that sort of a glance!

Still, he wasn't just nice to look at, he was a nice guy too, and after the morning they'd so far shared, it was nice to actually *meet* him.

And it felt so-o-o good to sit down.

So good not to be in that room where death was present. So good that, despite the horrors, despite the fact it was the foremost thing on both their minds, for most of their break they chose not to talk about it.

'So you're from Australia?'

'Queensland.' Imogen nodded.

'And you only just got here.'

'I didn't intend to start work quite so quickly. I was supposed to be finding somewhere to stay, but when I checked into the youth hostel there were already four messages from the hospital asking if I could ring them—I'd sent in all my paperwork and references a few weeks ago.'

'So what brings you here?' Angus asked. She didn't look like the regular travellers they got here—young nurses just qualified and ready to party. His eyes narrowed as he tried to guess her age—late twenties, early thirties perhaps. 'You said you've got a son?'

'I do…' He watched as her face brightened. 'Heath. He's here with his dad. Brad's working in London, so I thought I'd come over for Christmas.'

Angus's narrowed eyes were joined by a frown now and he fought quickly to check it. So what if her child lived on the other side of the world with his father? It certainly wasn't his place to judge.

'I was hoping to work just a couple of nights a week to cover the rent in a serviced apartment,' Imogen continued, 'but having seen the prices of temporary rentals that I *can* afford…' Imogen pulled a face. 'Well, let's just say they're not exactly the places I'd want to bring Heath back to! So it looks like I'm going to just have to take him sightseeing when I see him.'

'You're separated from your husband?' Angus checked.

'Divorced.'

'And he's English?'

'He's Australian.' Imogen laughed, enjoying his confusion. 'Brad's just working here.'

'So what does he do for a living? If you don't mind me asking.'

'He's an actor!' Imogen rolled her eyes. 'And not a very good one either—if you don't mind me saying.' Angus's frown was replaced by a grin as she smiled at him.

'Maria said that you're on television too!'

'She recognised me?' He could feel his cheeks redden. It was the one thing in his life that embarrassed him. He took his television appearances seriously, saw it as an excellent means for education, but lately personal questions had been creeping into the show, a sort of thirst for knowledge about him was being created, a celebrity status evolving that, unlike Gemma, he didn't aspire to. 'I have a regular spot on a current affairs show, discussing current medical trends, health issues… It's no big deal.'

'It is to Maria! She thinks you're marvellous!' Imogen winked. 'Says you're quite a hottie.'

'A hottie?' Angus queried then wished he hadn't, working it out before Imogen could answer.

'Cute!' Imogen grinned. 'But, I told her the camera *always* lies, and given I was married to an actor for years. I speak on good authority.' He couldn't quite make her out. She was very calm, laid back even, but she had this dry edge to her humour he liked.

'Anyway...' Angus went to bite into his toast '...I'm going to give it up soon.'

'Had enough?' Imogen said casually, but Angus, though apparently calm, was actually reeling inside! He hadn't told anyone that, had only *just* broached the subject with Gemma. It was just the sort of careless comment that he shouldn't be making. He hadn't even told them at the show, and he moved quickly to right it.

'I'd rather you didn't say anything.'

'About what?' Imogen asked.

'About what I just said.' Angus cleared his throat. 'It wouldn't look good if it got out.'

'I'll say!' Imogen grinned. 'We can't have everybody knowing that the amazing Dr Maitlin doesn't even know what a hottie is!'

In a morning where there should have been none, somehow she'd brought just a touch of laughter, and not just to him, Angus noticed, but to their patient too. Imogen Lake, the only shred of good fortune Maria Vanaldi had had today.

Emergency's gain, Maternity's loss, Angus thought,

thinking back to his obstetric rotation. She'd be great at that too.

'So you're a midwife too?'

'I am.' But suddenly she wasn't quite so forthcoming.

'You're emergency trained, though—clearly!'

'Yes.'

'And Heather said you had ICU qualification,' Angus pushed. 'So which do you prefer?'

'I don't know. I've been doing emergency for years now—since I qualified. I love it and everything, but…' He watched as she shrugged. 'Midwifery never really appealed to me till I had Heath. I've kept my hand in and I generally do a shift a month at the birthing centre at the local maternity hospital back home. I'm thinking of applying for a full-time job there when I get back. Actually…' she gave a tight smile '…I'm thinking about a lot of things.'

'Won't you miss Emergency?'

'That's a bit of a daft question to ask this morning,' she answered, and Angus would have loved to have spoken to her some more, was actually sorry when the quick reprieve was over when she drained her cup and stood. 'Speaking of which, I'd better get back to Maria.'

'I'll be there in a moment.'

'Thank you—' Maria held Imogen's eyes '—for being there today. I'm so glad it was you.'

'I'm glad it was me too…' Imogen answered, and even though today had been one of the worst shifts in memory and she'd have given anything to have missed it, would far rather have been bringing a gorgeous life into the world than helping one come to an end, somehow she was glad she had been there too, because she had helped. Imogen felt safe in the knowledge that she had done her job well—and Maria deserved that today.

She was a good nurse—Imogen knew that—and a good woman too, and today Maria had needed both. As painful as it might be, Imogen was actually glad that she *could* help this woman on her final journey.

'I don't want to die!' Loaded with morphine now, Maria's eyes were like pinpricks as she tried to focus on Imogen.

'I know.' Imogen stroked her cheek.

'I'm not ready.'

'I know.'

She could feel Angus, fiddling with the morphine, checking Maria's NG tube, lifting up the catheter and checking that there was still no output, and Imogen knew somehow that he was there for her. And as Imogen removed her mask, knowing it was pointless now, she felt him in the room as she did the hardest bit of nursing and gave a bit more of herself to her patient.

'I'm scared.'

And she could say I know again, only Imogen knew she had to give more, had to ask her patient for more, and Angus's hand on her shoulder was very gratefully received. The stab of his fingers in her shoulder actually hurt a touch as they dug in, but they were very welcome—that someone was standing silently beside her, supporting her as she tried to support Maria and tie up the loose knots in a life about to be taken too soon.

'What are you most scared of, Maria?' Imogen asked, because until she knew she couldn't possibly understand the most vital bits in Maria's life. 'Tell me and if I can help I will.'

'I'm scared for Guido. I'm scared that Rico's family will get him…' Maria screwed her eyes closed. 'Elijah knows.'

'Your brother?' Imogen checked.

'He knows what they're like. I don't want them raising him.'

'What about your brother?' Imogen asked. 'Can he raise Guido?'

'I don't know…' Maria sobbed. 'I don't know if he can, if he'll want to. He doesn't have children, he's not married… I need to talk to him. He knows how it is…' Maria's eyes pleaded for understanding that Imogen failed for a second to give, but thankfully there was a man behind her who stepped right in.

'Elijah will be here soon.' Still Angus gripped her shoulder as he spoke. 'And I promise you that we will come up with the very best solution we can for your son.'

Elijah rang his sister from the plane, and Imogen held the telephone while Maria spoke to him, but it was too much for Maria, sobbing into the phone despite her brother's attempts to calm her.

'She's getting more distressed…' Imogen took over the call, speaking to the man whose Italian accent was thick and rich. He sounded incredibly together, given the circumstances, but Imogen could hear the pain behind each word. 'She just needs to see you. I know you're doing your best to get here.'

There were no thank yous or goodbyes from either of them, nothing the other could say, both just dealing with it the best that they could.

Maria's condition continued to worsen, so much so that when Elijah rang again to check on his sister and to say that his plane would be landing soon it was becoming ever clearer that he might not get here in time. Angus wearily closed his eyes for a second before he began speaking on the phone. Maria was sobbing in earnest now, scared to see Guido and scared not to, and finally Imogen made the decision for her.

'You need to see your baby.' Imogen said softly. 'I'll go to the ward and get him.'

'Will you stay with me?'

'Of course…' Imogen soothed.

'Not just while I'm with Guido… Till Elijah…'

'Of course,' Imogen said again, because she would.

'Are you OK?' Angus asked as Imogen blew her nose at the nurses' station. She was waiting to be put through to the charge nurse on the children's ward to say that she was coming up to fetch Guido.

'Not really.'

'Do you want me to ask Heather if she can swap nurses? You've been in with Maria for ages, it must be—'

'I don't think Maria needs a fresh face appearing at the moment.'

'If it gets too much…' Angus offered, but she just

rolled her eyes and the conversation was terminated as the charge nurse on the children's ward came to the phone and offered to bring him down herself. But Imogen declined.

'I'll come and get him. I'm going to hold him while he sees her, so it might be better if I introduce myself to him up there on the ward.'

First, though, she went back into Maria to let her know that she'd see Guido very soon then arranged cotton sheets around Maria to hide the worst of her burns.

'How do I look?' Maria managed a brave feeble joke.

'Like his mum,' Imogen said gently. 'He'll cry because of the machinery, not you. Your face is fine.'

Guido didn't cry, just whimpered to get closer to his mum, and Imogen held him carefully, doing her utmost not to cry herself as Maria, aching for contact, pressed her cheek against her son and told him she loved him over and over. Even Angus was glassy-eyed when he came in to check on her, and finally when it was too much for Guido, when his mum wasn't holding him as he wanted, when the pain and emotion were just too much for Maria, Imogen made the horrible decision and took Guido back up to the children's ward, treating Guido as she could only hope someone would treat Heath if the roles had been reversed.

Stepping into the children's ward was like stepping into Santa's grotto—reindeer pulling sleighs lined the walls, snowflakes were sprayed on the windows and a wonderful tree glittered behind barriers at the nurses' station, only they didn't put a smile on Imogen's face.

Dangerously close to tears, irritated by the nurses' chatter at the desk, she told them that she was back and walked to Guido's room. He was too confused to cry now, the police, the hospital, his mum, these strangers all too much. Utterly exhausted and bewildered, Guido almost jumped out of her arms and into the metal hospital cot, clinging to a teddy bear, curling up like a little ball and popping his thumb in his mouth. Imogen quietly stroked his hair as his eyes closed and waited till he was asleep before heading back down to Maria.

As Imogen stepped back into Emergency she was greeted by a Santa Claus being pushed on an ambulance trolley and writhing in pain. 'Strangulated hernia—where do you want him?' the paramedic said, trying his best to sound serious.

'I'll take him.' Heather grinned. 'You're finished now, Imogen.'

Imogen glanced at her watch, surprised to see that it was already nearly one o'clock—the end of her shift. 'What's happening with Maria?'

'She's going up to ICU. They just rang to say they're ready.'

'I'll take her up,' Imogen offered. 'I'll go and get my time sheet. Just sign me off for one.'

'Imogen…' Angus called her as she headed out of the doors with Maria. Security was holding a lift for her, and the porters had sent an extra person along to ensure that the path was clear for a speedy run up to ICU. It really wasn't a ideal time to stop for a chat.

'Thanks for this morning.'

'No problem.'

'No, really, Heather or I should go over it with you. Come back down after ICU—'

'I don't have time.' Imogen shook her head.

'You have to make time.' Angus pushed.

'Really, I'm fine.' Imogen said, gesturing to the porters to get going, and there really wasn't much else Angus could say.

Speeding along the corridor and then handing over the patient to the ICU staff, Imogen sat down beside Maria, not as a nurse this time but as a friend.

At least until Elijah got here.

CHAPTER FOUR

WITH his entire day almost taken up with Maria Vanaldi, by the time his patient was wheeled up to ICU, a lot of things had piled up for Angus.

And not just at work.

Grabbing a coffee, he headed to his office for five minutes to ring Gemma, hoping that whatever the latest crisis was to blow up at home, it had somehow been diverted. 'Hey, Gemma.' He heard the cold silence of her answer, but still tried. 'Sorry about before and taking so long to get back to you—it's been hell here.'

'Well, it's not exactly been a barrel of laughs here!'

'We had this woman in,' Angus attempted. 'She's the same age as you, her husband died, they've got a toddler…' Only he could tell she didn't want to hear it, which made it impossible to share it. Oh, he knew he couldn't take it all home and, yes, it annoyed him too when she droned on and on about her own career, but sometimes he listened, sometimes he tried, and he really needed her to at least try today.

It just wasn't going to happen.

'Can we talk about *your* family for a moment, please, Angus?'

He didn't bother to tell her that he'd been trying to.

Instead he heard, rather sharply, how they were still minus a nanny a week before Christmas and how Gemma *had* to work tomorrow. And if there wasn't already enough to deal with, there was something else gnawing at Angus.

'It just doesn't make any sense. I can't believe that Ainslie would steal.'

'She's got money problems,' Gemma pointed out. 'Ainslie told you about that loan she had with her ex-boyfriend, well, maybe it was starting to catch up…'

'None of that was her fault, though.'

'Angus, whose side are you on here? I caught the nanny stealing—what the hell did you want me to do? Give her a pay rise?'

Frankly, yes! he was tempted to answer, if it avoided all this!

'So where is she now?' Angus asked instead.

'I don't know and I don't care,' Gemma huffed. 'She's hardly our responsibility.'

But to Angus she was.

Ainslie had been with the family for three months now. She had lined up the job with his family from her home in Australia and though at twenty-eight years old she wasn't some naive teenager, he didn't like the idea of her being kicked out onto the street with no money, no reference and just a week before Christmas. She was way too old to be his daughter, but if, heaven forbid,

Clemmie ever loaded up a backpack and headed to the other side of the world, he could only hope that someone, somewhere, would feel equally responsible.

Just as he did now.

And not just for Ainslie.

Imogen was from Australia, had landed here just a day or so before and had walked into a nursing shift from hell. In mid-conversation with his wife, Angus watched the red light on his phone flash, indicating that someone else was trying to get through, then his pager began to beep and the balls that Angus juggled, as he always did, suddenly all paused in mid-air.

Just this tiny pregnant pause as for a second everything just seemed to stand still.

Gemma's voice came as though from somewhere way in the distance as whoever it was on the other line gave up and the red light went off. Angus snapped off his pager before the second shrill and there was just stillness as the only thing on his mind was the woman he had worked with that morning. He could see her so clearly it was as if she was standing in front of him, those pale blue eyes blinking back at him, her freckly, kind face full of understanding, and he knew that she knew.

Knew, even though he'd denied it, that for him things were hell right now.

'Angus.' Gemma's voice snapped him to weary attention. 'You're going to have to take the day off tomorrow or ring your mother and ask her to come down. I simply cannot miss this shoot—you know how important—'

'Gemma...' His voice was supremely calm, but there was an edge to it, enough of an edge to tell Gemma that she'd better listen carefully. 'We've got more important things to worry about than a photo shoot, or whether or not I come in to work tomorrow, or finding a new nanny. Yes, I will see if I can get cover for tomorrow, but not so that you can go on your photo shoot. I'm going to ask my sister to watch the kids and then...' He took a deep breath and made himself say it '...we need to do some serious talking.'

'Hey!' Lost in thought, Angus nearly collided with Imogen as he headed for the staff lockers. 'I thought you finished ages ago?'

'I did!' Imogen nodded. 'I just didn't like to leave Maria on her own. I know the ICU nurses are fab and everything but, well, I got to talk to her, I guess I was there when she first came in, it just seemed wrong to leave her...'

'How about a drink? I'm sure I owe you one.'

'No thanks.'

'I can have a word with Heather,' Angus offered. 'I'm happy to speak to Admin about your hours...'

'I sat down all afternoon.' Imogen gave a watery smile. 'I made it very clear to the ICU nurses that I was there as a friend for Maria and nothing else. I don't want to be paid for it.'

'How is she?' Angus said slowly. He'd been asked to be kept informed but, given Imogen was here, he wondered if he was just about to hear the news they all expected.

'Not good. Her brother arrived half an hour ago. She's spoken to him, but she's starting to get distressed…' Imogen's eyes filled up, 'I brought Guido in again and she's had a good dose of morphine. The anaesthetist is going to intubate her soon. To be honest, I couldn't take it much more.'

'What will you do now?' Angus asked, not that it was his concern, of course, but he was worried about her, knew the toll today would have taken on her. The thought of going back to the cheerful, carefree world of a youth hostel certainly wouldn't appeal to him today and he doubted it would appeal to Imogen.

'I don't know.' She gave a tight shrug, blew her fringe skywards, and then said it again. 'I don't know.'

'Maybe see your son…' Angus suggested, though it wasn't his place, but with what she'd had to endure today, with all that she'd taken on, it was surely right that he was concerned, surely right that he didn't want her heading off alone. 'Do you talk to your ex?'

'Not about important things.' She gave a tight smile. 'I'll be fine.'

'Look, maybe—' Angus's voice stopped as quickly as it had started. The most stupid idea had come to mind, that maybe she could stay with him and Gemma for a few weeks, help out with the kids while Gemma went on her shoot and while they found a new nanny, but as her eyes darted to his, for reasons he didn't even want to fathom, he quickly changed his mind. 'Come and have a coffee—I've got time.'

'No, you haven't.'

'You're right,' Angus admitted. 'But I'm already so far behind today that I'm never going to catch up. Have a drink…'

'I'd really rather not…' She gave a pale smile. 'I'm not very good company.'

'I don't expect good company.' He frowned at her pale face and lips and was really quite worried now. 'You need a debrief, Imogen. I make sure our regular staff get to talk things through when there's been a difficult patient. It's hard enough for them, never mind agency staff, especially ones who have just landed in the country…'

'I'm fine.' She wouldn't accept his smile and she wouldn't accept his help. Except she wasn't fine, tears were filling those pale blue eyes now, the tip of her snub nose red, and all Angus knew was that he didn't want her to go, didn't want her heading off onto the wet London streets, with no one to unload to. 'How about you?'

'Me?' Her question confused him. They were supposed to be talking about her!

'This morning didn't upset you?'

'Of course it did, but I'm used to it—it's a busy hospital…'

'You can never get used to that.' She shook her head. 'I've been doing this for years and, believe it or not, we do get our fair share of trauma in Australia, even the occasional burn. But *that*, by anyone's standards, was awful.'

'Yes.' Angus admitted. 'It was.'

'So?' She demanded. 'Who debriefs the boss?'

'I get by…' Angus shrugged. 'I speak to the other consultants sometimes and Heather's pretty good. Mind you, I try not to…' His voice trailed off for a moment. 'Well—as you said, I'm the boss.'

'What about your wife?'

A short, incredulous laugh shot out of his lips before he could stop it and it was all evident in his bitter, mirthless laugh.

'You're fine too, then?' Her ironic words were the kindest, most honest he'd heard in a long time and Angus stood there. They both just stood there for the longest time, the moment only broken when Heather walked past.

'Oh, there you are Angus. There's a baby I'm moving over to Resus—not quite sure what's going on but very listless…' She gave Imogen a kind, tired smile. 'I'm glad to see you, Imogen. I was actually going to ring you. ICU just called—Maria's just passed away. Her brother wanted to thank you both for all you did for her…'

There was a long silence. Heather bustled off, Angus telling her he'd be there in just a moment, and still he stood and watched as a fat tear slid down Imogen's cheek and she quickly wiped it away with the back of her hand. Angus cursed how times had changed, how it was impossible these days to comfort a colleague with a quick cuddle, unless it was one you really knew well, as it could so easily be construed as inappropriate. He didn't even have a hanky to offer her, just a paltry 'I'm sorry'.

'She was never going to live…' Imogen sniffed and then wept just a little bit more, before pulling herself together. 'Told you I hated burns,' she said, hitching up her bag up and wishing him a good evening.

Inappropriate. As Angus checked over the baby, as he listened to its chest, checked the depressed fontanel, took bloods and started an IV, his mind was completely on the job, but later, filling out the lab forms and waiting to be put through to Pathology, his mind wandered back to Imogen. Oh, yes, it *would* have been inappropriate to hold her—because it wouldn't have just been about work.

The last year of his marriage had, by mutual agreement with his wife, been a loveless, sexless pit, but not once had he been tempted. Oh, sure, there had been offers and he wasn't blind enough not to notice a beautiful woman, only Imogen wasn't a classic beauty, Imogen wasn't his type at all.

But, then, what was his type?

God, but he'd wanted to hold her…

He actually shook his head as he sat there. He wasn't going to go there—even in his head. They'd shared the shift from hell, there was bound to be some sort of connection between them and anyone would be worried about her heading off alone. But even after speaking to Pathology and hanging up the phone, despite not a single rustle of paper, as he sat there Angus could feel the winds of change whistling through the department. He could feel the unsettling breeze swirling around him and knew, just knew, that things couldn't go on the way they were.

CHAPTER FIVE

'HI THERE!'

Walking through the car park, cursing the snow that had started to fall, lost in thought, dread in every cell of his body and grey with tension, Angus did a double-take as the vibrant woman greeted him.

Oh, my! was his first thought.

She should never wear white! was his second.

Wearing long, flat black boots, black stockings, black skirt and the softest grey jumper under a cropped black jacket, Imogen was somehow a blaze of colour with her red hair. There was a rosy tinge to her pale cheeks and those once fair eyelashes were now black too, a slick of mascara bringing out the blue of her eyes, and her soft smiling mouth was certainly pretty in pink.

'Sorry,' Angus blinked, 'I didn't recognise you without your uniform. How are you?'

'Great.' She smiled. 'Well, I'm starting to get over my jet-lag anyway! I just popped in to Admin to hand in my time sheet—I forgot yesterday. Oh, and I nipped in to see Mrs Kapur.'

'Mrs Kapur?' Angus frowned.

'She had a little girl, six pounds four and doing beautifully. She even let me have a little hold!'

'That's right, you were in the middle of a delivery…' Now the surprise at seeing her out of uniform was rapidly wearing off, Angus regretted prolonging the conversation. He had merely been trying to be polite, but now all Angus wanted to do was head into Emergency and do what he had to. He really didn't want to be standing in a car park, making idle chit-chat, only Imogen didn't appear to be in a hurry to go anywhere.

'How were things when you got home?'

'Fine.' Angus nodded and moved to go, before politeness forced him to ask, 'How about you?'

'Well, I'd hardly call the youth hostel home. I lasted about twenty minutes!'

She *had* been great yesterday, Angus reminded himself, and like him would have had no one to talk to about it so it would be rude now to cut her off, not to ask the question she was waiting for.

'So, what did you do?'

'I went and got my eyelashes dyed and then took a gentle spin on the London Eye and cried my eyes out. I must have looked a fright! I'm surprised the other passengers didn't press the emergency bell. What about you?'

'Me?'

'How are you?'

'I told you, I'm…' He was just about to make the usual polite response that meant nothing, just about to move on and get on with his day, but something stopped him. Whether it was the events of the last few hours that had him acting out of character, or whether it was her that made him change his mind, Angus wasn't sure and could hardly believe he said the words that slipped out of his grim mouth. 'Well, since you ask, I'm feeling pretty crap actually!'

And still she smiled, still she didn't move, just blinked those newly dyed eyelashes back at him and stared at him with those blue eyes. There were bits of snow in her hair now, Angus thought, one flake on her eyelashes, and just this…something. Something that made him stand there, that made him speak when perhaps he shouldn't, made the morning's events real when till now it had felt like a bad dream.

'My marriage just broke up.'

'Just?' A smudge of a frown was the only change to her expression.

'About four hours ago…' What the hell was he doing? Here he was standing in the car park and telling an agency nurse his problems, yet it was as if a ticker-tape parade was coming out of his mouth! Words just spilling out! All he could do was wait for the procession to pass as it all tumbled out. 'I'm just about to go into work—tell them I can't come in over the next few days. I've no idea who's going to fill in for me over Christmas…'

'How are the kids?' She dragged his mind back to the important part of the problem.

'My sister's watching them.'

'They're not with their mum?'

'No, she's gone.' She was frowning now and Angus didn't like it. He neither needed nor wanted her concern.

'She's just gone?'

'It's all under control!' Angus snapped, only it wasn't. He had a horrible feeling that there was a tinge of panic in his voice, it sure as hell sounded like it. He was an emergency consultant, for heaven's sake, was used to dealing with drama and problems, only it wasn't that his marriage was over that had him reeling—he'd dealt with that ages ago. No, now it was the thought of facing the kids, of telling them—what? He didn't know.

'Come and have a coffee.'

Was that her answer? Was she mad?

Angus certainly looked at her as if she was!

'I don't have time…' He didn't. He had to go into work and give them the news that the dependable Angus, one of only two emergency consultants covering the Christmas break, actually couldn't cover it. The thought of sitting in the canteen or the staffroom and talking, instead of doing, was incomprehensible.

'Come on…' She gestured with her head, and started to walk away from the hospital, offering the same wise words he had offered yesterday. 'You have to make time.'

'I don't have sugar…' Irritated, but not at her, he snapped out the words. His life was down the drain, he had a million things he *had* to get on with, yet here he was sitting in a packed café, surrounded by Christmas shoppers. Carols were frying his brain from the speakers overhead as she calmly came over with two big mugs of sickly, milky coffee and proceeded to load them with sugar.

'You do today.' Imogen shrugged as a strange sort of grin came to her lips. 'You're in shock!'

'Shut up!' He actually laughed. On a day when he never thought he would, when there was nothing, not a single thing to smile about, he started to laugh. Maybe he *was* in shock, Angus thought. Maybe this strange euphoria, this sort of relief that was zipping into him, was some sort of shock reaction, which a mug of something hot and sweet wasn't ever going to cure. But, as he took a sip, it somehow did. Not a lot, not even a little bit, but it sort of did do something.

'I'm not in shock,' he said finally when he'd taken a drink and put down his mug, 'because it really wasn't a shock—I just didn't think it would be today that it ended.'

'And certainly not the day after she sacked the nanny.' Imogen, as she always seemed to, Angus was realising, got right to the very point. 'How old are your children?'

'Jack's five, Clemmie's four.'

'Are they at school?'

'Jack is.' He nodded. 'Clemmie starts in September. Not that it makes any difference at the moment, they're on holiday and I'm rostered on all over Christmas. She sacked our cleaning lady last month as well,' Angus added gloomily. 'The house is like a bomb site!'

'Can you ask her to come back?' Imogen asked.

'Who—Gemma or the cleaning lady?'

'The nanny.' Imogen grinned, assessing him as she

would a patient and glad to see he had his sense of humour intact.

'Don't think so…' He shook his head. 'I went to see her this morning; I gave her her holiday money and a reference. She's actually already found another job—you'll never guess who for.'

'Who?' Imogen frowned.

'Guess.'

'I don't know anyone in London.'

'Guido!' He watched as her jaw dropped. 'As dire as my situation is, I think Maria's brother needs help more than I do right now—and Ainslie's great. It's good to know that Guido's being taken care of.'

'By a thief?' Imogen pointed out.

'No.' Angus took a long drink of his coffee. 'I'm pretty sure that I was right about that too…' He gave a tight smile as she sat there bemused. 'And I'd hazard a guess that the cleaning lady wasn't guzzling our gin either.'

'You've lost me.'

'Never mind. My loss is Elijah Vanaldi's gain…' Angus said evasively, 'that's all you need to know. Guido will be well taken care of by Ainslie.'

'So what happened?' Imogen asked. 'With you and Gemma?'

He gave a tight smile. He certainly wasn't going to go there—and certainly not with a stranger. 'I'm sure you'll understand, given that you've been through it yourself, if I don't want to talk about it.'

'No.' Imogen shook her head. 'Talking about it is the only way to get through it.'

'For you perhaps,' Angus clipped, but Imogen wasn't fazed.

'I'll show you mine if you show me yours.'

Why was he grinning again?

'Brad had an affair.'

'I'm sorry.'

'Oh, no.' Imogen gave him a startled look. 'Don't be sorry—it was absolutely my fault!'

'Pardon?'

'He had needs, you see…' Imogen said. 'Very Special Needs. He's very good-looking, he's an actor, you know…'

'Oh.'

'I mean, what was I thinking, Angus?' She shot him a serious look. 'I should have been at the gym if I'd cared about him, really cared about him. I'd have lost my weight straight after I had Heath, now, wouldn't I? And I certainly wouldn't have had a baby guzzling on my boobs at all hours of the night. I would have asked about his day more, wouldn't I, Angus?'

She was like icy water on an impossibly hot day, just this refreshing drench that stunned him. He didn't get her, yet he was starting to want to—never knew when she opened her mouth where it was going, yet every word gave him something, like this join-the-dot picture, as she revealed herself.

'If I had really wanted to keep him,' she continued, not lowering her voice, not caring who might hear, just utterly at ease with herself she carried on. He was half smiling, but very sad too as he stared at this amazing woman—sad for all she had been through, but smiling at the way she shared it. 'I would have stroked his ego more, I would have been tidier, remembered to put on my make-up before he came home, perhaps dressed a bit better. You see, Angus, I didn't understand how demanding his career was, but *she* did. *She* appreciated him, she understood his Very Special Needs—whereas I was fat, lazy and lousy in bed!' She ticked them off one by one on her hands. 'So, you see, it was absolutely my fault that he had an affair.'

'I'm sorry.'

'For what?'

'For what you must have been through. I'm sure you didn't deserve it.'

'I didn't,' Imogen said without even a trace of bitterness. 'And I'm not, by the way!'

'Not what?'

'Fat.'

'No,' Angus politely agreed, 'you're not.'

'I mean, I'm not supermodel material—I accept that—and, yes, I do like to eat, but I think there are better words to describe me than fat!'

'You're not fat.' Obviously getting hot now, she'd taken off her jacket, big boobs jiggling under her jumper. Her skirt was biting into her waist over her soft, round tummy, and Angus felt a terribly inappropriate stirring under the table. 'You're…' *Gorgeous* was what he'd been about to say, but that seemed too much. *Fine as you are* sounded patronising and just way, way too little, so he settled for 'lovely' instead, which seemed sort of safe and couldn't be construed as flirting, because he wasn't flirting. Well, he didn't think he was.

'And I'm not lazy.'

'I know that!' Angus answered, 'I worked with you yesterday—I know that you're far from lazy!'

'And…' Imogen gave a cheeky grin as he reached for his mug '…Brad was wrong on the final count too!'

'Quite!' He took a gulp of his coffee.

'Just in case you were wondering!' She winked.

He wasn't going to answer that one!

So she tried another question instead. 'Was she worried, Gemma?' Imogen flushed just a little as she fished. 'About you and the nanny?'

'Ainslie!' Angus shot her an incredulous look.

'Just wondering.' Imogen shrugged. 'Just you said that you went to see her this morning…'

'Because she was thrown out of my house!' He didn't even hide his annoyance at her suggestion. 'Because, like you, she's from Australia, and in the same way I was concerned about you yesterday…' He stopped in mid-sentence, because for the first time in the entire conversation he was veering from the truth. His concern for Ainslie had been as an employer, whereas his concern for Imogen… Angus swallowed hard. 'Look,' he said brusquely, 'I can assure you Gemma wasn't, neither did she have any reason to be, jealous.'

'Then consider me assured!'

'In fact—' Angus bristled with indignation '—it's Gemma who's been having an affair.'

'So things weren't happy at home?'

'You don't know that,' Angus started, but she was right, because the facts spoke for themselves. Eventually he nodded. 'She says she didn't intend to have an affair, but she fell in love.'

'Well, you can't plan for that,' Imogen said.

'You can when you're married.' Angus argued then gave in. 'OK, yes—things weren't good at home. We were both holding on till Clemmie went to school—it was over a long time ago. Gemma's a model,' he explained. 'She stopped working when we had the children, then when Clemmie was one she went back to it. Till that point, even before we had kids, it had been pretty low key, catalogues, brochures that type of thing. Then suddenly things just took off for her in a way neither of us expected really. I supported her at the start, well I hope I did. That's how I got into this blasted celebrity doctor spot—I was at a television studio where she was being interviewed and they needed an expert opinion…'

'Do you like doing it?'

'Sometimes,' Angus said. 'It's certainly a good forum for education—just sometimes…' He gave a tight shrug, not noticing her slight smile at the rather formal description. 'It started to take over and I pulled back. Gemma wanted me to do more of the celebrity stuff and wind things down at the hospital, but for me that wasn't an option. I guess, in the end, we just wanted different things.'

'Like what?' Imogen asked, but Angus didn't answer. 'Like what?' she pushed, but Angus just shook his head.

'I don't know,' he admitted. 'We've got great kids, a

great home, we love our work…' He blew out a breath of frustration. 'I don't know.'

'Tell me about it…' Imogen sighed then perked up. 'Except Brad's and my home wasn't actually that great and I wasn't particularly happy at work either, but we did have the great-kid bit!'

'Are you always so open?'

'No!' Imogen grinned. 'But given I'm not going to be here for long, and after yesterday I have no intention of working back down in your emergency room again, I think I can afford to be. You can be too!'

'We agreed last year things weren't working…' He gave a pensive smile. 'That makes it sound like we drew a neat conclusion, but it was the toughest thing we'd ever done. We both decided to stay together till Clemmie was at school.'

'In September?' Imogen checked.

'Yep.' Angus nodded. 'I'd signed up till then with the TV station, knowing that once they were both at school, I was going to give it up anyway and become the primary carer.'

'Not Gemma?'

'She figures she's only got a few years of modelling left—as I pointed out to her, the kids only have one childhood…' He drew in a deep breath then let it out. 'For the kids I could live a year or so in a marriage that was over, just not an unfaithful one. Gemma, it would seem, couldn't. After I got back from speaking with Ainslie this morning, we had an almighty row and the truth came out. Gemma did what I always knew she would in the end…' His eyes were two balls of pain. 'She walked out on the kids.'

'Do they know?'

'They know that she'll be away for a few days. I've told them she's away on a photo shoot, they're pretty used to that… I'm hoping that she'll see sense.'

'That she'll come back?' Imogen checked, but Angus shook his head.

'That we can work out properly what we're going to tell them—*then* tell the kids together. But, no—she's not coming back.'

'So what now?'

'Don't know…' he admitted. 'My mum's in Scotland. I'll ring her tonight, ask her to come and help out for a couple of weeks…'

'Will she be terribly upset?'

'I don't know,' Angus said. 'I'm going to have to ask her though…' He gave a small grimace as he realized how many other busy lives would be disrupted by his. 'She's going to visit friends for a few days for Christmas. I'll ask her to come after that—at least till I find a new nanny. My sister, Lorna, lives nearby. I'm sure she can help out sometimes, although she is working…'

'So you have got a plan!'

'Sort of.'

'Good.'

'Which doesn't help now.' He took another mouthful of coffee then screwed up his face. 'This is cold—do you want another?'

She didn't, but she nodded, and Angus idly watched

from the counter as she sat and checked her phone as he ordered a couple of coffees and two mini Christmas puddings, surprised himself at how much better he felt now just by talking.

'Don't you miss Heath?' Angus asked Imogen, though he was still thinking about Gemma. 'When he's with his dad?'

'All the time!' Imogen answered. 'I feel like I've permanently forgotten my keys when he isn't around. I confess to being the world's most overprotective mother—Brad always said he'd turn out to be a mummy's boy if I didn't back off, but he's turned out quite the opposite…'

'So how…' Angus frowned '…can you stand for him to live in London and you in Australia?' This time it was Imogen looking at him as if he'd gone stark raving mad in the middle of the café! 'You said he was here with his dad.'

'He is,' Imogen answered slowly, 'because I brought him here.'

'Oh!'

'Brad doesn't live here!' She smiled at his confusion. 'Brad and I pretty much share care back home in Queensland,' Imogen explained. 'Though, given the nature of his work, it tends to fall on me. When he got offered this role, well, it was huge for him. They've got time off over the Christmas break, but it would have been practically impossible for him to get home and he didn't want to be apart from Heath for Christmas. It's just a one-off—you see, he's got terminal cancer.'

'Oh, my God!'

'Not Brad!' Imogen grinned at his appalled expression. 'His character—Shane. He only took the part because it was short term—just three months. Brad would never come and live here and leave Heath. He's only going to be in England for a few more weeks, but even though I really wanted Heath to have some time in London, and some real quality time with his dad, I just couldn't stand to be away from him over Christmas. So I said that I'd bring him over, but that I'd stay pretty much in the background. I mean, Heath's having a ball, I've just taken him over to the studio now—he's watching his dad and all the cast are spoiling him. I don't want to interrupt that…'

'You're amazing,' Angus said.

'Amazing and broke!' Imogen admitted. 'This little jaunt to support my ex-husband's rising career has cost an absolute fortune—the airfares, the accommodation, my mad moment on the London Eye—'

'Worth it?' Angus broke in.

'Very much so!' Imogen smiled. 'I took Heath to see Buckingham Palace this morning, which was just amazing. Mind you, I'm already sick of taking him to cafes for lunch. I don't want him staying with me at the youth hostel—but I can't afford to stay anywhere else…' Her voice trailed off as she caught him frowning. Their eyes locked for just a fraction of time, then both rapidly looked away concentrating on their mini Christmas puddings.

'You could always…' Angus broke the sudden silence

then blew out a breath, before looking at her again. Serious, practical, yet somehow terribly hazardous, she offered a taste of a solution. 'Look, I'm minus a nanny. The nanny's empty room might not be the best on offer, but I'm sure that it would beat the youth hostel…'

'I don't want to be a nanny.' Imogen gave a polite smile. 'I am trying to have a bit of a holiday, believe it or not.'

'I'm not asking you for that.' Angus cleared his throat. 'Just helping out a friend and you'd be helping me too. It makes sense.'

'Why would you do that?' Imogen asked, and he opened his mouth to respond only Angus couldn't, because if it had been anyone else at work in her predicament, he wasn't sure that he'd make the same offer. In fact, he wouldn't even be having this conversation, would never dream of telling anyone at work so much about him and Gemma. There was just no point of reference—nothing familiar—and not a hope of answering her question.

'It would be bliss to actually have Heath stay over with me for a couple of nights during the week, and that's not going to happen at the youth hostel.' Her voice dragged him out of his introspection. 'I could juggle my shifts around yours… Are you sure about this, Angus?' Imogen asked.

'Absolutely.' Angus answered, without thinking, but when his brain caught up the conclusion was the same. 'Absolutely.'

'Just till your mum gets here?'

'Whatever suits you.'

'How soon…?'

'When can I…?'

They both laughed as they spoke over each other.

'Why don't I go home and speak to the kids?' Angus suggested. 'You go and pack up your stuff. Then, if it's OK, I'll dash over to the hospital and tell them….'

'Tell them what?'

'That I…' He opened his mouth, closed it, then opened it again. 'I'm on all day tomorrow… Are you sure?'

'Works perfectly for me!' Imogen answered. 'I'm on a day off.'

CHAPTER SIX

PACKING up her things at the youth hostel didn't take Imogen long. Angus had assured her his house was easy to find and was a mere two minutes' walk from an underground station. She had his address and phone number in her pocket, but as Imogen sat on the tube, her heart was hammering.

It had all made perfect sense at the time.

Sitting in the café with him, talking to him, confident and relaxed in his company, it had seemed an obvious solution for both of them. The last night at the hostel had been hell—the noise, the laughter, the sheer energy of the place just too much to deal with, when all she'd wanted was to flop in front of the television and *not* think about her day. It was also no place to bring Heath and although she was desperate to cram in as much sightseeing as possible with him, she was already tired of sitting in cafés with him. A homebody by anyone's standards, at the end of the day Imogen wanted to be in rather than out, wanted to just be with her son rather than think up things to amuse him.

It just didn't make perfect sense now.

Coming out from the underground station and finding Angus's street easily, Imogen was tempted to turn and run in the other direction as she wheeled her suitcase towards yet another destination unknown.

And how she hated them.

Hated the chaos her life had been plunged into when Heath had been just a baby. She had spent the last three years extricating herself from it.

Sensible might just as well be her middle name. She never took risks, never did things on impulse, well, hadn't done in a long time. As *amazing* as Angus thought she was for coming to London, he hadn't known the angst it had caused her to be hurtled out of the comfort zone she had created for herself and Heath back home in Australia. He wouldn't have a clue how out of character it was for her to have asked him for coffee, to sit in a café with a man she'd only just met and *then* agree to move in with him!

And he couldn't possibly have known how much courage it took for her to knock on his door and smile widely as he opened it.

'This is Imogen…' Angus introduced her as he led her through to the lounge. 'She's a nurse from the hospital and she's going to help out for a little while.'

'Will Ainslie come back?' Clemmie, her hair thick with curls and her eyes as green as Angus's, gave Imogen a bored glance then spoke to her father.

'No, Ainslie's got a job with a new family now,' Angus answered.

'Ainslie was fun!' Dark eyed and dark haired, Jack looked directly at Imogen as he threw down a challenge.

'I can manage fun.' Imogen smiled, unfazed. 'I like your Christmas tree!'

Actually, she didn't. On the positive side, at least it was a *real* Christmas tree, but it was so tastefully decorated it surely belonged in a department store. Large silver ribbons and not a lot else dressed the lonely branches, and several, beautifully wrapped silver boxes lay strategically underneath, causing the children to stand to rigid attention when Imogen strolled over and picked one up.

'You're not supposed to touch!' Clemmie warned.

'Whoops! Are they for display purposes only?' Imogen smiled, replacing the empty box.

'I made a decoration at school…' Jack scampered out and returned with several pieces of pasta stuck on a card and sprayed gold.

'That's fabulous!' Imogen beamed, placing it on the tree and standing back to admire it. 'Maybe we can make some more tomorrow when your dad's at work—if that's OK with you guys!'

'Imogen is *not* the new nanny,' Angus warned his children. 'She's a friend, helping out for now, so remember that.

'Come on.' He smiled. 'I'll show you around.'

The children didn't follow, and now, back in his company, chatting easily as he showed her around his home, it all made perfect sense again. Even though it was an enigma to Imogen, from the two busy schedules that were pinned up on the fridge the Maitlin family was obviously used to having staff, used to having people living in their home, cleaning their things *and* looking after their children.

'The children have a separate menu?' Imogen frowned as she looked at a piece of paper attached to the fridge.

'I'm not expecting you to follow it.' Angus laughed. 'That was for Ainslie. Anyway, the children have already had tea…' Which did nothing to fade her frown. 'At my sister's.'

'You mean dinner?'

Still, apart from the endless lists, the house was gorgeous.

Well, apart from the endless photos.

For the most part she was comfortable with her body. Sure, Brad's words had hurt at the time and for a good while after that, but, as her mother had pointed out, her whole family might be curvy, big bosomed and big bottomed, but they weren't unhealthy. Imogen's sister had also pointed out, furiously jabbing at a magazine to reiterate the point, that no woman who had had children could possibly, without a lot of airbrushing, look like that!

'When was that taken?' Imogen paused at a particularly spectacular image of a woman rising from the ocean in a man's white shirt.

'The year before last…' Angus frowned. 'When we went to Thailand, supposedly to try and make things work.'

'It's lovely,' Imogen said, deciding to take a photo of her own to send as a postcard to her sister!

Used to airy, open-plan houses, painted walls and floorboards, Imogen adored the old house. The carpets were thick and cream and the bold choices of colour on the wallpapered walls were so different to their own house—even the stairs would be a novelty for Heath. She could practically see him surfing his way down them head first. There was even a little box bedroom, which at first Imogen assumed was for her but was actually a spare that, Angus told her, she was welcome to use for Heath.

'This is yours.' He led her up yet another set of stairs to the 'nanny's accommodation', which translated to a converted attic decorated in white and yellow, with a skylight that had blinds and even a little kitchenette with a microwave, fridge and kettle.

'Does anyone actually eat together in this house?'

'I don't expect you to hide away in the attic,' Angus said. 'There's no bathroom facilities up here, though…'

'I wasn't expecting there to be.'

'Getting and keeping a good nanny is a serious business here,' Angus explained to a thoroughly bemused Imogen. 'Ideally they should have their own self-contained accommodation.'

'So you don't have to see them!'

'It's the other way around.' Angus laughed. 'They don't want to see us on their time off. Honestly, it's like a minefield.'

And one she had no intention of walking through!

Especially when at seven p.m., Clemmie informed Imogen that she'd forgotten to put her pyjamas out on her bed for her.

'Ainslie always did!' Clemmie said tearfully when Angus scolded her.

'Imogen is not the new nanny. I've told you she's a friend who's helping us out. Imogen's got a job at the hospital and her own little boy to look after.'

'How old is he?' Clemmie asked, suddenly interested.

'Four—like you. He's called Heath.'

'Well, my dad's on the television!' Clemmie said proudly.

'So's Heath's dad!' Imogen said, equally as proudly, then glanced at her watch. 'May I?'

'Help yourself,' Angus answered, somewhat bemused as the three of them piled on the sofa and proceeded to watch what was surely unsuitable viewing for a four- and a five-year-old, but from the squeals of recognition it wasn't the first time they had seen the show and from their rapt expressions it wouldn't be the last.

'Shane's Heath's dad?' Jack checked, clearly impressed.

'Cool!' Clemmie chanted.

And when surely he should be frantic, should be ringing round relatives, thinking about lawyers, trying to contact Gemma, for the moment at least he paused.

'Ten minutes,' Angus warned the children, 'then it's time to get ready for bed.'

Not that they were listening, all eyes in the room drawn to six feet two of bronzed Australian muscle, Shane's sun-bleached blond hair long and tousled on the pillow of his hospital bed. As if on cue Imogen's mobile began to ring.

'Hey, Brad!' Absolutely at ease, she grinned into the phone. 'I'm watching you now—tell them to go easy on the blusher next time…' Then she spoke with her son and Angus wondered if he and Gemma could ever get there, could chat and grin and even manage a laugh. Right now that world seemed light years away. Later, when Clemmie and Jack were in bed, and Imogen was rather expertly pulling a cork out of a bottle of her duty-free wine, Angus thought that perhaps now was the time he should be overcome with emotion, grief, panic, when *surely* now he should be thinking about tracking down his errant wife, or ringing his family, or getting started the million and one tasks that surely lay ahead. Instead, he pulled two steaks out of the freezer and watched as their dinner defrosted through the glass door of the microwave, watched as Imogen chopped onions and mushrooms and added a dash of wine to the sauce for the steaks, and it seemed incongruous how good he actually felt.

'To you!' Imogen tapped his glass and took a sip. 'To getting through.'

'I don't know how I would have, especially with it being Christmas…'

'You would have.'

'I would,' he agreed, taking another sip, 'but it would have messed up a lot of people's plans. This is really nice wine, by the way.'

'We do a good red.' Imogen smiled. 'I've got five more bottles upstairs!' Then she was serious. 'The kids seem OK.'

'They're used to people coming and going, and they're

used to Gemma being away. They seem more upset that Ainslie's gone at the moment… though they'll be devastated when I tell them about their mother and me.'

'Just wait till Gemma's calmed down,' Imogen said wisely. 'Things might look different.'

'We won't be getting back together.' The slight raise of her brows irritated him. 'Once I've made up my mind, Imogen, I don't change it.'

It was a nice dinner—a *really* nice dinner—just talking about work, and about Angus trying to cram in an eighty-hour working week at the hospital and also look after a family. They talked about Imogen's life in Australia and her colossal mortgage, how she missed midwifery and how she juggled her shifts around Heath and Brad and she told him how much easier things would be in a few weeks once Heath started school.

'Are you seeing anyone?'

Oh, so casually he said it—well, she knew so much about him, surely it was right to ask?

'No.' She frowned over her wineglass at him. 'You?'

'I've only been separated for…' he glanced at his watch '…oh, ten hours now.'

That wasn't what she'd been asking, but from the way he'd answered she didn't need to clarify the question. Somehow Imogen knew that the man sitting at the table, leaning over to top up her glass, was as decent and as nice as he appeared.

As he went to fill her glass, both shared a quick yikes look when they realised the bottle was empty.

'I'm going to bed.' Imogen stretched as she stood.

'It's not even nine o'clock.'

'Perhaps, but I'm still jet-lagged.'

'Sorry—I keep forgetting you've only just got here. You just seem so….' His voice trailed off, not sure himself what he had been trying to say. ''Night, Imogen, and thanks, thanks for all your help today.'

''Night, Angus.'

Familiar.

As he stacked the dishwasher Angus shook his head, unhappy with the description.

Comfortable.

Only that didn't fit either, because at every turn she shocked him, shocked himself too—he'd told her things he never thought he'd share.

She'd been right about so many things, though, Angus thought, and it had been good to talk, to be honest, to share some of what he was going through.

Though there was one thing that she'd got wrong…

Picking up the phone, he rang his mother, took a deep breath and paused for the longest time when she answered the phone.

'Is anybody there?'

'It's me, Angus.'

Yes, Imogen was wrong, because his marriage to Gemma really was over. Angus knew that for sure, or he'd never have made that call.

Imogen stared at the ceiling as she listened to the low murmur of Angus's voice drifting up the stairs as he spoke on the telephone. Suddenly she found she was holding her breath too.

In three years she'd barely even glanced at another man—let alone flirt.

Oh, and she had been flirting. Not deliberately—in fact, only now, lying in bed and going over the day, was Imogen blushing as red as her hair as she recalled some of the things that she'd said. They'd been the sort of cheeky, flirty things the old Imogen would have said a million years ago when she and Brad had been happy.

What *had* she been thinking? Imogen scolded herself.

Angus Maitlin was married to a model, for heaven's sake, or had *just* broken up with her. As if he'd even *think* of her in that way. And he was only being nice because he was glad she was here, that was all. Without her, a lot of people's Christmas plans would have been messed up and he would have had to fly his mother down from Scotland or try and arrange rapid child care just a week before Christmas. Yes, he was just glad she was here.

She was glad she was here too!

Everyone had said she was crazy, zipping over to London when she could least afford it, and had told her that she was being too soft on Brad, that he was taking advantage of her, but it was actually the other way around.

She needed this, Imogen thought. Lying in a strange bed, in a strange house, in a strange country, in the middle of an English winter—she actually felt as if she was thawing out.

As if the Imogen that had been placed in cold storage

when her marriage had broken down and she had struggled just to survive was making itself known again.

So what if she had been flirting? She was testing her wings, that was all.

As the phone pinged off, as the rumble of pipes through the house stilled, as she heard the heavy creak of the stairs, never had a house been more noisy, but as quiet filled her little attic Imogen stared up at the skylight, too tired to close the blinds now, a streetlight outside illuminating low clouds as they drifted past, the sky lighter than it had been at nine that morning, which didn't make sense, but she was too tired to work it out.

Yes, she needed this, Imogen realised, turning on her side and letting delicious waves of sleep wash over her.

Needed to be where no one actually knew her, so that maybe, just maybe she could find herself again.

CHAPTER SEVEN

AN EYEFUL of grey and the thick sound of nothing woke her up.

Staring at the skylight, struggling to orientate herself, the snowflakes falling was nothing like she'd dreamed of. The wad of grey slush peeled away from the edge of the skylight and slid down the glass and as Imogen climbed out of bed she found out for the first time what it *really* meant to be cold. She was tempted to tell Angus why he couldn't keep a nanny!

'Sorry!' Grinning, just back from a run, Angus looked as warm as the toast he was buttering. 'The heating timer's not working. I meant to put it on before my run. The house will warm up soon.'

'You run in snow!'

'It's not snowing!' Angus refuted. 'Though it is trying to. It's turning to slush as soon as it hits the ground.'

Handing her a cup of tea, Imogen wasn't sure if it was her breath or the steam that was coming out of her mouth. Disgustingly healthy, brimming with energy, Angus joined her, but she started to forgive him when he proceeded to spread thick marmalade on a mountain of toast. He *did* have nice hands, large yet neat, with short white nails and a flash of an expensive watch. Imogen noticed his left hand was now minus a wedding ring.

'Did you want marmalade?' He checked when he caught her looking.

'Thanks!' Imogen said, and forgave him completely when he didn't moan that she ate more than half of the toast.

'Any plans for today?'

'None as yet…' The whole day stretched out before her—three kids and the whole of London waiting to be explored, and she'd take her time deciding. 'I want to do the Duck Tour…' She misread his frown. 'I saw it on the Internet—this bus takes you around London then straight onto the river.'

'I know what it is—are you really going to do that?'

'Maybe…' Imogen shrugged. 'Or I might wait for a warmer day.'

It irked her that he laughed.

Imogen Von Trapp she was not, but with accommodation sorted, and her three little charges marching beside her with maps in hand, Imogen felt close. She snapped away with her camera as Heath, Clemmie and Jack teased the solider at the Horse Guard Parade—Clemmie furious she couldn't extract a smile. There was so much to see, and while she was here Imogen fully intended to see it all, but by mid-afternoon her charges were sagging. Cracking a bar of chocolate on the tube, she tried to inject some enthusiasm as they headed for Knightsbridge.

'I don't want to go shopping!' Heath moaned.

'Not even if you get to see Santa?' Imogen checked.

'It's not the real one!' Jack scolded. 'Everyone knows that they just send a helper to the shops!'

'Oh, no!' Imogen cajoled. 'Everyone knows that the *real* Santa only goes to Harrods!'

Every time he saw her she was more beautiful.

As if the first image of her had been in black and white, and not so gradually the colour was being turned up. She was wearing her black skirt and flat boots again only with fishnet stockings this time and a sort of dusky pink jumper that was clearly too warm for her in the kitchen, because there was a pink glow to her cheeks. He noticed this because she was wearing long silver earrings that caught the light as she smiled up at him from the table where she was sitting.

'Angus, this is Brad.' Imogen introduced them as Angus walked in the kitchen after an extremely long day.

'Hi, there!' Blond, long limbed and utterly at ease, Brad grinned up at him from the kitchen table, where they sat with two mugs of tea. Then Brad looked at Imogen, saw the tint that spread up to her cheeks, saw the slight flurry of her hands, the rapid way she blinked when she was suddenly nervous—and knew it was time to go.

'Hello!' Angus said politely, pulling out a chair and joining them, only his heart wasn't in it. There was this niggling pain in his stomach now, causing him to wonder if the stress might be catching up with him and he was getting an ulcer.

'And this…' Imogen said as six little feet charged down the stairs and into the kitchen, skidding to a halt, 'is Heath.'

'Hi!' Bold, confident and a mini-version of his father, Heath grinned up at him, showing a spectacular gap where his baby teeth had once been.

'Hi, there!'

Clemmie was dancing on the spot and thrusting a photo at him, 'Imogen took us to see Santa!'

'It's not the fake one!' Jack warned. 'Imogen took us to see the real one.'

'Fantastic!' Angus duly said, only it was a great photo—three beaming faces and one very flustered-looking Santa. Suddenly Angus was grinning too, 'Wow!' he added. 'You really did meet the real thing.'

'The food hall was fabulous too!' Imogen said, heading to the kettle to make Angus a drink. 'I thought I'd died and gone to heaven. I'm worn out now, though!'

'I'd better get going.' Brad smiled as the kids all scampered off to the lounge.

'Don't rush off on my account!' Angus offered, but Brad was already on his way out, standing at the kitchen door and calling for Heath to hurry up and say goodbye.

'Think about what I said, Imo,' Brad added as he waited. 'It might be nice for Heath to wake up on Christmas morning with us both there.'

'It would be too confusing for him,' Imogen called. 'I'll come over about ten.'

And even though Brad's voice was laid-back and casual, as Angus watched Brad watching Imogen, he knew he was anything but. Knew, that the, oh, so laid-back Brad, still fancied his ex-wife.

'Think about it!' Brad said, again calling for Heath and getting the little guy into his coat, then giving Imogen a bit more than a friendly kiss on the cheek. He ought to think about eating, Angus decided, because his stomach was really starting to hurt now.

'Come and see the tree!' Clemmie declared, once Brad and Heath had gone. 'Santa gave us glitter-glue and paper…'

'Oh, my!' Angus whistled through his teeth as he walked into the lounge. The once tastefully decorated tree was now a blaze of multicoloured stars and angels and some other shapes he couldn't quite decipher. 'It's brilliant!' Angus declared to the kids, and then added under his breath for Imogen's benefit, 'Gemma will have a coronary!'

'I did think about that!' Imogen admitted, 'but when Santa gives you glue and glitter pens and there's a tree just begging for colour…'

'You've got glitter in your hair.'

'I've got glitter *everywhere*!' Imogen responded, pushing the arms up on her V-neck jumper and revealing some glittery forearms. 'I'll never get it off!'

'You and Brad are friendly,' Angus commented a little while later, frying up chicken that was generously dressed with tarragon, while Imogen made a vast salad.

'We are now!' Imogen answered, pulling a mango out of the fridge.

'Where the hell did you get that?'

'The food hall at Harrods,' Imogen laughed, 'I told you it was fabulous. I just couldn't resist—it reminded me of home.'

'So, you're just friends now?' Angus prolonged the conversation, not the one about the fruit, which she was expertly slicing, instead broaching the other things that reminded her of home.

'Brad's a great guy and he's a wonderful dad...' Imogen shrugged. 'He's just a lousy husband!' She poured the hot chicken and oil over the cold salad, added the mango and tossed it all in together as the four of them sat down to eat.

'What's this?' Jack, who did his level best not to eat anything green, let alone salad in December, frowned at his dinner.

'Imogen's warm chicken salad,' Imogen announced, as if she'd lifted the recipe from a book. 'And it's bliss!'

It was, just the thing his grumbling ulcer needed, Angus decided, slicing a crusty bread stick, stunned again at the normality of it all, or rather the abnormality of it all, as for the second time in as many days he sat down to a nice home-cooked dinner.

'The agency rang, they asked if I could do a late shift tomorrow.' Imogen took a big gulp of water. 'I said I'd get back to them, but I just saw your roster on the fridge and it's got "OC" written over tomorrow—am I right in assuming that's "on call"?'

'It just changed to "OAN"—or "on all night".' Angus

grinned. 'Gus has a do to go to, but it's not a problem—I've already rung Lorna and she's going to have the kids tomorrow night, so take the shift.'

'You're sure?' Imogen checked. 'I can always ring the agency.'

'No need.' Angus said, helping himself to seconds. As easily as that it was sorted, no histrionics, no 'What about *my* career?'—just a simple solution to a simple problem, and for the first time in the longest time Angus actually felt as if he could breathe!

Until she stood up and leant over to load Jack's already empty plate with some more of the nicest warm salad imaginable on a cold December night and treated him to a glimpse of two very freckly, very glittery breasts.

'It gets everywhere, I tell you!' Imogen laughed as she caught him looking then blushed and looked away. 'I'm never going to get it off.'

Later, with the kids in their pyjamas, and the living room beginning to look a lot like Christmas, with the four of them watching Shane kissing a nubile blonde under the mistletoe, Imogen shot him a look.

'Are you OK?'

'Not sure…' Angus said, uncomfortably massaging his stomach. 'You know, I think I might be getting an ulcer.'

'Stress!' Imogen said, turning her head back to the television. 'Have a glass of milk.'

'How many times do I have to say it?' Angus responded, only she wasn't listening. 'I'm fine!'

* * *

'I've never seen so many Colles' fractures!'

'It's par for the course on this side of the world.' Heather grinned, as Imogen massaged her aching back.

After Maria, Imogen had never intended to go back to Emergency, but the agency had rung a few times, and comparing Heath's 'to-do' list in London alongside her bank account, a full late shift, even if it was in Emergency, was one Imogen couldn't really justify declining.

Thankfully it had proven far less eventful that her first shift in London. Oh, it had been busy, but dramas had been few and far between and heading towards her supper break, Imogen had just one more wrist to help plaster.

Colles' fractures often occurred when people put out their hands to save themselves from a fall, and the slushy, icy streets had meant that Imogen had seen more in one shift than she usually would in a year in Queensland. She was happily explaining this to Ivy Banford as she held up her hand while Owen Richards, the intern, plastered it.

'Well, I still feel like an old fool!' Ivy scolded herself. 'As if I'm not enough trouble to everybody already.'

'Trouble?' Imogen frowned, taking in the neatly done-up blouse and smart shoes, the powdered nose and the lips that still held a smudge of coral. 'Since when were you any trouble to anyone?'

Ivy Banford wouldn't know *how* to make trouble. She'd been sitting patiently in the waiting room since eleven a.m., called for an x-Ray at three, and only now, as the clock edged past seven, was her wrist finally having a cast applied. And all she had done was apologise.

'I'm supposed to be at my son William's for Christmas. I wanted to have it at mine, but they all insisted…told me I should relax and let them do it. Now all I'm going to do is get in the way.'

'So there will be no stuffing the turkey?' Imogen smiled. 'No laying the table or peeling a mountain of potatoes…'

'I said I'd get the parsnips,' Ivy fretted, pointing to her shopping trolley, 'and I said that I'd do the stuffing—'

'Ivy,' Imogen interrupted, 'I'm sure your son's wife is dying to impress you with her Christmas dinner.'

'She just wants to show me she can do it better.' Ivy pouted. 'She fancies herself as a gourmet chef—she's been waiting to get her hands on that turkey for years…'

'Give the baby her bottle!' Imogen said, her smile widening when she realised Angus had come into the plaster room.

'Meaning?'

'Let her do it all,' Imogen explained. 'Your job is to sit there with a big glass of sherry, play with the grandkids and let everyone spoil you for once. And,' Imogen added, 'even if the parsnips are burnt and the turkey's pink, you're to tell her it was the best Christmas dinner ever!'

'I will not,' Ivy thundered. 'What would that achieve?'

'Could be the start of world peace!' Imogen was holding her back now, grateful when Angus came and took the heavy arm from her as Owen continued to work on Ivy's wrist. 'Try it!'

'Huh!' Ivy huffed, but a small smile was forming. 'She'd get the shock of her life, mind!'

'And she'd know you didn't mean it!' Owen chimed in, as Imogen popped Ivy's arm into a sling.

'Just because you act like a sweet old thing…' Imogen winked '…doesn't mean you are one!'

'Your relatives are here,' Heather said as she ushered in a worried-looking man followed by his grim-faced wife.

'Oh, Mum, what have you been doing?'

'I'm fine, William!' Ivy said, refusing his help with her coat. Catching Imogen's eye, she relented and let him help her put it on. 'I didn't manage to get the parsnips.'

'Doesn't matter a scrap, Mum!' William soothed. 'Elise has got everything under control.'

'Such a relief…' Ivy smiled warmly at her daughter-in-law. 'I've a feeling this is going to be the best Christmas yet. Elise, dear, would you pass me my purse?'

But even before she'd pried out a note with one hand, Imogen was on to her.

'Don't you dare, Ivy!'

'Buy some sweets for your little boy!' Ivy insisted, pressing the note into Imogen's hand.

'I'll buy his sweets!' Imogen stuffed the fiver back in the purse and snapped it closed. 'You put it towards your sherry!'

'You're incorrigible.' Owen grinned as the trio shuffled off.

'I'm thirsty too!' Imogen smiled. 'I'm going for my break.'

'Good idea!' Owen agreed, following her out and telling Heather he'd be back in fifteen minutes. The sound of their laughter drifted down the corridor and Angus felt a kick in his stomach again.

'Everything OK?' Heather checked, as she noticed Angus rubbing his abdomen.

'Everything's fine!' Angus nodded then changed his mind, 'Actually, Heather, you couldn't get me some Gaviscon or Mylanta…?'

'For who? Did I miss someone?'

'It's actually for me.' Angus pulled a face. 'I think I've got an ulcer. I'm going to get some milk.'

It was a quiet evening—'The lull before the storm,' Heather warned, pouring out a dose of antacid then handing it to Angus. 'Better?' Heather checked, as Angus downed the chalky brew.

'Thanks.'

But walking into the staffroom, to find Imogen and Owen giggling as *Celebrity Doctor* calmly discussed some rather intimate issues, didn't exactly help.

'Do we have to watch this?' Angus snapped. 'It's actually a serious subject if you bothered to listen.'

'Sorry!' Imogen smothered a smile and though clearly not remotely sorry she did change the channel. However, this meant that he had to sit and watch a certain blonde head, *again*, writhing on the pillow, only this time in pain as the doctors battled to save Shane.

'He's gorgeous!' Another nurse, Cassie, had joined them now, gaping at the screen then over at Imogen, clearly unable to comprehend that someone as gorgeous as *Shane* could ever have married someone as plain and as overweight as Imogen. 'And he's such a good actor.'

'Do you think so?' Imogen sounded surprised. 'He's a complete hypochondriac. He carried on exactly like that when he had toothache.'

The storm didn't eventuate. The lull stretched on and when the night staff started to arrive, Heather had sent most of her regular staff home, knowing the night shift would dash around if there was an emergency. A few nurses milled around what patients there were and Imogen filled in the time by doing a restock as Heather and Angus chatted.

'Ready for Christmas?' Heather asked Angus as she updated the whiteboard.

'Hope so.'

'Don't worry—I'm sure Gemma's got it all under control.'

'Actually, Heather…Gemma and I broke up.' Imogen watched as Heather's hand paused over the whiteboard, her face aghast as she turned around. 'It's fine, Heather.'

'It's not fine!' Heather looked as if she was about to cry. 'Angus, why didn't you say?'

'I just did.'

'But…'

'Look!' Angus gave a wry smile. 'I'm just letting you know in case something unforseen happens—Gus has offered to help out if need be.'

'So where are the kids?'

'At home.'

'Where's Gemma?' As Angus gave a small eye roll, Heather sagged. 'When did all this happen? Oh, Angus…'

'It's all under control.'

'But how?' Heather asked. 'Who's helping with the kids?'

Imogen swallowed hard, her cheeks darkening a touch, wondering if Angus would say anything, and how Heather would react if he did. There was no need to worry, Angus's next comment making it spectacularly clear that his home and work lives were kept very separate.

'I've got some temporary help for now and my mother is coming down to stay after Christmas.'

He smiled over at Imogen, only she didn't smile back. In fact, she looked away.

Temporary.

Strange how much that word had stung her to hear.

Temporary.

Funny that the same word buzzed like a blowfly around Angus for the rest of his night shift.

And when she said goodnight, when the quiet department suddenly seemed empty without her, when he joined Owen later in the staffroom and had to listen to his junior tell him how great that red-headed agency nurse was, two weeks suddenly seemed too short.

His marriage was over, his life was supposed to be in chaos, Christmas was just a couple of days away and yet he was coping, would make sure that the kids coped, knew that they'd all get through.

The only thing that daunted him at this moment was the prospect of Imogen leaving.

That temporary solution he had found raised an entirely new set of problems all of a sudden.

CHAPTER EIGHT

ON SHEER impulse Imogen had purchased a red bikini and sheer silver sarong at the departure terminal in Queensland.

She'd had absolutely no intention of wearing them until she got home, and they'd nestled in her case with the labels still on. But, waking at the crack of dawn, her sleeping pattern still horribly out of whack, finally she had a reason to put them on.

Angus had point blank refused to take rent.

Admittedly she hadn't pushed the point, but the bliss of having a nice roof over her head for her time in London and as much work as she wanted meant Imogen could pay him back in other ways—like mangos—and at 5.30 a.m., when restless legs started twitching, she decided she could give the bathroom a rather overdue clean, because Mrs Gemma Maitlin certainly hadn't picked up the cleaning baton when she'd fired the cleaning lady!

Wrinkling up her nose, Imogen peered into the shower. Housework wasn't exactly her forte, but occasionally the urge hit, and it was hitting now. Turning up the heating and grabbing the radio as she located the cleaning gear, she padded to the bathroom, dropping her sarong in the hallway and frowning at her reflection in the bathroom mirror.

'Diet!' she warned herself, turning round and grimacing at her bottom, but at least it was tanned—brown fat was certainly more attractive than white! Yes, in the new year she was definitely going on diet.

'But after we get back!' she promised her reflection. Then she promptly forgot about it as she bopped along to the music, glad by the time that she'd finished and jet-lag had hit that Angus's kids were at his sister's and Heath was with Brad, so that she could now head down to the kitchen, grab a cup of tea and crawl back into bed before Angus came home.

Then she heard his key in the front door.

Eyes wide, her face red from exertion, Imogen wondered what she should do. She could just stand in the bathroom and hope he didn't notice or she could make a dash to her room. But if he looked up he'd see her running across the landing and she could hear his foot on the bottom step now so, not wanting to stink of bleach, she sprayed a generous dash of perfume and forced a smile on her face as she headed out to meet him.

Tired, grumpy and freezing, all Angus wanted to do as he put the key in the front door and headed up the stairs was to fall into bed.

Tired, because he'd been up all night.

Grumpy, because his shirt, suit and tie had lasted till seven a.m. but were now in a plastic bag, awaiting a trip to the dry cleaner's. Tossing the bag in the corner, he decided to deal with that unpleasant task later.

Freezing, because hair wet from a quick shower at work and dressed now in threadbare theatre gear, he'd found out five minutes from home that he really should have stopped for petrol at the last garage.

The heat hit him as soon as he stepped into the hall—the place was like a sauna!

He didn't have the energy to work out why—all he wanted was bed.

Till he saw Imogen standing on the landing.

'Morning!'

'Morning!' Angus gave what he hoped was a normal smile as he stood at the bottom of the stairs, trying not to look surprised or to comment on the fact that she was wearing nothing other than a red bikini. He failed miserably on both counts. 'Imogen!' He gaped. 'Why are you dressed like that?'

'I was just cleaning the shower…'

'You wear a bikini to clean the shower?'

'No!' She gave him a very old-fashioned look. 'Normally I wear *nothing* to clean the showers, but given this is your home…'

Picking up a sliver of silver fabric from the floor, she wrapped it around her rather magnificent bosom. 'Do you want some breakfast?'

'Nope!' Funny that he had to feign a yawn now. 'I'm

going straight to bed, I want to grab a few hours before I pick up the kids.'

'I'll pick up the kids,' Imogen offered. 'You should have something to eat and then you'll sleep well.'

He'd sleep well without something to eat, Angus was about to say, but she was walking down the stairs and was passing him now, and it would seem rude just to head on up. So Angus followed her into the kitchen, yawning again, but for real this time, as he sat on a barstool and poured some muesli into a bowl as Imogen screwed up her nose.

'I'll make you some pancakes.'

'Muesli's fine.'

'Not after a night shift!' Imogen said, tipping the lot into the bin and, Angus realised, refusing to look at him. 'It will only take a moment.'

'Great,' Angus said.

'There's some mango left…' She pulled it from the fridge, holding up half a fruit, and without waiting for his reply ran the knife along the plump fruit, scoring it into little crosses, then pushing her fingers onto the soft skin and inverting it so that all the fruit poked up into little squares and it felt strangely erotic.

She probably walked around like this at home all the time, Angus frantically reasoned. Wandering around the house in a bikini was probably the norm where she came from. Only there were kangaroos in Australia too, but he didn't expect to see one when he looked out of the window. Still, Angus told himself, she no doubt spent her entire day wearing as little as possible—only that thought wasn't exactly helping matters either!

The huge kitchen was claustrophobically tiny now, and he could see her freckly breasts jiggling before his eyes as she whipped up the batter.

'Won't be long!' Imogen smiled.

'The heating's high…' Angus said gruffly.

'Is it?' Imogen shrugged.

He could hear the batter sizzling as it hit the frying pan. Her back was to him and it was brown, this gorgeous brown that was so rare these days. Her tan not perfect because he could see the straps where another bikini must have been, could see the freckles that showered her back, only it looked pretty perfect to him…

'Here.' Leaning over the bench, she handed him breakfast and as she leant forward he could see the white of her breast as her bikini shifted, saw a little bit of Imogen that had never seen the sun. He knew she'd caught him looking because she was looking at him too, knew because the already hot room was stifling now. The bubbling steam from the kettle nothing compared to the cauldron sizzling between them. Three days after one's marriage ended was arguably the best or worst time to act on impulse—only Angus wasn't actually thinking about that.

For ages his marriage had been over and there was this assumption, from his mother, from Gemma, even from Imogen at first, that he must, in that time, have been seeing someone else. As if coping with the demise and subsequent end of his marriage couldn't have been enough to keep him occupied. Oh, they hadn't come right out and said it, but he could sense they thought there had to be more.

Well, there hadn't been anyone.

But, yes, there was more.

Pushing a plate towards him, loaded with pancakes and mango and syrup, Angus's mouth should have been watering, only it was a touch dry as he realised that there was way more to it than anyone knew.

And he was looking right at her.

Only now Imogen wasn't looking away, as she always had before. In fact, she was looking right at him. For the first time in the longest time, the first time for ages, the woman Angus wanted was looking back at him…

And with want in her eyes.

He *was* beautiful.

She'd known that from the start.

And he was nice.

She'd known that too.

But that this august yet tender man might actually want her in the way she wanted him was, for Imogen, a revelation.

Embarrassed at being caught in her bikini, she'd attempted casual—had, oh, so casually covered herself with her sarong and wished, as she often did, that she'd kept to her diet, or even considered that he might come home early. There were so many things Imogen hadn't factored in, and seeing the want in his eyes as she'd come down the stairs had been one of them.

Oh, she'd dismissed it, told herself she was imagining things.

But, standing in the kitchen, attempting to be normal,

she could hear the fizz of arousal sizzling around them. She tried to tell herself over and over that she was misreading things, that it was her want that she could sense and not his.

Only it was everywhere.

She could feel his eyes on her, burning into her back as she turned away, could feel his need in the stifling air she dragged into her tight chest. Awareness in every jerky movement, she was scared to turn around, scared that he might see the tumble of emotions that were coursing through her.

Because, as the kettle rattled to the boil, as she slid the plate she'd prepared towards him, Imogen knew it was impossible, knew that Angus Maitlin could have any woman he wanted…

Only he wanted her.

Watching him stride towards her, she could taste him almost before he kissed her. His mouth on hers had been the last thing she'd expected on awakening, yet it was everything she needed now. Angus made her feel like a woman again, one who had come alive.

For Angus it was the easiest walk of his life.

Used to making difficult decisions in an instant, this one was actually incredibly easy. Oh, he'd wrestled with it for days, had gone over every argument in his head as to why it would never happen, why it could never work, had told himself that he was imagining things, that this vibrant stunning woman saw him as nothing more than a colleague and a friend…

Till she looked up and he saw the pink flush that was

ever present in her cheeks spread across her neck and down her chest. He registered the tiny swallow in her throat, and for Angus, walking round the bench and over to her came as naturally as breathing—in fact, more naturally, because breathing was proving difficult right now, his lungs taut. His hands rested on the tops of her arms and he felt her tremulous body beneath them, a body that didn't want soothing, her skin soft and smooth beneath his fingers. He noticed a bergamot note to her perfume as his face neared hers, and it would have been so easy to kiss her then, but haste would have deprived him of seeing those pale blue eyes, black now with pupils dilated with lust. The scent of her skin filled his nostrils and the arousal between them intensified as the feel of her soft cheek grazed against his. He wanted to taste her mouth now so he did, placing his lips on hers and closing his eyes at the exquisite sweetness of ripe flesh that wanted to taste him too—and taste him she did, sucking on his bottom lip. Her hands on his shoulders, fingers kneading lightly as thoroughly he kissed her back.

'Oh, God, Imogen…' He moaned her name as he pulled back, knowing that at this point it should stop, should merit discussion, acknowledgement, something…but the bliss of wanting was here and now and the bliss of being wanted was mind-blowing. She kissed him back, her response moist, lingering, slow, like a river inevitably rolling. He could feel her hands slipping under his theatre top, inquisitive fingers exploring his stomach. He didn't want it to end, wanted also to explore this woman who wore a bikini and sarong on a freezing December morning—who had brought sunshine and warmth into what should have been the bleakest and coldest of winters. His hands, without guidance, were undoing the knot of her sarong, watching two red triangles strain against the gorgeous flesh of her breasts. He wanted to taste the woman who fed him fruit when he wanted bed, and pushing aside the bikini top he lowered his mouth. Her nipples were as hard as hazelnuts swelling in his mouth as he tasted her, his hand on her skin, her back, her waist, feeling the delicious, unfamiliar curves, the generous flesh that was for him, tasting the feel of want on his mouth, these myriad sensations as she kissed him back. And it felt so right—he'd come home this morning and it felt as if he were coming home to her now, to a kiss that had been waiting patiently, to a kiss that was almost *familiar*, because he'd been there before.

He may have said goodnight to her from the day she'd moved in, but he'd met her only a couple of hours later in his dreams. And dreams didn't match up to the real feel of her mouth on his, sucking him, kissing him, devouring him. Imogen, alive in his arms, and he was coming alive again too. In one easy shift she was sitting on the kitchen bench, sliding his theatre top over his head, and the moan of delight as she saw his torso had him so hard he had to slow himself down. Her fingers pressed harder into his shoulder, her hungry lips tasting his nipples now. Angus noticed there were still the last remnants of glitter on her nipple, this little glimmer of gold where there shouldn't be, and he sucked at it, yet still it stayed. He flicked at the fleck again with his tongue, willing himself to slow down, but she was playing with the ties of his theatre bottoms now, pulling them down with some difficulty over his erection as he dealt with the far easier task of her bikini bottom ties.

Alone in the kitchen, not a wedding ring between them, but there was a whole lot else. Staring into her pale blue eyes, seeing her blink, Angus knew she knew it too.

'We shouldn't…' he half heartedly attempted, kissing her again.

'We should,' Imogen purred as she kissed him back.

'You'll be gone soon…'

'I'm here now.' She guided his hands to her sweetest place and as the pad of his thumb took her most intimate pulse, he tried one last attempt at reason.

'It's too soon…' But her ankles were round his back and it felt like he'd been waiting for ever.

'Not for me.'

'I'm crazy about you, Imogen,' Angus gasped, hovering at her entrance, seeing the golden curls that beckoned him and desperate to enter, her breathless response all the invitation required as he plunged in blissfully.

'Me, too!'

It was like stumbling into paradise, feeling her legs coil around him as she dragged him in, smelling her, tasting her, feeling her. This stunning, beautiful woman was somehow as into him as much as he was into her. It *was* too much, and certainly *too soon*, and just as Angus tried to slow himself down, just as he forced himself to think about tax receipts and spreadsheets and anything mundane, she dragged him in deeper, her ankles coiling around his back, her head arching backwards, and he kissed the hollows of her throat. Angus knew that nothing was going to distract him now, and better still, as he felt her tighten, and heard these little throaty gasps come from the throat he was kissing, distraction was as unnecessary as it was impossible. He could feel the rhythm of her orgasm beating for him to join her in this heady place, and the only thing Angus was concentrating on was her, was Imogen, and how she made him feel. Then the heaven of his climax and the sheer pleasure of hers when it happened had his heart thumping a tattoo in his chest. As he held her after it all should have dimmed as reality invaded, as they were back in the kitchen having taken the biggest most reckless step of their lives. But, if anything, the world looked better.

'Oh, Angus.' Still inside her, still holding her, as blue eyes met his, there was no place he would rather have been. 'What do you do to me?'

'I could ask the same thing.'

And it should have been awkward, only it wasn't.

And guilt was curiously absent as he kissed her again.

There was not even a hint of uncertainty as she popped the pancakes in the microwave for all of thirty seconds, grabbed a fork and they both headed upstairs, just a tiny pause at the landing as he steered her to his bedroom.

'My room,' Imogen insisted. 'I can't do anything in there.'

'I can't do anything in the nanny's room!' Angus grinned. 'Anyway, it's a single bed!'

'Brilliant!'

'I thought I was getting an ulcer.'

'You need to eat more regularly.'

They were lying naked on her tiny bed, blinds closed on the skylight, the heating still up high and the radio still blaring, feeding each other mango in golden syrup, both discovering again what it felt like to be happy.

Not fine, or OK, or getting there, but actually happy.

Absolutely at ease, lost in the moment and just, well, happy.

'I keep getting this pain, you see….' Angus tapped his stomach. 'Well, not a pain as such…right here… right here in my solar plexus.'

'You poor baby!' Imogen soothed, bending her head and kissing it better.

'Every time I see your ex, either in the flesh or on the television, every time I hear Owen tell me how bloody fantastic that red-headed agency nurse is…' He blew out a breath. 'I didn't realise it at the time, but this little network of nerves, that really don't do much, scrunches into a ball every time…'

'Oh.' She looked up at him. 'Are you jealous?'

'I don't know.' Angus grimaced, because he'd never really been jealous before.

'Well, don't be!' Imogen frowned. 'Brad's like one of your boxes under the tree—beautifully gift wrapped, but sadly empty. There's nothing between us, nothing at all.'

Tired now, he watched as she slipped under the sheet, watched her lovely face on the pillow, those blue eyes smiling at him, and it felt utterly right to join her and spoon his body in behind her, to place his hand on the curve where her waist met her bottom and just hold her, and utterly wrong that in two weeks she'd be gone.

'Gemma's boyfriend's not Australian, by any chance?' Imogen said, much later in that time before falling asleep.

'Afraid not. Brad might get more work here…?'

'He's been offered a job on a children's show back home.'

'Oh.'

He wasn't remotely tired now. Too used to sleeping alone, he had been trying to accommodate to the feel of her in his arms, trying to fathom out that this was real, as his mind, which was used to coming up with them, raced for a solution, for something, some way to hold on to what they had only just found. Only at every twist of his thoughts he was thwarted…

Kids, careers, exes, schools—oh, and a tiny matter of ten thousand or so miles.

And she waited, stared at the wall and waited for him to say that they'd work something out, waited for him to tell her that it would all be OK, that somehow it might work.

Only he couldn't.

'We should keep it quiet,' Angus said instead.

'I wasn't going to rush into work and put up a poster.'

'I know.' He felt her body stiffen, could hear the irritated edge in her voice, especially when she continued.

'Don't worry, I won't damage your perfect reputation.'

'Imogen.' He put his hand up to her cheek, tucked a stray strand of hair behind her ear and tried to voice what he was feeling. 'It's not just about my reputation—you go home soon, all it will look like to others is a fling… It's about your reputation too.'

'I know.' She was glad she was facing away from him. Tears were stinging her eyes, knowing he was right and wishing it wasn't so.

'And it would be just so confusing for the kids….'

'Of course.' She gave a big sniff. 'They don't need to know anything.' Which was right and everything, but it just made it seem like a dirty little secret. As if all they shared, all that had felt so right, was seemingly wrong. 'You know…' Imogen gave a pale smile. '…I always wondered what Heath would be like, you know, if I met someone…'

'He hasn't met any of your boyfriends?'

'There haven't been any boyfriends.'

'But you and Brad broke up ages ago.'

'I wasn't ready,' Imogen said, and he rolled her towards him then, didn't want to talk to her back when he could see her instead, and he stared deep into those eyes that had entranced him from the second they'd locked with his. He knew then that he didn't really know her at all, only *how* he wanted to. He wanted to know everything about the shy but provocative, gentle yet sexy, completely stunning woman that had greeted him on the stairs, and who had just been his. 'I don't share my mango with everyone!'

She was attempting a joke, only he wasn't smiling,

the seriousness of their situation hitting home. Serious, Angus realised, because this deep, beautiful woman had trusted only him with her patched-up heart, and that was something he could never take lightly.

'Come here,' he said, as if the two centimetres that separated them in the bed was as vast as the distance that separated their future. Pulling her towards him, he kissed her deeply, though tenderly, blotting out the many questions with slow, deep answers, because for now there wasn't any rush. They didn't have to think about anything right now.

Imogen wasn't going anywhere today and neither was Angus.

CHAPTER NINE

'WHAT did you guys do today?'

'Nothing!' Looking up from smiling, pyjama-clad people mulling over a vast jigsaw, Imogen's smile was arguably the widest when Angus came home from work the next day. 'We just flopped.'

'Flopped?'

'Flopped around and didn't do much. We didn't even get dressed—did we, guys?'

'We brushed our teeth!' Jack said.

'I didn't!' Heath grinned, but one look from his mother and he hurtled up the stairs to the bathroom. Also in pyjamas, Imogen wandered into the kitchen where Angus was serving up some wicked-looking noodles.

'Thanks for this!'

'They're just noodles!'

'I mean this…' She gave a sigh of contentment as she looked around and beyond the kitchen. 'You have no idea how much it means to just do *nothing* with Heath. It's just been so nice to have a quiet day, instead of thinking up things to do or sitting in a burger bar, which is what I would have been doing today if I wasn't here.'

'Thank you too…' Angus smiled. 'It's been so nice to go to work and know the kids are happy and not have to worry about what I'm going to find when I come home. Have they asked about Gemma?'

'Clemmie has.' Imogen nodded. 'Gemma rang this afternoon and spoke to them for a couple of minutes, but Jack's asking when she's coming home. Have you spoken to her?'

'I've rung her,' Angus said, 'but I just got her voicemail. I've sent her a few texts—told her that we need to sort things out as to what to tell the kids. I've told her too that she needs to see them…' He raked a hand through his hair. 'I'm just in this holding pattern—till I see her, till I speak to her, I don't know…'

Which left Imogen in a holding pattern too.

Knowing that at any minute Gemma could come back, that with one phone call everything would change.

And it was selfish of her to not wish that for him.

How could she not wish that his relationship with Gemma was salvageable? How could she not wish that Clemmie and Jack's mum might suddenly come home—after all, home was where she would be heading soon.

'Have you sorted out the boxroom for Heath?' His question dragged her out of her introspection. 'There are spare pillows in the hall cupboard, I think.'

'I had hoped he'd want to sleep in with me, given we haven't spent a night under the same roof for a while, but times have changed apparently—he's got new friends now!'

'There's a trundle bed under Jack's,' Angus suggested.

'All options examined…' Imogen rolled her eyes. 'They want to camp out.' She gave a little wince. 'In the lounge.'

'Of course they do!' Angus grinned and she was so happy he did—so happy that a little bit of chaos didn't matter to him. 'Why would you want a soft warm bed when there's a cold hard floor?'

'They're planning a midnight feast too.' Imogen giggled. 'Though we don't know about that.'

And she loved it that he lowered all the crisps and treats to a lower shelf, loved it that he put a few cans of usually forbidden fizz in the fridge and pulled the ice cream to the front of the freezer. Loved it that he couldn't just *get* the blankets for the kids to make the fort, but *had* to help them too. And with growing amusement Imogen came back from a long soak in the bath to find some rather impressive-looking tents, all of which Angus had to go in and check for size and comfort.

'Mine's the best!' Clemmie demanded. 'Isn't it, Imogen?'

'It's fabulous!' Imogen declared, checking it out for herself. 'I might sleep here myself.'

And later, when the living room was a no-go zone, and Imogen had eaten the last of the noodles while Angus finished off the crossword in the newspaper, when she was sitting in a dressing-gown at the kitchen table as Angus headed off to the shower, when his mother called and she had to knock for him to come out of the shower, it was just too much.

Standing in the kitchen dripping wet with a towel around his hips, trying to find a pen to write down his mother's flight arrival time, Imogen knew that if she spent a second longer in the same room with him and didn't touch him, she'd surely self combust, and she could take no more.

'I'm going to bed.'

'It's only nine o'clock!' Angus said, cursing as the crayon he was using to write, suddenly snapped. 'What did I say the flight number was?'

Only she couldn't answer. Simply couldn't tell him how much she wanted him, or how it was killing her inside to know that this magical evening doing *nothing* with the kids, this slice of heaven they had found, couldn't be shared with others and certainly couldn't last.

'I'll make you a cup of tea…' He was halfway to the kettle and she'd half decided to stay up a bit longer when the phone rang. She watched the set of his shoulders stiffen, watched his free hand rake through his damp hair and even before he said her name, Imogen knew that it was Gemma.

Knew she wouldn't be getting her cup of tea.

Closing the kitchen door, she checked on the kids—smiling at their excited faces and joining in the fun, leaving him to it, because his marriage ending had nothing to do with her.

But it was hard.

Especially when the phone in the living room

clicked off and she knew the call was over, but he still didn't come out.

Especially when later, much later, the kids charged into the kitchen, with Imogen racing to stop them, only to find Angus with his head in his hands at the table.

'Are you crying?' Clemmie said accusingly.

'Don't be daft!' Angus grinned but looked distinctly glassy-eyed. 'I've got a cold.'

And later, lying in bed, she could hear the commotion downstairs, kids giggling, the fridge door opening, and as the bedroom door pushed open and he sat down on the side of her bed, she hated the tears that greeted his hand when he stroked her cheek.

'Sorry!' She shuddered the word out.

'For what?'

'You were right….' Imogen gulped. 'It is too soon.'

'Not for me.'

'You miss her—and it's right that you miss her…'

'Imogen, have you any idea how unbearable the last few days would have been without you?' Still he stroked her cheek. 'And have you any idea how unbearable my life was before I met you?'

'No.'

'She's coming over tomorrow. We're going to tell the kids—that's what's beating me up.'

'It's nearly Christmas,' Imogen croaked.

'Which gives us a little time to get our act together for Christmas Day.' Angus screwed his eyes closed. 'Couldn't she have waited?' Then he cursed himself. 'I shouldn't have pushed things—'

'No.' Imogen interrupted. 'Angus, you can't plan these things and Gemma couldn't either. She didn't just *decide* to fall in love…'

'Don't expect me to forgive her…' Angus shook his head.

'Would it have been any easier in September?' Imogen asked. 'With Clemmie all excited about school… Or maybe you could have held out till Easter…'

'Imogen, don't…'

But she did.

'Or last year when you knew things were over…'

'No,' Angus admitted. Gazing down at her, the muddied waters cleared a touch as he realised in many ways that time had actually been kind, because somehow she was here beside him. 'What would I do without you?'

'You'll find out soon enough.'

His mouth was gentle. A kiss so tender, so kind, so merited that for that second, even if the kids had rampaged up the stairs and caught them, it would have surely been justified.

So justified that when the crisp packets were empty, when the carefully built tents had long since collapsed and three little people lay curled up on the floor, with Angus and Imogen tucking blankets around shoulders, it seemed right that he take her hand as they headed up the stairs to bed. Somehow it would be wrong to sleep alone tonight.

'Put the chair against the door.' Imogen gulped, shy all of a sudden, hating the body he seemed to adore, not as bold as before and wishing he'd turn the lights off or would turn around long enough so that she could jump under the covers without him seeing her.

But see her he did.

One touch and she was comfortable.

One kiss and he soothed her.

Chased away the insecurities with every caress.

And never had his love been as sweet as it was bitter.

The depth of his kiss almost annulled by its sheer impossibility. Like a barnacle on a rock, she clung to him, couldn't bear that soon they would be ripped apart. Her single bed was just so much better for the intimacies they shared, to feel the muscle of him beside her, every roll, every kiss, every tumble bringing them closer until he was where he belonged—inside her.

And it was the saddest, sweetest love she had ever made. Every stroke, every beat of him pushing them to a place they'd never been, to mutuality, affinity, to a space in the world that was solely for them.

Sweet to have visited.

So sad to leave.

Her single bed huge when later, much later, he crept from the room.

CHAPTER TEN

OH, YOU can smile and distract, you can make soothing noises, you can ignore and deny and you can really try to hide things, but children always know.

Especially at Christmas.

'Mum's coming in an hour.' Clemmie was sitting on the stairs, watching as Imogen pulled her boots and coat on. She was taking Heath on the London Duck Tour, would ride around Central London then plunge into the Thames in the same amphibious vehicle.

Heath had been bright-eyed with excitement when Imogen had told him about it.

Jack and Clemmie hadn't even asked if they could go.

'That's good,' Imogen said, looking at her little angry face and truly not knowing what to say.

'I'm going to play in my room.'

Imogen didn't call out goodbye to Angus and didn't call it out to the children, relieved just to open the front door and escape the oppressive atmosphere.

'Hello, Imogen.'

The camera did lie. Because standing on the doorstep,

close to six feet tall in high-heeled cream boots and a soft cream coat, dark hair billowing around her pale face, Imogen hadn't braced herself for Gemma's absolute beauty, or that she might know her name.

'Angus said he'd arranged some temporary help…'

Oh, she needn't have worried, Imogen realised, because not for a second would this stunning woman ever consider her a threat. It wouldn't even enter her head that Angus might want someone as dowdy and as plain as her.

'The children have raved about you on the phone… Thank you so much for taking care of my babies,' Gemma continued in a flurry, and Imogen realised the woman was actually beside herself with nerves, still standing on the doorstep of her own home, as if it was up to Imogen to ask her inside.

Truly not knowing what to say, Imogen was saved from answering as Angus came down the hallway.

'Hello, Gemma.'

'Oh, Angus.'

Of course she didn't need to be asked in, Imogen thought as she stepped out into the street. Of course, when Gemma burst out crying, Angus would comfort her as together they faced the most appalling task together. Only she had never expected to like her, had never expected to be moved by the raw tears that had spilled from her eyes, the throaty sob that had come from her lips. And if it moved her, then what must it have done for Angus?

Maybe they might make it work, Imogen thought,

huddled up with Heath, freezing as they sped through the streets taking photos and quacking at passersby. Heath whooped with delight as they plunged into the river and even though it was fun and brilliant and a day she'd remember for ever, Imogen felt as if her heart was being squeezed from the inside.

Especially after she dropped off Heath at Brad's and went back to a house that felt different somehow, no matter how Angus tried to act normal.

A new normal.

A new normal where Angus went into work for a few hours and Gemma came over on Christmas Eve to take the children out and Imogen attempted some last-minute Christmas shopping. Heath was easy to buy for and Jack and Clemmie were too. Brad? Well, thankfully, given it was December, sunglasses were drastically reduced in price, which took care of that.

If only Angus was so easy.

Along with the last of the frantic last-minute shoppers she wandered around vast department stores, trying to find the perfect present for the perfect man—and knowing she had one chance to get it right.

That this could be their only Christmas.

And it would take more than a miracle for it to be a happy one. There was just way too much hurt all around.

'Get everything?' Angus asked, when laden with bags she nearly fell through the door.

'If I didn't, it's too late now! How are the kids?' Imogen added, as he helped her stuff the bags in the stair cupboards.

'They seem OK…' His jacket and tie were off, his shirt coming untucked at the hips, but he was still the most impressive man she had ever seen, Imogen thought as he waited till they were alone before discussing it again. 'They really do seem OK. You know, we clung on for a year, thinking we were doing the right thing, but I'm starting to wonder if we—'

'My tooth fell out!' Clemmie burst into the kitchen, dripping blood and smiling at the same time.

'That's what happens if you keep tugging at it.' Angus grinned, getting a wad of kitchen roll and dealing with the casualty. 'She's hoping for bonus points if Santa and the tooth fairy both come on Christmas Eve!'

Clemmie grinned her gappy smile and it reminded Imogen so much of Heath it hurt. Oh, she adored Clemmie, adored Jack, only they weren't her babies.

Her first Christmas Eve without Heath beside her and surely no one in the world knew how she felt.

Except one.

'Mum's on the phone!' Angus called later as he was putting two excited children to bed. Imogen sat in a room bathed with fairy lights, feeling sick on her third mince pie, missing Heath so much it hurt. As she watched a rerun of Shane, all Imogen could wonder was how grown-ups got it so wrong.

How did they mess up so badly—and who was it that suffered the most?

And then she thought of Maria.

Tears sliding down her cheeks, she thought of how, even if it was a difficult life sometimes, she'd so much rather live it. She thought of little Guido, and prayed he was OK without his parents to love him. She barely looked up when Angus walked into the lounge, laden with boxes that *weren't* empty for underneath the tree.

'Still hurts, huh?' Angus asked, staring for a minute at the TV and Shane, then back at her.

'Always,' Imogen answered, as his pager trilled.

And because he was a consultant, because the pubs were turning out and because Gus had promised to come in at six next morning if he could just have Christmas Eve undisturbed, she nodded and took over.

Lugging the presents under the tree as he sped into the night.

She left the Christmas lights on and took bites out of four mince pies then bit on the carrot that had been left for Rudolph. Then she headed up the stairs and quietly filled their stockings, before having to go back down because she'd forgotten that the tooth fairy was coming tonight too. By the end it was a relief, just a blessed relief, to finally close her bedroom door.

It would take more than a miracle to make this Christmas a happy one, Imogen thought, staring up at her little skylight, hearing the wail of sirens in the distance and the swoosh of cars as they sped through the night. Finally she gave way to the tears she'd held in as she'd hung Clemmie's stocking and fiddled with Jack's; as she'd kissed two little faces goodnight, and had done all the right things for Gemma's children…

While all the while missing her own.

CHAPTER ELEVEN

THERE was one advantage to putting two overexcited children to bed on Christmas Eve.

It was actually past eight when the ringing of the phone pierced the house. Sitting up, blinking through swollen lids, Imogen *just* had time to grab her sarong and wrap it around her before two thoroughly over-excited bundles burst into her room.

'Mummy's coming!' Jack yelped. 'She's coming over!'

'Santa's been!' Clemmie chimed in.

Various squeals pierced her brain as two mini-tornadoes spun out of her room and charged down the stairs, leaving Imogen to ponder that things really did seem better in the morning as she was greeted by one tired unshaven sexy blond in a pair of hipsters.

'They seem OK with it.' She could hear the relief in his voice. 'Gemma called me at work. We're going to do Christmas dinner here.'

'That's great.'

'I'm not so sure…' Angus frowned. 'Won't it be too confusing for them?'

'They don't seem confused!' Imogen said, and then looked at him, really looked at him, because Angus didn't seem confused either. The tense man she had met that first day, the strained man she had seen on the day everything had fallen apart, seemed light years away from the one who stood before her now. 'Merry Christmas, Angus.'

'It looks like we might just manage to scrape one together,' Angus answered. 'Merry Christmas, Imogen.'

Standing on the landing with a lovely soft mouth that thoroughly kissed her, and a morning erection that had them both wondering if they could leave it to the kids to find out what Santa had bought them, while Daddy and Imogen concentrated on being naughty and nice, it actually started to look like it might be.

'When did you get back?' Imogen asked directly into his mouth.

'Seven.' His mouth answered into her kiss.

'Daddy!' Clemmie wailed from downstairs.

Christmas really was magic.

Imogen had seen it in her training when she'd worked a shift on the children's ward—seen how, no matter how dire, everyone pulled together and made the impossible work on that day. She'd seen it in her own family a few short years ago and was seeing it now with Angus's.

Angus, with an hour's sleep to his name, trying to work out what parcel Santa had left for whom, because he'd been sure when he'd wrapped them that he'd remember! Smiling and holding it together and doing his very best for the two little people who mattered most.

Or rather three little people.

Imogen pulled out her phone and chatted excitedly to Heath, who was ripping open parcels of his own, and then to Brad, instructing him to turn down the turkey and telling him that she'd be there by ten.

And Gemma must be feeling the same, because she rang again, laughing and talking to the kids and reminding them she'd be there by eleven.

And by the time the kids were whizzing around the room, building Lego castles and playing with dolls, Angus had his little pile of presents left to open and Imogen was blinking at her rather big pile.

A big pile she truly hadn't been expecting.

'Go on, then!' Angus prompted.

'You first,' Imogen replied, just wanting to get it over, kicking herself at the choice she'd made, of all the stupid, soppy, romantic things to go and buy him.

Not that Angus thought it was.

'A waffle-maker?' She could hear the sort of bafflement in his voice as he stared at his kitchen appliance.

'It's going to be your new best friend.' Imogen smiled. 'Brilliant for a quick lunch, or a nice breakfast for the kids...sort of like a pancake mixture...' She saw a smile flare at the side of his mouth as he examined his gift rather more closely.

'Heart-shaped waffles!' Angus said.

'And they only take a few moments to make!'

She saw his tongue roll in his cheek, saw the shake of his head as he got it—all the hours searching for the perfect gift more than worth it now, her humour his.

His loss hers.

'It looks like I'm going to be eating a lot of waffles when you're…'

He didn't say it, he didn't have to—they both knew what lay ahead. And Imogen actually got it then—she'd been waiting, waiting for the wave of grief to hit him, and she realised then that it already had. That hellish year he had lived through had been his mourning time, and Angus really was ready to move on.

It nearly killed her that it wouldn't be with her.

'From the kids!' Angus said, as she opened her smellies.

'From me…' he said gruffly, as she pulled back the wrapper on a vast silk bedspread. 'I'll pay the excess baggage—figured if I can't be with you…'

And it was so nice…too nice, just a whole world away where she'd have to cuddle up to this instead of him, it was easier to open her next present than to think about it.

'From me too…' Angus said as she unwrapped a beautiful glass snow globe, shaking it up and watching the snow fall on Knightsbridge.

'I can see the food hall!' Imogen joked, pretending to peer into the tiny windows. 'Ooh, mangoes!'

'Keep opening.'

'There's more? Angus you shouldn't have…'

'I didn't. You seem to have built up quite a fan club since you've been here.'

'Lollies?'

'Sweets in England!' Angus grinned. 'Read the card.'

Dear Imogen,

I asked Elise to drop these off for you and your lovely little boy.

I felt awful at first being so helpless, but Elise said she doesn't mind a bit!!!

Enjoy being spoiled.

I do!

Ivy Banford

'Cheeky old thing!' Imogen grinned, but her eyes were brimming. 'What's this?' she asked, turning over a silver envelope.

'I'm not sure. I saw Heather putting it in the agency nurse's pigeon hole and I swiped it for you.'

'Probably just a card from Heather…'

But it wasn't. She barely made it past the first line… handing it to Angus who after a moment read it out loud.

'Dear Imogen,

'You spent time with my sister when I could not. Maria worried about her house, she told me you understood—that meant a lot to her—to be understood on that day.

'Forgive me if you find this gift offensive—my hope is to make you smile as you think of my sister.

'With deepest thanks,

'Elijah and Guido Vanaldi'

'That's quite a fan club you've got there,' Angus said, his voice just a touch gruff, reading the gift card more closely. 'You have a cleaner for a year.'

'A cleaner?'

'Actually, you have the crème de la crème of cleaners, to do with what you will for a year… What sort of a present is that?'

'The perfect one.' Imogen crumpled. 'Only I won't be here…'

And she truly didn't know if she was crying because she'd miss him and the children or crying because right now she missed Heath, or crying for Maria, or for the fact that the one time in her life she had the crème de la crème of *everything* lined up and at her service and raring to go, she was in absolutely no position to take what was on offer.

'Come on…' Angus summoned her to the kitchen. 'We've got cooking to do.'

Jack, wearing reindeer ears, poured the batter, and Clemmie insisted on being chief taster. Breakfast really was delicious, but as wonderful as it was to be with Angus, Jack and Clemmie on Christmas morning, there was somewhere else she needed to be.

Wanted to be.

'I'm going to go.'

It was barely after nine, but long before that he had sensed her distraction, knew she wanted to be with Heath. Watched as she applied mascara, lipstick, pulled on her boots, hugged the kids and told them to have a great day.

Watched as she left.

Then waited for Gemma to arrive.

And Christmas really was magic, because somehow

he wasn't quite so angry. Somehow he managed to just put it all on hold.

He had understood when he'd seen Gemma's puffy eyes and nervous face that she had been scared—scared of facing him, scared of telling the kids, scared of the future too, no doubt.

So they had one thing in common at least! And now they had two, both wanting to give their kids a good Christmas to remember.

'Wow!' Gemma beamed as the kids showed her the graffiti job they'd performed on the tree. 'You two have been busy!'

'Imogen helped us make them.'

'Imogen?' She glanced over to Angus. 'The kids do seem fond of her. Can she stay on?'

'Afraid not!' Angus busied himself picking up wrapping paper. 'But Mum's coming in a couple of days and I'll put an ad in in the new year.'

'Well, between us all…' Gemma was picking up paper too, holding a garbage bag for the first time in years and actually cleaning up the mess so they could enjoy the day '…we'll work it all out.'

Yes, magic, because when, after a vast Christmas dinner and a couple of very welcome glasses of Imogen's red wine, he didn't explode when Gemma asked if she could have the children with her that night where she was staying.

'You're staying with him?'

'Yes, but he's not there tonight—he's going to visit his family. I thought it might be better for the children to see where I'm staying for the first time without Roger being there…' She swallowed hard as she voiced his name. 'I think that would be too confusing for them.'

Oh, and there was such a smart retort on the tip of his tongue, but he swallowed it down with another swig of wine and managed a curt nod.

Magic, because later, when the house was unbearably quiet, when the living room was littered with toys and no kids, and all the beds upstairs were empty, when for a second he didn't think he could stand it, there she was. He watched from the window as Brad dropped Imogen off, grimacing just a touch as she kissed her ex goodbye. In turn Imogen sniffed Gemma's perfume in the air when she walked through the door.

'How was it?'

'Great!' Imogen beamed, depositing a large amount of bags, not noticing the set of his jaw as she opened a box and pulled out a pair of soft suede boots. 'He remembered my size.'

'How's Heath?'

'Asleep!' Imogen giggled. 'Not for long, though. With the amount of cake and drinks he's had, I wouldn't be surprised if he's up a few times in the night. But we had a great day. I was so worried how it would be, but it turned out to be wonderful. How about for you?'

'It went pretty well,' Angus said, 'given the circumstances. We just put everything on hold and tried to give the kids a great day—which I think we did.'

'Are they in bed?'

'They're at Gemma's.' He saw her eyes widen just a

fraction. 'They really did seem to have a good day. They're going to stay again in a couple of nights if all goes well. They went about half an hour before you came home.' She watched him flinch at his choice of words and gave a soft smile.

'It feels like home.' Imogen said, because it did. Getting out of the car and walking up the steps, for the first time in the longest time she actually felt as if she was coming home. This peace to her soul that he brought, a connection that was blissfully familiar. 'And well done, you.'

Yes, it felt like home and it felt like Christmas when, full from the day's excesses, they still managed to gorge on Ivy's presents as they sat cuddled up on the sofa beside the twinkling Christmas tree, watching the same slushy movie that was surely on the world over on Christmas night. It felt like home and it felt completely right.

So right it hurt.

CHAPTER TWELVE

'I'M SCARED.'

At three in the morning and after a long and exhausting labour, Roberta Cummings had every reason to be scared. Her labour hadn't progressed but, determined to deliver naturally, she had held on. Imogen had come in often to check and finally the resident had sent for his registrar when, at still only five centimetres dilated, the baby's heart rate had started to dip during contractions and an emergency caesarean had been decided on.

'You're going to be fine.' Imogen assured Roberta.

'What about the baby?'

'Hey!' Imogen held the terrified woman's hand and it was such bliss to be able to reassure her, 'We've been watching you closely all night and we're doing this now, *before* the baby gets into too much distress... When you wake up, you'll have your baby!'

There was a quiet assuredness in Imogen, which she imbued in her patients. Here on Maternity, even though things could go wrong, even though they did, Imogen was confident in the process of birth, even when it was a complicated one. With the right team and the right approach, this emergency would turn into something wonderful and *that* for Imogen made it the place she wanted to be.

'Now, do you understand what's happening?' Smiling down at his patient, despite the flurry of activity going on in the theatre, the obstetrician, Oliver Hanson, was calm and unruffled. 'We can't wait for the epidural to take effect, so the anaesthetist is going to put you to sleep…'

'Think baby thoughts.' Imogen smiled as the anaesthetist placed a mask over Roberta's face, and Imogen held her hand, watched her relax and then stiffen. Then, as medications were slipped into her IV, she jolted as her body resisted, and then relaxed again as the anaesthetist swiftly intubated.

'Let's get this little guy out,' Oliver said. Only now, with the patient safely asleep, did he show the haste this procedure required if the baby was to be born safely. Making his incision, strong arms had to work hard as the baby's head was deep into the birth canal. A wrinkly purple bottom followed by two floppy legs was delivered onto the drapes, and even though it was the third delivery Imogen had seen that night, still it never ceased to amaze her. She watched as he was expertly lifted, a theatre nurse receiving the precious bundle and heading over to the cot as the team vigorously rubbed the baby, his navy eyes open, not even blinking.

'Let's cover that ugly head before Dad sees you!' Rita, a senior midwife said with a laugh as the baby's head was elongated from his difficult attempt at birth. They all knew it would all settle down soon, but could often scare new parents. 'Right, Imogen, do you want to take him to the nursery?'

Which was the best bit for Imogen, introducing the little fellow to his dad, who sat and held him as they waited for his mum to be ready to meet him too. Oh, and she could have bathed him and dressed him up in one of the little outfits his mum had brought in for this day, but she chose to wait and let Roberta see him all sticky and messy and covered in vernix.

'Imogen?' Rita popped her head in just as Imogen was introducing a very tired but elated Roberta to her son. 'The nurse co-ordinator's on the telephone. Now that we've quietened down here, she wondered if you'd mind popping down to Emergency for the last couple of hours of your shift.'

'Sorry about this!' Heather apologised the moment Imogen hit the department and she walked her over to Resus. 'The place is steaming. I had to send two staff home at midnight with this wretched flu that's going around—that's why I'm stuck on nights too—then we had this one bought in…

'Gunshot wound!' she added as they walked briskly. 'To the right upper chest, and from what the police say there might be a couple more on the way!'

'Can we roll him over?' Angus didn't acknowledge her and she didn't expect him to as she joined the rather sparse trauma team and helped to roll the patient over so that Angus could examine the exit wound. She knew she was just another pair of efficient hands as they raced to put in a chest drain and push through blood in the hope of getting him up to Theatre before he bled out. For the second time that night Imogen hit the theatre doors, running alongside Angus, the thoracic team having run ahead and already scrubbed and gotten in place.

'Sorry!' Both slightly breathless from the run and adrenaline, it took a while for Imogen to answer.

'For what?' Imogen stopped at the water cooler and took a long drink. 'I don't expect you to kiss me hello!'

'For telling Heather to get you from Maternity.'

'You told Heather that I was working?' Imogen frowned.

'I said that I'd bumped into you in the car park.' Registering her frown, he spectacularly misinterpreted it. 'It was hardly the place to say that I knew you were at work.'

'I'm not worried about that.' Stopping midway in the corridor she angrily confronted him. 'I was actually enjoying my shift. I assumed that the nurse co-ordinator had requested me. You had no right to tell them to pull me off Maternity.'

'Imogen, a guy was bleeding out. We had staff dropping like flies and Heather frantically trying to call people in. I *knew* that there was an experienced emergency nurse up on Maternity. We needed you—'

'Needed me?' Imogen furiously interrupted. 'Or was it just terribly convenient that I happened to be there?'

'Well done, guys!' Heather's weary face greeted two

stony ones. 'Thanks so much for that, Imogen—I don't know what we'd have done without you.'

'Survived, no doubt!'

'Probably.' Heather yawned. 'But you made things a lot easier. Hey, Angus, I was going to drop round this afternoon when I woke up. I've made up a few meals…'

'You don't have to do that.' Angus smiled and shook his head. 'Anyway, I'm going to the airport to pick up Mum.'

'Well, tomorrow, then,' Heather pushed. 'I can pop them over—'

'And offend my mum!' Angus's smile froze in his face as he met Imogen's eyes. 'Honestly, Heather, we're fine. You don't have to worry.'

'You were right.' Angus arrived home a couple of hours after Imogen, and she could have pretended to be asleep but couldn't be bothered with games. Instead, she just lay there as Angus placed a mug of tea on her bedside table and nudged her knees just a little bit to make room for him when he sat down. 'I shouldn't have told Heather that you were working— I should have left it to the co-ordinator to work it out. I just didn't think. The department was bursting and we needed help quickly…'

'I get all of that,' Imogen said, staring up at the skylight, 'but don't…' blue eyes snapped to his '…choose when it's convenient to know me.'

'I don't.'

'Come on, Angus. You're not leaving for the airport

till five—don't tell me if I wasn't here that Heather wouldn't be welcome to drop over.'

'I don't need food parcels, Imogen.'

'Perhaps, but if Heather drops by and sees me here, then work will know, which wouldn't look too good for you, would it?'

'What do you want me to say here?' Angus asked. 'That we should tell everyone? Tell them at work, tell Gemma, tell my mother, tell the kids… And then what? You'll go. You'll be on that plane and back to your life in Australia and I'll still be here. Surely it's better if it's just between us.'

'Which is why I think I should go. I don't think it can work with your mum here. I think it might be awkward…' Imogen gulped. 'I mean, it's hard enough keeping it from the kids.'

'She doesn't still tuck me in at night.' Angus attempted a joke, only she didn't return his smile.

'It's not about that…' Tears were welling in her eyes. 'It's about us. I mean, she'll know I'm not the nanny or just a friend helping out. She'll see what we're like….'

'Like what?'

'Like this.'

And she answered the question that he hadn't been able to back at the café. When she'd asked him what the different things had been that he and Gemma had wanted, he hadn't known how to answer, but *this* was what he wanted and *this* was what he couldn't have.

'Stay.' He didn't know if he was asking for the next few nights or for ever, but he knew her answer covered both.

'I can't.'

'Don't go.' His eyes closed on the impossibility of it all, then opened again, his voice firmer now. 'Look, I've got to pick up the kids at three. Come to the airport, stay for a couple of days, at least till after New Year. You can't stay at the hostel for that…'

'I might want to go out partying!' Imogen tried, but they both knew she wouldn't.

'Stay a bit longer and let the kids get used to the idea of you going…'

'They're not going to miss me….'

'Oh, they will.' Angus insisted. 'I can assure you my mum won't notice a thing. And if by some miracle she does…' he blew out a breath '…then I guess I'll have to just deal with it.'

'You're so pretty!' Clemmie sighed as, feeling anything but, Imogen peered in the mirror at her puffy face and dragged a brush through her hair.

'Really? Well, so are you.'

'Oh, I will be,' Clemmie nodded assuredly, 'when my teeth stop falling out.'

They were just adorable.

Used to dealing with kids, it still took her by surprise how quickly she'd come to *like* Clemmie and Jack. Oh, all kids were cute and all kids were nice and funny if you stopped to look, but too many years in Emergency had knocked some of that sentiment out of her.

Till she'd had Heath and till she'd met Clemmie and Jack.

Jack, as direct and as serious as his father could be. Clemmie, as offbeat and as funny as her father could sometimes be too!

And she adored them both for it—for the way they'd made Heath feel welcome, for the tiny moments like this one as Clemmie stood in the bathroom and told Imogen she was wonderful then promptly steered the conversation back to herself.

'I wish I could look pretty for the party tomorrow.'

'That's right.' Imogen smothered a smile as Clemmie worked her way up to whatever it was she'd be asking. 'You and Jack have got a party to go to.'

'I don't want Nanny to do my hair.' Clemmie came over and fiddled with her hairbrush. 'She hurts when she brushes it and she doesn't do it very nice—she always puts it in bunches. But if you're my nanny too…'

'I'm not really a nanny, and your Nanny's a different sort of nanny…' Imogen attempted, but it was too hard. 'But, yes, I am helping look after you and, if you want, I can do your hair.'

'With that sparkly stuff that was in my stocking?' Clemmie checked, finally getting to the point she had been wanting to make all along!

'Sure.' Imogen grinned.

The drive to the airport was pretty fraught, the traffic moving at a snail's pace, giving Angus and Imogen plenty of time to pause for thought as they watched the planes take off and land. Three weeks had stretched endlessly ahead, when Imogen had first landed. A long,

long holiday then she'd go back home with Heath. At first it had felt like for ever, only now, as all good holidays do at the end, the days were starting to fly by fast. New Year's Eve was just around the corner and then just a few days after she would be on her way home.

She'd made so many plans, there had been so many things she'd wanted to do in her time here, and she'd achieved them all—just never when she'd made those plans had she expected to fall in love.

Yes, love.

Oh, she'd told herself it was a holiday romance, only that didn't quite fit.

Holiday romances didn't work, apparently because you were lying on a beach by day getting nice and tanned and out at night sipping cocktails, which didn't translate to the real world.

Yet they'd lived in the real world.

Through the rain and the gloom they'd still managed to find laughter, so it couldn't be a holiday romance. And it certainly wasn't a fling…at least not for her.

Heathrow was as daunting as it had been when she'd arrived with Heath—people everywhere, trolleys, noise, tension, and that was just the car park! But standing in Arrivals she couldn't help but get caught up in the excitement. Clemmie, dancing on the spot, arguing with Jack as to what presents Nanny might bring. Imogen wondered what Angus's mother would be like. She imagined some stern, serious, forebidding-looking woman and reeled a touch when all four feet eleven of Jean was introduced to her. Imogen realised before they'd even made it back to the car that Angus's mother was completely potty and really quite lovely.

'Could you make me a cup of tea?' She smiled sweetly at Imogen as they stepped into the house and Angus baulked.

'I told you, Mum, she's not a housekeeper. Imogen's a friend who's helping out.'

'Then she won't mind making me a cup of tea!'

'I don't mind at all,' Imogen answered, smothering a smile as she filled the teapot.

'She'll be back soon!' Jean said, as if Gemma had gone on day trip.

'It's over, Mum.'

'Marriage takes work, Angus.'

'And we did work at it.'

'It wasn't all perfect for your father and I. But we worked at it.'

'Mum, Gemma's met someone else.'

'Maybe she's got that postnatal depression or something.'

'Give me strength!' Angus gritted his teeth as Jean headed off to the bathroom. 'Clemmie's four!'

'She just doesn't want it to be over.'

'But it is.' Angus gave a wry shake of his head. 'Why am I the only one who believes it?'

Still, as delightful as Jean was, as nice as dinner was, as Imogen lay in bed that night she knew there'd be no getting up for a glass of water. Knew Angus was right, that it would be unfair on Jean to tell her, unfair on the kids.... It was just unfair all round.

That glimpse of Heathrow airport, just too real to ignore, meant she couldn't pretend it wasn't happening any more.

CHAPTER THIRTEEN

'SORRY, no, I've actually got plans for New Year's Eve!' Imogen snapped off the phone just a little pink in the face as Angus knew she was lying.

'What are they?' Angus asked.

'Bath and bed!'

'Go on,' Angus pushed, 'I'm working it. It would be fun.'

'New Year's Eve in Accident and Emergency really isn't my idea of a fun night. Now, if they offered me Maternity, I might consider it.'

'Morning! Anything I can do?' Not quite so potty, Jean had retired to bed when it was time to do the dishes, had woken only after the children had eaten breakfast and was now pouring a drink from the pot of tea Imogen had just made.

'Did you hear the kettle, Mum?' Angus grinned, as Imogen's mobile shrilled again.

'Go on.' He smiled. 'It will pay for Madame Tussaud's.'

He wasn't smiling a moment later when he saw her face pale.

'Talk about what, Brad?' Imogen said as she stood up and left the room. For Angus it was almost impossible to carry on chatting to his mother as if nothing was happening. It was hell for him to just sit there and drink tea and pretend it didn't matter that for the first time since he'd known her she'd left the room to take Brad's call.

'I have to go out,' she said when she came back.

'Problem?' Angus asked, his face as strained as hers and both trying not to show it. 'Is Heath OK?'

'Heath's fine.' Imogen gave a tight shrug. 'Brad's got something he wants to discuss. I should only be a couple of hours—I'll be back in time to do Clemmie's hair.'

'Who's Brad?' Jean frowned, the second Imogen had gone.

'Imogen's ex-husband.' Funny, that of all the new phrases he'd been getting used to these past couple of weeks, that one came out the hardest.

'Nice that they're civil.'

She must be becoming a local, Imogen briefly thought as she raced up the escalator instead of just standing. She hadn't even noticed the other passengers on the tube, had just sat there staring blindly out of the darkened windows, trying to fathom what Brad could possibly have to say. Oh, he'd pulled out more than a few surprises in their time together, and a few in their time apart. She'd considered herself quite unshockable where Brad was concerned, till now.

She'd never heard him so nervous.

Laid-back Brad, suddenly supremely polite and, yes, definitely nervous.

He'd met someone, Imogen decided, taking the lift up to his apartment, just like she had... Only that wouldn't faze Brad! But maybe this one *was* serious... Maybe, Imogen gulped, this one was pregnant and there was going to be a brother or sister for Heath.

Knocking on his door, Imogen blew out her breath, sure she'd covered all options.

'Hey!' He kissed her on the cheek, just as he always did, and she played with Heath for a few moments, just as she always did, then Brad asked Heath if he'd play in his room for a moment because Mum and Dad had something they wanted to talk about.

'I don't know how to say this...' Brad wasn't his usual laid-back self as, instead of lounging on the sofa opposite he stood up and paced. 'Actually, I don't even know if I should say this. But if I don't tell you...'

Oh, she hadn't covered all her options, Imogen realised, sitting on the sofa, listening to what he had to say and realising that even after all this time Brad still had it in him to surprise her.

They were *extremely* civil, Angus thought darkly, sitting in an empty lounge, trying not to notice the semi-darkness, trying not to care that two hours had turned into six.

Only he did care.

A lot.

To ring or not?

For the hundredth time he picked up the phone, and

for the hundredth time he replaced it and stared out of the window as if willing her to appear.

She'd gone to see Brad for a couple of hours, six hours ago. She'd told Clemmie she'd be back to do her hair for the party—but she hadn't been. Clemmie was at the party wearing Jean's bunches, though Angus had managed to avoid tears by spraying them silver.

Would it look like he was checking up on her?

Was he checking up on her?

But what if she was hurt?

What if something had happened and he hadn't rung, hadn't rung because he didn't know if he was allowed to check up on her.

Seeing Brad's car pull up, seeing her pale face as she climbed out huddled in her coat, Angus's load didn't lighten. He could see the set of her shoulders, could see as she came up the steps the tension in her pale face, and as she turned the key in the door, somehow he knew it wasn't going to be great. Even before he saw her tear-streaked face and eyes that couldn't quite look at him, he knew that she had something difficult to tell him.

'I'm sorry I didn't get back earlier.'

'It's fine.'

'Was Clemmie OK?'

'She's fine too. Mum's taken them to the party…' He managed a smile. 'I had a go with the sparkly stuff.'

'I wanted to ring…' Still she couldn't look at him. 'Only I didn't know what to say.'

'That's OK…'

'Brad kind of sprang something on me, something I wasn't expecting…'

And it was Angus who didn't know what to say now, Angus who really just didn't.

'I need to think, Angus.' Now she did look at him, tears pooling in her eyes. 'I know you must think—'

'I don't know what to think Imogen.'

'We were just talking about things.'

'What things?' His candid question was merited, and she looked up into those questioning jade eyes and it would have been the easiest thing in the world to tell him, to reveal to him her quandary, to ask this knowledgeable, strong man if maybe, just maybe he could show her the way. Only Imogen knew she had to find the answer herself, had learnt long ago that the easy option often turned out to be hardest in the end.

'What would you call this?' She saw his perplexed expression at her strange response. 'Us,' she elaborated. 'A fling, a relationship, a holiday romance? I mean, if you had to describe it…' The pause was interminable. Watching, waiting for him to answer, seeing the hesitation, the indecision gave Imogen the first taste of bitterness. 'But, then, you wouldn't have to describe it, because no one knows about us, do they?' She stared at him for the longest time. 'Is there any chance for you and Gemma?'

'I've already told you.' His answer came readily this time. 'We're finished.'

'Because if there is a chance,' Imogen said, ignoring his response, 'then you need to explore every option and I don't think you can do that while we're together…'

'Who are we talking about here, Imogen?' Angus asked. 'Do you really think I would have embarked on this if my marriage wasn't completely over?'

'This what, Angus?'

And he didn't know what to call it because it wasn't a fling and it wasn't some knee-jerk response to freedom either and it certainly wasn't a holiday romance, because he was right here at home and Imogen had been there for him during the most difficult of times.

Yet it couldn't be love, because if this was love, then very soon he was going to lose it, and out of all of this, it was the thing he couldn't stand losing the most. Couldn't risk loving her, only to lose her.

'Brad and I have some things that we need to sort out, and so do you and Gemma.'

He didn't even have it in him to be angry, even when later Brad's car pulled up to collect her, because as Heath thundered in and Brad waited in the car for her, though Imogen wasn't crying, she was the saddest, most confused he'd ever seen her.

It should have been easy too, for the kids to all say goodbye. Used to comings and goings, surely people who'd been in their lives for only a couple of weeks shouldn't hurt so much to lose. But they'd been through a lot together, and three tearful children didn't help matters.

'You can write…' Angus attempted.

'I can't write,' Clemmie wailed.

'Well, you can ring then.' His eyes met Imogen's. Maybe she was right to just go, because if two weeks hurt like this, imagine what it would be like in three?

'Ring me!' He fiddled with the buttons on her coat. 'I might see you at work.' He managed a weak smile. 'I promise not to haul you off Maternity again.'

'You can!' Imogen said. 'I'll call you—before I go back, I mean.'

'Do.' He didn't care if his mother was there and if he might have to explain later, didn't really care about anything, except that she was going, and he pulled her into him. Despite her bulk when he held her close, because he couldn't bear to let her go, never had someone felt more fragile.

'He's not worth it.' For the first time he crossed the line, entered a discussion where he didn't belong. 'He'll let you down.'

'I have to think,' Imogen mumbled into his shoulder, then pulled away, 'and so do you.'

CHAPTER FOURTEEN

'READY for action?'

Smiling, even though it was false, Angus walked into the staffroom at ten minutes to nine, depositing a couple of cakes and bottles of fizz on the table as he greeted the team that would witness probably the busiest of nights on the Accident and Emergency calendar year.

Oh, Christmas Eve was impossible once the pubs closed, and Christmas Day always managed to pull a few unpleasant surprises out of the hat, but the fireworks that heralded the new year weren't exclusive to the London skies. Come midnight the department, or rather the patients, would, no doubt, put on a spectacular display of their own, and extra security guards had been rostered on along with the most experienced medical staff.

'Ready!' Heather grinned—a true emergency nurse who was actually looking forward to the night. 'I've bought in a vast turkey curry—it's in the fridge, just help yourself!'

'Oh, I will!' Angus agreed, doing just that and picking up a couple of mince pies to get him started. The mood was festive almost, and although he'd brought food in and would join in with the crazy, alternative New Year's Eve party the staff would have—every breath hurt.

Hurt because a year that needed to end was about to.

Another year was starting, only he didn't quite feel ready.

He would have, though.

If Imogen hadn't entered his life.

If she hadn't waltzed right in and given him a taste of how good, how wonderful, how normal and just delicious being good and wonderful and normal could be.

He was supposed to be busy getting divorced at this point.

Not nursing a broken heart for someone else.

'Have a slice now.' Barb, one of the nurses misread his watery gaze and pushed a massive pavlova towards him, lashings of meringue laced with sugared mango. 'Imogen gave me the recipe.'

How long would it last?

How much longer would her name pepper the department? She'd worked a few shifts and it was as if she'd left a flurry of glitter wherever she'd been.

And he didn't want it to diminish.

Didn't want to take down the Christmas tree, even though Jean kept telling him to.

Didn't want to forget, even though it hurt to remember.

'Go on, have a piece—you know you want to.'

Oh, he did want to. Wanted to ring her up and tell her to get the hell away from Brad. That he didn't deserve her, had hurt her once and would do it again. But what right did he have to do that?

Except that he loved her.

Right there and then Angus admitted to himself what he didn't want to. Didn't want to love her, because he knew he was going to lose her.

They'd both known from the start that it could never go anywhere, that circumstances, geography would keep them apart but, apart or not, Angus knew he didn't need her name to be mentioned to remember the morning they'd found each other. In fact, kneed in the groin with longing, Angus knew that he'd never look at another morning without remembering her.

'Hi, guys!'

Her voice was just utterly unexpected, like some auditory hallucination as he bit into the pavlova.

'Imogen—thank heavens!' Heather practically fell on her as she walked in the staffroom just as the team headed out for handover. 'I begged the agency to send you—I had two of my senior staff ring in sick for this shift just before I went home this morning. I was desperate.'

'The agency said—the *third* time they called!' He watched as she smiled, as she deposited a vast tray on the coffee-table, kebab sticks spiked with pineapples, strawberries, kiwi fruits and mango—bringing summer into the room in so many ways. As she gave him a tight smile, blinking rapidly a few times, he knew that this was hard for her too.

Knew she didn't want to be here—but he was so glad that she was.

'Grab a drink and bring it round,' Heather ordered. 'We'll be having our coffee breaks at the nurses' station tonight. And I am sorry,' she added, 'for pestering you.'

'It worked.' Imogen smiled.

'Still, I shouldn't have asked them to ring you at the hostel when you wouldn't answer your mobile.'

And for a minute it was just the two of them. Imogen dunking a tea bag in her cup and heaping in sugar as Angus fiddled with his stethoscope.

'How have things been?'

'Good,' came her noncommittal answer.

'I didn't expect to see you tonight.'

'I didn't expect to be here, but the agency kept ringing…'

'You're staying at the youth hostel?'

'Where else would I be?' Imogen started, and then paused, two little spots of red burning in her cheek, not from embarrassment but anger. 'You think I'm back with Brad?'

'Well, you did go to him.' All the anger, all the hurt and the bitterness was there in his sentence.

'To talk…' Her words were as laced with anger and bitterness as his. 'I told you that we had things to discuss. Do you really think I'm so available that he could just snap his fingers and I'd run back?'

'Of course not.'

'That I'm so lucky to have him want me—'

'Imogen…' Angus broke in, but she didn't want to hear it.

'I told you it was over with him. I don't change my mind about things Angus…' She gave a twisted smile. 'Except when the blasted agency keep ringing and I end up doing a shift in the last place I want to be.'

'I'm sorry things are so awkward between us.'

'It's actually not all about you, Angus…' She gave a pale smile as Angus frowned. 'I'd better get round there.'

The department was fairly quiet, as it often was early on New Year's Eve, almost as if everyone saved their dramas for later. Heather made sure that her staff took themselves off for extended breaks and filled themselves up on the mountain of food they had brought, while they still had the chance. Imogen wished they were busy, wished the lull would end so the night would be over more quickly.

Wished she knew what Angus was thinking when she caught him looking at her.

'We've got a paediatric arrest coming in!' Angus's face was grim. 'Drowning.'

'Now?' It was a stupid comment. People didn't plan their dramas, didn't know that they were supposed to be quiet till midnight, and it certainly wouldn't enter the family's head that their desperately ill child was the very last thing Imogen wanted to deal with right now.

'New Year's Eve party…' Heather came off the phone from a further update from Ambulance Control. 'The bath was filled with ice for the drinks, and he fell in. Dad found him—it was his party. They can't get hold of his mum—apparently she's working tonight. We don't know how long he's been down.'

'How old?' Imogen croaked.

'Three or four,' Heather answered, 'I can't get a clear answer, it sounds pretty chaotic.'

'It's not Heath.' He could see her hands shaking as she pulled out the leads for the cardiac monitor and opened the pads for the defibrillator, knew exactly what she was thinking.

'You don't know that.'

And he put his arm around her and gave her a squeeze, because now he could, Imogen realised, because now she'd been there a little while longer, now she was considered one of them, it was deemed appropriate.

Only it wasn't.

A friendly cuddle from him was the last thing she needed tonight.

'I'm going to wait for the ambulance,' she said, slipping his arm off and heading outside, shivering as she heard the sirens draw closer, trying to make small talk with a chatty security guard as the nine hours left of her shift stretched on endlessly.

It wasn't Heath.

The second the ambulance doors opened, her mind was put at ease, but the dread stayed with her as she took over the cardiac massage as the paramedics unclipped the stretcher and ran in. Drowning she was more familiar with than burns—nearly every garden in Australia had a pool, and sadly, and all too often, this type of patient presented.

'He's in VF…' The paramedics reeled off the list of treatment and drugs that had been given at the scene and en route, and even though it looked dire, the news was actually as good as it could be.

He was two, not three or four, Imogen heard as she pressed the palm of her hand on his sternum, and an ice-filled bath a far better option for an unsupervised toddler to tumble into than a hot one. He'd have been plunged into hypothermia, which meant the demand for oxygen to his brain would have been rapidly diminished, which gave him a better chance of being left without brain damage. He was still in VF, which meant there was some activity happening in his little heart too.

All of this went through her head as she continued the massage, stepping back every now and then as Angus shocked the little body...blocking out the cries and shouts of his family from the other side of the doors and focussing on the little boy who was clinging to life.

'Do you want to swap?' Barb offered to take over the massage, but she was getting a good rhythm on the monitor and Imogen shook her head.

'I'm fine.'

'Let's go again...' The defibrillator was whirring and Imogen felt as if she were watching from above, could see the warmed fluids dripping into his veins, could see herself going through the painful motions, and later saw the relief on everyone's face when they got him back. And, yes, she had said the right thing when she comforted the parents as Angus gave them the tentative good news and, yes, she did all the right things as she took the little boy up to the Intensive Care and handed him over. But as she walked out of the paediatric section and past the adults, she could see the bed where Maria had been, only with another person in it. And as she walked down the corridor and back to Emergency, all she knew was that she didn't want to make that walk again.

'You look exhausted!' Heather grinned as she came back. 'The night hasn't even started!'

'Fifteen minutes till lift-off!' Imogen glanced at her watch and smiled back.

'Why don't you have a break?' Heather suggested kindly. 'Take the lift and go out on the fire escape…'

'The fire escape?'

'You'll get a good view of the fireworks—if anyone deserves to see London at its best tonight, it's you.'

'This is my last shift in Emergency.' She didn't turn her head when Angus walked out onto the fire escape to join her, had seen him look up when Heather had been talking, had known that he would come.

'Your last?' The cold air caught in his throat, making it hard to keep his voice light. 'So you're ready for home, then?'

'I meant…' Her face was pale, her eyes like glass in the darkness as she turned to him. 'It's my last ever shift in Emergency. I can't do it any more. I'm going back to midwifery. I know you can't always guarantee the outcome, but I'm going to work with the lowest-risk mums and hopefully spend the rest of my nursing time bringing in lives instead of watching them end. I just can't do it any more. I can't go home and cry myself to sleep, I can't stand all the violence and the death, I just…' She shook her head. 'I just haven't got it in me any more.'

And Angus realised then, that no matter how much he might love her, he didn't really know her. That as close as they had been, there hadn't been time to get close enough, because this beautiful, talented, consummate professional actually bled inside every day she came to work.

'You're burnt out,' Angus said softly. 'It happens. Maybe take a break, do something else for a while.'

'I was hoping to do that here, only once they find out you're emergency trained…' she gave a tight smile '…well, you've seen first hand what happens.'

'I'm sorry.'

'Don't be,' Imogen answered. 'It's helped in a way. I know I've had enough of it. I know the money's going to be less—I'm at the bottom rung in midwifery and at the top in Emergency, but some things are just more important. I'm going to apply for a full-time job in maternity.'

'You might change your mind.'

'I already told you, Angus, I *don't* change my mind.'

She was telling him something and it hurt to hear it—any relief he'd felt earlier that she wasn't with Brad countered by the agony of the future she was mapping out without him.

'Look Imogen…' It was Angus's turn now to open up. 'I haven't been completely honest with you.'

'Did you sleep with Gemma?' There, she had been brave enough to say it, a few years older and brave enough to confront what she hadn't been able to a few years ago.

'Why do you always do that, Imogen?' Angus asked. 'Why do you have to dash to the worst-case scenario all the time?'

'Because it usually is.'

'Was,' Angus said gently. 'Imogen, it's over between me and Gemma. Even my mum's starting to believe it. We went out for lunch last week, but that was more to see if we could handle the divorce without lawyers.'

'Can you?'

'Nope!' Angus gave a half-grin.

'So when weren't you honest?'

'When I said why I didn't want anyone at work to know.' He blew out a breath, and she knew it was a long one because the freezing night made it white and it went on for ever. 'Everything I said, I meant—I mean, I did feel uncomfortable about people knowing, especially given how soon after Gemma it happened and how long you'd be here, especially that you were leaving… But that wasn't entirely the reason…'

'Just say it Angus.' Her eyes brimmed with tears that she hoped he couldn't see.

'I didn't want Heather to know. I felt it would be unfair to her.'

'Heather?' Imogen did a double-take.

'I'm trusting you with this…'

'You and Heather?' She saw him frown. 'I'm sorry—of course you can trust me not to say anything.'

'She's got a bit of a thing for me…' He said it only with kindness. 'She had too much to drink at one of the work Christmas parties a couple of years ago and out it came. Nothing happened, of course,' Angus said, and she was grateful she had bitten her tongue to refrain from asking. 'And I told her nothing ever would happen, you know, that I was flattered and everything, but that I was happily married… She was mortified the next day—rang me in tears, even offered to resign, but look…' He gave an uncomfortable shrug. 'I sort of pretended that I'd had too much to drink and couldn't really remember all she'd said. It made it easier for her…' And that he would do that for Heather made her eyes fill with tears for entirely different reasons.

This, one of the many reasons she loved about him.

Loved him.

Which was why she'd shown him all of her—or most of her.

'I just think it would be a bit of a kick in the teeth for her,' Angus explained further. 'She's rung a couple of times, I've tried to put her off.'

'Maybe she just wants to be friends now.'

'She is a friend.' Angus nodded. 'Which is why I don't want to hurt her.

'Imogen…' She knew what was coming, knew what he was going to ask, knew he wanted the rest of her that she was so very scared to give. 'Why do you think I don't want people to know?'

'Because it's too soon…' she attempted.

'Why else?' Holding her hands, even if he wasn't looking at her, Imogen knew that he'd seen her, not just here and now and not just naked, but that he could see inside her very soul, see the bits she thought she had long ago dealt with and never wanted to show again. And the bits she'd sworn she'd never let another man see.

'Brad was embarrassed to be seen with me.'

'Then he's a fool.'

'Look at Gemma and look at me…'

'I'm not comparing.'

'Of course you are.' Imogen snapped. 'I do! I look at Brad and I look at you and you're both good-looking, all the women adore you, you're both on television—'

'How's this for a comparison, then,' Angus broke in. 'We're both crazy about you and while Brad, I'm sure, is regretting losing you, I know that I'm about to face the same…'

'Then do something about it.'

'Like what?' Angus asked, only there wasn't an answer. 'I hated geography at school,' Angus said. 'Now I know why.'

She didn't smile at his joke and neither did he—just stood in endless silence, wanting the agony over but never wanting it to end. 'A couple more minutes…' he glanced at his watch and tried to lighten things up. 'Hey, it's already New Year's Day for you! What's the time difference in Australia?'

'No, it's New Year's Eve for me too,' Imogen corrected him, her voice utterly steady, her eyes holding his as she conveyed the seriousness of her words, 'because everything I love most in the world is here, right now, in London.'

It could never be wrong to kiss her.

Even if it could never last, never work, even if in a few days she'd be gone, it could never be wrong to kiss her, and it would never be pointless to prolong it.

Because pulling her into his arms, feeling the sweet taste of her as he parted her lips with his tongue, every second, every minute that he kissed her, held her, adored her was another minute he could remember for ever.

'Hey…' Ever the chameleon, she pulled back just a fraction, their warm breaths mingling. 'If you make love to me here, at least we won't have to say we haven't had sex this year…'

'As much as I might want to…' Angus grinned even though his eyes were glassy '…I am not going to have sex on the fire escape at work!'

'Spoilsport,' she teased.

'Imogen…' He kissed her again, but was adamant. 'It's a measure of how much I love you that I'm not going to.' He stopped then, stopped because he'd never meant to say it, had never really let himself feel it. Love wasn't supposed to come along just yet.

Love was something in the distance, something that would maybe happen in his life later, much later, but love was what it was, right here, right now, and he was holding it in his arms.

'I love you, Imogen.'

Only she didn't say it back. Instead, she stared back at him for the longest time, then blinked a few times before she gave her strange answer and turned to go.

'Then you'd *really* better do something about it.'

* * *

'How were the fireworks?' Heather asked as they returned to the still quiet department.

'Spectacular.' Imogen grinned, picking up a fruit kebab and making Angus's stomach fold over on itself as she licked the tip of a strawberry. Then she added for Angus's benefit, 'But they fizzled out at the end—not quite the big bang I was hoping for!'

'Could you hurry up and see her, please?' Heather said as she handed Angus a chart. 'The husband's getting a bit worked up.'

'Sorry?' Angus frowned.

'Louise Williams, the abdo pain in cubicle four. Oh, sorry.' She gave an apologetic smile. 'It was Gus I spoke to about her—she's twenty weeks pregnant, had a miscarriage earlier in the year, oh, it's last year now…'

And Imogen saw it then.

Saw how often Heather called for Angus if there was a problem, how Heather arranged her breaks around his and probably her shifts too—and saw how hard it would be, not just for Angus but for Heather too, if the truth came out.

Not that she had time to dwell on it, not when at fifteen minutes past midnight on New Years Day the fireworks went off again.

CHAPTER FIFTEEN

'WE'VE GOT multiple stabbings coming in.' Heather had to practically shout as a group of young men spilled out of the waiting room, security men quickly onto them as the waiting room started to fill. 'Gus is onto it and the surgeons are coming. Imogen,' she called out, 'can you take the abdo pain?'

The noises in the department did nothing to soothe the terrified woman and Imogen held her hand as Angus gently probed her abdomen, Louise's anxious husband hovering.

'You've had no bleeding?' Angus checked.

'None. Just this pain. I'm losing my baby, aren't I?'

'Let me take a look at you,' Angus said firmly, 'before we rush to any conclusions. Now, have you had any nausea or vomiting?'

'I feel sick,' Louise said, 'but I haven't been sick.'

'How's your appetite?'

'I can't eat.'

'OK...' Angus checked the card which had her observations recorded. 'I'm just going to get the Doppler.'

'Doppler?' Louise's eyes darted to Imogen.

'It's just a little machine, so he can listen to the baby's heartbeat.'

'Oh, God!'

'Just try and take it easy,' Imogen said gently, but even though she was calm and reassuring, Imogen did let out a breath when, after only a few seconds of trying to locate it, the delicious sounds of a strong, regular foetal heartbeat was picked up.

'OK…' Angus gave a thin smile at the heartbeat. 'That's certainly good news. You're a bit dehydrated. I see Heather put in a drip and took some bloods—I'm going to get those sent straight to the lab and I'm going to get some IV fluids started on you…'

'Aren't you going to examine me?' Louise flushed. 'I mean…'

'I'm not going to do a PV,' Angus said, 'because the obstetrician is going to want to do one and if your uterus is a bit irritable, I don't want to disturb things. I'm just going to speak with a colleague and then I'll come back and talk to you.'

'What do you think is wrong?'

'Let me just have a quick word with the surgeon and then I'll be back.'

'The surgeon!' Louise startled, but Angus was already gone, leaving Imogen to deal with a less than impressed husband.

'What?' he demanded. 'Are we too menial to even be told what he's thinking?'

'We've got a surgical emergency in Resus,' Imogen

said calmly. 'I suspect he wants to catch the team before they race off to Theatre.'

'Oh.'

Which was exactly the case, as it turned out. The surgical consultant made a brief appearance and examined Louise, then went outside the cubicle to talk to Angus as the couple became more agitated. Once Louise had been for an urgent ultrasound, Imogen did her observations regularly and tried to reassure them, only she was practically running between patients as the waiting room filled fit to burst, nurses, doctors everywhere calling out for assistance. If they'd had double the staff on tonight, it still wouldn't have been enough.

'Will someone please have the decency to tell us what the hell is going on!'

Imogen, wearing gloves and holding up an inebriated patient's tea towel–wrapped hand that contained a partially severed finger wasn't really in a position to calm the furious Mr Williams as he stormed out of the cubicle. 'My wife's in bloody agony and all you lot keep saying is that you're waiting for blood results.'

'The obstetrician's on his way down,' Imogen said, 'just as soon—'

'I don't want to hear how busy he is!' Mr Williams roared, coming up to her, shouting right in her face. 'I don't want to know about other patients, when my wife…'

As his voice trailed off Imogen actually thought he was going to hit her, could do nothing to defend herself as she held on to her patient. She could see the hairs up his nose and the veins bulging in his forehead, could hear her patient slurring obscenities in her defence, and then she realized that he *was* going to hit her. She could see his fist, and behind that Angus dropping the phone and racing over, but Security got there first, grabbing his hand before it made contact, coming between the relative and the nurse, taking control of the situation, as they often did.

It was a non-event really—something that happened, something she was more than used to dealing with. She was just utterly weary to the bone of being *used* to dealing with it.

'I'll take him for you.'

Cassie saw Imogen's pale face and relieved her of her drunken patient as Imogen peeled off her bloodied gloves while Angus read the Riot Act.

'If you ever threaten or verbally abuse my staff again I will have you removed from the department and arrested!' There was no doubt from his voice that he meant every word.

'I didn't threaten her!'

Even though Angus was completely in control, his anger was palpable, contempt lacing every word as he responded to Mr Williams.

'When a six-foot man gets in the face of a woman and shouts, believe me, sir, it's extremely threatening. And when that same man raises his fist…'

'I wasn't going to hit her!'

Debatable perhaps—only there simply wasn't time.

'Now…' Angus let out a long breath. 'Even though it seems you have been here ages, it has, in fact, been an hour. In that time your wife has been examined by myself and the surgeon, she has had an IV started and bloods taken and has been sent for an ultrasound. I was actually on the phone just now getting some results and was about to come in and talk to you.'

'Hi, there.' Whistling as he walked, grinning as he came over, Oliver Hanson, incredibly laid-back, dressed in theatre scrubs and oblivious to all that had occurred, joined the little gathering. 'Hi, there, Imogen—good to see you.' Then he raised his eyebrows to Angus. 'I hear you've got a suspected appendicitis for me to see—twenty weeks gestation.'

Which wasn't the best way to deliver the potential diagnosis, but then the whole exercise had been a bit of a disaster. A touch pale in the face and a bit grim-lipped, Imogen followed the doctors and Mr Williams into the cubicle as Security hovered outside.

'I'm sorry!' Mr Williams glanced over at Imogen, who nodded.

'He didn't mean to scare you.' Louise was in tears. 'He's just worried about me.'

'Let's listen to the doctors.' Imogen forced a smile, told herself that it wasn't Louise's fault she was married to this man. It was simply her job to put the patient at ease, only it was getting harder and harder to do.

'We think you have appendicitis,' Angus started. 'It's difficult to diagnose in pregnancy as there are some tests we can't do because they may affect the baby. Some of the changes in blood that happen during pregnancy make the lab findings more difficult to interpret too. The ultrasound of your abdomen appears normal, which has ruled out some other tentative diagnoses and I've spoken again to Mr Lucas, the surgeon who saw you, and he agrees that appendicitis is the most likely diagnosis. However, until you have the operation, we won't know for sure.'

'But isn't that dangerous for the baby?'

'It's far more dangerous for the baby if your appendix ruptures,' Oliver explained. 'That's why we'd prefer not to wait. Yes, there is a chance that the surgery might cause premature labour, but I'll start an infusion that should hopefully prevent that, and we'll work closely with the anaesthetist. We all want your pregnancy to continue.'

'So there's no real choice?' Mr Williams's voice was gruff.

'No.' Angus spoke to his patient. 'Mr Lucas is in Theatre and he'll be ready for you soon, so the best thing we can do is get you up as quickly as possible. You've had some IV fluids so you're better hydrated now and the anaesthetist is going to come down and talk to you but, yes, we'll get you up as soon as possible.'

'You'll be OK.' Imogen smiled once all the doctors had gone and she prepared Louise for Theatre, collecting all her notes and going through the endless check lists.

'I never even thought it could be appendicitis—I thought I was losing the baby.'

'It's always your first thought when you're pregnant, but appendicitis is just as common during pregnancy as it is at other times—just more complicated. You'll go up to Maternity after the operation so they can watch the baby closely.'

'You've seen this before then?'

'I'm a midwife.' Imogen nodded. 'So, yes, I've seen it before.'

'A midwife?' Louise frowned. 'So what are you doing working here?'

'Earning a living.' Imogen answered, as the porter clicked off the brakes on the trolley and they headed through the bedlam of the emergency department, tears stinging her eyes as she gave the wrong but honest answer.

'You've been marvellous as always, Imogen!' Always generous with praise for her staff, Heather thanked Imogen profusely as she signed her time sheet at seven-thirty a.m. The place was still full, patients everywhere, linen skips and bins overflowing, but order was slowly being restored. 'Have a look at the roster before you go and take your pick—there are plenty of shifts to be filled this week.'

'No, thanks!' Pulling off her hair-tie, Imogen hoisted her bag on her shoulder. 'I'm done.'

'I thought you were here for a little while longer?'

'I mean with Emergency.' Oh, so casually she'd said it, but Heather quickly noticed the wobble in her voice. 'I'm calling it a day.'

'Imogen!' Heather's voice was full of concern, causing a few nurses to turn round. 'Did that incident with Mr Williams—?'

'I'd made up my mind before that,' Imogen interrupted. 'I'm just…' she gave a helpless shrug '…tired of it, I guess. Burnt out—isn't that what they say? I love Emergency and everything. It's just getting too much, since I had Heath.'

'Excuse me!' Looking nothing like the angry, raging man from earlier, Mr Williams appeared at the nurses' station. 'Louise had her operation and the baby seems fine.'

'That's good to know,' Imogen said, and the smile she gave was genuine because it *was* good to know.

'About before.' He was red in the face again, but for different reasons this time. 'I really am sorry for what happened.'

His apology was genuine, Imogen knew that.

And she was about to open her mouth, to tell him it was OK, that he had been stressed and worried about his wife and the baby and that it didn't matter.

Only it did.

It mattered a lot.

Mr Williams wasn't the reason she was giving up a job she loved, but the Mr Williamses of the world were a big part of it.

And somehow sorry wasn't enough for Imogen this morning.

His apology, no matter how genuine, just one she couldn't accept any more. Without a word she walked off and left him standing there, tears streaming down her face as she exited through the ambulance bay, before finally she said the words she'd really wanted to.

'So you should be!'

CHAPTER SIXTEEN

SHE so did not need this.

Stamping through the slush, Imogen wished she'd been more assertive, wished she'd just stuck to her guns and refused to take the shift.

OK, they'd assured her that she wouldn't actually be in Emergency, that the nurse unit manager had agreed that she could stay in the observation ward. Only that made it worse somehow—being there and not doing anything, hearing the buzz of Emergency and not being a part of it.

Seeing Angus again.

The only thing worse than that was the thought of *not* seeing him again.

It had been four days since they'd last kissed, four days since she'd, cryptically perhaps, laid her heart on the line and four days when he hadn't done a thing about it.

No phone call.

No text.

Nothing.

So what if he'd said he loved her? For all he knew

she could be on a plane already winging her way back to Queensland with Heath, which was probably what he wanted, Imogen thought, her face stinging as the heat of the hospital hit her frozen cheeks. Yes, once she was safely out the country there would be no chance of their embarrassing little interlude coming out, no explanations necessary.

The heat had nothing to do with the tears that suddenly pricked her eyes.

'Hi, Imogen…' Cassie greeted her warmly. 'Go and grab a coffee before handover.'

'I'm in Obs.' Imogen forced a smile. 'I'll just head straight round there.'

'You've got time for a coffee,' Cassie insisted. 'Actually, I'll join you. I never got my break this morning, the place was bedlam as usual…' She chatted away as they walked, two nurses heading off to the staff-room. Cassie could never have known how much it hurt Imogen to glimpse Resus, see the machines, the patients, the buzz of Emergency that she loved but which didn't love her back, that just hurt too much to stay.

She actually wanted to turn and run—she could turn and run. She was an agency nurse, easily replaced, could plead a migraine, anything, as long as she didn't have to put herself through it.

'Surprise!'

Opening the staffroom door, it really was one.

Colleagues and friends she had only just made all standing there to greet her, the table laid with Chinese take-aways and cola and crisps. Emergency staff only ever needed a teeny excuse to throw a party, but that they might throw one for her—an agency nurse who had done just a very few shifts—was unfathomable.

'Now…' Heather handed her a cup of cola and took the floor. 'We don't do this for everyone, but we're not losing an agency nurse—the nursing world's losing a good emergency nurse and we figured she deserved a bit of a send-off! How long have you been one of us?'

'Ten years?' Imogen gulped.

'Then you've more than earned a party.'

They'd signed a card and her eyes blurred as she read the messages, especially Angus's. Short and sweet, he'd wished her luck in her new career, thanked her for her hard work here and signed it without love, and with very best wishes for her future—just not theirs.

Which was to be expected, of course.

It just hurt.

Hurt too that he couldn't make it, Heather explained, because he was recording his TV show.

And when the party was over, sitting in the obs ward, her one head injury patient snoring his head off, Imogen knew that ten cardiac arrests and a few stabbings would be much easier to deal with than her own thoughts.

Sitting in a busy department in a busy city, never had she felt more alone.

'Why don't you have your break?' Heather bustled round. 'I'll watch Mr Knight.'

'I've been sitting down for three hours!' Imogen pulled her head out of the book she was desperately trying to concentrate on. 'I don't need a break.'

'Well, I do!' Heather said, sliding into the seat beside her. 'I really am glad you came in today.'

'I am too. It was really thoughtful of you all…' Imogen flushed. 'I wasn't expecting it.'

'Not just for that. That incident with Mr Williams…I didn't want you leaving on a bad note…'

'He's not the reason I'm finishing up.'

'I know that, but it did upset you.'

'It didn't used to,' Imogen explained. 'I used to be able to shrug it off. I just can't any more. So now it's either get upset or get hard and cynical—and I don't want that to be me.'

'That isn't you,' Heather agreed. 'I do know how you feel, after the week we've had here, what with Maria Vanaldi and everything…'

'Maria?'

'You haven't seen the news?'

'They don't have televisions in the rooms at the youth hostel—what about Maria?'

'It wasn't an accident.'

'The car lost control…'

'It had been tampered with. It was her husband's family apparently.'

And Imogen closed her eyes, knowing in that moment that the choice she'd struggled so hard to come to had, for her, been the right one.

'Go and have your break,' Heather said again, and this time Imogen didn't refuse.

His voice in the room hurt.

Imogen was glad that even though she'd joked with

Maria about it, she'd never actually thought to record Angus's show because, seeing him, hearing him and not being able to have him hurt in a way it didn't when she watched Brad.

She knew that if she did have a recording, she'd torture herself over and over, watching his beautiful, proud face, slightly defiant as the carefully scripted interview commenced.

She put more bread in the toaster and stood in the empty staffroom, tears streaming down her face as she rammed the lovely buttery toast into her mouth and waited for the next round to toast, wishing it would fill the hole in her soul. She listened as they spoke about viewers who were lonely and ill over Christmas, listened as they talked about the miracle that should be Christmas but in reality how incredibly hard it was for some people at this time of year.

And then came the difficult part.

Imogen could hear the shift in tone from the interviewer and watched Angus's chin lift a fraction, ready to face the public music. Only it wasn't quite the tune she was expecting to hear.

'A lot of our viewers are going to be sorry to hear that this is to be your final regular appearance on the show.'

'That's correct.' Angus nodded.

'We've seen in the newspapers this week—' his colleague, no doubt his friend, cleared her throat just a touch '—that your own marriage just ended.'

'It did.' And because he was a so-called celebrity, because part of his job was asking people to bare their lives, Imogen screwed her eyes closed as Angus, this private, beautiful man, was forced to open up—if not for the good of himself, then for the good of all.

'Did that have any impact on your decision to leave the show?'

'Of course,' Angus answered brusquely, and Imogen could only smile at his closed-off expression, the same one she'd seen when they'd sat in the café that first time together.

'It must be a painful time.'

'It's a…' There was a pause, just a beat of a pause that had her open her eyes, that had the interviewer frowning just a touch, as maybe, just maybe, Angus deviated from the script. 'It's a *searching* time,' he said carefully, but on behalf of so many, so, so eloquently he added, 'For all involved.'

'It's been reported that there was another party involved—do you have any comment you'd like to make to that?'

And she went to bite into her toast but changed her mind, her throat so thick with tears that there wasn't room for anything else. She waited for his polite rebuttal, for his clipped 'No comment', for his request for his family's privacy—only it never came.

'My wife, without malice or intent, fell in love with someone else.'

'Oh!' Imogen saw the slight, frantic dart of the interviewer's eyes. She smiled, despite her tears, as with candour, honesty and integrity he reached into living rooms everywhere and showed the world a little bit of why he really was so special.

'And you don't fall in love with someone else if things are good at home,' Angus continued, borrowing Imogen's script for a moment then reverting back to his own. 'And for that I take my full share of the responsibility.'

'That's very forgiving.'

'You don't choose with whom, when and where you fall in love,' Angus responded coolly. 'I didn't understand that, but now, thanks to a very special person, I do.'

'So…' The interviewer was shuffling her papers now, staring at them as if willing something to leap out and tell her what the hell to say. 'You're saying that you too—'

'Absolutely.' Imogen's gasp came as the staffroom door opened, knew without turning it was him, could feel his arms wrap around her as he held her from behind and stared at her from the screen. 'There is the most wonderful woman in my life at the moment and I intend to keep it that way. I'm going to learn from my mistakes, which,' he added, 'we actually do all make.

'Gemma and I decided to be honest.' His words were soft and low in her ear. 'She doesn't deserve to be portrayed as the guilty party in this. We both just want it over, so we decided to be upfront and just get it all over and done with. Gemma has my support, even if it nearly killed me to give it on national television…'

'I'm so proud of you.'

'I'm proud of me too,' Angus said. 'And I'm proud of you too.'

'For what?'

'For being you. For making me see.' And he didn't add '*sense*' or '*things more clearly*.' He didn't need to, because his eyes were open. Now he really could see that there was so much more than two sides to a story, that the two sides had other sides, and those other sides had other sides too. People were people and that was OK. That was what made them real.

'You didn't call me.'

'I didn't know what to say,' Angus admitted. 'I knew I had to offer you something, only I didn't know what. And then things got busy… Maria Vanaldi…'

'I heard it wasn't an accident.'

'It got nasty—the police contacted me to ask if Maria had said anything, and I went round to see Ainslie. I was worried about her being caught up in it all and not knowing what was going on. I spoke to Elijah…'

'Guido's uncle?'

'He's his guardian now. And that sounds simple, only this man lives in Italy, a rich playboy who hops on planes the way we take the underground and he didn't even know if he wanted to do it—and then he fell in love with his nephew. A few days with Guido and he's turning his life around if it means that he can keep him.'

And that Guido was safe, that he would be loved and looked after was the nicest thing she could have hoped to hear, or, Imogen admitted, gazing into jade eyes that adored her, almost the nicest.

'You were never the easy option,' he said, turning her to face him. 'You were never a quick fling or convenient or not good enough or any one of those things you beat yourself up with. You were the most difficult option possible, Imogen.'

'Why?'

'Because you live on the other side of the world, because in a few days you'll be back there with your Heath and I'll be here with Clemmie and Jack. You were absolutely the last person it made sense to fall in love with.' He pulled up her chin to make her look at him. 'You were never a threat to my marriage—it was over long before you came along. The only threat you were was to my sanity. The craziest thing I could do was fall in love with you, but I did. I love you. I absolutely love you. And I don't know how, but I know it can work.' She opened her mouth to talk, but it was Angus's turn still. 'I can't bear the thought of you on the other side of the world without me there beside you every day, but it's a far better option than losing you. I don't care if people say long-distance love can't work, because those people don't know me and they don't know you...

'I don't change my mind either and I won't change my mind about this. If I have to spend every minute of annual leave flying to see you, if I have to work every shift I can so I can fly you back to see me just as much as you can, if we can't properly be together till the kids are much older—we'll still be together, if only you'll have me.'

That he would give her his heart, and let her go with it, that he trusted her enough to return with it whenever she could was the greatest gift of them all—a miracle really, Imogen thought, smiling through her tears as he kissed her swollen buttery mouth till it was she who pulled away.

'It's a Christmas miracle!'

'It is...' Angus grumbled, not caring that Heather had

just walked in, not dropping Imogen or pulling back, just wanting to kiss and taste her again, because she was his—she really was.

'No…' Imogen gave a giggle. 'Shane's going into remission.'

'Shane?'

'Shane!'

'But he's only got two weeks to live!' Heather's shocked gasp had Imogen giggling. Heather loved the show—loved, loved, loved it, taped every episode and was always pumping Imogen for inside info. 'It's completely incurable—Dr Adams said so last night.'

'It's a miracle, I tell you!' Imogen said, waving her hands like a gospel singer, then as Angus watched on, bemused, the two women doubled over in a fit of laughing.

'Don't breathe a word!' Imogen warned. 'If the story line ever gets out…'

'Praise be!' Heather said, grinning, slipping out and, unbeknown to them standing guard on the other side of the door so that no one could possibly disturb them.

'She knows?' Imogen checked.

'I told her.'

'So the party…'

'The party was their idea. Heather just told me that you'd be back today. Imogen, when did you find out about Brad?' Puzzled eyes frowned down at her. 'Is that what you two had to discuss?'

'Brad and I had to talk.' She was suddenly serious and always, always beautiful. 'He's been offered another year's work here and he wants to take it.'

'And you couldn't tell me that?' He didn't get it. 'Imogen, have you any idea what I've been through, trying to think of ways we could be together, trying to come up with a solution? And all the while you had one.'

'I had a temporary solution, Angus, and we both deserve a lot more than that. Brad just dropped it on me—his character proved popular and they offered him a year's contract. Of course, my first instinct was to say yes, but it wasn't a solution. What happens in a year when his contract's up, what happens if I hate it here? And why should I leave a home and family I love because Brad's been offered a job? If you and Gemma got back together or if you and I didn't work out, I needed to be sure I was staying for the right reasons…'

And he got it then, got what a huge decision it must have been for her. 'It took a glass or two of wine and a lot of tears but we actually managed some very grown-up talking—something neither of us are very good at. He had to get it that I can't just follow my ex-husband around the globe, and I had to get my head around the fact that you couldn't come into my decision either.' She saw him frown. 'This had to be about Heath and I.' She took a big breath. 'Whether I could stand to be in London without you.'

'Could you?'

'I can stand anything, Angus.' She gave him her soft smile. 'But I'd rather do it with you.'

'Then you will.'

'But what about next year…when his contract…?'

'Who knows?' Angus hushed her with his lips. 'This, I do know, though, we'll work it out.'

'Will we?' And he saw her blink a couple of times, just as he had that first day. He saw again that this soft, utterly together woman sometimes got nervous, sometimes got scared, and it thrilled him that he could read her, could comfort her and could love her.

'Always!'

EPILOGUE

'I FEEL so fat!'

Angus looked over to where Imogen lay.

'I could think of so many better ways to describe you.'

Oh, and he could.

Dressed in her favourite red bikini, they'd been enjoying a gentle dip in the pool after a massive Christmas barbecue and now Imogen was on the lounger, her belly ripe with their baby, her skin freckled by the hot Queensland sun. It was still as if each day the colour in his world brightened.

What could potentially have been the worst year of his life had been the best.

Clemmie and Jack thriving, as their parents did the same.

Thanks to Imogen.

Thanks to this funny, complicated, beautiful woman who had stepped into the path of an oncoming train and somehow made them all change track.

Christmas in Australia!

Who'd have thought?

Hauling himself out of the pool and lying on the lounger next to her, dripping water as he went, Angus watched the three kids splashing and playing in the water, then grinned over to where Imogen lay. 'They're having a ball.'

'They're killing me,' Imogen groaned. 'They've been up since five!'

'It's been a long day, having all your family over and everything, but we can go to bed soon,' Angus pointed out. 'Brad will be here soon and Gemma and Roger just texted to say they were on their way.'

'Good!'

Who'd have thought?

Angus lay back as Imogen heaved herself up again and then joined the kids in the pool for one last play before they headed off to enjoy the rest of Christmas Day with their other families.

She'd wanted to have their baby in Australia.

Which should have been impossible as they'd all wanted Christmas with the children.

But because, through it all, Imogen had been consistently nice and kind and infinitely understanding, somehow that sentiment grew and somehow, when needed, the universe gave back.

Taking some long overdue leave, Angus was even doing the odd stint in Australia, realising in years to come he might well do many shifts more. The home she'd struggled so hard to keep for Heath was now a furnished rental that the hospital used, only not these past weeks. Tentative plans put forward had been made so much easier when Gemma and Roger had decided that bringing the children for a holiday in Australia might be rather nice. Brad too had taken time off from his very busy schedule and was even planning to negotiate four weeks off each Christmas.

Impossible almost, yet they'd worked it out.

For Imogen.

He was quite a nice guy really, Angus conceded as, sunglasses on, long hair so blond it was white now, Brad sauntered into the back yard and the kids leapt out of the pool to greet him.

Yes, quite a nice guy for a thickhead, Angus thought as Brad knelt down and kissed Imogen on the cheek.

Oh, his solar plexus still got the odd workout, but nothing too major. And a bit of jealously was OK, Imogen had pointed out, if it kept him on his elbows!

'Hey, Angus!'

'Merry Christmas, Brad,' Angus responded, just a touch formally.

'Do you want me to watch them?'

'Watch them?' Angus could see his frown in the mirrored sunglasses.

'Till Gemma gets here.' He nodded in Imogen's direction and Angus was on his feet in an instant. Her forearms were resting on the edge of the pool, a look of intense concentration on her face. Suddenly Brad wasn't the thickhead here, because a doctor and a midwife they may be, but it had taken the actor to first realise what was happening. Irritable, restless, Imogen wasn't tired and cranky—she was in labour.

Imogen had worked it out, though, by the time he got poolside.

'I wanted a water birth…' Imogen stopped talking then, her face bright red and screwed up in agony for a long moment till finally she blew out. 'But I'm not having it in the pool!'

'Heath took for ever,' Brad drawled, 'but doesn't the second one usually come quicker? At least, that's what you used to say…'

'Thanks, Brad!' Angus snapped. 'Just watch the kids, bring the car round…'

'Just get me into the house,' Imogen groaned through gritted teeth. 'Brad, call an ambulance.'

This was so not how she'd planned it. A full-time midwife practically till the moment they'd flown back to Australia, she'd worked out her birth plan, and being hauled up the pools steps and led to the house, her ex-husband the one ringing for an ambulance and watching the kids as Angus steered her inside, wasn't a part of it.

'Let's get to the bedroom.' Angus was trying to be calm, but Imogen could hear the note of panic in his voice and it panicked her. Nothing fazed Angus, nothing medical anyway.

'The bathroom…' Imogen gasped. 'I don't want to ruin my silk bedspread…'

'Never mind the bloody bedspread.'

'But I broke the snow globe.'

The silk bedspread wasn't ever going to be an issue, the living-room floor having to suffice, Angus sweating despite the air conditioner on full blast as he pulled off her bikini bottoms.

'I wanted drugs.'

'I know.'

'I wanted to go in the spa.'

'I know…' Angus gritted his teeth. 'Just try and breathe through it. The ambulance will be here soon.'

'Angus…' As another contraction hit and she just really, really had to push, she also really had to ask. 'There's something wrong.'

'There's nothing wrong.' Angus tried to steady himself, attempted a reassuring smile. 'It's got red hair!'

'Poor thing.' Imogen tried to smile back but started crying, because she could see the panic in his eyes, see the grim set of his jaw, knew that he was seriously worried. 'I've worked alongside you—I know when something's going wrong.'

'Nothing's going wrong,' Angus said, only it didn't soothe her. 'It's just never been you before.' And in her panic it didn't make sense, but in that moment between contractions, that last moment between birth and born, the mist cleared.

He loved her.

Absolutely loved her.

And love made things a bit scary sometimes because the stakes were so high.

'It's all good.' Angus said. 'All looks completely normal.'

And it was.

Scary but good. Agony sometimes, but completely and utterly healthy and normal—this thing called living.

Imogen got to deliver her herself, with a bit of help from Angus, lifting their daughter out together and watching in awe as blue eyes opened and she screamed her welcome. A blaze of red, from kicking feet and fists that punched in rage, right to her little screwed-up face and tufts of red hair.

'She's perfect…'

'She is,' Angus said, because it was all he could manage, actually relieved when the paramedics arrived and he could just be a dad.

'Born under a Christmas tree,' the paramedic greeted them. 'You're going to have some fun picking names.'

'Do I have to go to hospital?'

'You need to be checked,' the paramedic said. 'The little one too.'

'You can have that spa,' Angus said temptingly when her face fell. 'And champagne and…' He grinned. 'I can ask Gemma if she minds cleaning up the mess!'

And they were the nicest paramedics, Angus thought, high on adrenaline and loving everyone. They were in absolutely no rush, even happy to let her freshen up a bit once they'd got her on the stretcher and Imogen had decided that she really didn't want Gemma to see her coming out looking quite this bad!

'I want Heath.'

So Angus got him. His usually happy face, pinched and worried, but relaxing into a smile when he saw his new sister. Jack looked pretty chuffed too and Clemmie burst into tears because she'd desperately wanted a boy so that she'd still be the only girl. And then Heath looking worried again when it really was time to get them to the hospital.

'He'll be OK.' Brad assured them, and Angus had to swallow, not jealousy now, maybe even a tear as he saw a slightly wistful look on Brad's face as he gave Imogen a fond kiss goodbye. 'I'll bring him up to see you later tonight.' He looked over at Angus. 'If that's OK with you guys.'

'That'd be great.'

'Us too?' Clemmie asked.

'Yes, you too!' Gemma smiled but her eyes were a little bit glassy, a wistful look on her face as for the first time she met Imogen's eyes. 'Congratulations!'

'Congratulations!' Brad shook Angus's hand and Roger did the same.

Yep, just a bit painful sometimes, Imogen thought as they wheeled her off—for all concerned—but worth it.

And what better way to spend Christmas night? Tucked up in bed, champagne in hand, choosing from a massive chocolate selection with Angus cuddled up beside her, choosing names for a certain little lady who didn't have one yet.

'Holly?' Imogen said again.

'Natalie?' Angus frowned. 'You know, there really aren't that many to choose from.'

'I know!' Imogen breathed, staring over to her daughter, her hair all fluffy after her first bath, her complexion creamy now, fair eyelashes curling upwards, her little snub nose covered by her hand as she sucked on her thumb.

'Summer!'

'Summer?' Angus creased up his nose. 'That's not a Christmas name.'

'She was born in summer.'

'But Christmas is in winter in England, it won't make sense.'

'It will to us.'

'A December baby called Summer!' Angus looked over to his sleeping new daughter. A little ray of sunshine, a little bit of summer, no matter how cold the winter, and, yes, he conceded happily, Imogen was right and he kissed her to tell her so.

'Summer Lake…' Imogen sighed, coming up for breath.

'Summer Maitlin,' Angus corrected, kissing her again.

'Summer Lake-Maitlin.' Imogen said, and then she smiled. 'We'll keep working on it.'

EMERGENCY AT BAYSIDE

CHAPTER ONE

PULLING off her ID tag and stethoscope, Meg threw them into her locker and, as the changing room was empty, expended some of her frustration by slamming the door shut, then, for good measure, slammed it hard once again.

It didn't help.

She hadn't really expected it too.

'Morning, Meg.' Jess ran in and without pausing for breath started to undress at lightning speed. 'This is the first time in more than thirty years of nursing I've been late. Can you believe it?'

Had it been anyone else Meg wouldn't have believed it, but coming from Jess it was probably true. Trained in the days of starched uniforms and matrons, Jess ruled her world by the little silver fob watch neatly pinned to her crisp white blouse.

'Was that Carla the student nurse I saw leaving here in tears?'

Meg nodded but didn't elaborate—a move she knew would infuriate Jess, who liked to keep her finger on everyone's pulse.

'I thought she was doing really well; at least she has been on days.' Jess's Irish accent was as strong and sharp as Meg's own mother's. Maybe that was the reason Meg's defences seemed to go on high alert whenever Jess approached; she always felt as if she were about to be scolded. 'So, what did you have to tell her off about?' Jess wasn't being nosey—well, maybe a bit—but as they were both Associate Charge Nurses, any problems with the staff had to be discussed.

'I wasn't telling her off.' Meg had pulled on her shorts and T-shirt and was now concentrating on combing the long dark curls, that had been clipped up all night, into some sort of shape before tying her hair loosely into a ponytail. 'She was just upset about a patient we had in last night.'

'Oh, were you busy?'

'No, we were actually quiet for once, which was just as well.' Meg paused before continuing, taking out her scrunchy and combing her hair again before adding, 'We lost a child last night.'

Jess stopped filling her pockets with scissors, forceps and the other paraphernalia that Emergency nurses seemed to magic up at appropriate moments and stood still for a moment. 'How old?'

'Two.' This was where most nurses would have gone into detail. Sat on the bench and told their colleague about the little kid who had been in the bath with no one watching him. The tiny lifeless bundle the paramedics had run in with. The prolonged resuscitation that everyone had known was useless, but no one had wanted to be the one to call. The agony of talking to the parents. The utter desolation at such a senseless waste of a promising young life.

But not Meg.

Meg finished her hair and turned around. 'I'm the peer support person for Emergency so I thought I ought to go over it with her. She's still pretty upset; it was her first death,' Meg added.

'Poor Carla.' Jess took a deep breath. 'Sure, your first death's bad enough when it's a ninety-year-old, but to have a child… Would you like me to have a quiet word with her?' Jess's intentions were well meant, but Meg shook her head.

'She's off for a couple of days—the break will be good for her. But I might get her phone number and give her a ring—see if she wants to catch up for a coffee and go over anything again.'

'What about you, Meg?' Jess's voice was wary; she was unsure of the reaction she might get. 'Do you want to talk about it? I mean, I know you're the peer support person, but that doesn't mean *you* don't need to go over things.' She waited for a response but Meg just stood there. 'If you're upset….'

'I'm fine; this sort of thing comes with the territory. It was hard on Carla because she hadn't witnessed anything like it before; I'm used to it.'

'I know. It's just—' Jess swallowed hard '—this sort of thing affects us all, and if you do need to talk I'm here for you.'

Meg gave a dismissive smile. 'I'm fine, Jess. Honestly.'

To be fair, Jess might be a little irritating, might be a drama queen, but Meg knew she meant well, and had they been sitting in the staff room with a cup of coffee, then maybe she would have opened up a bit. But that was the problem with debriefing, with peer support or trauma counselling, or whatever new name Admin dreamed up for it: sometimes emotions couldn't just be switched on. Jess—busy, rushing to start her shift—together with Meg—weary, teary and ready to go home—wasn't exactly the ideal combination. It just wasn't going to happen this morning.

Jess knew when a conversation was over and decided not to push it, instead choosing sensibly to change the subject. 'Are you staying to meet the new consultant?'

'I'd forgotten about that. Is it this morning he starts, then?'

'Yep, the canteen's even putting on a breakfast in the staff room. Surely you're not going to miss out on a free feed *and* the chance to meet the new boy wonder?'

Meg gave a wry smile. 'He doesn't sound that wonderful to me. From what I've heard, Flynn Kelsey has spent the last two years doing research.'

'Ah, but his research has all been in trauma and resuscitation.' Jess wagged a finger. 'It's all relevant—at least that's the propaganda being fed to us from Admin. The truth is, they're just relieved someone's actually taken up the position; poor old Dr Campbell can hardly run the department alone. Who knows? They might have actually got it right for once and Flynn Kelsey will turn out to be the fantastic doctor that they're promising.'

'If he's that good, what was he doing with his head buried in books for the last two years? Hands-on experience is more relevant,' Meg said firmly. 'We can all sit and read about it. Rolling your sleeves up and getting on with the job does it for me every time.'

'So you're not staying to welcome him?'

'I'm sure I'll meet him soon enough.'

'Come on,' Jess pushed. Meg's red-rimmed eyes were worrying her. 'Just for a quick coffee?'

Meg feigned a yawn. 'Honestly, Jess, I'm exhausted. My bed sounds far more tempting right now.' Picking up her bag, Meg slung it casually over her shoulder. 'Bye then.' As she got to the door Meg paused for a second. 'Oh, Jess, I've left all the paperwork from Luke—the child last night—in the Unit Manager's office. Dr Leighton needs to write up all the drugs that were given; I've left the list clipped to the casualty card.'

'Sure.'

As Meg turned to go she let out a small sigh. 'Poor kid.' Her voice was soft, more a whisper, really, and Jess knew that the words had come out involuntarily. But Meg recovered quickly, smothering her display of emotion with another huge yawn. 'I'm dead on my feet; I'd better get home.'

Meg wasn't tired, not in the slightest. In fact as she drove her small car out of the car park she debated whether or not to stop at the shops and pick up some groceries, knowing that when she got to bed all she was going to do was lie there staring at the ceiling, going over and over the night's events. But shopping was more than she could deal with this morning. Choosing between wholemeal and white, full cream or low-fat milk seemed so trivial, so irrelevant, when a child was dead.

Poor kid.

Driving along Beach Road, for a second Meg hesitated, her foot poised over the brake, wondering whether or not to stop at her parents'. Tea, toast and sympathy from her mother sounded wonderful, but, given the fact that tensions on the home front were running at an all-time high, Meg decided against the idea, instead flicking on her indicator and heading up the hill for home.

Wincing as she changed gear, Meg remembered why her hand was hurting this morning. Remembered Dr Leighton looking over to the flat line on the monitor.

'We've been going for forty-five minutes with no response. I think we should call it. Does anyone have any objections?'

The ampoule of adrenaline Meg had been holding in her hand had shattered then, but she hadn't let on. 'Perhaps we should keep going while I talk to his parents. It might help them to come in and see us still working on him.' Throwing the shattered ampoule into the sharps bin, Meg had wiped her hand and applied a plaster to the small deep cut, then taken a deep steadying breath before heading for the interview room and walking in and delivering the shattering news. The look of utter desolation on Luke's parents' faces as she'd gently broken the news, then walked them the short distance to resus, had stayed with her throughout the night. The utter grief as they had done what no parent should ever have to.

Said goodbye to their child.

Up the winding hill she drove, the stunning view of the bay that filled her car window doing nothing to soothe her. Instead the conversation she had had with Luke's parents replayed in her mind so clearly that it might just as well have been coming from the car's stereo.

Meg had driven this road hundreds, maybe thousands of times. She knew every last bend in it, knew the subtle gear changes that ensured a smooth ride home. But this morning the painful image of Luke and his mother that flashed into her mind, the tears that sprang from her eyes, the sob that escaped from her lips, were all it took to make her lose her concentration. And in that tiny second the bend she had taken so easily, so many times, suddenly loomed towards her. With a start of horror Meg realised she had taken it too fast. Before she could even slam on her brakes the car shot off the road. There was no time to attempt to gain control, no time for anything—just a panicked helplessness as she heard someone yelling out, heard the slam of metal, the pop of glass as it shattered around her.

An ear-splitting shriek seemed to be going on for ever. It reminded her of Luke's mother. Only when the car somersaulted and she felt the impact of the wheel thudding into her chest did the screaming stop, and in a moment of clarity before she lost consciousness Meg realised that the person who had been screaming was her.

CHAPTER TWO

'IT'S all right Meg. We're going to get you out of there just as soon as we can.' The familiar voice of Ken Holmes, one of the paramedics Meg knew from her time in Emergency, was the first that welcomed her back to the world.

Everything was familiar: the hard collar holding her neck in position, the probe attached to her ear measuring her oxygen saturation. Meg had been out to many motor vehicle accidents with the Mobile Accident Unit and she knew the routine, knew all the equipment that was being used down to the last detail. But the familiarity brought no comfort. None at all.

The morning sun shone painfully into her eyes, and only then did Meg begin to realise the precariousness of her situation. Her car, or what was left of it, was embedded into the trunk of a huge tree. Its ominous creaking, Meg knew, was a sign of its instability. She sat there angled backwards, watching a massive chain slowly tightening around the trunk, and felt a huge jolt as the chain took up the last piece of slack. Every bone in her body seemed to be aching, her tongue felt swollen and sore, and she could taste blood at the back of her throat.

'How much longer until we can free her?' A deep voice from behind her left ear was calling out.

A deep voice that most definitely wasn't familiar.

It was the first time Meg had realised someone was actually in the car with her.

'They're still trying to secure the tree. More equipment's on the way.' Ken's voice was calm and even, but Meg could hear the undercurrent of urgency.

'How long?' She heard the edge of impatience in the deep voice and the hesitancy in Ken's before he answered.

'Twenty minutes—half an hour at most.'

'I want to get another IV line into her and check her injuries. Ken, you come and hold her head. I'll get into the front beside her.'

'Do you want to wait for the rest of the equipment before you move?' Again an ominous note was evident in Ken's voice.

'No. Do you?' There was no scorn in the strange voice, no impatience now, and if Meg hadn't quite grasped the danger she was in, hearing Ken being given a choice served to ram home just how vulnerable her situation was.

But Ken didn't miss a beat. 'I'll come in round the other side.'

'Good man.'

Her fuddled mind fought to recognise the masculine voice that was calmly giving out orders as Ken moved into the back and took over holding her head, while her unknown companion climbed over the passenger seat and into what was left of the seat beside her. It took for ever; every tiny movement seemed to ricochet through her body. Unable to move, all Meg could do was listen: listen to his heavy breathing and the occasional curse as a branch or piece of mangled metal halted his progress.

'It's Meg, isn't it?'

She tried to nod, but the hard collar didn't allow for movement. Opening her mouth a fraction, Meg tried to talk. But her mouth simply wouldn't obey her.

He seemed to recognise her distress in an instant. 'It's okay. Don't try to talk. My name is Flynn Kelsey. I'm a doctor, and I'm just going to put a needle into your hand so we can give you some more fluids before we move you out.'

He was talking in layman's terms and Meg realised he didn't know that she was a nurse. He probably assumed the paramedics had got her name from her driver's licence or a numberplate check. It was funny how her mind seemed to be focussing on the tiniest, most irrelevant details. Funny how her mind simply wouldn't allow her to take in the horror of her own situation, trapped and helpless in her precariously positioned car.

Through terrified eyes she watched Flynn Kelsey as he set to work. He was a big man, and the small area that had been cut away was fairly restrictive, but he didn't seem bothered by the confined space. The only concession he made was to take off the hard orange hat he was wearing before he set to work quietly. She searched his face, taking in his grey eyes, the high, chiselled cheekbones, the straight black hair neatly cut. Though he was clean shaven, she could see the dusting of new growth on his strong jaw.

Occasionally he would shift out of focus, her immobilised head making it impossible for her to follow him, but through it all Meg felt him beside her. Felt the steadying presence of his touch, the gentle reassurance of his regular breathing. Shifting into view again, for a second his cool grey eyes caught her petrified ones and he gave her a reassuring smile. Only the appearance of another flask of fluid indicated to Meg that the IV bung was already in; a scratch in the back of her hand was small fry compared to the agony everywhere else.

'We're going to be here for a little while yet.'

'Why can't they get me out now?' It was the first time she had spoken and her voice was husky and strained, no more than a whisper, really, and Flynn had to move his head closer to catch her words.

'Once the car's a bit more secure we can get you out.'

Which didn't answer the question. His careful evasion only scared Meg more.

Watching her closely, Flynn registered her deep intake of breath, saw her eyes screw tightly shut.

He recognised her terror.

'You're a lady that likes the truth, huh?' He paused for a moment before continuing, 'Your car came off the road at Elbow's Bend—do you know it?' Meg did know it; she knew it only too well. The sharp bend of road, cut into the rocks, was a favourite lookout point, and, if her memory served her correctly, the only view was that of the bay a hundred metres below. 'Luckily a couple of trees broke your fall, and we're on a nice sturdy ledge which has given us all a bit of room to work.'

She could hear her teeth involuntarily chattering as Flynn continued talking in quiet calm tones. 'The trees are holding the car and the firefighters have secured us; we're fine for now, but until the rest of the equipment arrives it's probably safer not to try moving you.'

He didn't add just how tenuous her position had been before the emergency services had arrived—didn't casually throw in how both he and Ken had literally put their lives on the line by climbing into the car to be with her.

He didn't have to; Meg had been out to enough accidents to know the score.

'You're going to be okay.'

'Stay,' she croaked, her eyes still screwed tightly shut.

'Oh, I'm not going anywhere; you're stuck with me for a good while yet. Do you know where you are?'

It seemed a silly question, especially given what he had just told her, but Meg knew he was testing her neurological status. 'In my car.' Her voice sounded gravelly, shaky. 'Or what's left of it.'

'That's right.' He squeezed her hand as she started to cry. 'But it's only a car; you're what's important here. Do you remember what happened? Can you remember what caused the accident?' He watched the tears squeezing out of her closed eyes and, realising he was distressing her further, decided instead to try a different tack.

'We'll go through it all later, at the hospital. Let's talk about nicer things. Tell me about yourself, Meg.'

She tried to shake her head, but the collar and Ken held it still. 'I'm tired.'

'Come on, Meg. If I'm going to stay with you, the least you can do is talk to me.' His voice was sharp, forcing her out of her slumber. 'Have you got a husband? A boyfriend? Tell me about him?'

'We broke up.'

'Ouch.' He gave a low laugh. 'Trust me to say the wrong thing.'

Her eyes opened a fraction, wincing at the bright morning sun glimpsed through the broken tree. Golden-brown eyes, he noticed, almost amber in the bright sunlight, thick black eyelashes framing them, glistening with a new batch of tears. She turned her amber headlights to him. 'He was cheating.'

That was a simple way of putting it, but she was too tired and it was all just too damn complicated to explain.

'Then he's a fool.' Flynn said decisively. 'Forget him.'

'That's what I'm working on.'

Flynn laughed. He was shining a pupil torch in her eyes now. 'I meant while you're stuck here. Think of something you really like. I'm not suggesting anything this time; I'd probably just put my foot in it again. What cheers you up?'

She didn't answer; frankly she couldn't be bothered. Closing her eyes, Meg wished he would just go away, leave her alone to rest a while.

'Meg!'

Reluctantly she opened her eyes. 'I'm tired.'

'And I'm bored. Come on, Meg—talk to me. If I've got to sit here with you, the very least you can do is entertain me.'

'The beach.' Running her tongue over her dry blood-stained lips, Meg cleared her throat as best she could. 'I like going to the beach.'

'Do you live near it?'

'Not really.' She was really tired now, her eyelids growing heavy again, the need to sleep overwhelming.

'A bit too expensive, isn't it? Come on, Meg, stay awake. Stay with me here and tell me about the beach.'

'Mum and Dad...'

'Do they live near the beach?'

'On the beach,' she corrected

'And I bet you're round there more often than not?'

She actually managed a small laugh. 'Mum says I use the hotel...' No, that wasn't right. Everything was coming out muddled. Meg forced herself to concentrate. 'I use the house like...' She never finished her sentence, her eyes gently closing as she gave up trying to explain.

'Like a hotel?' The torch was blasting back in her eyes now. 'I bet you do. So, come on, what do when you go to the beach? Body surf? Water ski?' There was a tinge of urgency creeping into his voice. 'Open your eyes and tell me what you do at the beach, Meg!'

The sun was shining brightly when she did, warm and delicious. The same sun that warmed her when she sunbathed, the same birds chirping, the same lazy, hazy feeling as she stretched out on a towel and drifted off. Closing her eyes, feeling its warmth, she could almost hear the ocean, almost imagine she was lying on the soft sand, listening to the children patting sandcastles into shape. The hum of the firefighters' drill was almost a perfect Jet Ski in the distance…

'Meg!' It was him again, breaking into her dream, utterly refusing to leave her be. 'What do you do at the beach?'

'I sleep.'

She heard him half-laugh, half-curse. 'She's practically hypnotised herself here, Ken. Tell them to step on it.'

Whether it was Flynn's insistence or whether the tree was finally secured Meg didn't know, but suddenly the 'jaws of life' were peeling the roof off her car as easily as the foil top on a yoghurt carton. The noise was deafening, the movement terrifying, but through it all Flynn was beside her, holding her hand, soothing her with his presence, until finally a firefighter appeared above them, giving the thumbs-up sign. For the last hour all Meg had wished for was to be free from the mangled wreckage, but now the moment was here suddenly she was scared again.

Bracing herself for movement, she gripped Flynn's hand tighter. 'It's going to hurt.'

'You're going to be fine. Once you're in the ambulance, and I've checked you over, I'll give you something for pain.'

'Promise?'

He gave her a smile. 'Trust me.' He was easing his fingers out of her grip. 'I'm just going around to your other side so I can support your head as they bring you out. I'll speak to you again in the ambulance.'

And with that she had to be content.

He held her head as they skilfully lifted her, taking charge from the top as they started the slow, painstaking ascent back to the road, relaying his orders in clear, direct tones, carefully ensuring that her neck never moved out of alignment, assuming at all times the worst-case scenario: until an X-ray showed no fracture of her neck it was safer to assume that she had one. And though Meg had never been more scared in her life, never been in more pain, amazingly she felt safe, knew that she was in good hands—literally.

Strong hands gently lowered her onto the cool crisp sheets on the stretcher, and she felt the bumps as they wheeled her to the awaiting ambulance. Fragments of the conversations between the police and the firefighters reached her as they jolted along.

'…no skid marks…'

'…the witness said she just veered straight off.'

'…just finished a night shift…'

It was the type of conversation Meg heard nearly every working day, the tiny pieces of a jigsaw that would painstakingly be put together, adding up the chain of events that had led to an accident. Only this time it was about her.

As they lifted her into the ambulance and secured the stretcher she ran a tongue over her dry blood-stained lips.

'Where's Flynn?'

Ken patted her arm. 'He'll be here in a moment.'

'He said he'd be here.' Suddenly it seemed imperative that she see Flynn and tell him what had happened.

'Just give him a moment, Meg, he's had a rough morning.' Ken's words made no sense. She was the patient, after all, and the way Ken was talking it sounded as if Flynn was the one who was upset.

'What's she moaning about now?' It was Flynn again, a touch paler and a bit grey-looking, but with the same easy smile and a slight wink as he teased her.

'Are you all right?'

Meg opened her mouth to answer but realised that Ken's question had actually been directed to Flynn.

Flynn muttered something about a 'dodgy pie' and, after accepting a mint from Ken, again shone the beastly pupil torch back into her eyes.

'She's in a lot of pain, Flynn.' Ken was speaking as he checked her blood pressure. 'All her obs are stable. Do you want to head off to the hospital now?'

'I'll just have a quick look first.' Whipping out his stethoscope, he gently moved it across her bruised, tender ribcage. 'Good air entry,' he murmured, more to himself than to anyone else. 'Is it hurting a lot, Meg?'

'I didn't…' Her voice was merely a croak, but it was enough to stop Flynn listening to her chest. Pulling his stethoscope out of his ears, he bent his head forward.

'What was that, Meg?'

'I didn't fall…' But she couldn't finish her sentence. Huge tears were welling in her eyes, sobs preventing her from going further as the emotion of the morning, now she was free from the wreckage, finally hit home.

'It's all right, Meg. Don't try and talk. You're safe now. I'm going to give you something for the pain.' His lips were set in a grim line and she could see the beads of sweat on his forehead, but Flynn's voice was kind and assured as he continued talking. 'The main thing is that you're safe.' His grey eyes seemed to be boring into her, and Meg found that she couldn't tear her own away. Even as the sirens wailed into life and the ambulance moved off she found herself still holding his gaze, her eyelids growing heavy as the drug he had injected took effect and oblivion descended.

'Meg O'Sullivan, we weren't expecting you till tonight. Don't tell me: you just can't stay away from the place.' Jess chatted away good-humouredly, her Irish accent thick and strong, as the team lifted her onto the trolley. There was nothing Emergency staff dreaded more than being wheeled into their own department, but unfortunately it happened now and then, and the staff dealt with it with a very special brand of humour—intimate, yet professional.

'Perhaps she's checking up on you.' Ken Holmes carried on the joke as they swapped the paramedics' monitors and equipment for the emergency department's own.

'Or…' Jess smiled as she wrapped a blood pressure cuff around Meg's bruised arm '…she decided that she did want to meet the new consultant after all.'

'She works here?' Apart from leading the count as they'd lifted her over it was the first time Flynn had spoken since they had arrived in the unit.

'*She* does.' Fifty milligrams of Pethidine on top of a sleepless night had not only controlled her pain but also taken away every last piece of Meg's reserve, and her comment came out rather more sarcastically than intended. She saw his perfectly arched eyebrow raise just a fraction as he skilfully palpated her abdomen.

'And what is it you do here, *Meg*?'

'The same as Jess.'

'And what does Jess do?'

God, why all the questions? All she wanted to do was sleep. Closing her eyes, she ignored him, but Flynn hadn't finished yet.

'Meg, what job do you do here?' His voice was sharp, dragging her out of her slumber.

'I'm a nurse,' she answered reluctantly. Maybe now he'd leave her alone.

'What day is it today?'

The interrogation obviously wasn't over. He was testing her reflexes now, lifting her legs slightly and tapping at her knees as he repeated the question. 'Come on, Meg, what day is it today?'

'Pay day.'

Jess laughed. 'It is too. Thank God,' she added. 'My credit card bill is crashing through the roof. Now, come on, Meg—tell the good doctor here what day it is so he can get off to his welcome breakfast.'

'Tuesday.' No, that was yesterday. Meg always got

mixed up when she was doing nights. 'Wednesday,' she said, more definitely. 'Today is Wednesday.'

The same small affirmative nod he had used at the accident scene was repeated and Meg gave a relieved sigh.

'Do you remember what happened yet?'

'I had an accident.'

Flynn gave her a thin smile. 'You certainly did. I meant before the accident. Do you remember what caused it?'

She opened her mouth to answer, to tell him exactly what had happened in the hope of finally being allowed to rest, but as she tried to explain Meg felt as if she was trying to recall a dream. Little flashes of the morning would pop into her head, rather like watching a photo develop, but before the picture appeared it would vanish again, and no matter how she fought to remember the images just slipped away.

'Can you remember?' His voice was gentle, as if he realised how much she was struggling.

'No.' The simple word terrified her.

'You will. Just give it time, Meg.'

Turning to Jess, Meg listened as Flynn ordered what seemed an inordinate amount of tests. 'We'll get her over for a C. spine and head CT now, and I want one of her abdomen. She's tender over the spleen. Chest and abdo films, and I want those bloods back from the lab stat, in case she needs a transfusion. It might be better to pop in a catheter.'

'No.' This time the simple word was said much more forcefully, and Flynn and Jess both turned to her simultaneously. 'No,' she repeated. 'I'm not having a catheter.'

'Okay.' Flynn relented. 'But if you haven't passed urine in the next hour I'm getting one put in.' He turned back to Jess. 'Obviously keep her nil by mouth for now. I'd best go and do a quick duty speech, and then I'll be back to check on her. Call me in the meantime if you're in the least concerned.'

He came over to the trolley then and looked down at her, her hair fanning out on the pillow, knotted and full of glass, streaks of blood on her cheeks and her lips bruised and swollen. Yet there was an air of dignity about her, coupled with a wary, but somehow superior look that brought the beginning of a smile to his lips. 'And try not to give her any more Pethidine. I want to do a full neuro assessment when I get back.'

'Are you going?' It was a strange question, one Meg couldn't believe she had just asked.

'Just for a little while, then I'll be back to review you.' That seemed to placate her, and she relaxed back onto the pillow. 'If you're very good Jess and I might even save you a Danish pastry.' He smiled then, properly, for the first time since their eventful meeting.

It was like being rescued all over again.

Closing her eyes, his face still etched in her bruised, muddled mind, Meg let sleep finally wash over and, utterly oblivious to the world, even the hourly neuro obs the staff performed at regular intervals, she slept through what was left of the day.

'She's waking up.'

'Leave her, Kathy. The nurse said not to disturb her.'

Mary O'Sullivan's voice had that sharp warning edge that would have sent Meg scuttling straight back to her chair, but it had little or no effect on her sister.

'That was two hours ago. I just want to see she's all right for myself.'

'Do as your mother says, Kathy.' Ted O'Sullivan had as little impact on Kathy as his wife, and as Meg came to it was to the all too familiar strains of her family bickering.

Kathy stood there peering anxiously over her. 'You're awake.' Kathy's eyes filled with tears as she looked down at her big sister.

'No thanks to you,' Mary interjected. 'Can you not obey a simple order, Kathy? The nurse said to leave her be.'

'Hello, Mum,' Meg croaked. 'Sorry for all the trouble.'

'No trouble—apart from a coronary when the police came to the door.' Mary's attempt at a joke felt more like a telling off, and Meg closed her eyes again, the bright lights of the Emergency observation ward too much for her fragile head. 'Are you all right, pet?'

Keeping her eyes closed, Meg nodded. Now the collar was off at least she was able to do that. It was about the only thing she could do; her chest felt as if a bus was sitting on it. Mary fussed and chatted for a while, but Meg could almost sense her relief when six o'clock came and her mother had a valid reason to go home.

'That lovely Irish nurse, Jess, has kept us up to date. She's away home now, to her husband, but she said that you were to rest as much as possible. Now that you've come to, I might get your father home for his dinner. His insulin was due half an hour ago. I'll be back in first thing tomorrow and we'll ring the ward tonight.'

Again Meg sensed the sting of disapproval.

'Are you coming, Kathy?'

'No.' Meg felt the bed move as Kathy perched herself on it. 'I'll stay with her. Jake can always give me a lift later.'

'She was only joking about the police,' Kathy said when their parents had finally gone.

'Since when did Mum joke?'

'There's always a first time. I was in the hydro pool and Jess let Jake know. It was Jake that went and told her.'

Meg looked at her sister. Her uncombed, spiky blonde hair and the faint scent of chlorine certainly held up her story. 'So the police didn't come?'

'No.' Kathy laughed, but her brimming eyes belied her casual chatter. 'Actually, you did me a favour. They've got a new chief of physio and the workout they were putting me through felt like an army training camp—and, despite what she says, Mum's had a grand afternoon gossiping to Jess about the fair Emerald Isle.'

Meg attempted to smile, but it died on her lips.

'She was upset, you know.' Kathy squeezed Meg's hand. 'Really upset.'

'And now she's angry.'

'You know what Mum can be like.'

Meg did know—only too well. The last few months had been a nightmare. It was bad enough finding out that your boyfriend of eighteen months, the man you'd adored, actually thought you had a future with, was in fact married.

And not just married. Married to your colleague's sister, who just happened to go to the same church as your mum. So not only had Meg felt the wrath of disapproval from her colleagues at Melbourne City Hospital, there had been the wrath of her mother to deal with.

Mary O'Sullivan wasn't sure which was the greater of the two evils. The fact her eldest daughter had been branded a home-wrecker, or the undeniable fact that Meg wasn't a virgin.

And now she had trashed her car.

'I hate this year.'

'I know, but there's always next year.'

'Next year will probably be just the same.'

'It won't.' Kathy insisted. 'You've got a new job, new friends, a whole new start. All you have to do is loosen up a bit.'

'Loosen up?'

'Try letting people in. It's a nice world out there. I know Vince hurt you, but not all men are the same.'

Just the mention of his name bought forth a whole fresh batch of tears. Meg hadn't cried since the day they broke up, and certainly not in front of anyone, but the egg on her head combined with the pain in her chest was such a horrible combination that for once crying came naturally.

'I've got some news that might cheer you up,' Kathy said desperately. Seeing her sister, who never cried, sobbing in the bed was torture. 'How do you fancy being a bridesmaid?'

Like a tap being turned off, Meg instantly stopped crying, her eyes swinging round to her sister.

'You're engaged?'

'I have been for…' Kathy glanced at her watch. 'Twenty hours now. He asked me last night.'

'Who, Jake?'

Kathy gave a gurgle of laughter. 'No, the tram conductor. Of course it's Jake. Who else?'

'What does Mum have to say about it?' Meg asked slowly.

'Well, the fact we want to get married so quickly—on Valentine's Day, actually—led to a few sticky questions, but we've finally managed to convince her that it's not a shotgun wedding. We're just head over heels and want to do it as soon as possible. She's tickled pink, actually, and insisting that we have an engagement party. But I've told her that the most we want is a casual dinner.'

Meg gave a wry laugh. 'So no doubt she'll spend tomorrow on the telephone, ringing up hundreds of relatives.'

'Probably,' Kathy conceded. 'But after she's been in to see you, of course,' she added hastily. 'Whoops, look like I'd better make myself scarce—here comes Flynn now.'

Meg screwed up her forehead. 'Flynn? Do you know him?'

'He's a friend of Jake's…' As Flynn approached the bed Kathy's voice trailed off.

'Good evening, Meg—Kathy.' He gave her sister a friendly nod.

'Hi, Flynn. I'll leave you to it; see you in the morning, Sis.' Popping a quick kiss on Meg's cheek, Kathy limped off.

'How are you feeling?'

'Better. Well, sore but better.' The beginning of a blush was creeping over her cheeks.

'That's good. You've had a very lucky escape, Meg, all your tests have come back as normal. Apart from a lot of bruising, which is going to hurt for a while, and a mild concussion, you've got off very lightly.' He peered at his notes for a moment, and Meg watched as he fiddled uncomfortably with his pen. 'Can you remember what happened yet?'

Meg shook her head. Normally she would have left it there, but there was something about Flynn, something about the way he had smiled at her this morning, the drama they had shared, that made her take the plunge and for the first time in ages prolong a conversation. 'No, but I do remember you offering to save me a Danish pastry. You didn't, by any chance, did you?'

Her attempt at small talk was instantly to her dying shame rebuffed.

'Apparently the police seem to think that you might have fallen asleep at the wheel.'

Embarrassed at his businesslike tone, Meg felt her blush only deepen. 'I didn't!'

'There were no skid marks at the scene, and apparently you were exhausted when you left this morning—though Jess told only me that, I hasten to add. I haven't written it in my notes.' He ran a hand through his hair, an exasperated tone creeping into his voice. 'Why the hell didn't you get a taxi?'

She knew he was wrong, knew somehow that the

picture he was painting wasn't how it had happened, but her total lack of recall didn't put her in the best position to argue the point.

'I didn't fall asleep,' Meg intoned.

'The police…'

'The police are wrong,' she retorted quickly. 'And anyway, it's none of your business.' She knew she was being rude, but something about Flynn had her acting completely out of character. The little hint about the Danish pastry, the blush that wouldn't go away—and now she was answering him back. It wasn't actually out of character. It was more the old Meg. The Meg before Vince had extinguished every last piece of her fiery personality.

Flynn begged to differ. 'Oh, but it is my business, young lady. It became my business at precisely four minutes past eight this morning, when I stabilised your neck in the wreckage of your car.' His voice was curt and formal, with no hint of the man who had held her hand just this morning, cajoled her to stay awake—who, even in the most dire of circumstances, had actually managed to make her laugh. 'It became my business when I found out that one of the nurses in my department was so damned tired after her night shift she nearly killed herself. And,' he added, standing over her so she had no choice but to look at him, 'had you wiped out an entire family, no doubt it would have been left to me to deal with it. So you see, *Meg*—' his lip curled around her name '—it is my business.'

Despite his anger, it wasn't a no holds barred attack, Meg realised. Not once had he mentioned the very real danger he had put himself in by staying with her throughout the ordeal, and his modest omission somehow touched her.

He stood there for a moment, his eyes challenging her to respond, but she was too tired and too utterly defeated to argue. 'Right, then. I've spoken to your parents, and I'm happy for you to be discharged tomorrow as long as you go and stay with them.'

'That's all I need,' Meg muttered ungraciously.

'I want the physio to see you before you go and run through some deep breathing exercises. Your chest is badly bruised and it's important he sees you.'

'No.'

Flynn let out an exasperated sigh.

'The catheter I can understand your objection to—but physio, for heaven's sake? Do you have to argue about everything?'

'You don't understand.'

'So enlighten me.'

'Jake Reece is the Emergency physio,' Meg started, her eyes darting around the obs ward to check that Kathy had definitely gone.

'So why is that a problem?

'He's marrying my sister.'

Flynn's face broke into a grin then, and for a second he looked like the Flynn from this morning. 'Jake and Kathy are getting married? That's fantastic news.' He seemed to remember she was there then, and stared at her, perplexed. 'So why on earth don't you want him to see you?'

'Because, unlike you, I'm not exactly thrilled with the news.'

'Why?' He seemed genuinely bemused and Meg couldn't believe that he didn't understand how she was feeling.

'He's her physiotherapist, for heaven's sake. Kathy's handicapped. It's wrong.'

His face changed. She saw his bemused look change to one of distaste.

'Please don't try to tell me that you're so politically correct you haven't even noticed.'

'Of course I've noticed. Kathy has also told me about it herself. Unlike you, she doesn't seem to have a problem with it. From what I can remember of our conversation, she has mild cerebral palsy from birth, which has left her with a limp and a minor speech impediment. What she didn't tell me, but I soon found out for myself, is that she happens to be a fun, happy, caring and very attractive woman.'

'He's ten years older than her.'

'Hardly a hanging offence.' He paused then, eyeing her carefully before continuing. 'As you yourself pointed out, he's her physio, not her doctor. They will have spent a lot of time together. If you got down off your high horse and actually spent some time with them, instead of judging them, you might find yourself pleasantly surprised.'

And, after signing off her discharge papers, he left her lying there.

Lying there for all the world wishing the ground would open up and swallow her.

CHAPTER THREE

MEG'S childhood had ended at nine years old.

The day Kathy was born.

She had spent endless afternoons sitting after school in a waiting room doing her homework while Mary took her youngest daughter to a seemingly never-ending round of appointments. Paediatricians, speech therapists, occupational therapists—the list had been endless.

The only person who had taken it all in her stride, literally, had been Kathy. Defying the doctors' grim prognosis, she had cheerfully picked herself up, over and over, until finally at the age of four she had taken her first steps. Her optimistic, sunny nature had served her well in the playground also, with Kathy making friends easily and keeping them. A group of little girls Meg had referred to as 'Kathy's army'. But Kathy's army hadn't always been there for her, and the playground hadn't been the only place a child like Kathy could run into trouble or become the victim of a cruel and thoughtless taunt.

So, from the day Kathy had come home from the hospital, Meg had taken it upon herself to look out for her. It was almost as if Meg had been fitted with an inbuilt radar, constantly on the alert, always looking out for her little sister.

And even though the callipers had long since gone, even though Kathy was nineteen years old now, and, as Flynn had pointed out, extremely attractive with a social life that would exhaust anyone, Meg's radar was still there. The protective feelings Meg had for her little sister hadn't faded one iota. That was why she was cautious of Jake. She certainly wasn't the bigot Flynn had implied. Her concern here was only to save Kathy from being hurt. After all, Meg knew better than most how easily your heart could be broken.

But a couple of weeks at home, hiding away in her old bedroom, reading again the wonderful books that had fuelled her childhood and eating the inordinate meals that appeared every few hours, had given Meg plenty of time for reflection and introspection, and somewhere along the way Meg had finally realised that Kathy neither wanted nor needed saving.

But Kathy wasn't all that Meg had dwelled on as her sick leave days ticked by into double figures. Hesitantly, painfully, Meg had travelled the bittersweet journey of the brokenhearted. Bitter because, bruised and battered, and with a good excuse to cry, Meg had allowed herself to finally grieve—grieve for the man she had lost, the man she had thought Vince was. And sweet because, despite the pain, despite the soul-searching as her blackened chest turned to a dirty yellow and her swollen lips finally went down, for the first time in six months Meg actually knew she was finally over him.

'I've brought you some soup.'

Meg screwed up her nose as Kathy peered around the bedroom door, a laden tray in her hands. 'I'm sick of soup.'

'How do you think I feel? I wasn't even in an accident and I'm having lentil broth forced down me twice a day. At least you can afford to put some weight on; I'm going to be huge for my party at this rate.'

'What happened to the "casual dinner"?'

Kathy laughed. 'Mum got involved, that's what happened. How she's managed to book a hall and caterers at such short notice I've no idea. I shudder to think what the wedding's going to be like. Half of me just wants to get a licence and get it over and done with, without all the fuss.'

Raining salt on her soup, Meg didn't look up. 'And the other half?'

'The other half of me is starting to buy all the bridal magazines and is wrestling between crushed silk and organza, and lilies as opposed to freesias. I guess the upshot is I can't wait to be married.'

This time Meg did look up. Seeing her sister sitting on the edge of her bed, her face glowing, her eyes literally sparkling, Meg knew she had never seen Kathy looking happier. 'You really love him, don't you?'

'I really do.' Kathy paused for a moment. 'And the best bit of it all is that I know Jake loves me—all of me—even down to my limp. He says that if it wasn't for my limp we'd never have met, which is a pretty nice way of looking at it.'

It *was* nice, Meg admitted to herself. Actually, in the last few days she had found herself looking at Jake rather differently. He had treated Meg with professional friendliness at the hospital, and as—thanks to Flynn Kelsey—she had been forced into spending the last two weeks at home, there had been plenty of time to watch Jake and Kathy together. Jake even took Mary's somewhat overbearing nature in his stride.

'How do you feel about going back to work tomorrow?'

Meg shrugged. 'It will be nice to get away from the soup.'

'I wouldn't bet on it. Mum's just bought a massive stainless steel vacuum flask; you'll be supping on her Irish broth for weeks yet.' When Meg didn't laugh Kathy continued tentatively. 'A bit nervous, huh?'

Meg nodded. 'A bit,' she admitted. 'It doesn't help that everyone thinks I fell asleep at the wheel.'

'It will be old news soon. They'll soon find something else to talk about.'

'I just wish I could remember what happened.'

'You will.'

Meg fiddled with her spoon. 'I feel as if I've been away for months, not just a couple of weeks. I'm more nervous than when I first started there.'

'Once you've been there a couple of hours you'll soon be back in the swing of things. They seem a nice bunch of girls; you should try to get to know them better. That Jess was lovely to us while you were sleeping.'

'Oh, Jess is nice. She can be a bit overbearing, but it's all well meant. She's probably the one I'm closest to, but a night out with Jess isn't going to do my social life wonders—it would be like going out with Mum.'

'What about the rest of them?' Kathy asked.

'They all seem nice enough,' Meg replied. 'But I don't really know them. I mean, we chat about work and what we did on our days off, but apart from Jess I don't really know much about any of them.'

'And whose fault is that?' Kathy said gently. 'Look, Meg, I know you've had it tough recently, but it's really time to move on, let the world in a bit.'

Meg nodded. 'I know it is.'

Kathy put a hand up to her sister's forehead, an incredulous look on her face. 'Quick—call a doctor! The girl must be delirious. You're not actually agreeing with me, are you?'

Meg grinned as she pushed Kathy's hand away. 'For once I am. Bloody Vince.'

'Absolutely,' Kathy agreed, grinning broadly. 'That's more like it. There's a whole world out there full of gorgeous *single* men.'

'Hold on a moment,' Meg said quickly. 'A relationship's the last thing I want at the moment. I'm talking about resuming a social life, nothing else. I mean it,' she added as Kathy gave her a questioning look.

'I believe you,' Kathy said, but just as Meg started to relax a meddling look flashed across her sister's face. 'But if there was anyone you wanted me to add to the party list, you know you'd only have to ask?'

For a nanosecond Meg's mind involuntarily flashed to Flynn—the Flynn who had sat with her in the car, not the jackbooted doctor who had visited her in the obs ward—but resolutely she pushed all thought of him away. That was one path she definitely wasn't heading down—and anyway, the last person she wanted to help with her love life was her little sister; a girl had to have some pride! 'I'm quite capable of sorting out my own social life, thank you very much.'

Kathy grinned, not in the slightest bit bothered by Meg's haughty tones. 'Okay, okay, it was only a suggestion.' Picking up the last of Meg's bread, she popped it into her mouth. 'At least it's a start.'

A small start, perhaps, but to Meg it felt monumental. This time when she pulled on her uniform and clipped on her badges she forced a smile as she made her way out to the department, utterly determined that when someone suggested heading off to the bar after work, or a house party next weekend, instead of murmuring her usual excuses she would smile warmly and agree to go.

'Morning, Meg, welcome back.'

'Good morning, Carla, how are you?'

Unless it was Carla.

Meg quickly made a sub-clause in her self-imposed contract. A students' bash with cheap wine and even cheaper comments from the medical and nursing students she could do without. She wasn't that desperate.

Yet.

'Fine.' Carla flicked her long blonde fringe out of her

eyes and Meg watched as it promptly fell back over them, tempted to tell her to take a bandage from the trolley and tie the shaggy mess back. But, in the spirit of it being her first day back, Meg said nothing. Jess could sort Carla out later.

'Where are you working this morning?'

'I'm in the cubicles at the moment, but Jess said that if anything comes into resus I'm to go in.'

Meg heard the nervous note in the young student's voice. 'You'll be fine. No one will expect you to do anything, you're just there to observe, and when you're feeling up to it you can join in.'

'Thanks. Will you be in there?'

Meg was saved from answering as Jess appeared, crisp and fresh in her white linen blouse. 'How about it, Meg? Do you fancy starting back in the deep end? We're a bit low on numbers this morning, and I'm supposed to be going to an occupational health and safety lecture at ten. I can't believe it's been two years since my last.'

'No problem,' Meg answered, before turning to give Carla a reassuring smile. 'Dr Campbell is really nice to work with in resus.'

'Except he's on two weeks' annual leave.' Jess rolled her eyes. 'Flynn's on this morning. If it's quiet he wants to lecture the students and the grad nurses in CPR—or BLS, as it's called now. Why do they have to keep changing things? And when does this place ever stay quiet?' she asked, but as usual didn't bother to wait for an answer. 'I've told him Annie is off having her arm stitched back on, but he still wants to go ahead.'

'What happened to Annie?' Meg asked. Annie, the plastic doll the staff practised their lifesaving skills on, was a popular member of the staff, and the concern in Meg's voice was genuine.

'My lips are sealed,' Jess said dramatically, which meant she was pausing for breath before she continued. 'Let's just hope that next time our dear Dr Kelsey tries to show the new interns how to reduce a dislocated shoulder, he'll leave poor Annie alone. The man doesn't know his own strength.' Tutting away, Jess turned her attention to Carla. 'In my day—and, I hasten to add it wasn't *that* long ago—we wore hats, and with good reason. Now, go and do something about that blessed fringe of yours or I'll make you wear a theatre cap for the rest of your rotation.'

As she bustled off Carla rolled her eyes and turned to Meg. 'She talks as if she trained during the Second World War; just how old is Jess?'

'Fifty-something,' Meg mumbled.

'Oh, well, I guess that explains it,' Carla replied, accepting the bandage Meg offered her and managing to still look gorgeous with a massive white bow on the top of her head.

'Which means she's got a lot of experience,' Meg said pointedly, annoyed at Carla's surly comments. 'I know first-hand what a good nurse she is—and not just from a professional point of view. Jess is the first person you want to see when you're coming through those doors on a stretcher. Tying up your hair and looking smart might seem minor details, but they're important ones; it goes a long way to instilling confidence in the patients.'

Suitably chastised, Carla followed Meg into resus.

'I know it seems *boring* how we constantly check all the equipment, but it really is vital,' Meg explained as she painstakingly checked and restocked all the back-boards behind the resus bed. 'Everything has its own place in s resuscitation room. There isn't time to be rummaging through shelves when someone is desperately ill and staff are already tense. It's much easier all round if everything is well stocked and in order.'

'I couldn't agree more.'

Meg didn't need to look up to know who the deep voice that filled the room belonged to. But in the spirit of her new-found openness she forced a smile as she battled with a blush, painfully aware that the last time they had been together in this room she had been dressed only in a skimpy hospital gown with a good dose of Pethidine on board. Not the best of looks!

'Morning, Flynn,' Carla announced cheerfully, and Meg frowned at the rather too familiar tone.

'Morning, Carla.' Flynn did a double take. 'Have you got a toothache or something?'

'Nah.' Carla shrugged. 'Apparently my hair was a health hazard.'

'Good morning, *Dr Kelsey*,' Meg responded, casting a pointed look at Carla, but Flynn didn't seem remotely fazed by the student's familiarity.

'Flynn will do. Dr Kelsey's my father.'

Meg realised she was gnashing her teeth; between the two of them they had managed to make her feel as if she was about to start drawing her pension. 'Well, in that case,' she said in a rather falsely cheerful voice, 'good morning, Flynn.'

At least she wasn't the only one blushing, Meg realised—Carla was positively beetroot. But then who could blame her? Students had hormones too, and Flynn was a pretty impressive sight for seven-thirty in the morning. Everything about him oozed masculinity—not just his huge, powerful build, but also the husky voice, the spicy tang of cologne, even the hint of legendary strength, added a touch of zest to an otherwise routine morning.

'You're looking better than the last time I saw you. How are you feeling?'

'I'm fine, thank you.'

But Flynn didn't look convinced. 'I wasn't expecting to see you back so soon. That was a nasty accident you were involved in.'

'Which I'm over.' Meg bristled, unnerved by his scrutiny.

'Hey, I'm just the doctor.' Flynn grinned. 'Still, if it does turn out too soon for you to be back just let me know and I'll sign you off.'

'Wouldn't you just?' Meg muttered, but Flynn wasn't listening. Instead he was looking around the room, pulling from the walls half the equipment Meg had only just replaced.

'What are you doing?'

'Setting up for my lecture. Where's Annie?'

'But I haven't finished checking resus,' Meg argued.

'And Jess said she'd already told you that Annie was off being repaired. Someone,' Meg said accusingly, 'apparently used her as a sparring partner.'

'I did not,' Flynn said defensively. 'I was trying to show the interns how to reduce a shoulder.' He flashed a smile and Meg knew there and then that he'd get his lecture. 'Hey, Carla, any chance of rustling me up a coffee and then grabbing the other students? I'd like to get started.'

Only when Carla had willingly dashed off did Flynn speak again. 'Before you tell me off, I don't usually use the students as tea girls, but I wanted to get you alone and apologise.'

Meg was caught completely unawares, and in an attempt to cover up her embarrassment at suddenly finding herself alone with him her words came out far sharper than intended. 'For wrongly accusing me of falling asleep at the wheel or insinuating that I'm a bigot?'

But Flynn just laughed. 'Feisty, aren't you? And to think I thought it was the Pethidine!'

Meg sucked in her breath. Damn this man, he really managed to get under her skin. 'I thought this was supposed to be an apology?'

'So it is.'

She waited, not quite tapping her foot, but her stance showed her impatience.

'About Kathy,' he started. 'Look, I just went off at the deep end. I was more riled at you falling asleep at the wheel.' He saw her open her mouth to argue and put his hands up. 'Or "allegedly" falling asleep. I took Jake and

Kathy out for a celebratory drink the other night and had my ear bent about what a wonderful sister you are. I won't embarrass you by going into detail, but the upshot is I know now that I was way out of order.'

He didn't look particularly sorry. 'Is that it?'

Flynn shot her a surprised look. 'Do you want it written in blood? Tell you what, how about I take you out for a drink or dinner? Show that there's no hard feelings?'

Sub-clause B, Meg thought quickly as she shook her head. 'That won't be necessary, thank you.' Delicious consultants with an over-supply of confidence and sex appeal were a definite no-no.

'Oh, come on,' Flynn said easily. 'It would save us both a heap of trouble—I've got a feeling your sister's in a matchmaking mood. Maybe we should just get it over with, before she deafens us both singing the other one's praises.'

'Are you always so romantic when you ask a woman out, Doctor? Because if the way you've just asked me is an indication of your usual approach, it's no wonder you need my sister to help you.'

Flynn just roared laughing. 'Is that a no, then?' he asked as the students started trickling in.

'Yes,' Meg muttered blushing to her toes. 'I mean, yes, it's a no.'

'Pity,' Flynn murmured, and with an easy smile turned his attention to the gathered crowd.

Meg had to hand it to him. Within seconds of starting he had the students and nurses enthralled. BLS, or basic life support, was a subject they would all have covered at college, and on their ward rotations, but here in Emergency, given that it was an almost daily event, they would practically be guaranteed a chance to witness and, if at all possible, practise the life-saving skill.

And Flynn held them in the palm of his hand, explaining that what they learnt today and in their weeks in Emergency might never be needed in their entire career, depending upon their chosen field. 'But…' He paused, those expressive grey eyes working the room, ensuring he had everyone's attention. 'Statistically speaking—and I'm not talking about while you're at work; I'm talking about when you're at the library or doing the groceries, or dropping a video off at the shop—somewhere in the future, someone in this room will utilise this skill, possibly on a stranger, but maybe on someone you love. And you, as nurses, have a chance of doing it right; have a chance of saving a life. Pretty exciting, huh?'

He grinned at the rapt faces. 'So how about a practice?'

'We can't. Annie's still being repaired.' Meg pointed out again.

'Good.' Flynn grinned. 'Then we'll practise on a human—far more realistic than a doll, don't you think? Come on, Meg.'

She hesitated—and for more than a brief moment. Had it been Dr Campbell or Jess—anyone, in fact—Meg would have leapt up on the trolley without a second thought. After all, in her six months here she had been strapped to the ECG machine, been plastered, even had blood taken all in the name of practice. It was part and parcel of the job. But it wasn't Dr Campbell asking her, it was Flynn Kelsey, and lying on the trolley pretending to be a mannequin… Well, suffice it to say there was nothing remotely mannequin-like about the butterflies flying around in her stomach.

'Come on, Meg,' Flynn said impatiently. 'Unless you need a refresher course as well?'

Reminding herself she did this sort of thing all the time, Meg climbed on the trolley and lay back against the pillow, wishing her beastly blush would fade.

'Now, this patient looks well, as you can see. Her colour's excellent—quite pink, actually.' Meg was tempted to take a swipe at him as their audience started laughing. 'But don't be fooled. High colour in an unresponsive patient could be an indication of any number of things. Any ideas?'

'Carbon monoxide poisoning?' Carla said, and Meg made a mental note to praise her later.

'Excellent,' Flynn said warmly. 'Flats with old heaters, suicide attempts, house fires—all these can cause carbon monoxide poising. The patient might look pink and healthy but in reality they're exactly the opposite. Okay, so we've dragged this poor woman out of her flat, she's as red as a beetroot and completely unresponsive—so what now?'

'Check her airway,' a couple of the students called out.

'Good start.' She could feel his fingers on her jaw—firm, warm fingers, Meg noted, squeezing her eyes closed and desperately attempting to relax her face as he gently pulled her chin down. 'Yep, airway's clear. If it wasn't, here in resus obviously I'd use suction. Out on the street it would be with more basic means.' He held up a finger and the students groaned. 'Now what?'

'Check her pulse.'

'She can have the strongest pulse in medical history,' Flynn replied quickly, 'but if she's not breathing what is her heart pumping? Certainly not oxygenated blood. Come on, guys—ABC, remember? We're heading into danger time here; this long without oxygen and you're starting to look at brain damage. Okay—A for airway, B for breathing. Watch her chest to see if it's moving.'

Meg felt ten pairs of eyes on her chest and wondered if he expected her to hold her breath to make things more realistic. A distinct impossibility as suddenly her breath was coming out in short, rapid bursts.

'So, she's not breathing and I'm feeling for a pulse—which…' Meg heard the tiniest hint of a laugh in his voice as he placed his fingers on her neck and felt her fast, flickering pulse '…is absent. Right, because she's an adult I'm going to tilt her neck to open the airway; on an infant you wouldn't do this,' he added, sliding a hand under her neck and jerking her head backwards. 'Babies' necks are shorter and straighter. In an adult pinch the nostrils, so all the air you breathe in doesn't escape. Again it's different for a baby. In that instance you would place your mouth over both the nose and mouth. Anyway—' he coughed slightly '—this isn't a child, this is a full-grown woman. So we tilt the neck, pinch the nostrils and give two effective inflations.'

She could feel his fingers around her nose, gently

pinching her nostrils together. One hand was pulling her mouth open and Meg realised with alarm she could feel him moving closer, feel his hot breath on her cheeks. Opening her eyes in alarm, Meg found herself looking into the deep pools of his. Surely he wasn't going to actually do it? This was a practice, for heaven's sake!

But before she could react, register a protest, even if she had wanted to, he had moved his face and given two fast breaths into mid-air, just as any professional would. But there was nothing, *nothing* very professional about the sudden sharp shift in tempo, the crackling awareness that made every touch, every tiny movement send a massive voltage of charged energy tearing through her body. He might just as well have grabbed the defibrillator beside him and charged it to two hundred joules.

'Right.' His voice was perfectly normal. 'Now we can get some of that oxygenated blood pumping through her system. Feel for the bottom half of the sternum and place the heel of your hand on the chest. Very importantly, remember your own strength. By now you'll be pumping with adrenaline yourself, and you don't want to crack the ribcage before you've started.' Mercifully, he removed his hands, then turned to his audience. 'Obviously you never practise massage on a person, so we'll have to wait for Annie to fully recuperate before you all have a turn. But if there's a cardiac arrest in progress in resus and you feel up to it ask one of the trained staff if you can have a go. Nothing beats first-hand experience.'

The BLS demonstration might have been finished,

but Meg's questionable hell wasn't over yet. The lecture went on for ages, with the students learning—courtesy of Meg's neck—the finer points of cricothyroid pressure to assist the doctor during intubation. Her limbs were also subjected to the clumsy students' attempts to place her in the recovery position. All in all, by the time Flynn had finished, and Meg was wearing a blood pressure cuff and possibly the same hard collar she had worn for her accident, despite all her earlier good intentions she wasn't in the best of moods.

'Can I get up now?' she asked rather indignantly when the students rapidly dispersed for their fifteen-minute tea break.

Flynn roared with laughter. 'I'd better give you a hand.' Looking down at her, he grinned. 'A certain *déjà vu*, don't you think?'

'I'd rather not be reminded, thank you.' Taking his offered hand, she let him sit her up, then ripped the blood pressure cuff off as Flynn undid the neck collar. 'Hold still. Some of your hair has got stuck in the Velcro. Here, hold your hair up.' He took her hand and guided it to the pile of curls he had unceremoniously dumped on her head.

'Ow,' Meg squealed as he ripped open the fastening and took half her hairline with it in the process.

'Sorry,' Flynn muttered, but he didn't sound it in the slightest. 'Sorry,' he said again, but this time with more conviction.

Her acceptance died on her lips as she looked up into his eyes. The humour and arrogance had gone; instead his eyes were suddenly serious, and the personal space he had so haplessly invaded suddenly felt inviting and strangely familiar. For Meg there was no question of not moving towards him, no thought of anything other than their lips meeting, a tender yet definite need that pulled them closer.

It was, quite simply, a kiss that had to be.

'Just as I thought,' he murmured, gently pulling away. 'Most kissable.'

'You shouldn't have done that.' Confused, embarrassed, Meg stood up.

'I didn't sense much resistance.' The same easy smile was back, and Meg was sure he was laughing at her, positive that he had kissed her just because he could. Just because she had let him.

'It was an accident,' Meg retorted, furious with him, but more so with herself for succumbing so easily.

Flynn laughed. 'We're in the right room for it, then.'

An uncomfortable silence followed—at least it was for Meg; Flynn didn't seem remotely bothered and made no effort to break it. He was probably, Meg thought angrily, used to necking with willing nurses at inappropriate moments. Used to endless reams of willing woman prepared to jump for his attention, happy to share him around so long as they had their moment in the sun with him.

Well, gorgeous he might be, and sexy and irresistible too, Meg thought reluctantly, but if Flynn thought he was going to use her to boost his already inflated ego then he had another think coming. He might have got away with a quick kiss when she wasn't paying attention, but she wasn't going to let down her guard again.

No way.

From somewhere outside a car was sounding its horn, loud enough to drag Meg back to reality, and she set about clearing away the inordinate amount of equipment Flynn had used for his demonstration, determined not to let him see how his teasing kiss had affected her.

'Meg, look, maybe we should…' The car horn broke into whatever he was about to say and Meg realised that she was frowning.

Flynn noticed it too. 'Something wrong?'

'I don't know.'

Cars tooted all the time, but there was something urgent about this hooting, something forcing Meg's attention. It was nothing she could explain.

Not logically anyway.

Without further explanation Meg swiftly made her way outside at the same time as Mike, the porter. The car was tooting incessantly now, and Meg broke into a run. Pulling open the door, she looked at the terrified and shocked face of a young woman, her large pregnant bump immediately obvious.

'I'm bleeding.'

Looking down, Meg swallowed as she watched the bright patch of blood spreading over her dress.

'What's your name?'

'Debbie. Debbie Evans.'

'How many weeks are you, Debbie?'

'Thirty-three. I'm supposed to be going to my antenatal appointment.'

Turning, Meg addressed the porter, who was patiently awaiting her instructions. 'Mike, grab a trolley and call for some help.' Meg turned back to the woman. 'It's okay, Debbie, we're going to get you inside now.' A small crowd had gathered now, as Meg got what further details she could from the pale woman.

'What have we got?' Flynn rushed the trolley forward

'Thirty-three weeks pregnant. She was on her way to the obstetrician when she started bleeding.'

'A lot?'

Meg gave him a worried nod as she made her way around to the passenger side. Slipping in beside Debbie, she undid her seatbelt, helping as much as she could from her end as the strong arms of Mike and Flynn gently lifted the woman onto the waiting trolley.

By the time Meg had extracted herself from the car the trolley had disappeared inside and, slightly breathless from exertion and nervous energy, she followed them, instantly going to Flynn's side to assist in taking blood and establishing IV access. Oxygen was already being given to the shocked woman, and Meg shouted her instructions in clear tones as Jess assisted. Carla, back from her coffee and hesitant at first, soon forgot her nerves and even ran an IV infusion of Hartmann's through the giving set, passing it to Meg as intravenous access was established.

'Good work,' Meg said encouragingly, without looking up.

'Debbie, my name is Flynn Kelsey. I'm the Emergency consultant.'

Passing Flynn the necessary tubes for an urgent FBE and cross match, Meg set up another flask of fluid as Jess appeared.

'Need a hand?' Mike was still discreetly hovering, knowing he would soon be needed. As part of the Emergency team his role might not be hands-on, but his input was just as vital as the medical staff's if the department was going to run smoothly.

'Please, Mike. These bloods need to go, stat, as soon as Flynn signs off the form. Make sure the lab knows they're urgent.'

Picking up the telephone, Meg punched in the radiography department's number. 'It's Meg in Emergency. We need an urgent obstetric ultrasound in resus.' Meg paused.

Flynn was busy examining Debbie's abdomen. He felt the baby's position for a moment, before attempting to find the heartbeat with the Doppler machine Jess had just passed him. The tiniest collective sigh as a heartbeat was picked up made Meg realise she hadn't been the only one holding her breath.

'Your baby's got a good strong heartbeat.' Flynn's words were calm and assured and he held Debbie's gaze. For an instant Meg felt her mind flash back to the accident, and those same grey eyes as he told her she was safe, that everything was going to be okay. She watched Debbie relax a fraction, the utter fear in her face fade a touch. Flynn was certainly a good doctor;

he managed to combine a relaxed bedside manner with an air of concentrated efficiency and direct honesty. 'But you are bleeding a lot, Debbie. I'm going to do an ultrasound to see exactly what's going on. Has anyone told you that your placenta is lying low?'

Debbie nodded. The loss of blood was making her drowsy. 'Stay with me, Debbie.' The same sharp voice he had used on Meg was dragging Debbie back to consciousness.

'I was going to have a Caesarean. Placenta pr…' Her voice trailed off and Meg watched as she closed her eyes.

'Come on, Debbie.' It was Meg speaking sharply now, forcing Debbie to stay awake as Flynn concentrated on the ultrasound.

'Placenta praevia,' Flynn said, confirming the assumed diagnosis. 'What's her blood pressure?'

'Eighty over fifty.'

'Will she be transferred to the maternity hospital?' Carla's voice was a loud whisper, and Flynn looked up and made his way over.

'Good question. But no. She needs to go straight to Theatre.'

Carla's eyes widened. 'But there's no Obstetrics here at Bayside.'

Flynn nodded 'If Mohammed won't go to the mountain…'

Carla gave him a completely nonplussed look.

'Meg will explain. Call me the second you're worried.' With a brief nod he left the room. Meg knew he would be on the telephone, safely out of earshot of Debbie.

'What was that about mountains?'

Meg grinned. 'The mountain will have to come to Mohammed. It's a saying. He'll be ringing the emergency obstetric team to hotfoot it over here.'

'They'll do the Caesarean in the Theatre here?'

Meg nodded.

The first unit of blood had arrived, along with a breathless Mike, and Meg thanked him for his speedy work. As it required two qualified nurses to check it, Carla observed as Jess and Meg ran through the formalities, carefully checking the patient's identity badge with the corresponding number on the bag of blood. The painstaking checking was all the more essential now the patient was barely conscious.

'We're going to put the blood through the blood warmer,' Meg explained. 'This blood is cold, and as we want to transfuse her quickly this will warm it to body temperature.' She showed Carla the long coil inside the machine that would warm the blood. 'The usual obs apply—close checking of pulse, blood pressure and respirations—but variations due to the blood are harder to detect in someone so sick, as their obs are unstable anyway. Any rash or rise in temperature is of particular importance and must be reported immediately.'

'Debbie?' Flynn returned, the consent form in his hand. 'Debbie!'

Her eyes flicked open, too shocked and exhausted now to be scared. 'We need to perform an urgent Caesarean.'

'It's too soon.'

'Your baby has to be born.'

Debbie rallied a bit then, her maternal instinct forcing her to concentrate to stay awake and fight for her baby.

'It's too soon,' she repeated.

'There's no choice.' His words were forceful, yet gentle. 'Debbie, we have to get your baby out, for both your sakes. You're thirty-three weeks—it's early, but not impossibly so. Your baby really needs to be born.'

Meg watched with compassion. She knew so well how Debbie was feeling—that overwhelming urge to just close your eyes—yet Debbie was struggling to focus.

'Will you do it?' Debbie asked.

Flynn shook his head. 'No, the obstetric team are on their way. But if they don't get here in time and it becomes necessary then I will. I'm going to do everything I can for you and your baby.'

Her pale hand accepted the pen and, shaking, Debbie managed a weak signature on the paper.

'My husband…'

'We've contacted him, and he'll be sent straight up to Theatre when he gets here.'

Meg smiled at the woman and then looked up to Flynn. 'Shall we get her up?'

'Yep.'

Mike didn't need to be asked even once. He arranged the IV pole and the cardiac monitor onto the trolley and switched Debbie's oxygen piping over to the portable cylinder as Meg collected the emergency boxes containing drugs and resuscitation equipment.

If Debbie suddenly went off *en-route* the safest thing

would probably be just to carry on running as, realistically speaking, Theatre was her only chance. But, as Flynn had only so recently pointed out, oxygenated blood was vital for Debbie and her baby. Slipping an airway and ambu bag under Debbie's pillow, silently hoping she wouldn't need to use them, Meg made a final quick check that everything was in order.

Going out with the Mobile Accident Unit was probably the most exciting thing in Emergency—the kick of adrenaline as you pulled on your gear, the call of the unknown as the ambulance drove off with sirens wailing, running through blood, checking equipment *en-route*, the crackling details coming in over the ambulance radio. But running through a busy hospital at high speed—curious stares, the lift held as you dashed past, the rush of excitement a true crisis generated in an Emergency nurse's stomach—well, usually that came a close second.

But not today.

Today Meg was just desperately concerned for her patient and the unborn baby. All she wanted was to get them to Theatre—get her patient the help she needed. It was as if a light had gone off inside her: the adrenaline buzz that emergency nurses survived on just wasn't happening for Meg as they ran along the corridor. And run they did. Flynn gave them no choice, his long legs making the dash seem effortless.

It was all right for him, Meg grumbled to herself as they stood in the lift. Meg was struggling to catch her breath while Flynn stood there calmly eyeing the cardiac monitor. It was all right for him, *he* didn't have a ribcage that felt like a used football.

'All right Meg?'

'Couldn't be better,' she answered dryly as the lift door opened and the mad dash to Theatre started again.

But there was no rushing once they stepped into the hallowed grounds of the theatre. Here the staff were never ruffled, were almost relaxed, even, as they accepted the patient and lifted her over onto the operating table. Everything was in place already—the resuscitation cot in the corner of the room, the packs being opened. No one would have guessed that an emergency Caesarean hadn't been performed in the small theatre for well over two years. Theatre, like Emergency, had to be prepared for every eventuality.

'We'll take it from here, thank you.' The theatre sister smiled as the anaesthetist appeared. 'The team's just arrived and they're on their way up.'

Which was a rather polite way of telling the trio to leave. But they didn't want to; Meg could sense even Flynn's reluctance. There was a baby here about to be born. Debbie was their patient, and letting go was sometimes hard.

'Can Carla stay? She's a student.' It was worth a try—Meg knew it would be great experience for her.

The theatre sister hesitated for an age. 'Show her where to change—but she has to stay at the back of the room.'

Meg grinned widely. 'She will. Thanks.'

Carla was so excited Meg practically had to dress her. 'Here's your blues. Come on, Carla, quickly or you'll miss it. Now, just grab some clogs—they'll do—and tuck your hair into this hat. If you think Jess is strict, wait till you meet the theatre sister! Now, *come on*.'

Pushing her through the black swing doors, Meg just managed to call out, 'Good luck!' and then she was gone.

'That was nice of you.'

Looking up, she was both surprised and embarrassed to see Flynn waiting for her to walk back to Emergency.

'Asking if Carla could stay—she'll really enjoy it.'

Meg realised she was frowning. Just what was it with those two? 'Just so long as she doesn't faint.'

'Oh, she won't. She's been hanging out to get into Theatre for ages.'

Meg felt her frown deepen. Since when did consultants take such an interest in nursing students? Silly question, Meg realised with a stab of disappointment. Especially when you didn't want to know the answer. 'It will be good experience for her,' she replied in efficient tones. 'She's only in her second year, so she hasn't done Theatre yet. You can pore over the books, but nothing beats it first-hand.'

'Absolutely.'

'I had an ulterior motive,' Meg admitted. 'At least I'll get a first-hand, in-depth report of what happened—not some cool message from Theatre.' He didn't respond, and they walked along in silence, flattening themselves against the corridor as a team pushing a huge incubator rushed past them. 'There's the mobile PICU,' Meg observed. 'They made good time as well.'

'Meg?' They were still standing against the wall and

Meg turned, hearing the serious note in his voice. 'About that kiss…'

'What about it?' Meg replied airily, setting off at twice their previous pace.

'Don't you think we ought to talk about it?'

Meg gave a scornful laugh. 'Why? Are you worried I'm going to dash off to Personnel and squeal sexual harassment?'

'No.'

'Then forget it.' She even managed to shrug. 'I'm not expecting you to follow it up with a marriage proposal. It was just a kiss—a bit of fun.'

She was lying through her teeth. It had been far more than a bit of fun for Meg—her lips were still scorching from his touch—but she certainly wasn't going to let Flynn see the effect he'd had on her. Unless one of them handed their notice in they were going to be seeing a lot of each other, and she was determined not to let him see how his reckless bit of fun had sent her into a spin.

'When do you think they'll transfer Debbie to the maternity hospital?'

It was a pointless question, an obvious attempt to change the subject, and Meg felt herself flush. Verbal diarrhoea wasn't a condition she usually suffered from.

'This afternoon, I guess, once she's a bit more stable. She's lucky she got to us. Heaven knows how she didn't have an accident, given the state she was in when she arrived.'

'Oh, well, at least you'll have time before she goes to give her a quick lecture on the dangers of driving while haemorrhaging.' It was a cheap shot, but she was still smarting at the harsh way he had spoken to her when she was a patient. Again Flynn didn't answer. 'So what do you reckon the baby's chances are?'

Flynn pondered for a moment before answering. 'Good,' he said finally, and Meg rolled her eyes.

'That's it?'

She watched his eyebrows furrow. 'What did you want me to say?'

Meg shrugged. 'Good, I guess, but a bit of padding would be nice.'

'I'm not one for small talk.'

'Well, you could have fooled me. You never stopped talking when I had my accident, and you hardly hold back with the students.'

Flynn shrugged. 'So I don't treat the students like a bunch of gormless subordinates. It is the twenty-first century, you know, and as for the accident…' It was Flynn stepping up the pace now, striding off down the highly polished corridor, forcing Meg to half run to keep up with him. 'It was my job to keep you awake.'

Which should have made her cheeks scorch—but something stirred inside Meg. Something akin to anger. 'And was it "your job" to dress me down in the obs ward?'

Flynn didn't seem remotely fazed by her accusatory tones. With a wry smile he finally slowed down and, turning, caught her eye. They had arrived at the emergency department now and he held the door for her as they entered. 'No,' he admitted. But her victory was short-lived when he continued, 'That was more a moral duty.'

For once the place was deserted and Jess greeted them with a smile. 'Why don't you grab a coffee, Meg, before I head off for my meeting?'

'Good idea,' Flynn answered, and, silently fuming, Meg followed his broad back around to the staff room.

Sitting down, she slipped off her shoes as Flynn headed straight for the kettle. 'White with one,' she said cheekily, and as he turned around with the kettle in his hand Meg gave him a smile. 'Oh, sorry, Flynn. Didn't I tell you? I'm not one for small talk.'

Okay, so the earth didn't move. Meg didn't suddenly become the social butterfly of the Emergency Department and Flynn didn't roar with laughter and crack open a packet of chocolate biscuits. But he *did* make her a coffee, and he did sit on the same side of the room as her and ask how she felt she was coping on for her first morning back after her accident.

'Better now.'

'Is my coffee that good, then?'

Meg stood up and spooned another teaspoon of sugar into her cup, and just to annoy him added a touch more coffee. 'No. I meant that I finally feel back in the saddle, so to speak. I know I've only been off a couple of weeks but it seems much longer.'

He turned then to the television, and for something to do Meg gazed unseeing at the screen. 'What was it like for you? I heard you did research for a couple of years before you took up this post.'

'That's right.' He took a long sip of his coffee before continuing. 'It was a bit hard, I guess,' he admitted finally. 'It still is.' There was something in his voice that made Meg look over, that told her she had just hit upon a raw nerve.

'In what way?'

'Four pounds two, with eyes of blue.' Carla burst into the staff room brimming with excitement, her smile so infectious even Flynn's suddenly serious face broke into a grin.

'What did she have?' Meg immediately asked.

'A little boy. He's so tiny, but just beautiful. Thanks so much for asking if I could stay, Meg. It was just amazing—and so quick!'

'Sit down. I'll get you a coffee—I reckon you've earned it!' Meg laughed. 'How's Debbie doing?'

'Well, they're stitching her up, and the sister said that she'd be in Recovery for a while before they transferred her, but the anaesthetist said to tell you, Flynn—' another blush crept across Carla's face as she addressed him '—that they're happy with her obs and she's haemo...haemodynamically stable now.'

'That's good. Ideally we would have liked to transfer Debbie with the baby in utero—there's no better incubator than the mother. But in this case we had no choice but to deliver there and then...'

Meg watched as he went into detail, patiently explaining the merits and pitfalls of the crucial choice he had made that morning in resus. And though he spoke about nothing but the patient, though he was nothing but friendly and professional, Meg couldn't help but notice how easily and readily he chatted with the student. How familiar they seemed with each other. And, more pointedly, even if she had wanted to, Meg couldn't miss the rapt expression on Carla's face, the flirty way she looked up at him from under her eyelashes.

There was something going on here that Meg didn't quite understand. And what was more, Meg realised as she left them to it and slipped away unnoticed, she wasn't entirely sure that she wanted to.

CHAPTER FOUR

'ANYONE there catch your eye?' Kathy breezed into the living room and Meg hastily put down the guest list she had been stealing a look at.

'There must be a hundred names there!' Meg exclaimed.

'I'm sure Mum can stretch to one hundred and one if there's someone I've missed out.' Kathy's voice was loaded with innuendo and Meg deliberately chose to ignore it.

'I'm sure there's enough there to be going on with.'

There was. The one name Meg was interested in—Flynn's name—was right there near the top. Unfortunately Kathy had listed the guests randomly, so there was no way of telling if the 'Maria' above his name or the 'Louise' below it was his partner. And more worrying was the utter relief she felt that Carla's name most definitely wasn't there. But if she asked Kathy, Meg might just as well take out a full-page advertisement in the local paper telling the world she had a crush on Flynn Kelsey.

A bit more than a crush, Meg admitted to herself reluctantly, but she wasn't in any rush to give her heart away again—and certainly not to someone so effortlessly divine, so overtly charismatic as Flynn Kelsey. After all, hadn't she left her last job because of a disastrous relationship? Even though Vince hadn't worked with her, his infidelity had permeated her workplace. A casual fling—and Meg thought glumly that that was all it would be to Flynn—was a recipe for disaster. It wasn't just her heart she had to look out for either, her resumé simply wasn't up to another update. Inevitably it would end in tears—most probably hers—and three jobs in six months wasn't a record Meg wanted to achieve.

And yet…

In the past few weeks Meg had found herself glancing at the medical staff's roster with more than a passing interest, and to her dying shame had agreed to an overtime shift just because Flynn was on duty. And though she loved working with him, adored the constant verbal sparring, the undeniable flirting, each shift was tempered with a sense of frustration, a need to finish whatever it was they had both started, to somehow let them draw their own natural conclusion.

Flynn Kelsey was more to Meg than just another colleague, and to deny it would be an outright lie.

'What are you daydreaming about?'

Meg shook her head. 'Nothing.' How she would love to confide in Kathy—ask her for some insight, find out once and for all if she was wasting her time. Contrary to what Flynn had said about Kathy playing matchmaker, Flynn's name had never even been brought up once. But Meg knew her sister only too well, and subtle certainly wasn't her middle name. If Meg even remotely asked about him, and *if* Flynn did turn out to be single, Kathy would think nothing of seizing the day and engineering a dance or three at the party, or some quiet little dinner with Flynn and Meg making up the numbers—by chance, of course! That was the sort of help she could do without. It was far safer all round to keep quiet and steer the conversation back to the party and the wedding.

'I know that look.' Kathy picked up the list. 'Come on, Meg, surely someone there catches your eye? What about Lee—six foot two, blue eyes…?'

'I don't think I'm ready for a man with three kids,' Meg said dryly.

'Okay, point taken. How about Harry, then? At least he comes without baggage, and he's a plastic surgeon so he must be loaded.'

Meg gave a cynical laugh. 'He's certainly not loaded with personality.'

'So you want personality *and* a clean slate?' She ran her eye down the paper. 'Well, that rules out just about everyone here. Looks like you'll be dancing round your handbag with me and Mum.'

'You'll be with Jake, remember?'

Kathy poked out her tongue. 'Jake's the last person I'll be dancing with; he might be gorgeous to look at, but, believe me, propped up at the bar is the best place for him; dancing really isn't his forte.'

'That's right; I'd forgotten! Do you remember when Vince and Jake got up and danced at that nightclub? The bouncers thought they were drunk and they'd only been on orange juice all night.'

'Oh, my goodness.' Kathy blinked slowly a couple of times, her face breaking into a grin. 'That's the first time I've heard you mention Vince without getting that misty look in your eyes.'

Meg nodded. 'I'm *so* over him, Kathy. That accident was probably the best thing that ever happened to me. Hanging upside down in a smashed up car is a pretty good reminder of how precious life is, and a couple of weeks licking my wounds, with an excuse to cry if I wanted to, was just the tonic I needed. Vince could walk through the door this moment and tell me he's left his wife and I'd just promptly show him the way out. I've wasted enough of my time on him.'

'Well, good for you.' Kathy's beaming smile belied the trace of doubt in her voice, but Meg homed in on it straight away.

'I'm over him,' Meg insisted.

Kathy put her hands up in mock defence. 'I believe you! And to prove it, how about I treat you to a glass of champagne to celebrate the demise of "bloody Vince"? There's a new wine bar just opened on the Bay Road…'

'Not for me. I'm on a late shift.'

'Well, an iced coffee, then? I need to get some shoes for the party. I could really use your opinion.'

Meg shook her head. 'When did you ever need my opinion on anything? Anyway, you know I can't walk in a shoe shop without buying something. I've already spent enough on my dress—speaking of which, that's why I'm here. I'm heading off to the beach to get a bit of sun; I'm so pale you can't tell where the fabric ends and my legs start. Look, tell Mum I'm sorry I missed her. I'll pop back for a shower before I go to work, but tell her I've already eaten or she'll be warming up the soup in the freezer!'

'If you don't stay for lunch you know she'll moan that you're using the house as a beach hut again?' Kathy warned

'I'll risk it.' Grabbing her bag from the couch, Meg gave her sister a cheery wave and, savouring the delicious morning, walked the couple of hundred yards from her parents' house to the beach.

Slipping off her sarong, Meg laid it on the sand before stretching out luxuriously on it. Closing her eyes, she waited for the little dots dancing before her eyes to fade, wriggling her toes into the warm sand and feeling the heat of the late morning sun bathing her body. This was the best time of year to be at the beach; apart from a couple of mothers with young children, and a few older couples strolling along, the place was practically deserted. It would be a different story in two weeks' time, when the schools broke up for the summer break. Then she would have to share the beach with seemingly hundreds of screaming children and overwrought parents, but for now it was pretty near perfect.

Perfect, even.

An alarm clock would be good, though, Meg thought

as she drifted off, her mind flicking back for a moment to her accident, remembering Flynn beside her, holding her hand as they waited for the firefighters to secure the tree, imagining the sound of the ocean. It was almost a pleasant memory, made better because this time she could close her eyes, this time she could sleep…

At first Meg felt only relief when a child's screams dragged her awake. Focussing on her watch, she stood up with a yelp and shook the sand out of her sarong. Never mind the soup, there wouldn't even be time for a shower at this rate. Fuzzy from sleep, and the bright midday sun, it took Meg a second or two to register that the screaming hadn't stopped—in fact it had multiplied. A woman was screaming.

Loudly.

Swinging around, Meg watched in horror as she saw a woman running hysterically along the beach, twisting and turning, carrying a screaming child in her arms.

A bleeding child.

That second was all it took for Meg to break into a run, to shout her orders to the stunned onlookers who were watching helplessly, frozen with shock.

'Get me a towel. Someone call for an ambulance.'

The screaming grew louder, and Meg acknowledged with relief that the child was screaming also as the woman practically threw the infant into her arms. 'He stood on a bottle. Oh, God—help him, please!'

'It's all right, darling.' Despite her own fear Meg spoke soothingly to the child. Lying him down, she immediately raised his leg. The blood was pouring from his foot. Meg swallowed hard. It wasn't pouring; it was pumping. He had a large arterial bleed. Immediately she applied pressure behind his knee, holding the leg as high as she could as an elderly gentleman thrust a towel at her.

'Here—can you use this?'

'I can't let go of his leg.'

'Tell me what you want me to do.'

Meg nodded, relief washing over her. Her fear was real. Nothing scared her in Emergency—there she knew what she was doing, could put her hand on the necessary equipment in an instant, summon help at the touch of a button or the buzz of an intercom. But here she was on her own. Apart from this man no one had done a single thing to help—all were standing uselessly. Meg didn't blame them for a moment, but it didn't help matters in the least. But this man was sensible. The sweat was pouring off him, and there was a grey tinge to his lips, but he was at least listening, ready to help. 'Hold his leg up and push like I am behind his knee. I need to have a look before I wrap it up.'

As soon as Meg released the pressure the blood started spurting again. By now the child had stopped screaming; he was lying there shocked and pale, which worried Meg far more than the noise.

'Has someone called for an ambulance?' she asked as she examined the foot. There was no glass visible so, taking the towel, she wrapped it tightly around the foot, pulling it as hard as she could in an attempt to stem the flow of blood. 'Has someone called an ambulance yet?'

One of the women was frantically pushing the buttons on her mobile. 'It isn't charged.'

'Has anyone else got a mobile?'

'I could run up to one of the houses,' the man offered. Meg looked down at the child. He was becoming drowsy, and despite her best efforts already the towel was bright red. 'Or my car's just there. My wife could drive…'

Meg did a swift calculation. By the time he had run up, and assuming he got straight in to someone's house, it would be at least another ten minutes until the ambulance got here—and that was if their luck was in. If they dashed to a car she could have him straight in within five minutes.

'We'll go by car. I have to keep pushing—keep his leg up.'

He nodded. 'June—go and start the car.'

Spurred into action, the assembled crowd finally moved, helping to carry the boy the short distance along the beach to the waiting car. The mother sat in the front, sobbing loudly as Meg and her helper squeezed into the back and the car jerked away.

'Drive carefully,' Meg warned the woman.

'But step on it, love.' The man gave Meg a small smile. 'She's as slow as a snail normally. My name's Roland.'

'Meg.'

It was only a short drive, and even as the car pulled away Meg instantly felt calmer. Everything would be fine now. The hospital was in sight, and by emergency standards this wasn't particularly serious—not in the controlled setting of a hospital anyway.

'Thank goodness you were there.' The woman had

stopped sobbing now, and was swallowing hard to compose herself.

'What's your son's name?'

'Toby. I'm Rita.'

Meg smiled down at the little boy as the car pulled into the ambulance bay. 'We'll have you sorted in no time, Toby.

'June, grab a trolley from the entrance and bring it up to the car,' Meg instructed. But Mike the porter, grabbing a quick smoke between jobs, had already beaten her to it. Pulling the back door open, he popped his head in. 'Here you go, Meg—anything I can do to help?'

'We just need him on the trolley, but I'll have to keep his leg up and the pressure on.'

'No worries.'

Anywhere else they would have looked a curious sight—four adults dressed in their bathers pushing a trolley with a bleeding child—but here at the Bayside Hospital they barely merited a second glance.

'You're starting your shift a bit early!' Jess joked. 'You really can't stay away from the place, can you?'

'I was supposed to be topping up my tan,' Meg groaned. 'It's pretty deep,' she added in low tones, so as not to frighten Toby and his mother. 'Arterial bleed. He lost a lot of blood at the beach.'

'Right.' Jess nodded, bandaging a huge wad of Combine firmly into place and elevating the foot of the trolley, then taking over pressing behind Toby's knee. 'We'll not disturb it until the doctor gets here. Speaking of which…' She turned and smiled as Flynn entered.

'What have we got here?' He barely glanced in Meg's direction, his eyes firmly fixed on Toby. 'You've been down at the beach, I see, young man.'

'I stood on a broken bottle.' It was the first time Toby had spoken, and Meg smiled at the little lisping voice.

'There was blood everywhere; he must have lost a gallon.' This was a slight exaggeration from Rita, but Meg nodded.

'He did lose a lot—the bleed's arterial. I stopped it with popliteal and direct pressure and we've kept it elevated.'

'Good.' Still his eyes stayed fixed on his young charge. 'Toby, I'm going to put a little needle into the back of your hand so I can give you some medicine to take away the pain. It will only hurt for a second. I know that you've been so brave up to now—can I ask you to be brave for just a moment longer?'

Toby nodded, but his mother wasn't convinced. 'Can't you numb it first? He hates needles.'

'He'll be fine,' Flynn said confidently. 'Numbing it would take twenty minutes or so to take effect, and I'd like to give him some fluid thorugh a drip and take some blood. He looks a bit shocked, and I'm sure he'd appreciate something to settle him before we take the dressing down.'

But Rita wanted an anaesthetic. 'He'll scream the place down.'

Meg watched Flynn's shoulders stiffen a fraction. The only person who was getting upset was Toby's mum, and if she carried on Toby was likely to start getting anxious again.

'Look, Rita,' Meg suggested, 'why don't we go and grab a cool drink and let the doctor get on with it? It must be very upsetting for you to watch all this.'

'Surely it would be better if I stayed?'

Meg took a deep breath. Honesty was the best policy, and all that, but she wasn't sure how well it was going to be received. 'It's probably better if we go and get a drink and calm down. The drip will be up by the time we get back and you'll feel a lot better then.'

Rita seemed to accept this, and after a rather tearful kiss and hug with Toby allowed herself to be led away.

'Is there anyone you'd like to ring?' Meg offered once they were in the staff room. Given that both women were dressed in their bathers, apart from the skimpy sarong wrapped around Meg, the waiting room hadn't seemed an appropriate place to send Rita. Anyway, Meg was desperate for a long cool drink and was sure Rita could use one.

'Just my husband—he's going to have a fit when I tell him.' Her hand was shaking as she picked up the telephone. 'Do you think Toby will need an operation?'

'Yes.' Meg said simply. 'It wouldn't be fair on Toby to try and repair it under local anaesthetic. Do you want me to dial for you?'

Rita nodded. 'Useless, aren't I?'

Meg shook her head. 'Don't say that. You're his mum; you're allowed to be upset.'

As predicted, Toby's dad didn't take the news too well, and after Rita had ducked off to the toilet for another quick cry Meg took the opportunity to ring her mother. Mary wasn't in the best of moods either.

'You just can't stay away from trouble, can you? And you haven't even had lunch. How can you do a full shift without a morsel of food in your stomach and no work clothes?'

'I've got some spare shoes here, and I can wear Theatre gear. I'll be fine,' Meg assured her.

'Fine, my foot.' Not the greatest choice of words. 'I'll bring you up a Thermos of soup.'

'Please, Mum, don't bother. I'm okay. Honestly,' she added, but with zero effect.

'Tell that to the patients when you're fainting over them. I'll warm it up and bring it straight over. Do you need anything else?'

Meg looked down at her blood-splattered sarong and her sand-dusted legs. 'A toiletry bag would be nice.'

'I'm on my way.'

'Where's Rita?' Jess popped her head around the door.

'In the loo. How's Toby doing?'

'He's going straight up to Theatre. The plastics had a quick look and they want to get him up now. They need her to come and sign the consent form. How are you?'

Meg stood up. 'Desperate for a shower. If my mum comes can you ask her just to drop all my stuff in the changing room? I'll be round to start my shift when I'm looking a bit more presentable.'

'Sure. Take your time, Meg. I reckon you've earned it.'

Rita appeared then, and Meg left them to it. Her shift hadn't even started and already she felt as if she'd done a day's work.

'There you are.' Flynn loomed into view. 'Where's Toby's mother? The plastics need her to—'

'Sign the consent,' Meg finished for him. 'I know—Jess is already onto it. I'm just heading off for a shower.'

'Oh.' For the first time since her arrival he actually managed to look at her, his eyes flicking down her body. For the last half-hour Meg had been wandering around barefoot, her modesty protected only by a sheer sunflower-emblazoned sarong, yet totally unabashed. Now, under Flynn's scrutiny, she suddenly felt exposed and woefully inadequately dressed.

'There wasn't really time to get changed first,' Meg joked feebly.

'Of course not.'

His eyes were looking somewhere at the top of her forehead as he cleared his throat, and Meg could have sworn that the beginning of a blush was creeping over his usually deadpan face. She should have gone then—nodded politely and dashed to the refuge of the changing rooms. But for some reason her legs simply wouldn't obey her and she stood there mute, staring back at him, forcing his eyes to meet hers.

'How was the beach—before all this happened, I mean?'

'Wonderful.'

Something strange was going on. Something strange and delicious. An apparently sedate, normal conversation was taking place, but there was nothing normal about the white-hot look passing between them, and definitely nothing sedate about the pulse flickering relentlessly between her thighs or the sudden swell of her nipples, jutting against the flimsy fabric of her sarong, inching their way closer to Flynn with a will of their own.

His hand moved up to her face. Meg didn't flinch, just stood there. The pad of his thumb gently brushed across her cheek. 'You've got sand on your face.' Her instinct was to reach up and capture his hand, to hold it against her cheek and then guide it down slowly to her aching engorged breasts. But there was nothing she could do except stand there, terrified she might be misreading the blazing signs, painfully aware that a hospital corridor wasn't the best place to make a complete fool of yourself if sand was the only thing on his mind.

'Thank you,' she said simply, the tension unbearable. 'I'd best get on.'

The changing room was only a few steps away but it seemed to stretch on for ever.

'Meg?'

She turned slowly, not trusting herself to speak.

'I'm looking forward to the party on Saturday.'

Meg nodded, gripping onto the door handle for dear life. 'Me too,' she managed to croak, and, attempting a nonchalant exit, waited until the changing room door was safely closed before slipping onto a wooden bench and resting her burning face in her hands.

How was she going to survive the afternoon, let alone last until Saturday?

Of course the one time Meg really wanted to be busy and appear professional, the department was practically deserted. Toby was cleared out quickly, and apart from a couple of gastros and the usual lumps and bumps they remained frustratingly quiet.

'Come on, Carla, we can practise your BLS on Annie.'

'Oh, spare her, Meg—the poor lass spent two hours with her this morning,' Jess responded cheerfully. 'She's probably seen Annie more than her boyfriend this week, haven't you, Carla?'

'Actually, I haven't got a boyfriend.'

'What? A pretty young thing like you?' Jess clucked. 'Surely there must be some young man you've got your eye on.'

Carla shrugged, but not before her cheeks darkened, and Meg watched her gaze flick over to Flynn, who was obliviously writing notes in the corner of the annexe.

'Well, there must be some cupboards that need to be sorted,' Meg said quickly, before Jess followed Carla's gaze.

'All done—by my own fair hands. Now, why don't you go and have your afternoon tea? And maybe for once the early shift can get out on time—though I've probably just jinxed myself and there'll be a busload pulling up now.'

'Well, if we're expecting a rush on…' Flynn recapped his fountain pen '…I might get myself something from the machine to tide me over.'

Jess clapped her hand to her forehead. 'That reminds me—the machine's not working, I'd best ring the canteen.'

The kitchen seemed to have shrunk to minuscule

proportions as Meg attempted to make coffee. The brief display of affection, the reference to Saturday—all seemed to be crackling in the air around them as Flynn opened the fridge and pulled out a rather sad-looking yellow jelly. 'Not exactly what I had in mind.'

Meg screwed her nose up. 'Yuk—*and* it's diabetic jelly,' she added, looking at the hospital canteen label.

'Any bread in the bread bin?'

'What? At three o'clock? We're right at the end of the food chain, bar the night staff.'

Even the cornflakes box was empty.

It was only then that Meg remembered her mother had dropped her off some supplies. Knowing Mary, there would be enough to feed a small third world country. She dashed off to the changing room and returned triumphant with a large thermo bag packed full with a flask and a mountain of sandwiches. 'At least some of us come prepared,' she said, depositing the bag on the kitchen bench. 'Help yourself.'

'What's this?' Flynn asked, opening the bag with all the relish of a child on Christmas morning.

Why Meg fibbed at this point she never knew. What she hoped to gain by having Flynn think she was a whiz in the kitchen not only eluded her, it also belied all Meg's feminist principles. But the small white lie was out before she could stop it. 'Just some soup and sandwiches I made.'

'Great.' Pulling out the shiny foil packages, he turned casually. 'What's in them?'

It was an obvious question and one, to Meg's dying

shame, she realised she couldn't answer. Ignoring him, Meg concentrated on spooning sugar into two mugs.

'What's in the sandwiches?' Flynn persisted.

'I don't know,' she responded, flustered. 'Ham, cheese—whatever was in the fridge. It's hardly decision of the day!'

'I only asked,' he muttered, carrying them through to the staff room as Meg followed with the drinks.

Just as they started eating Jess appeared. 'Oh, you found them. Flynn *did* remember to tell you that your mum had dropped off your lunch—I thought he might have forgotten.'

'This chicken's just delicious, Meg,' Flynn said with a mischievous glint in his eye as he took a huge bite. 'You must give me the recipe.'

Jess flashed him a quizzical look. 'Nice to see a man who enjoys cooking. Now, Flynn, this lass with the ulcer in cubicle three—did you want me to use Comfeel or Aquacel for her dressing? You didn't write it on the cas card.'

'Oh, I don't know,' Flynn quipped, grinning at his own warped humour. 'Comfeel, Aquacel—whatever's on the dressing trolley. You choose, Jess. After all, it's hardly decision of the day.'

As a slightly bemused Jess wandered off Meg picked up a magazine and pretended to read, ignoring his grin.

'Great sandwiches.'

'So you've already said.'

'What's in the flask?'

'Soup—help yourself.' Meg looked up. 'And, no, I

didn't make it.' Turning her eyes back to the magazine, Meg pretended to be engrossed in an article about the latest Hollywood scandal.

'No, thanks. I'm not a fan of soup.'

Meg didn't respond, just carried on pretending to read, her cheeks still flaming.

'These will tide me over. I might head off to the new wine bar on the beach front tonight; it's supposed to be good. Have you tried it?'

'No.' Why couldn't he leave her alone to die of shame quietly?

'What time do you finish tonight?'

The blush that had only just started to recede was coming back for an encore.

'Nine-thirty,' she responded, as casually as she could with her heart in her mouth. Surely this wasn't what it sounded like?

'Do you fancy joining me?'

Turning the page of her magazine, she found a glossy supermodel grinning back at her, brown, lithe and with an overabundance of self-confidence.

'I would,' Meg said lightly, though her heart was doing somersaults. 'Except I don't think I'd get in in a bikini and blood-stained sarong.'

'Oh, I don't know.' Flynn laughed. 'The dress code's supposed to be pretty laid-back. Still, we could stop at your place if you want to get changed.' Standing, he screwed up the tin foil and casually tossed it into the bin. 'How about it?'

Her resolve was weakening—the threat of changing

her resumé a poor argument in the face of such delicious provocation. It was only a drink, Meg reasoned, and after all lots of nurses moved around. If the worst came to the worst she could always join an agency.

The clock was ticking as Meg wrestled with her conscience, and she knew that if she didn't answer quickly then Flynn might realise the profoundness of his invitation. 'Okay,' she answered, in such a voice that would make even the laid-back Carla sound edgy. 'Sounds good.'

'Great, I'll catch up on some paperwork, then. Give me a knock on my office door when your shift finishes.' And he strolled out of the room as if he'd just asked her to drop by a pile of admission notes.

The supermodel was still grinning at her, and Meg found she was grinning back.

An evening with Flynn Kelsey.

Now, what girl could ask for more?

CHAPTER FIVE

SHAVING your legs with a disposable hospital razor could be risky at the best of times. But shaving them in a hand-basin with a heart-rate topping one hundred and hands shaking with nervous anticipation was a feat in itself, particularly as she was only supposed to be nipping out to the loo for five minutes. Eying the shaky lock, Meg debated whether to risk shaving under her arms.

Stop it, she warned herself. It's just a casual drink, and even if it was a date—a real date—she was hardly going to rip off her clothes and jump into bed with him.

Hardly.

Tossing the plastic razor into the bin, Meg took a deep breath. Gorgeous he might be—stunning, even—but she was on the rebound, just getting over a broken heart, and more to the point casual sex simply wasn't her style.

Yet…

There was nothing casual about Meg's feelings for Flynn. Since the day she had met him, since those moments trapped in her car, there had been an attraction—an undeniable attraction. The kiss they had shared hadn't been an accident, hadn't been a passing whim. It had been an inevitable consequence—a necessary outlet for the pressure cooker of steam that seemed to build up whenever they were thrown together. The occasional bickering, the sometimes stilted conversations, were more an attempt to stem the tide, to defuse the atmosphere, than a sign of incompatibility. And now they were finally doing something about it.

Who knows? Meg tried to reason. After a glass of wine he might not look so appealing—and if that was the case at least they'd know. But then again, Meg thought with a fluttering excitement that gnawed at the very pinnacle of her being, suppose things did move on? Suppose by the time the last drinks were served, the attraction was still most defiantly mutual…?

Mary O'Sullivan must have thought someone was walking over her grave as Meg rummaged guiltily through the bin and retrieved the razor. Her mother would never understand, Meg realised, but then how could she be expected to, when Meg herself didn't understand the feelings Flynn Kelsey ignited in her? How six months of steely resolve and heartfelt resolution could so easily be discarded by the crook of his little finger…

'All finished?'

Meg nodded. She'd been willing the shift to pass, but now the time had come suddenly she longed for the relative comfort of work, half hoped Flynn's pager would go off and there would be a legitimate excuse to end whatever they had started here and now. But his pager didn't go off, and it was a tentative, nervous Meg that walked quietly alongside him out to the car park.

'Flynn!'

The voice calling out in the darkness made them both jump a fraction, but, seeing Carla rushing towards them, Flynn instantly relaxed.

'Carla, what's wrong?'

'The car.'

Flynn groaned. 'Again? You're going to have to do something about it, you know.'

'I know,' Carla replied breathlessly, eyeing Meg with some suspicion. 'Look, sorry—I didn't realise you were on your way somewhere. I can call out the breakdown services.'

'That's okay,' Meg finally found her voice. Suspicious of Carla's motives she might be, but acting all proprietary when they hadn't been for so much as a drink together wasn't her style, and anyway, fanning the flames of the hospital grapevine was the last thing she needed after her time at Melbourne City. 'Flynn was just giving me a ride home. Given what happened with Toby at the beach, I'm a bit stranded today.'

In an instant the slightly petulant expression that had been marring Carla's usually pretty face vanished. 'Of course.'

Handing Meg his keys, Flynn pointed to a rather impressive silver sports car. 'Meg, why don't you wait in the car? It's a bit cooler. I'll just see if I can work my magic on Carla's pile of junk.' He winked at Carla as if sharing an old joke. 'Again.'

Meg sat there trying desperately to relax. She watched him hunched over the bonnet, watched Carla leaning against it, tossing her shaggy blonde hair, her little bust jutting out of the skimpy top she was wearing, and just knew that it wasn't an outfit Carla had casually thrown on after her shift.

When Carla slipped into the driving seat Meg rolled her eyes and gave a cynical snort as, lo and behold, the car started first time.

'Sorry about that.' Grinning, slightly breathless, Flynn slid in the car beside her.

'What was wrong with it?'

'Search me. It's happened a couple of times. I've told her to get it seen to.'

'Flynn?' The single word was out before she could stop it and she watched as he turned to her, a searching look on his face. 'There's nothing wrong with her car.'

'Meg, it's a pile of junk. It's no wonder it's always breaking down.'

'So it's happened a few times?'

She watched his hands grip hard on the steering wheel and wished she could somehow retrieve the words that had just slipped out of her mouth, take back the accusing, slightly jealous tone that had crept into her voice.

'Yes, it's happened a few times. And for the record, your honour—' he was trying to make a joke, but neither of them were smiling '—Carla's father is an old colleague of mine. I know her family well.'

'You don't have to explain. I mean, I wasn't suggesting...' Her voice trailed off and she felt like opening the car door and making a bolt for it. The night was ruined and they hadn't even left the car park yet!

'I know you weren't.' His voice was softer now, and when Meg looked up she realised he was smiling at her. 'How about we make a move? I've still got to stop for petrol, and at this rate we'll be lucky to make it for last orders at the bar.'

'Sounds good.' Meg forced herself to smile back, and as he started the engine and the car slid off she leant back in the soft leather seat, willing herself to loosen up, to relax. But she couldn't. All their sparkling repartee, the backchat and witty answers, seemed to have vanished, and they drove in uncomfortable silence for the next couple of kilometres.

'I'd better stop at this garage or it will be me calling out the breakdown services.'

'Sure.'

'Do you want anything?'

Meg shook her head, letting out a rather strained breath as he closed the door. God, he was probably wondering what had possessed him to ask her, she thought as he filled the car with petrol. The forecourt was bright, and Meg watched as he strode across to pay. His wallet sitting on the dashboard caught her eye about two seconds after Flynn started patting at his pocket, and she held it up as he grinned and beckoned her over.

Maybe it was nerves, or just her rush to fetch it for him, but as she dropped his wallet on the forecourt Meg felt as if her world had suddenly ended. The photo Flynn kept in his wallet was smiling back at her. There, younger, a touch slimmer, but unmistakably him, stood Flynn—and Jake too, for that matter. Both men were smiling happily, not a care in the world, their arms wrapped around the woman between them.

The *bride* between them.

And from the adoration in Flynn's eyes Meg knew that the bride was his.

Flynn was walking towards her, calling her name as his eyes darted from the open wallet in her hands back to her stricken face.

'When were you going to tell me?' She threw it at him. 'After you'd taken me out? Or were you going to sleep with me first?'

'Meg, I can explain.'

'I'm sure you can.' Her voice was rising and people were starting to look, but she didn't care. 'What? Doesn't your wife understand you? Come on, Flynn, try me. But I can guarantee I've heard it before.'

'Meg, just listen, will you…?' He grabbed at her hand, pulling her towards him, but Meg refused to be quiet.

'Or maybe she doesn't realise the pressure you're under at work. Or is it that she's too wrapped up in the children and doesn't pay you enough attention?' Tears were coursing down her cheeks—choked, angry tears. She was utterly unable to believe it was all happening to her again. 'I suppose Carla couldn't make it tonight so you thought I'd do to pass the evening! My God, why don't I ever learn?'

'She's dead.' He loosened his hand and Meg's arm fell to her side as the words hit home. 'Lucy's dead.'

He crossed the forecourt to pay.

Mortified, all she could do was stand there—stand there and watch him through the glass, going through the motions, nodding at the checkout girl. Every eye was watching, waiting for the next instalment.

'I'm sorry,' was all she could manage as, grim-faced, he walked back towards her.

'Get in the car. I think we've provided enough entertainment for one night.'

He didn't say anything, not a single word as he shot out of the garage, while Meg sat silent next to him.

'It's left here,' she muttered as they approached the exit for her flat. Ignoring her, he carried on, and Meg sank back in the seat. 'I didn't know.'

Flynn glanced over, then looked back to the road ahead. 'That's your fault; you didn't give me a chance to tell you.'

'I know,' she admitted. 'Where are we going?'

'Here.' Indicating, he pushed a button, and Meg watched as the garage door of a townhouse opened and they glided in. For a second they sat in silence, before Flynn pulled on the handbrake. 'Come on—we'll talk inside.'

She felt him brace himself as he opened the door, and once inside Meg understood why.

Lucy.

Their wedding photo, almost the same shot he had in his wallet, was the first sight that greeted her. Sitting on the hall table right next to the telephone.

She needed a moment—a moment to collect her

thoughts, to calm down and work out just how she could even begin to apologise to him.

'Can I use your bathroom?'

'Sure. It's up the stairs on the left.'

Lucy was there too. Oh, there wasn't the usual paraphernalia that women collected, there wasn't a mass of heated rollers and hair tongs, tampons and moisturisers, but her perfume collection still stood on the shelf, and the picture hanging on the wall was so overtly feminine Meg knew at a glance Flynn hadn't chosen it. And what man would ever put an incense burner on the bathroom ledge?

'I'm sorry,' she said for the second time, coming down the stairs. 'I really am.'

Flynn nodded and handed her a glass of wine. 'The worst part,' he started as Meg took a sip, 'was losing a wife who actually did understand me.'

Meg winced, recognising the hurtful words she had so recently thrown at him.

'I was going to tell you tonight, actually.'

Meg nodded. 'I know that now. Flynn, I shouldn't have jumped in; it's just I had no idea—none at all. You don't seem like…' Her voice trailed off.

'Like a widower?'

Meg nodded. It was such a sad, lonely word, conjuring up images of pain and desolation. Nothing like the vibrant, easygoing man she was beginning to finally know.

'How do you expect me to be?' He didn't wait for an answer. 'Walking around with a permanent air of sadness? Crying into my beer at the local pub every night?'

'No,' Meg said slowly. 'It's just that you seem so

content, so unruffled. You don't look like someone who's had an awful past.'

'But I haven't.' His words confused her and Meg looked up, her mouth falling open but no words coming out. 'I've had a wonderful past, with a very special woman. It ended too soon, far too soon, but we still had a great marriage and shared an amazing journey together. I'm not going to spend the rest of my life being bitter, feeling cheated, when in truth I've been luckier than most.'

He sounded so sure, so confident that Meg almost believed him.

Almost.

'How did she die?'

'A car accident.' He took a large slug of wine. 'A truck driver fell asleep at the wheel; he walked away with a bloody nose. I shouldn't have taken it out on you that morning, and for that I'm sorry. I don't often get worked up about it, but it was all a bit too close to the bone. You're about the same age, and when I heard that you'd fallen asleep…'

'I didn't fall asleep.'

Flynn shrugged. 'It's not important now.'

'I was crying.' She was speaking almost to herself, and Flynn looked up, startled at her words. But Meg just sat there, that morning's events slowly coming back to her, terrified to look up, to move, in case the images evaporated.

'I was crying because a child had died. Jess had tried to talk to me and I'd pushed her away, told her I wasn't upset. But I was. I pretended I was tired.' It was all coming back now, flashing into her mind with painful clarity. 'I'd cut my hand on an ampoule.' Looking down, she saw the thin white scar. 'Look.' He took her hand, running his finger along the pale raised flesh. 'I can remember changing gear. It hurt, and I started crying. The next thing I knew I'd missed the bend and a tree was coming towards me.'

'And then?' He was holding her hand, kneeling on the floor beside her.

'You were there.' Meg laughed through her tears. 'Actually, I think it might have been Ken Holmes, the paramedic.'

Flynn gave a dry laugh. 'Don't ruin the picture.' Then his voice changed, urgency taking over. 'Meg, you can't let it get to you like that.'

His statement surprised her. She had been expecting a lecture, to be told in no uncertain terms how she should have opened up to Jess. Not this. 'Doesn't it get to you?' she asked, bewildered.

Flynn shook his head. 'I don't let it.'

'But it must.' She stared at him, genuinely astounded.

'It's a job Meg. A labour of love, maybe, and painful and heartbreaking sometimes, but at the end of the day it's a job. You do your work to the best of your ability and then you go home. That's how you survive it.'

'I can't just walk away and switch off,' Meg argued. 'It's just not that easy.'

'You have to.' He took a deep breath. 'Meg, you smashed your car. You could have been killed—you nearly were,' he added darkly. 'Do you know how many emergency doctors and nurses go home and uncork a bottle, or down a couple of pills so they can get to sleep?'

'I'm not that bad!' Meg protested.

'No, but hell, Meg, you nearly died!'

'I know.' She was on her feet now. 'But it *was* an accident, Flynn. Don't make it more than that.'

'You can't let it get to you like that.'

Meg nodded. 'Lesson well and truly learnt. Look, Flynn, I've been having a hard time recently. I left my old job because everyone—and I mean everyone—seemed to be discussing my personal life. I had an affair with a married man.'

'Vince?'

Meg nodded. 'I didn't know he was married at the time. When his wife found out so did everyone else, my mother and work colleagues included. It's just been a rough few months; that's probably why I'm not coping as well as I usually do.' She flushed, suddenly embarrassed. 'Here's me banging on about myself. It must be ten times worse for you. How do you cope, seeing accidents and everything? It must be agony.'

But Flynn shook his head, refusing to be drawn. 'I just try not to compare.' He was swirling the wine around in his glass. 'I'm over Lucy. I've dealt with it.'

But something in his voice warned Meg he was trying to convince himself more than her. 'What was she like?'

'Lucy?' His face brightened up. 'Funny, happy-go-lucky, smart—take your pick. She was into adventure, always planning the next holiday—bungee-jumping one summer, white water rafting the next. Actually, you remind me a bit of her.'

Meg gave a shaky laugh. 'I hate to shatter your illusion here, Flynn, and I'm touched—thrilled, actually,' she half joked, 'that anyone could ever consider me adventurous. But the most adventurous thing I've ever done is go on the big wheel at the fair. And I only agreed to that because otherwise Kathy wouldn't have been allowed to go on.'

Flynn grinned at her grimace. 'What happened?'

'I screamed so loudly they had to stop it, and then I promptly threw up. Dad had to give me a fireman's lift home. And as for happy-go-lucky.' Meg took a deep breath. 'I'm the least happy-go-lucky person I've ever come across. It's only fair to warn you in advance that this conversation will be analysed, scrutinised and distorted beyond repair. So you see, there's really no comparison.'

Flynn pulled her down beside him; putting down his wine glass, he took her hands. 'I meant funny, smart and beautiful…' He swallowed then, his face achingly close, his full lips so near, so kissable. 'And just a little bit crazy'

'So where to now?' Her voice was trembling. His hand was still wrapped around hers, and when he didn't immediately answer, Meg continued tentatively. 'Now we know each other's dastardly pasts.' She flushed then. 'I didn't mean you and Lucy…'

'I know.' His face was moving nearer, his voice low and seductive, his lips just a whisper away. It only took the tiniest motion to move forward, but Meg knew as she did it would have monumental consequences.

His lips were cool—that was her first conscious thought—and they tasted of wine—that was her second and last as she lost herself in his touch, moved herself closer, felt his arms wrap around her, tasted the passion as his tongue met hers.

'Where to now?' He repeated her words as she broke away, her lips tingling, burning from the weight of his touch.

'Home,' Meg said softly. 'I think we both need some time.'

'What are you scared of, Meg?'

'You,' she said honestly, but without a trace of malice. 'Myself, even. Take your pick.'

'Just because I loved Lucy it doesn't mean there isn't room for someone else.'

'I know that,' Meg admitted. 'But…'

'Why does there have to be a but?'

Meg swallowed. 'We've both been hurt.'

'Maybe it's our turn to be happy.'

Oh, she wanted to believe him, wanted to believe it was all that simple. But how could it be? She needed a clear head, needed clarity before she dived into the sea again only to be bitten. She'd been up against sharks before.

'Please, Flynn, it's better this way.'

He closed his eyes and Meg held her breath. She wanted him, wanted him so badly it hurt, and she knew how much he wanted her. But not tonight. Tonight was precious and sweet; tonight they had bridged the gap—found out so much about each other. The last thing she needed was to sense regret in the morning, for either of them.

'I know you're right,' he grumbled. 'But don't ask me to smile as well.'

'I won't. Just call me a cab.'

He didn't, of course. They drove back to her house in amicable silence, his hand resting gently on her leg between gear changes, and when they approached her street he indicated without prompting.

'Just pull in behind the red car there.'

'Which one's yours?'

Meg pointed to the top floor of a small apartment block. 'You see the balcony with all the Buddhas, statues and wind chimes?'

He gave her a slightly startled look before nodding.

'Well, mine's the one next to it.'

Flynn laughed. 'Thank heavens for that. I don't think I could stretch to the lotus position.'

It was a joke, a tiny insignificant joke, but in Meg's present state of mind even the surf report on the radio seemed to have massive sexual connotations.

'Do you want to come in for a coffee?' Her steely resolve was melting like molten lava now.

'I do,' he said slowly. 'But I'd better not.'

It was what she had wanted him to say, and yet opening the car door and peeling herself out of the seat beside him took an unimaginable effort.

'Meg?'

She turned and lowered her head into the car through the open door, the streetlight illuminating her fluffy curls, her eyes shadowed so he couldn't read her expression.

'Shall I pick you up on Saturday? We could go together.'

'I'd like that, but…'

In the darkness he couldn't see her features, but Flynn just knew that she was nervously chewing her lip. The endearing image brought a smile to his face. 'But what?'

'If we arrive together…' Meg hesitated. How could she explain this without sounding as if she was fishing? How could she ever expect him to understand the strange unwritten rules of her family? 'If we arrive together, my mum will expect…she'll think…' Meg was practically stammering now, and Flynn put her out of her misery and finished her sentence for her.

'She'll think we're an item?'

Her blush was so deep that even if he couldn't see it Meg was sure he must at least be able to feel the heat radiating from her. 'Something like that,' she mumbled. 'Mum doesn't know the meaning of the words "casual date".'

'Would it help make up your mind if I told you that there's nothing casual about the way I'm feeling?'

Nervous but pleased, Meg nodded as Flynn continued. 'Would you believe me if I told you that nothing your mum's going to be thinking hasn't already crossed my mind?'

She did believe him. After all, the last few weeks all she had thought about was Flynn. However reluctant, however suppressed, her mind had been only on him, and now he was telling her he had felt it too.

'So.' He cleared his throat. 'Am I coming to get you or not?'

Suddenly, her reasons for holding on to her heart seemed woefully inadequate; so she might live to regret it, might rue the day she succumbed to his charms, but nothing would ever compare to the regret she would feel if she turned and walked away now. 'Yes, please.' She hesitated for a moment, longing to ask him again to join her, but knowing if she did this time he would say yes. 'I'd best get inside.'

He nodded as she closed the car door, then sat and watched as she walked up the driveway. Only when he saw the light on the top floor flick on did Flynn start the engine and drive slowly home.

The house, always silent, always empty, now had a slightly different feel—the lingering scent of Meg's perfume, the two glasses side by side on the coffee table. It was the first time in two years Flynn actually felt he'd come home.

CHAPTER SIX

'WHAT did Mum say?' Meg asked nervously as Kathy breezed in.

'Oh, she thinks you're covering for me and I'm off for a midnight rendezvous with Jake. The fact she caught me swiping a bottle of cream liqueur didn't help much.' Producing a bottle from under her flimsy cardigan, she grinned. 'I thought it might loosen your tongue a bit. I'm warning you, Meg. I want *all* the details. Don't leave a single thing out.'

'You're here to fill me in, Kathy, not the other way around.' Meg grinned.

'We've got all night. Now, come on, Sis, I need food.'

They had to make do with toast, but there was something strangely therapeutic about a pile of warm buttered toast and a glass of ice-cold liqueur.

'Why didn't you tell me he was widowed?' Meg started.

'I did. I've often spoken about Jake's friend. You probably weren't listening, as usual.'

She had a point. The minute Jake appeared in a conversation Meg had more often than not changed the subject or simply switched off.

'Though I haven't brought him up recently,' Kathy admitted.

'Why?'

'You said you didn't want baggage, remember? And, as much as Flynn might deny it, he comes with a pretty big load.'

'Lucy?'

Kathy nodded.

'Did you ever meet her?'

'No, she died a couple of months before I met Jake. It's actually how we first became close. He was having a tough time with his friend, and I guess I provided a pretty good sounding board. I'd just had my last operation so my physio sessions were pretty long. Sometimes Jake would be tired, or a bit flat, and you know how nosey I am—I just sort of dragged it out of him.'

'Like what? Was Flynn really upset?'

To Meg's utter revulsion Kathy dunked her toast in her drink. Normally Meg would have scolded her, but not this time. She wanted to hear what Kathy was about to say next. 'The opposite. Flynn just accepted it there and then. Told Jake how lucky he was to have had her for so long, how the last thing Lucy would want was for him to mourn her.'

'So why was Jake worried?'

'Come on, Meg, they'd been so close, so happy. No one deals with death that easily. Anyway, next thing he threw in his job in Emergency—said he was going to make

Lucy's death count and go into research to find out more about the "Golden Hour". What is that, by the way?'

'The hour after an accident,' Meg answered automatically, but her mind was on Flynn. 'Depending upon the treatment the patient receives then, it dramatically affects their chance of survival.'

'Well, whatever it is, Jake was really worried about him. For the first six months we went out I think Jake spent more time with Flynn than me, sure that each night was going to be the night that Flynn would actually crack, show a bit of emotion.'

'But he didn't?'

Kathy shook her head. 'That's just the problem—he never has.'

'But he seems so together, so laid-back,' Meg mused. 'Maybe he just deals with things privately. Not everyone wears their heart on their sleeve. And as to Flynn going into research—well, I can understand that, see why he might want to do something pro-active; his wife died in an accident, which is his speciality after all.'

Kathy didn't answer for a moment. 'It's worse than that, Meg. Flynn was on the Mobile Accident Unit that went out to her.'

'No!' Unimaginable scenes flashed through Meg's mind; her attempts to justify Flynn's laid-back attitude were dashed in that instant. Every fatal accident she'd been out to had left its mark, but to have actually known one of the victims, to have loved them? The pain Flynn must have experienced, the sheer hell he must have been through was impossible to fathom.

'Apparently he recognised the car as soon as they pulled up at the accident, but Flynn didn't tell the paramedics it was Lucy involved. I guess he knew they'd make him stay back.'

'Was she…' Meg swallowed. 'Was she already dead?'

Kathy shook her head and her eyes filled with tears. 'No. But her injuries were so appalling that they knew within moments of freeing her she'd be dead. Flynn sat there with her in the car, held her hand and talked to her…' Kathy stopped as Meg noisily blew her nose.

'He told her he loved her, how happy she'd made him, that sort of thing.'

'Did Flynn tell Jake that?'

Again Kathy shook her head. 'Flynn never spoke about it. Jake got it all from Ken, one of the paramedics.'

'How does he do it?' Meg asked. 'How did he go through all that and still manage to come back to Emergency?'

'I honestly don't know. The job at Bayside Hospital came up and apparently Flynn jumped at it. Jake was worried what might happen if there was a fatal car accident, he even confronted him about it, but Flynn was his usual laid-back self. "Come on, Jake, stop worrying. I'll be fine. And anyway, it might be months till I'm called out."'

'And look what happened,' Meg said slowly. 'Half an hour into his first shift and I go and wrap my car around a tree.'

'Go gently, Meg.' Kathy's voice had an ominous note to it. 'For all Flynn's easygoing, fun-loving attitude, you're the first person he's asked out since Lucy. I know you've been hurt, but if it's a temporary fix you're after then steer clear.'

'I thought you were on my side, here,' Meg interrupted.

'I am,' Kathy said. 'I'm just warning you to think twice before you jump in. There's a lot of pain there. I know you think you're over Vince…'

'I *am* over him.'

'Good.'

But Kathy's lack of conviction rattled Meg. 'He's married, Kathy—as if I could even think of going out with him again.'

'I know. Look, Meg, Flynn's one of the nicest guys I know. He's been to hell and back and has somehow managed to come out intact. He's kind, funny—a bit opinionated, mind,' Kathy added, rolling her eyes. 'There's nothing I'd like more than to see the two of you together…'

'But? Come on, Kathy, I assume there is one.'

'But there's nothing I'd hate more than being around if it ended. And before you jump in and tell me you're not going to hurt him that's not all I'm worried about, Meg. I'm worried that Flynn might not be as over Lucy as he lets on.' Looking at Meg's pale face, Kathy moved over on the sofa and gave her sister a hug. 'I'm probably just being over-dramatic—you know me, anything for a bit of scandal.' She was trying to lighten the mood, but her words had only echoed the nagging voice that Meg had been trying to ignore.

'Now, we've spoken about you long enough—it must be my turn now.' Rummaging in her bag Kathy pulled out a bridal magazine, happily ignoring Meg's groan of dismay. 'I need help with the cake…'

Proud was the best way Meg could describe her feeling as she walked into the party with Flynn on her arm. Proud of her sister, who looked flushed and radiant in a red, crushed velvet dress sweeping the floor, with her blonde hair framing her elfin face. Proud that Kathy had defied all the odds and had made it in the world. And proud of herself too. How could she be otherwise with Flynn on her arm, recalling the tender kiss they had shared when he had picked her up, a teasing taste of what was to come?

And when Jake stood up and spoke to the assembled guests, told everyone how honoured he felt to be betrothed to Kathy, Meg felt her eyes fill with tears. She watched the sheer love in his eyes when he spoke about his fiancée.

'Hey, what are you getting all choked up about?' Flynn whispered as he stood beside her. 'This is supposed to be a happy occasion.'

'I am happy. I'm really happy for them. That's the problem: I feel really bad about the things I said about Jake. It's just…'

'Come on.' Taking her arm, Flynn led her outside. The manicured gardens were beautiful and he led her to a wrought-iron bench, the sound of a fountain a soothing backdrop.

'You had every right to be cautious,' Flynn said once they were both sitting down. 'And I had no right to judge you without knowing all the facts.' He stared at the water for a while before continuing. 'Kathy's pretty good at playing things down, isn't she?'

Meg managed a watery smile. 'That's one way of putting it.'

'From the way she described things to me it sounded as if her limp was never much worse than now. It was a lot worse, wasn't it?' He didn't wait for her to answer. 'I'm not asking you to break any confidences; I already know. I asked Jake about it.'

'Why?'

'Because I wanted to understand.' Those beautiful grey eyes were staring right at her now, and there was nothing she could do but stare back. 'I wanted to know about you, and Kathy's a big part of you.'

'She was pretty bad,' Meg admitted.

'And it must have been hard on you.'

Meg shook her head. 'What have I got to complain about?'

'That sounds to me like your mother talking.'

Meg blinked, startled by his insight. 'She feels guilty, though there's no reason why she should…'

'She's her mother. And sometimes, when you're scared or guilty, it's easier to be angry. I know—I've been there.'

Meg didn't say anything; she knew the conversation was turning to Lucy, and that she needed to hear this if ever she was truly going to know the real Flynn.

'When Lucy died, I got angry. Not just at the driver who caused it; that would have been too simple. I ranted at the paramedics—sure if they'd got there sooner, instigated treatment, called for medical back-up earlier, somehow she might have lived. Hell, I spent eighteen months doing research—as if somehow I could change the outcome, find something that should or could have been done on the day.'

'And did you?'

Flynn's foot was scuffing the ground. 'No. Oh, the research was valuable—there's a couple of things that are done differently in the Golden Hour thanks in part to me—but at the end of the day nothing that would have saved Lucy.' He stopped looking down at his foot, and so did Meg, their eyes lifting to meet. 'Your mum's probably angry, feeling cheated, and it's her way of dealing with it—the same way you deal with it by vetting anyone that tries to get close to Kathy.'

'It's not just that.' Meg's words surprised even her.

'What, then?'

She shook her head. 'I can't tell you.'

'Yes, you can. Hey, Meg, it's me you're talking to.' Pulling up her chin with his fingers, he forced her to look at him, and though she had only known him the shortest time, though in some ways they were just in the infancy of their relationship, it was as if he were looking into her very soul. 'You can tell me anything.'

'It's too embarrassing.'

Flynn started to smile, but it was without a trace of mockery. 'Not the old "three times a bridesmaid" bit, is it?'

Meg let out the tiniest wail of frustration. 'How did you know? Is that what everyone's thinking?'

'It hadn't even entered my head till now.' Flynn laughed, but seeing her embarrassment he quickly changed it to a cough.

'Stop it.' Meg brushed his hand away, but despite herself she could feel a smile creeping on her grumbling lips. 'It's not how I feel, I just know that's what all my aunts are thinking—Mum too, probably. Kathy's not even twenty and she's got it all sorted, and here's old Meg.'

Flynn roared with laughter then and didn't even try to hide it. 'Old Meg! God, just how old are you?'

'Twenty-eight,' Meg muttered.

'Thank heavens for that! I thought you were about to tell me you were in your late forties with a brilliant plastic surgeon. Come on, Meg, you're hardly going to be on a Zimmer frame when you walk up the aisle.'

'I know all that,' Meg wailed. 'I don't even particularly want to get married. It's just what everyone's thinking. I'll be trailing up the aisle behind Kathy and they'll all be whispering into their hymn books about Vince, and how all I can land is someone else's husband.'

'You scarlet woman.'

Her smile was starting to spread, 'You don't think I'm terrible?'

'No,' he replied honestly. 'But that doesn't mean I wouldn't like to get my hands on this Vic.'

'Vince,' Meg corrected. 'Or "bloody Vince", as Kathy and I call him.'

'That's much better,' Flynn agreed. 'And no one thinks you're a washed-up old maid. You're just a beautiful *young* woman with a very bruised ego.'

'Who's had too much champagne.'

Flynn shrugged. 'It's a party—your sister's engagement. If you can't have a glass or three and get a bit emotional, then what fun is there in life?'

Meg shrugged. 'I was wrong about Jake; I can see that now.'

'He adores her,' Flynn said assuredly. 'And to prove it I'm going to tell you something that must never go further, no matter what happens to us.'

Us. That single word had the most delicious ring to it, and Meg found herself hanging on to it, dwelling on its implications as Flynn continued.

'Jake hates working in Emergency.'

'Jake?' Meg dragged herself back to the conversation. 'But I thought he loved being a physio.'

'He does.' Flynn nodded. 'He loves rehab—even back in uni it was all he wanted to do. And then he met Kathy. Ten years younger and with a mother like a lioness with a cub.'

A smile was tugging at the corner of her lips. 'Is that a polite term for a battleaxe?'

'It's anything you want it to be. He asked me what to do. Technically he wasn't doing anything wrong in asking her out, and I said the same to Jake as I did to you—he wasn't her doctor. But Jake knew what people might say, and he just didn't want Kathy to be put through the mill any more than she already had been. He applied for the Emergency position before he even asked her out.'

'He did that for Kathy?'

Flynn nodded. 'In a heartbeat. Jake hates handing out

crutches and, as nice as he might have been to you, advising people how to cough isn't what he wants to be doing. But he grins and bears it.'

'For Kathy.'

'Pretty nice love story, huh?'

Meg nodded, shocked by what Flynn had told her, yet pleased—so pleased for Kathy.

'You know what you should do?' When Meg looked at him, bemused, he carried on talking. 'Go back in there and congratulate them—both of them—for finding each other; they'll know you mean it now.'

Meg nodded; Flynn was right. But as she went to stand he pulled her back.

'Hey, not so quick.' Wrapping his arms around her, he moved her closer towards him. 'There's something that needs to be taken care of first.'

'What?' Her mind was with Kathy and Jake, and putting right a hundred wrongs, but as she saw his face moving towards her everything bar the moment flew out of her mind like petals in the wind.

'This,' Flynn muttered, his breath warm on her cheek, the solid strength of him drawing her closer. Their lips met, tremulous yet certain, the cool shiver of his tongue against hers, their breath mingling in delicious union. A kiss full of depth and desire and a delicious glimpse of what was surely to come…

'Megan.' Her mother's accent was unmistakable.

They broke apart, laughing like naughty schoolchildren as they hastily arranged their clothes before Mary appeared in view.

'It's Megan when she's annoyed,' Meg explained. 'Which is quite a lot recently.'

'Talk about timing,' Flynn muttered, but Meg just laughed as Mary bore down on them, her face flushed from her one glass of champagne.

'Just what exactly are you doing out here, Megan?' She cast a disapproving look at Flynn, who was wearing a rather flattering shade of crimson lipstick.

'Where do I know you from, young man?'

Flynn coughed, and Meg was amazed to see this strong confident man for once actually lost for a flippant reply. 'The hospital. I'm the doctor who spoke to you when Meg had her accident.'

But Mary O'Sullivan had dealt with too many doctors in her time to be impressed or intimidated by a medical degree.

'Well, then, can I safely assume you've had a good education, and therefore you know that it's bad manners to leave during the speeches?'

Meg smothered a grin as her mother's steely expression turned to her. 'And as for you, young lady, you haven't even said hello to your aunty Morag.' Marching on ahead, she turned briefly. 'Try and remember to ask about her gall bladder.'

Following subserviently, Meg nudged Flynn, who absolutely refused to catch her eye. 'A lioness, remember?' Meg whispered.

'Maybe,' Flynn said glumly. 'But I'm the one holding her cub.'

* * *

The party was in full swing when they returned. With the speeches safely over, everyone in the packed hall was intent on having a good time.

'Flynn!' Kathy screeched as they entered. 'Meg! Mum has been looking everywhere for you.'

'She found us,' Flynn said dryly, which Kathy seemed to find hilarious.

'What's so funny?' Jake came over, handing Kathy a fresh glass of champagne.

'Mum just caught these two outside.'

'So?' He looked over at the two blushing faces. 'Oh,' he said, and started to laugh. 'Thank God for that. It might take the pressure off me a bit.'

And that was that. As effortlessly and as easily as breathing it seemed to be accepted that Flynn and Meg were a couple, and as Flynn dived on a passing waiter carrying trays Meg knew the time had come to let Kathy and Jake know that, at last, she recognised them as one.

'I just wanted to say congratulations, and how happy I am for you both,' she said with feeling as Flynn slipped a supportive hand in hers. 'You're lucky to have each other.'

'You really mean it?' Kathy asked, her face suddenly serious, as if Meg's opinion really mattered.

'I really mean it.' With a slightly unsteady hand Meg accepted the glass of champagne Flynn handed her. 'To both of you.'

'I'll drink to that.'

'While we're all being soppy and emotional, Jake's got something to ask you, Flynn. Haven't you?' Kathy prompted, nudging Jake none too gently in the ribs.

'I have.' He cleared his throat. 'I was wondering—I mean, we were wondering if you'd be my best man?'

The glass that was on the way to his lips suddenly paused, and with a flash of pain Meg knew what Flynn was thinking; they all did. Suddenly the foursome were quiet, knowing how poignant this must be for him, how he must be remembering asking Jake to do the same for him.

For him and Lucy.

'I'd be honoured,' he said quietly, and Meg felt his hand tighten on hers. But even as she returned the small gesture, even as she offered what small support she could, the moment was over, and suddenly it was all slapping backs and hugs and handshakes, all smiles and laughter, toasting the future.

Lucy was Flynn's past, Meg realised, and as much as she might want to share his pain, lighten his load, Flynn wasn't letting anyone in.

'Did you remember to find out about your aunty Morag's gall bladder?' Giggling, immoderately they half fell into her flat.

'Find out!' Meg exclaimed. 'In glorious Technicolour detail! I swear they did it without an anaesthetic the way she went on about it. Can you believe she had the stones in a jar in her handbag?'

Pouring what was left of the cream liqueur Kathy had brought over into two glasses, Meg handed Flynn one.

'And do you think your mother bought our story about sharing a taxi?'

'Not for a second,' Meg replied happily. 'Flynn, I'm old enough to look after myself. I left home eight years ago.'

'I know.' He winced. 'God, she could cut you with a look, your mother.'

Meg laughed, but the laugh faded in a second as she heard what Flynn had to say.

'Maybe I should just be done with it and make an honest woman of you.'

'Flynn?' Meg wasn't sure she had heard right.

'I'm serious, Meg.'

So was she. Incredible as his words were, as much as they had taken her completely by surprise, it was as clear to Meg as crystal that she loved him. 'We hardly know each other.'

'I know that I love you.' He put down his glass and crossed the room. 'Don't ask me to tell you when it happened, because I can't be sure. But looking down at you in resus that morning, yours eyes like a wary kitten, bits of glass strewn through your hair, I wanted to pick you up and take you home. If there's such a thing as love at first sight then it happened to me.'

He ran a finger along her cheek. 'Meg, I never thought I'd be saying this again, but being with you just feels so right.'

'I know it does—but marriage?' She looked up at him. 'Flynn, we haven't even slept together.'

He gave a low, throaty laugh, his tongue tracing the length of her neck, making her toes curl as he nuzzled deeper. 'We can soon put that right.'

One hand was stealing along her waist, searching

fingers locating her zip and sliding it down as his warm hand slid inside. With a low moan she felt his hand on the soft mound of her breast, his finger and thumb massaging her nipple. His other hand was brushing her strappy dress down over her shoulders and, moving back slightly, he watched with unmasked admiration as it fluttered to the floor. His tie, already undone, was easily removed, and with almost indecent haste they both attacked his shirt. The need to feel him naked against her was an instinct as natural as breathing. The heavy buckle of his trousers and the tiny silver zip were teasing obstacles for her long nails. Tugging at his trousers, she ran her hand along the solid dusky-haired thighs, the taut, muscular buttocks.

There was nothing now to stop them—no physical obstacle anyway. Just one big question that Meg needed the answer to.

'Are you sure?'

He nodded, the same affirmative nod she had grown so used to, but it had bigger ramifications now. 'Are you?'

Oh, she was sure. Never had she been more so. 'I don't want you to regret…'

'Shh.' Pulling her up, he held her close for a moment. She could hear his heart pounding in his chest, and his fingers were lost in her long dark curls as she closed her eyes and let his words wash over her, soothe yet simultaneously excite her. 'I know how I feel, Meg, and I know how you make me feel. And as long as it's right for you then there's nothing for either of us to regret.' He wrapped his arms tighter around her, pulled her closer if that was possible. 'Is it, Meg? Is it right for you too?'

She nodded into his chest, salty tears of love and joy slipping down her cheeks, moistening his glistening skin beneath her. He laid her down on the floor gently, slowly. Each kiss, each touch, was measured, calculated to bring her to the very edge of reason, the very edge of oblivion. He parted her soft thighs, his fingers tracing the yielding flesh of her womanhood until she groaned for mercy, quivering with desire, almost begging him to enter her welcoming warmth. As he entered her a strangled gasp was forced from her lips, muffled by the weight of his kiss. Then her hips were rising to meet his, grinding in unison, pulling him deeper. He was taking her further than she had ever been in her life, the throbbing intensity of her sweet surrender causing her to cry out his name.

She knew she shouldn't compare—Vince and Flynn were two different entities entirely. And in truth there was no comparison. The exquisite tenderness of Flynn's lovemaking, the adoration in his eyes, should have washed away all the pain of her past. But when Flynn scooped her up in his arms and carried her to the bedroom, gently laying her down and pulling the sheet over her, she felt a surge of panic as he smiled down at her and moved for the door. This was the point when Vince had left. When he'd suddenly remembered an early client, or the car service, when he had kissed her goodbye and said that he'd ring her in the morning.

'Where are you going?' Her voice was tentative, the

tiniest note of panic creeping in, and Flynn turned with a quizzical look in his eyes.

'To get some water. Do you want some?'

Relief washed over her. 'Please.'

'Where did you think I was going?' He stood there, naked and gorgeous. Evading the question, attempting a diversion, Meg stretched seductively on the bed.

But he didn't respond and, looking up, she could see the hurt in his eyes.

'Meg, where did you think I was going?' His voice was slightly louder, more insistent.

'Home,' she admitted finally.

'You think I'd just get up and leave? We just made love, for heaven's sake. Didn't anything I said count?'

Meg rolled on her side, facing the wall. Anything other than see the pained look in his eyes. 'Of course it did.'

'Then why did you think I was going home?'

'Just leave it, Flynn. Please,' she added. But Flynn was having none of it. In two short steps he crossed the room. Sitting on the bed, he raked his fingers through his hair, hardly making a mark in his jet black hair.

'I'm not leaving it, Meg. I went to get a glass of water and you—'

'I made a mistake,' she interrupted. 'Vince—'

It was Flynn that interrupted now, his voice angry, trembling with fury, but Meg knew that it wasn't aimed at her.

'I'm not Vince. Don't ever compare me to him.' His eyes flashed to her and in a second the anger evaporated. Seeing her lying there on the bed, confused, he felt his heart melt. 'I'd never hurt you, Meg. Don't let that excuse for a man ruin it for us.'

'He won't,' she said, her voice trembling. 'He won't,' she said again with more conviction.

He pulled her into his arms, burying his face in her hair, breathing in her sweet perfumed scent and feeling her fragile and vulnerable beneath his touch. Nothing else but that moment mattered. All he wanted to do was love her, adore her, and all she wanted was him.

Their lovemaking was slower this time, gentler, but the passion, the breathtaking rollercoaster ride of discovering each other, was just as enthralling. And afterwards, as they lay spent in each other's arms, there was no shame in her tears, no turning away and pretending to sleep. Just the gentle peace of acceptance, the utter joy of a new love born.

CHAPTER SEVEN

IT SHOULD have been perfect.

It almost was.

Meg awoke slowly, lying on her stomach, feeling the heavy weight of his leg over her, an arm draped over her back and the soft kiss of his breath on her shoulder. Wriggling slightly, she turned her head, watching Flynn sleep. Watching the sun on his face, the full sensual mouth, the dark hair, his eyelashes short jet spikes, and she waited.

Waited for the pang of guilt, the shame of the morning after, the desire to pull the sheet over her head and groan with embarrassment.

It didn't come.

Instead Meg realised she was actually smiling. Smiling as she watched him wake—the way his eyes screwed up and his lips curled, the restless movements of a body coming out of a deep long sleep. One lazy eye opened, immediately closing as a shaft of sun hit it.

'Morning.' Meg grinned.

He ran a lazy hand over her bottom and despite his

grumbling as he awoke Meg knew he was delighted to feel her there from the way he luxuriously touched her. 'Is it morning already?'

'Has been for ages.'

He ran a tongue over his lips. 'I shouldn't have had that liqueur.'

Meg laughed. 'Tell me about it! Do you want some coffee?'

He nodded gratefully. 'And a gallon of water.'

Slipping on a robe, Meg padded out to the kitchen. It was only when she was alone, watching the water spurt through the filter machine, that the demons crept in. What if he thought less of her? What if he was lying there across the hall right this minute regretting every moment? What if that dig about drinking a liqueur was his way of saying that he'd never have slept with her if he hadn't had too much too drink?

Stop it.

Pulling the ice tray out of the fridge, she broke some on the bench and filled a long glass. His intentions had been clear long before they had even arrived back at her flat. He had told her he loved her, practically proposed to her! Meg ran the glass under the tap, mentally shaking herself. She was being an idiot.

And anyway, the grin that greeted her when she padded back into the bedroom, balancing a tray and a mountain of Sunday papers, was more than enough to suspend any doubts.

'God, I love Sundays.'

'Me too.'

He read every last piece of the papers, his hand running over her body now and then and taking breaks to kiss her, to laugh with her. Somewhere between the business page and the colour supplement he made love to her all over again, and for a while there Meg thought she had died and gone to heaven.

For a while.

'Hey, sleepy head.' Flynn broke into her postcoital doze.

Sitting on the bed, his unkempt hair and the dark stubble on his chin emphasizing the crumpled white shirt of his dinner suit, Meg thought she had never seen a man more beautiful.

'I have to go.' He watched her force a smile, attempt to mask the disappointment in her eyes.

'Sure.'

'There's a few things I need to take care of.'

Meg glanced at the bedside clock; it was two p.m. after all. 'Okay.' She hesitated a moment before continuing, not sure if she was pushing things too hard. 'I'm on a late tomorrow. Will I see you?'

'I certainly hope so.' He picked up her hair and gently moved it off her face. 'But do we have to wait until tomorrow?'

Hope surged in her and Meg's smile finally caught up with her eyes.

'Do you want to come over to mine tonight? I'll ring for a takeaway.' He was pleating the sheet, his eyes not quite meeting hers, and Meg realised he was nervous too. 'You could bring your uniform—if you want to, that is?'

She did want to; there was nothing Meg wanted

more. And this time when he got up to go there was nothing playing on her mind, nothing but all the thrill and promise tonight held.

He hadn't left her much hot water—Meg's tiny flat wasn't exactly designed for two—but it didn't stop her singing or rubbing conditioner into every strand of her hair and body oil into every crevice of her body. Tonight was going to be perfect. She walked back into the bedroom, surveying the tousled bed and the newspapers littered everywhere, and was hard pushed to wipe the grin off her face as she set about tidying up. The place looked as if a bomb had gone off, and when the phone rang it took a moment to locate it under the pile of her hastily discarded clothes.

'Has he gone?' Kathy's voice was a loud whisper, bubbling with excitement.

'Kathy!' Meg exclaimed indignantly. 'We shared a taxi.'

'You might be able to fool Mum…' Kathy let out a low chuckle. 'Actually, you can't. She was out first thing for Mass, and now she's upstairs doing the Rosary. Praying for your sins, no doubt.'

'Well, there's no need.'

'Not feeling guilty, then?'

'Not a bit,' Meg said firmly.

'Good. Well, hold that thought and I'm on my way.'

Meg's stomach let out a huge rumble, and before Kathy could hang up she called her back. 'Stop at the bakers on Beach Road, would you? Bring some croissants.'

'Hungry, are you?'

'Starving,' Meg admitted without thinking, and Kathy started laughing. 'Just bring the pastries.'

Hanging up, Meg dressed quickly and put on the coffee pot for the second time that day. Just as the jug was filling and the flat was taking on a semblance of normality her doorbell rang loudly, and with a wide grin Meg opened the door.

Her grin didn't last long.

'Vince?' He was the last person on earth Meg had been expecting to see, and the shock was evident in her voice.

'I only just heard. I came as soon as I found out.' He ran a hand through his blond hair—straggly hair, Meg noted. And he looked thinner now, with dark rings under his eyes.

Meg gave him a bemused look. 'What on earth are you talking about?'

'Your accident.'

'But that was ages ago.'

'What you must have been through.' He stared at her with sorrowful eyes. 'And I wasn't there to help.'

'Of course you weren't,' Meg said stiffly. 'You were with your wife. How is she, by the way?'

'Meg don't bring Rhonda into it…'

'She's your wife, Vince. I know you seem to find that little fact rather easy to forget, but I for one can't.'

'Please, Meg.' There was a note of desperation in his voice. 'Can I just come inside?'

Her instinct was to scream no, to slam the door in his face and retreat to the safety of her flat. But what would that solve? A slanging match in the hallway she could do without. 'Just for a moment, then,' Meg mumbled, standing back stiffly to let him in.

'Hell, Meg,' he said once the door was closed and the only sound was Meg's pounding heart. 'I've missed you.' When she didn't respond his voice took on a slightly pleading note. 'Please, Meg, when I heard about the accident…'

'Does your wife know you're here?'

'Meg, just listen, will you…'

She swung around then, her eyes blazing with fury. 'What were you expecting, Vince? That we'd fall into bed? That we'd carry on as before?'

'Of course not,' he spluttered.

'Then what?'

'I just wanted to see for myself that you were okay.'

'Well, you've seen.' She held her hands up and slapped them quickly down to her thighs. 'I'm fine. Now, if you'll excuse me, I'm expecting company.' Undoing the latch, she went to wrench open the door—but his hand got there first.

'Please, Meg.' His hand was over hers, and in a reflex action Meg pulled it away. But not quickly enough. The door flew open at that moment, and as Kathy burst in, her arms full of greasy paper bags, the happy smile on her face died in an instant.

'Oh,' she said her eyes turning questioningly from Vince to Meg. 'The adulterer's here.'

'Kathy.' Meg's voice had a warning ring to it, but Kathy hadn't finished.

'He looks like a duck.' She walked over to the bench

and put the bags down as Vince stood there, a muscle pounding in his cheek. 'Walks like a duck.'

'I don't need this from you!' Vince had finally found his voice.

'And quacks like a duck!' Kathy finished triumphantly.

'Vince was just leaving.' Meg flashed Vince a look. 'For good.'

'I am allowed to be concerned,' Vince said from hallway the as Meg finally ushered him out. 'We were together for a long time, and they were good times, Meg. You know that as well as I do.'

Meg closed the door behind Vince. Leaning her head against it, she took a deep cleansing breath before turning to Kathy. She had expected a sympathetic grin, or at the very least a look of understanding, not the suspicious, even hostile stare that was coming from the usually easygoing Kathy.

'What the hell are you doing, Meg?'

'He just turned up out of the blue, honestly,' Meg said somewhat taken aback by the accusing note in Kathy's voice.

'I didn't ask what Vince was up to. I couldn't care less about him and neither should you.'

'I don't.'

'Then what were you doing letting him in?'

Meg shrugged. 'What was I supposed to do? Discuss things in the hall so all the neighbours could hear?'

'You shouldn't have anything to discuss.'

'We don't. Look, Kathy, he just found out about the accident. He was worried.'

'I bet he didn't tell his wife he was dropping by.'

'We were together a long time; he was bound to be concerned,' Meg reasoned, but Kathy was having none of it.

Kathy, happy-go-lucky Kathy, who never got rattled, never, ever got cross, was suddenly on her feet, literally shaking with rage. 'Oh, grow up, Meg. Just grow up, will you?'

'What's that supposed to mean?' Instantly Meg was on the defensive. She had truly done nothing wrong and couldn't believe how Kathy was reacting.

'Exactly that. The best thing that's ever happened to you has just rung Jake. He's asked him to go over—wants to move things on in his life.'

Meg shook her head, bemused, not understanding where Jake came into all this.

Kathy threw up her hands in despair. 'Flynn's sorting out his house—clearing things away. He doesn't want to upset you with constant reminders of Lucy when you come over tonight. And what are you doing? Having a cosy afternoon tea with Vince, that's what!'

'Kathy, will you listen to me?' Meg's quiet deliberate tones were such a stark contrast to Kathy's angry rantings that she actually snapped her mouth closed, her suspicious, angry eyes turning to Meg.

'Vince arrived two minutes before you. I honestly had no idea he was coming.'

'Honestly?'

'Kathy, this is me you're talking to. I'm your sister—have I ever lied to you?'

Kathy sniffed. 'Yes.' Her anger was abating and Meg saw a flash of the old Kathy as a reluctant smile wobbled on her lips. 'You told me you'd taken those books back to the library and I found them under your bed.'

'Seven years ago,' Meg pointed out. 'I meant about anything important.'

Grumbling, Kathy picked a bag off the bench. She selected a pastry for herself first then tossed the rest of the bag to Meg. 'I still had to pay the fine.' Closing her eyes for a second, Kathy let out a little sigh. 'I'm sorry, Meg, I just overreacted—seeing that creep here, knowing the hell he's put you through. I just don't want to see you get hurt again.'

'I'm not going to get hurt,' Meg said resolutely. 'At least not if I've got any say in it.' She took a small bite of her croissant. Funny, but after seeing Vince she suddenly didn't feel so hungry.

'Are you going to tell Flynn?' Kathy asked. 'That Vince was here, I mean.'

Meg swallowed the pastry, it tasted like cardboard. 'I don't know. I've done nothing to be ashamed of, but if what you told me about him clearing out the house is true, I don't think it would be exactly great timing. Are you going to tell Jake?'

Kathy looked at her sister thoughtfully for a moment. 'No,' she said slowly. 'But I'm not covering up for you, Meg, and don't ever expect me to. I just don't think Flynn needs it, today of all days.'

* * *

'Meg.' He kissed her warmly and fully, right there on the doorstep. 'I was just about to ring and see where the hell you'd got to.'

Meg looked at her watch. 'I'm not even late.'

Flynn pulled her inside. 'I guess I just missed you.'

The first thing Meg noticed, or rather didn't notice when she stepped inside was his wedding photo. It was still on display, she saw when he led her through to the living room, but on the dresser. His eyes followed hers and she felt his hand tighten around her fingers.

'I can't just put it away.'

'I'd never expect you to.'

He cleared his throat. 'I just didn't want you to be overwhelmed.' He showed her around briefly, depositing her bag on the large double bed, and even though Meg had never been in the bedroom before, a woman's instinct told her that the freshly polished smell and the incredibly clean dressing table were the results of a poignant afternoon. Her instinct was confirmed when she excused herself to the loo.

The picture was still on the wall, but the incense burner was pushed back a bit and the perfume bottles had been moved from the bathroom shelf. Maybe she shouldn't have looked, maybe she was being nosy, but even as she opened the bathroom cabinet Meg knew what she would find. There, nestled amongst the combs, shaving brushes and aftershaves, were Lucy's perfume bottles. Sure, he'd moved things around, tried not to overwhelm her, but she knew that when push had come to shove he simply hadn't been able to do it. Taking a bottle down, Meg sniffed at it for a moment, her eyes welling with tears as she inhaled the heady fragrance. Tears for a young life lost. For all Lucy had lost and for all the pain Flynn had been through.

Oh, Flynn.

All she wanted was for Flynn to be honest—not just with her, but also with himself.

But honesty was a two-way street. Replacing the bottle, Meg took a deep breath, and as she headed down the stairs her mind was whirring. She couldn't start with lies, no matter how white, no matter how small. A lie by omission was still a lie, and it was the one thing she dreaded Flynn doing to her.

He had to know.

He handed her a glass of red wine as soon as she stepped in the kitchen. 'I didn't know how you took your coffee,' he admitted. 'And if you don't like red wine, we might as well call it quits now. Joking,' he added seeing her serious face.

'I know.' She took a sip. 'It's delicious.' She didn't know how to start, wasn't sure that she wanted to. But all Meg knew for certain was that she had to.

As it turned out, Flynn made the opening for her.

'I saw Jake this afternoon. He said Kathy was heading your way. How was she? Still on cloud nine after last night?'

'Not exactly,' Meg muttered, swirling the wine in her glass. 'Flynn, there's something I have to tell you.'

'Sure.' He was staring at her so openly, not a trace of concern on his face. Meg had the same feeling that plagued her when she was about to give a baby an injection. That rotten feeling as they smiled at you, trusting and gorgeous, not remotely aware that you were about to stick a two-inch syringe into their fat dimpled legs.

'Vince came over this afternoon.'

'Vince?' His eyebrows creased for a moment. 'You mean "bloody Vince"?'

'The very same.'

'Are you all right?'

Meg looked at him, a touch startled by his question. 'I guess so. It was just a shock. I thought it was Kathy when I opened the door, and there he was.' She took a large slug of her wine. 'Apparently he'd heard about my accident—said that he was coming to see how I was doing.'

'A bit late,' Flynn snorted, but the scorn was directed at Vince, not her.

'I know.' She simply couldn't believe how well he was taking it. 'I got rid of him as quickly as I could.'

'And he didn't give you a hard time?'

Meg shook her head.

'Good. So why's Kathy upset?'

Meg was staring at his back now. He was pulling open an overhead cupboard and grabbed a large bag of potato chips, tossing them in a bowl as she tentatively continued.

'I think she thought it was a bit inappropriate.'

'Inappropriate? Has she been taking lessons from your mum?' Flynn laughed, really laughed then, and unbelievably, after all her angst of just a few moments ago, Meg found herself joining in.

'She was just worried you might be upset.'

'Had you rung him the second I'd gone, begged him to come over and jumped into bed with him, *then* I'd be upset.'

'How do you know that I didn't?'

Flynn shrugged. 'If you did, why would you be here?' He came over and, taking her wine glass from her, picked her up and deposited her none too gently on the bench, pushing his groin into hers, Meg found her legs instinctively coiling around him as he quietened her with a deep, slow kiss. 'Meg,' he said, pulling away, cradling her face with his hands. 'You don't have to earn my trust; you've already got it. Now, enough about Vince already,' he whispered. 'Let's think about dinner.' He gestured to the fridge door. 'Pick a menu.'

Never had she seen so many takeaway menus. Indian, Thai, Chinese, Mexican—a cultural melting pot right there on his fridge. 'Or,' he said seductively, 'we could skip the main and head straight for dessert.'

'What is there?' Licking her lips, Meg suddenly realised she was really hungry. Her appetite was eternally whetted, though, when Flynn reached over and pulled open the fridge door. Taking out a can of instant whipped cream, he pulled off the lid with his teeth, shaking the can vigorously as Meg let out a gurgle of excited laughter.

'It's anything you want it to be,' he said in a seductive drawl. 'The possibilities are endless.'

CHAPTER EIGHT

WAKING up next to Flynn was, Meg decided, enough of an incentive to turn her into a morning person. Instead of slamming her hand on the snooze button and burying her head further under the pillow, she lay for a somnolent moment, revelling in the warmth of his body, the bliss of feeling his arm around her, recalling the tender, sweet love they had made.

'Hey, sleepy head.'

Meg opened her eyes, the delicious sight of Flynn better than any dream. 'I wasn't asleep.'

'Fooled me.'

It was the tiny glimpses of domesticity Meg adored, like listening to him in the shower as she prepared breakfast. Not exactly a feast of culinary delights—all Flynn's larder stretched to was bread, some dubious-looking jam and a scraping of butter—but taking it back to bed and sharing it with a newly showered Flynn, Meg might just as well have been eating at a five-star hotel, it tasted so divine.

But the real world was out there, waiting, and as the

clock edged past seven Flynn reluctantly got up from the crumpled bed and started to dress. 'I'd better step on it.'

'Can't you be late?'

'Charge Nurse O'Sullivan!' Flynn mimicked Jess's strong Irish accent. 'Is that any example to set the students?' Reverting to his own gorgeous deep voice, he removed the breakfast tray from beside her on the bed. 'I'll see you for your late shift. Don't lift a finger. I reckon you've earned a rest—and anyway the cleaner comes in this morning.'

'You've got a cleaner?'

'Best money I've ever spent.' He laughed. 'She's an old sourpuss, so don't bother with small talk.'

'So why do you keep her on if she's so miserable?'

'She can be as miserable as she likes,' Flynn said glibly, knotting his tie with ease. 'She's brilliant at housework, and it's not as if I see her much. The perfect woman, really.'

He gave a wink to show he was joking before leaning over and kissing her goodbye unhurriedly. She could smell the sharp citrus of his shampoo, the musky undertones of his aftershave, and she thought her insides would melt.

'How am I going to keep my hands off you?' he murmured. Resting back on the pillow, Meg half dozed as he filled up his pockets with pagers, a wallet and the usual collection of pens and loose change. 'Just let the answer-machine get the phone.'

'Mmm,' Meg murmured.

'And, Meg, maybe don't say anything to anyone

about us just yet.' Her eyes flicked open as he spoke. 'At work, I mean.'

'I wasn't exactly going to walk in with a megaphone.' Sitting up, Meg wrapped the sheet around her breasts, trying and failing to read the expression on his face. In truth she had already decided the same thing—it was just too early and too soon to be the focus of the hospital gossip columns—but hearing Flynn suddenly so cagey was all too painfully reminiscent of Vince.

'I know you weren't,' Flynn replied reasonably. 'There's just a couple of things going on—I haven't time to go into it now.' He glanced at his watch and grimaced. 'I'm seriously behind already. I'll explain tonight. You do understand, don't you?'

Meg nodded, attempting a bright smile, but she didn't understand. How could she? Hadn't Vince always told her to ring his mobile, not to blab too much about them, only allowed a select few friends to see them together? With the benefit of hindsight it was so easy to see why. To see how easily she had been lied to, to see exactly where she had been a fool.

And it wasn't going to happen again.

It was almost a relief when the front door closed. When she could wipe the fake smile off and attempt to gain control of her jumbled thoughts.

Flynn was nothing like Vince.

Nothing.

She was in his house, for goodness' sake, and she would see him at work. Maybe he wanted to be the one to tell his boss—wanted to let the land lie a while so it didn't sound like a brief fling. Dr Campbell was a stickler for the old school ways, and Flynn might be an independent professional, but he still had to toe the line and be seen to do the right thing.

Meg had almost convinced herself, almost assured herself that she was overreacting, reading far too much into a harmless few words. Flynn loved her—he had told her so, and Meg believed him.

Then the telephone rang.

Even if she'd wanted to answer it she couldn't have as the answer-machine picked it up on the second ring. She lay there smiling as she listened to Flynn's rather flip, short message, but her smile vanished as she heard the young, slightly breathless but completely unmistakable voice of Carla on the line.

'Flynn—only me. Pick up if you're home.' So Carla didn't even need to introduce herself. Meg lay there gripping the sheet with clenched fists as Carla paused before continuing. 'I must've just missed you. No worries, I'll see you at work.' She gave a throaty laugh, then lowered her voice, but despite her apparent casual chatter Meg could hear the note of tension in her voice. 'Hey, Flynn, are we ever going to get around to that meal? I'm off next Saturday and so are you. I've checked your roster, so no excuses.'

The beeping of the machine ended the message, but for Meg the agony had just started.

Carla.

Carla leaning over the bonnet of her car. Carla blushing when she spoke, calling Flynn by his first name. Carla the 'family friend'. Who thought nothing of ringing him at seven-thirty on a Monday morning.

And there, Meg realised with a spasm of pain that defied description, was the reason for Flynn's reluctance to go public.

Her instinct was to ring him, to confront him there and then and ask just what the hell was going on, but Meg knew it was pointless. She had to wait—wait until she had calmed down and give Flynn a chance to explain before she judged him. But at the pit of her stomach Meg had already returned her verdict. The result was a foregone conclusion.

Somehow she got through the morning—showering quickly before dressing and heading for home. Not quickly enough, though, to avoid colliding head on with Flynn's cleaner.

'Oh, good morning,' Meg said nervously as she came down the stairs.

The cleaner looked Meg up and down slowly.

'I'm a friend—a friend of Flynn's.' Well, that was one way of putting it she thought wryly.

With a rather curt nod the woman headed off for the kitchen, leaving Meg standing there with her cheeks flaming. Everything, it seemed, had been turned on its head. From her joyous awakening she had been reduced to feeling like some cheap two-minute fling.

All through the day Meg swung erratically between hope and despair. Hope that the love she had discovered in his arms was as true and good as it had felt, and despair that yet again she had allowed herself to be conned.

Any hope of an early answer or resolution was quickly dashed as she entered the department. Trolleys were everywhere, the waiting room humming, and from the frazzled look of the staff as Meg approached for the hand-over she knew there wouldn't be a chance of grabbing Flynn for a coffee.

He was there, though, in the thick of it, listening to a patient's chest in resus. Standing at the white board, Meg tried to concentrate on the hand-over, but her eyes kept dragging back to Flynn, watching as he even managed to make the unwell-looking patient laugh. He must have felt her watching, sensed the weight of her stare, for he looked up, the laugh turning into a small intimate smile as he stilled for a moment. Meg smiled back, a stiff forced smile, and she saw the question in his eyes, the slight furrowing of his eyebrows.

'All right?' he mouthed, and Meg nodded briefly, glad of the excuse to turn away and concentrate on the hand-over.

'I'll hand over cubicle four here.' Jess's attempt at a whisper was fairly fruitless; she could call cows from the top field at the best of times. 'I don't want her husband to hear. Her name is Sonia Chisolm and she came in with facial bruising—the story was that she caught the side of her face on the top bunk, while she was making the children's beds this morning.' Jess paused for effect, her china blue eyes widening, but

Meg didn't rise. She really wasn't up to manufactured drama this afternoon; the facts would do nicely.

'Anyway,' Jess continued when it was obvious her audience wasn't going to play, 'unless she was making the bed at ten last night her story doesn't add up. The bruises are at least twelve hours old.'

'Did you ask her how she got them away from her husband?' Meg said wearily.

'I was just getting to that. The husband had to go to a meeting at work—and I mean had to. It was obvious he didn't want to leave. So I had a bit of a gentle chat while I got her undressed.' Jess missed Meg rolling her eyes. 'There are bruises everywhere and every colour of the rainbow. Anyway, Flynn had a long talk with her. Apparently this is her second marriage—her first husband did the same to her and she left him, but she's sticking by this one. Apparently he didn't mean it—the usual: pressure at work, if she'd only had the house a bit tidier, the kids in bed—all that type of thing.'

'So what are we doing for her now?'

Jess shrugged dramatically. 'I've offered her a social worker and spoken at length about the women's refuge, the police—even Flynn's tried until he's hoarse. But she's simply not budging. Her husband's back now, and he wants to know when she can go home.'

'What does Flynn say?' It was like getting blood from a stone, getting Jess to wrap up a story when she was on a roll.

'Well, what do you know? He wants to admit her to the obs ward for neuro obs. I've told him that we can't.

We haven't got enough staff at the best of times, without using it as a women's refuge. There's no medical reason she should stay and she clearly doesn't want any help.'

'So that's it?' Meg felt a flash of anger. 'We just leave it there?'

'What *can* we do, Meg?'

'We could buy her a bit of time. Arrange a social worker to at least attempt a chat.'

'She doesn't want it,' Jess pointed out. 'And at the end of the day she's a grown woman.'

'So it's her fault?'

'I didn't say that. Nobody deserves to be treated like that, but if she doesn't want to be helped there's not a lot we can do. You can only take the horse to water, Meg.'

'Oh, spare me the proverbs.'

'Are we talking about Sonia Chisholm here?'

Meg deliberately didn't look up as Flynn came over.

'Yes,' Jess replied crisply. 'I was just explaining that we haven't got enough staff on to open up the obs ward this evening. If you want to admit her she'll have to come in under Trauma.'

Flynn pushed Sonia's X-rays onto the viewfinder and searched them without answering.

'You can look all you like, Flynn, there's no fracture.'

Emergency was one of the few places in a hospital where a nurse could get away with challenging a consultant to this extent. Here the nurses were more aggressive and more forthright than on the wards. And with good reason. Huge volumes of patients came through the department and it was a constant juggling game to balance policy with patient care. Technically Jess was right, but Meg had a feeling Flynn was about to pull rank.

'Open up the obs ward,' Meg said, handing the keys to Carla, who was obviously enjoying the power struggle. 'I'll do all the admission notes and you can stay round and watch her.' With a sigh Meg ran her fingers through her long dark curls before daring to look up at the livid face of her colleague. 'Jess, you know as well as I do it will be hours before Trauma come down, and by then he'll have persuaded her to discharge herself.'

'And how are we supposed to cover the obs ward? We're two staff down as it is.'

'Suppose it was a genuine head injury?' Meg asked. 'What would we do then?'

'We'd have to ring the agency,' Jess replied, flustered. 'But this isn't a genuine admission.'

'It doesn't mean she doesn't need our help. Look, Jess, if there's any flak for this I'll take it.'

'Doctor!'

Meg didn't need an introduction to realise that the impatient tones were coming from Mr Chisholm. 'My wife's been here for five hours now. Has anyone reviewed her X-rays?'

'I'm just doing that now, sir.'

There wasn't even the tiniest hint of derision in Flynn's voice; there couldn't be. One hint that the staff thought this more than a simple accident and the discussion would be over there and then, with Sonia the only loser.

'Good, so can she go home now?'

Meg watched as Flynn shrugged slightly. 'Look Mr…er…' He looked down at the casualty card he was holding. Meg could only admire him. No one would have guessed they had only just finished discussing Mr Chisolm. 'I don't want to worry you unduly, but I am a touch concerned.'

'Why?'

'Here.' Flynn pointed to the X-ray. 'There's no visible fracture, but your wife is extremely tender—particularly over the temple, and that can be a dangerous spot.'

'But you just said there's no fracture.'

'That doesn't mean she mightn't run into problems. I feel it would be better to err on the side of caution and admit her overnight.'

Mr Chisholm immediately shook his head. 'Not possible. Look, she'll rest at home—I can get my mother in to keep an eye on her. She's just got a small bump on her head—and I thought the health service was stretched for beds?'

Flynn turned back to the X-rays and scratched his head thoughtfully.

'You're obviously a busy man, and admitting Sonia might cause you some inconvenience, but I'm sure you'll agree that your wife's safety is paramount. There is a question as to the length of her loss of consciousness, so I'm really not happy to send her home just yet. We'll keep her in the obs ward, where the nurses will do her obs hourly, and all being well she'll be ready for discharge in the morning.'

The way Flynn had put it Mr Chisholm really had no choice but to agree. He sucked air in between his teeth, and Meg found she was holding her breath as she awaited his verdict.

'Okay, then. If it's better for Sonia.'

Flynn nodded. 'It is. Now, if you'll excuse me, I'd better get on.' And after briefly shaking Mr Chisholm's hand he casually turned and walked off.

Sonia wore an apologetic, anxious-to-please smile while her husband was present, and Meg noted as she ran through her admission history how Sonia's eyes would constantly dart to her husband's before she answered even the most basic question about herself. It was only when his mother arrived and the crying children were obviously ready for an afternoon sleep that he finally left.

The change in Sonia was dramatic. You could almost feel the tension evaporate from the room when he finally left.

'Okay.' Meg smiled. 'Carla will keep an eye on you now. I'll leave you to get some sleep.'

'Is that it?' Sonia asked, a suspicious note in her voice. 'I thought the second he'd gone there'd be a social worker at the end of the bed.'

Meg looked at her questioningly. 'I thought you didn't want one?'

'I don't.'

Meg nodded. 'Then that's your decision and we respect it. Try and sleep.' Meg knew that pushing Sonia now would only put her on the defensive. It had to be Sonia taking the initiative.

* * *

'Thanks for before.' Flynn finally caught up with Meg a few hours later, while she was dressing some ulcers on Elsie, an elderly woman who chatted away happily as Meg set about her work. 'Is Jess still upset with you?'

Meg shrugged. 'She'll get over it.'

'How about you? How are you feeling?'

Meg concentrated on cleaning the ulcers. 'I'm fine. Jess's moods don't bother me.'

'I wasn't talking about Jess.'

Meg knew he wasn't, but a patient's bedside wasn't the place to say the things she wanted to. It was easier for now to dismiss him.

'I'm fine.'

'When's your coffee break?'

'I doubt I'll be getting one,' she answered honestly, but with a slight edge to her voice.

'I'll catch up with you later, then.' He smiled at the patient, and after hovering just a moment finally left, when it was obvious the conversation was going nowhere.

'Nice-looking man,' Elsie commented when he had gone. 'I bet he has to fight them off.'

Pulling a piece of Tubigrip over her dressing, Meg gave Elsie a tight, non-committal smile, which Elsie happily interpreted. 'My George was a looker—real sharp in his day. The girls swarmed over him.' Accepting Meg's help, the old lady lowered herself from the trolley before straightening herself to all four feet eleven of her tiny frame, a wistful look creeping onto her face. 'Only trouble with George was he didn't try so hard to fight them off.' Pulling a compact out of her handbag, Elsie reddened her lips with a sharply pointed lipstick before turning back to Meg. 'How much do I owe you, my dear?'

'Nothing,' Meg said gently. 'How are you going to get home?'

'On the bus, of course.'

'Would you like me to see if I can arrange a taxi?' Meg offered. 'Those ulcers must be very painful.'

Elsie patted Meg's arm. 'The bus will be fine. Now, my dear, why don't you go and get that coffee? Surely they can manage without you for five minutes?'

They'd just have to, Meg decided. If she didn't sort things out with Flynn once and for all she was going to explode. The only trouble was, now she'd taken the initiative and told a still fuming Jess she was taking a well-earned break Flynn was nowhere to be found.

She headed off to the staff room for a coffee she neither wanted nor needed, and the vision of Carla and Flynn sitting together on the obs ward talking quietly, the curtains drawn around Sonia's bed, wasn't exactly a sight for sore eyes.

'How,' Meg said in a crisp voice, rather reminiscent of Jess's, 'are you supposed to observe your patient, Carla, if the curtains are closed?'

Carla stood up abruptly, but Flynn just sat there, not even managing to look remotely guilty. 'The social worker's in with her. Flynn was just writing the referral. I thought I might give them a bit of privacy.'

'Oh.' Meg beat back a blush. 'Did Sonia ask for her?'

'Yep.' Flynn signed off the piece of paper he was scribbling on. 'She asked Carla to fetch me, we had a chat, and Sonia seemed pretty adamant. So I paged the social worker, who came more or less straight down. Did you need me for anything else?' he asked Carla, scraping the chair as he stood up. Without waiting for an answer he turned to Meg. 'Can I have a word, Meg, in private?'

'Sure. I was just going on my coffee break.'

Meg had been all set to confront him, but standing in the deserted staff room she was somewhat taken back when Flynn closed the door and in no uncertain terms turned the tables, his angry voice unfamiliar. 'What's the problem Meg?' Not leaving her time to answer he continued, obviously rattled. 'What am I supposed to have done now?'

'Meaning?'

'Oh, don't play games. You've been avoiding me all afternoon. We made love last night, for heaven's sake. I left you in my bed this morning and everything was fine—more than fine. Something's happened and I want to know what. What am I being hung for this time?'

Meg swallowed, hesitant to tell him, realising how petty her accusation would sound, how stupid she had been to doubt him. 'Nothing. I'm just tired, I guess.'

'So there isn't anything upsetting you?' His eyes were searching her face, his voice almost pleading for an answer.

Meg shook her head and smiled. 'I was trying not to make things too obvious, I guess I must have gone too much the other way.'

'So we're fine?' He put a hand up to her cheek and Meg held it there.

'We're more than fine.'

'You'd tell me—if there was something worrying you, I mean?'

Meg nodded, and as he placed the gentlest of kisses on Meg's lips she regretted doubting him.

'Good. Look, I'm off at six. How about I go home and fix up some dinner?'

'You mean ring for a takeaway?

'A guy's gotta eat.'

'How about you go home and have a sleep and *I* pick up the takeaway?'

Flynn gave a low, pleased groan. 'Keep going—don't stop now. Bed, food, then you—sounds great.'

Meg laughed. 'How about bed, me, then food?'

'Better and better.'

The intercom summoning them both to resus was the only thing that stopped them kissing. Rushing around setting up for the cardiac arrest being brought in, they shared a tiny secret smile, and Meg thanked her lucky stars she hadn't confronted him about Carla. She would talk to him tonight, sensibly and with a level head. Flynn had made it clear he would put up with anything except irrational jealousy.

The house was in darkness as Meg pulled up. A storm had broken and rain lashed her as she scooped up the takeaway. Locking up her car, she wished she had a key to Flynn's home. Not for any proprietary status, just for the delicious thought of slipping in unnoticed, climbing into the warm bed where he slept and waking him in the most intimate of ways…

The doorbell would have to do for now, and as she rang it Meg fully expected a couple of soggy minutes' wait in the pouring rain while Flynn orientated himself and staggered downstairs. She was somewhat taken back when the door opened almost immediately.

'Were you asleep?' Meg asked, stepping inside.

'No.' He took the bags from her and headed off towards the kitchen. 'Just thinking.'

'In the dark?' It was only then Meg realised that he hadn't kissed her hello, that he didn't seem particularly thrilled to see her.

'I had a light on,' Flynn replied in a heavy voice. She couldn't read his expression in the darkness, but there was nothing relaxed about the atmosphere. Flicking on the hall light, he gestured upstairs. 'Come on—I'll show you.'

It was exactly as they had decided—bed then dinner—but Meg knew she wasn't heading upstairs to be ravished, and with a sinking feeling followed him.

'See.' He pushed open the bedroom door and walked in behind her. The room was in darkness, the only light coming from the flashing answer-machine—a tiny red light, indicating trouble. Walking over, he played the message, and Meg stood there not moving as she listened to Carla's voice for the second time.

'Seven thirty-two,' Flynn repeated, his voice imitating the electronic American accent that concluded the message. 'Which no doubt means you were lying in bed listening to it?'

Meg nodded.

'And, unless your pet goldfish died and you wanted to spare me the grief, I'd pretty much put money on it that this message was what was upsetting you when you came to work. You were going on about Carla when you found out about Lucy. All that rubbish about us not being too obvious was a lie.'

Again Meg nodded, standing there frozen as he sat on the edge of the bed, resting his head in his hands with a sigh. Even in the darkness he looked beautiful.

'I can't do this, Meg.' He looked up and a flash of lightning illuminated his face, casting shadows on his high chiselled cheekbones, the darkness of his unshaven jaw, his eyes dark pools of pain.

She took the two steps necessary to cross the room, but the void between them was much wider than that. Putting her hand out, she touched his bare shoulder, felt the slump of his usually taut muscles, sensed the despair in him. 'Flynn, don't.' She felt like crying but held it back. She needed to be rational, calm now. Her insecurity had already done enough damage.

'I can't walk around on eggshells.'

'You won't have to,' Meg pleaded. 'I was just upset. Carla's got a thing about you…'

'That doesn't mean I've got a "thing" about her.' He brushed her hand off his shoulder, and the pain of his dismissal was as unbearable as the anger in his voice.

'Flynn, she rang you at seven-thirty in the morning and asked you out for a meal…'

'I've explained—she's a family friend.'

'Who's nineteen and gorgeous, with a king-size crush on you.'

Flynn shook his head angrily.

'She has,' Meg insisted, but Flynn wasn't shaking his head at her statement, more at her absolute refusal to see the problem.

'So?' Leaping to his feet, he stood there, angry and confrontational. 'She rang me, Meg, she asked me for a meal—not the other way around.' Again he shook his head, a weary sigh coming from his parted lips. 'She's nineteen, for heaven's sake, I'm thirty-four.'

'Hardly a hanging offence,' Meg quipped, her intentions to stay calm evaporating as she leapt to her own defence. 'Your words, Flynn, not mine. Is Carla the reason you wanted to keep quiet about us at work?'

Flynn nodded, but there wasn't a trace of guilt on his face. 'I wanted to talk to you about it, see how I was going to handle it. I know her parents well, and I'm going to have to see her long after her crush has ended. I just wanted to give her the out with her dignity intact.'

'Oh, very noble.'

Flynn snorted. 'The most stupid part of it is I was hoping you'd understand—give me some insight as to how I was going to deal with it. Seems I was wrong on all counts.'

'I would have understood, Flynn. If only you'd told me.'

'That's the crux of it, Meg. What do you expect me

to do? Sit with you over the dining room table and run through my life story, just in case something pops up that might be misinterpreted? I can't even get a glass of water without you thinking I'm about to do a bunk.'

'That was a mistake; it happened once.'

'The trouble with you, Meg,' Flynn said slowly, ignoring what she had said, 'is that you're so sure you're going to get hurt. So sure that if you open up and actually let the world in it will end in tears.'

'Looks like I'm right,' she said as a salty unwelcome tear splashed down her cheek. Flynn seemed to wince when he saw the tear, his hand reaching up for a second, then pulling away. Instead he ran the frustrated hand over his face.

'I can't live like that, Meg. I can't be constantly looking over my shoulder, wondering what I've said or done to upset you. Things like this don't go away. The deeper we get, the worse it's going to be. It's better this way.'

'You're probably right.' The calm dignity in her voice surprised even Meg. 'But I think you're being a bit harsh, blaming this all on me.' Walking over to the dressing table, Meg picked up a photo of Lucy. 'Before you say it, no, I'm not jealous of her. And something tells me, Flynn, that you were looking for an excuse to end it. Maybe you're not as over Lucy as you make out.' She placed the picture on the bed beside him; it didn't make a sound as she rested it on the thick duvet. He turned and looked at it for a moment, before sitting back down and staring ahead.

'I know I'm not trusting, Flynn. A year and a half of

deceit put paid to that. But I'm working on it. I know I can be jealous, and doubting, but if you really loved me, if you really wanted to, you would understand. We got together too soon. You might not admit it, but we're both on the rebound—we've both been hurt. I'm not comparing my grief and pain to yours—we both know you'd win hands-down.'

'It's not a competition,' Flynn said, his voice a raw whisper.

'I know,' Meg admitted. 'And I'm pretty sure you love me, Flynn. I think you even meant it when you spoke about marriage.'

She watched as he screwed his eyes closed. 'I did mean it, but…'

That horrible three-letter word ended all her dreams, and Meg knew there and then she had lost him. 'Here's the "but", Flynn: it was just all too good too soon, and neither of us were really ready. I can see that now.'

'This isn't about Lucy,' he insisted, but the certainty had gone from his voice. 'I'm over her.'

'So you keep saying. You can shuffle her pictures about, move her things and pretend that you've dealt with it, but it can never be that easy, Flynn. Something tells me that you're just as scared and just as mistrusting as me. The only difference is that I don't hide it as well. So, either we be honest with each other and admit our weaknesses and try to work through them, or we walk away. Is that what you want, Flynn?'

Almost imperceptibly his eyes darted to the photograph, then back to Meg's. 'This isn't about Lucy,' he repeated.

'I take it that means you're choosing the latter?'

His slow nod was the final nail in the coffin, and, making for the door, Meg stifled the sob that was welling in her throat, holding onto the door handle when his voice called out to her.

'What are you going to do?'

Hesitantly she turned. He was still sitting there, and Meg fought an irresistible urge to rush over and wrap her arms around him, to cry with him as they held each other, and kiss away the pain they both felt.

'Get on with living. I've got a bit of catching up to do.'

'You'll be all right?' Trust Flynn to ask, to break her heart and then check to see that she would be okay.

'That's not your concern.' But even as she said it Meg knew the bitterness in her voice wouldn't help either of them. 'I'll be fine,' she said gently, her face softening, her voice a touch unsteady but her words heartfelt. She even managed a tremulous smile. 'Swollen eyelids and a cracked nose tomorrow, no doubt, but you can't begrudge me that!'

Flynn tried to smile back. 'I'm sure I'll look the same.'

CHAPTER NINE

BUT he didn't.

It was as if their brief affair had never happened. Not a trace of a blush, not a shadow of pain marred his perfect features. If Meg had been worrying about how she was going to face him, then it had been unnecessary. He set the tone the very next day—jokey, pleasant and utterly normal.

Somehow she limped through seeing Flynn at work. Somehow Meg got up each day, showered and put on her make-up. Hell, on a good day she even managed to share a joke with him—about work, of course. Their private lives were off limits, and neither of them ever crossed that line. And, though she searched for a chink in his armour, the tiniest sign that the demise of their relationship had caused him even a millionth of her own agony, not once did she see it.

Well, what had she expected? Meg asked herself. He had got over the death of his much-loved wife; how could a brief fling with a colleague even begin to compare with that?

But it had been so much more than a brief fling for Meg, so very much more. And, despite her best attempts to put it behind her, to build a bridge and somehow get over it, as Flynn forged ahead in his career, as his colleagues warmed to his affable character, as the department lifted under his knowledgeable leadership, the gulf between them widened. Meg, never the most outgoing in the department, never the most popular, struggled through each day, the pain she witnessed in the name of duty only adding to her grief. And she knew that it was only a matter of time before the winds of change forced a resolution.

As she arrived for an early shift one day, the disarray in the unit for once didn't match Meg's emotions. Finally, after much soul-searching and the best part of a bottle of red with Kathy, Meg had made a decision—a big one. Now all she had to do was see it through.

'What's going on?' Meg asked Heather, the Night Charge Nurse, who was busily setting up resus. A couple of the staff were pulling over trolleys to make up extra beds and the overhead tannoy was crackling into action, urgently summoning the trauma team to the department.

'Multi-car pile-up on the Beach Road—two fatalities and five serious injuries. We've just sent our Mobile Accident Unit out to it.'

Meg rolled her eyes. 'Where do you want me?'

The radio link to the ambulance buzzed then, and Heather rushed to get it. Meg didn't wait for further instruction and started to run some Hartmann's solution through a giving set, simultaneously connecting an ambu bag to an oxygen outlet as she did so. Five multi-traumas at one time was enough to stretch even the biggest of departments.

'One's being directly lifted to the Trauma Centre,' Heather said as she returned. 'But apparently there's another pile-up on the Eastern Freeway, so everyone's stretched. Looks like we could get the remaining four. The first is already on the way.'

'We'll cope,' Meg said assuredly. 'The day staff are all arriving now. Have you called Dr Campbell and Flynn?'

Heather nodded as she worked. 'Dr Campbell's on the way, but Flynn was already here with a query epi-glottitis. He went out with the Mobile Accident Unit. I felt wrung out when we'd got the child safely intubated and airlifted to the Children's Hospital, and now this! What a night.'

Meg gave a half-laugh. 'It ain't over yet, kid,' she joked, but her heart wasn't in it. Her mind was with Flynn. Out facing his demons. Stuck on the freeway with two fatalities and serious injuries. And the worst part of it, the hardest bit of all, was that it was no longer her place to be there for him. He had made that perfectly clear. 'Looks like we're pretty much set up? What's the ETA?'

'Five minutes for the first,' Heather glanced at her watch. 'Which is up.'

'I'll go and meet the ambulance.'

She stood on the forecourt, watching as Security pulled cars over to clear the hospital entrance, aware of the curious looks of staff who had hung around to see what was arriving. Normally Meg loved this bit. The pit-of-the-stomach thrill of excitement as the sirens neared, the first glimpse of the flashing lights, the slight headiness at an impending drama, showing off a touch, knowing everyone was watching.

But not today.

Today her heart was too heavy and her mind too filled with what Flynn must be suffering to enjoy her work. As she pulled on the shiny silver handle of the ambulance door and saw the paramedics massaging the stilled heart, saw the bloodstained mangled wreck of a life, all she felt in that tiny silent second was sadness. Sadness for the people going to work, setting about their day, and ending up fighting for their lives. Sadness for the relatives who had to sit and drink machine coffee for hours, their world temporarily on hold as they rang around chasing people up, trying to be strong as they awaited their loved one's fate. And sadness for the staff who dealt with it. The staff who, day in and day out, pulled on their uniforms just to pick up the mess of other people's lives. Who bandied about expressions such as 'avoiding burn-out', or 'peer support', when they all knew it caught up with you in the end. You wouldn't be human otherwise.

Climbing in the ambulance, she took over the cardiac massage from Ken, and for just a second they shared a knowing look.

Life was bloody awful sometimes.

But there wasn't time for introspection, not when people's lives depended on you. So Meg ran along with the stretcher, massaging the unlucky woman's chest as they raced through to resus. They lifted her over on Dr Campbell's count and she concentrated on the moment, fought hard to save the life of someone she'd never met, nor probably would again. As the other resus beds filled up with the victims, as other teams attended the wounded, Meg battled along with her team. Pushed through bag after bag of blood, drew up drugs, wrote down the hastily shouted obs, set up equipment and picked it back up off the floor when a doctor threw it across the room in frustration.

And when it was over, as everyone who had worked on the woman had known it would be, Meg sat with the relatives as Dr Campbell delivered the terrible news. The only saving grace was that they could look them in the eyes and say that they'd given it their all—that, though it mightn't help now, somewhere down the track it might comfort them to know that their beautiful wife, mother and daughter had had the best treatment available.

Only sometimes it wasn't enough.

'No good, then?' Ken caught up with Meg as she came out of the interview room.

Meg shook her head. 'She just lost too much blood. The faster we put it in, the faster she lost it.' Looking down, she saw he was holding a patient card. 'Another one?'

'Only me. I cut my arm when we were lifting the last one; it just needs a couple of steri-strips whenever you've got a moment. I know it's been hell.'

Meg peeled back the wad of gauze from Ken's arm. 'I think you need more than a couple of steri-strips.'

'It's no big deal.' Ken was in his fifties; he'd been there and done that too many times to get worked up over a small cut. 'I'd have stuck a plaster on it and forgotten abut it if Flynn hadn't seen it.'

Meg felt her insides flip just at the mention of his name. Focussing on replacing the gauze, trying to keep her voice casual, she popped open a bandage and wrapped the gauze in place. 'How was he? At the accident, I mean.'

'Great. You know Flynn—had everyone organised in two seconds flat and still managed to crack the odd joke…' His voice trailed off and he searched Meg's face questioningly. 'You know, don't you?'

Meg nodded.

'Not many do,' Ken said thoughtfully. 'He doesn't exactly make it public knowledge.'

'So how was he this morning?'

Ken took a deep breath. 'Well, he didn't throw up like he did after we got you out, but if his colour was anything to go by I'd say he wasn't far off.'

'He was sick?' Meg's recollection of her accident was hazy at the best of times, but Ken's words stirred her deeply buried images—waiting for Flynn to come to the ambulance, the concern in Ken's eyes when he'd finally appeared, grey and sweaty. She knew for a fact, then—knew for a fact that her instincts were right. Flynn could scream from the rafters that he was coping, deny the world had hurt him, but the truth, however vehemently opposed, was crystal-clear.

Lucy's death had devastated him.

Meg's jealous insecurity, her crippling self-doubt, might have played a part, but she and Flynn had been finished before they'd even started. Like the poor patient lying in resus, from the moment of impact, the moment their two worlds had collided, the end had been inevitable.

'You know, Meg, I've seem some bloody tragedies in my time. But that day, going out with Flynn and seeing what he went through…' Meg was horrified to see Ken's eyes mist over. 'Well, no one should have to go through what Flynn did. I know it's a different hospital, and a couple of years on, but given what he's been through that guy deserves a medal for what he did this morning.'

But Flynn didn't get a medal. He got a cup of cold coffee. And by the time the last of the motor accident patients had been moved out of resus, and the shelves had been restocked and the floor mopped in preparation for the next unfortunate who needed it, Meg's half-day was almost over.

'Bet you're glad to be finished?' It was the first time they had actually caught up that day, and Meg was writing her notes, trying to remember if it was the left or right elbow she had just examined on a screaming two-year-old.

'That's an understatement. Left,' she added, and Flynn gave her a quizzical look. 'Sorry—there's a query epicondylar fracture for you in cubicle two. I was just trying to remember which arm.'

'Thanks.'

'How are you feeling? I mean, I gather it was pretty messy out there this morning.' They might not be lovers any more, but they were still colleagues. It was only right that she ask.

Flynn took the child's casualty card from her before he answered. 'It wasn't great—but, hey—' he gave a shrug '—that's what we do for a living, Meg.' Picking up his stethoscope, he draped it around his neck and flashed his usual smile. 'Catch you later, then.'

Meg just stood there; suddenly she was tired. Tired of the stupid game they all played each day; tired of pretending she was coping. She realised there and then that the decision she had made was the right one. Now all she had to do was tell him. 'Just who do you think you're fooling, Flynn?'

'Don't start that again, Meg.' He held out his hands, joking to the last. 'See, not the tiniest tremor.'

'Flynn, will you just stop for a moment?'

His smile faded as he heard the serious note in her voice.

'There's something I have to tell you.'

'Are you worried about the wedding rehearsal? If you are then there's no need. I won't let on for a second there's any tension…' His voice trailed off as Meg shook her head.

'It's not that.'

'So what is it? Tell me.'

The annexe was deserted, but Meg shook her head. 'Not here.'

His office was tiny, more an overgrown cupboard, really, and the piles of notes and X-rays littering the chairs and desk only made it appear smaller.

'Before I start, I'm only telling you this because…' She was struggling to find the words, acutely aware it was their first time alone since the break-up. 'I just don't want you to feel responsible. This has nothing to do with you. I'm only telling you first because you'll find out soon enough anyway.'

One look at his paling face and Meg realised what he was thinking—realised what her jumbled attempt at an explanation must have sounded like.

'I'm not pregnant,' she blurted out. 'God, you didn't think I was pregnant, did you?'

Flynn gave a relieved laugh. 'Well, see it from my side. Six and a half weeks after we make love you're looking like you haven't slept in a while and asking to see me in my office.' He put a hand up to her chin, pulling her eyes up to meet his. But it wasn't the gesture of a lover, more of an affectionate friend. 'We'd have coped if you were, Meg. I'm not that nasty!'

'I never said that you were.' His eyes were doing the strangest things to her, and Meg dragged hers away, knowing she couldn't get through this if she had to look at him as well.

'I'm handing in my notice, Flynn.' Meg was looking at her feet as she spoke.

'No.' The word was instant, decisive. 'No,' he repeated. 'Meg, you don't have to do this. We're fine, no one knows—'

'It isn't because of us,' Meg interrupted.

'Then why?' His fingers were back, forcing her chin up, forcing her to look at him, and suddenly she couldn't bear it. There was nothing friendly about his touch and nor would there ever be. Pushing his hand away, Meg took a deep breath.

'I can't do it any more, Flynn. I've loved Emergency, adored it, but not any more. I'm simply not enjoying it.'

'You're just tired,' Flynn insisted. 'Everyone feels like this sometimes, but it doesn't last for ever. Sooner or later the sparkle comes back and you remember why you're here in the first place.'

'Is that what happened to you?' She saw the shutters come down and immediately regretted her words. 'Sorry, Flynn, that's not any of my business.' She closed her eyes, searching for the words to articulate her feelings, trying to explain what she didn't understand herself. 'I'm going to go and lay out a body now. It should have been done hours ago, but we didn't have the staff and we didn't have the time.'

'Because you were busy looking after the living, Meg,' Flynn reasoned. 'I can't believe you want to throw it all away. You do love it, Meg, you do. When Debbie had to be rushed to Theatre…'

'She lived, Flynn.'

'And so did three of the motor accident victims that came in this morning. They lived because of us. Because people like Ken, the police and the firefighters were on the ball. Because when they arrived here they had staff who were up to date and trained to their back teeth. Yes, there's a body, but there are also three people who are going to go on and have good, productive lives. Forgive me if I sound conceited here, Meg, but it's because of people like us.'

'I know that.' She was almost shouting. 'But it isn't just a body to me, Flynn, and it isn't just a job. I nearly died because I was so broken up at losing a child. The emergency line bleeps and I go cold, Flynn, when I used to get excited. To work here you have to be an adrenalin junkie, and it's just not me any more. All I want is to come to work, do my job and then go home.'

'So what will you do?' She could feel his eyes on her, yet still she couldn't bring herself to look at him.

'There's a Charge Nurse position being advertised on the surgical day unit.'

'Oh, come on, Meg,' Flynn scoffed. 'Lumps and bumps and circumcisions—you'd be bored stiff in a couple of weeks.'

Meg gave a low, tired sigh. 'Sounds perfect.'

'And there's nothing I can say to make you change your mind?'

Meg shook her head. Tears were threatening now, and the last thing she wanted to do was break down.

'We'll all miss you.'

'I doubt it. Oh, maybe when Jess does the roster, but I don't think I made much of an impression down here.'

'You did on me.' His simple honesty made Meg look up. 'I'm going to miss you.'

'Thanks.'

'Does anyone else know?

Meg nodded. 'Kathy. She's coming over again tonight; she's been really good.'

She turned to go, but there was one question bugging

her—one final thing she needed to know. 'Flynn, can I ask you something?'

He was sitting on the desk, his long legs dangling, tapping a pencil on his thigh, and he looked up at the questioning tone in her voice. 'Ask away.'

'Why did you come back? Was it because you missed it so badly, or to prove that you could still do it?'

For an age he didn't speak, the only sound the tapping of the pencil on his thigh, and when finally he answered Meg was almost knocked sideways by the confusion in his voice. 'I don't know, Meg,' he said slowly. 'I really don't know.'

Closing the door, Meg realised it was the first time she had heard Flynn sounding anything other than assured.

Through all the turmoil, all the hell of the past few weeks, her staunchest ally had been Kathy. Kathy—who had warned her, tentatively forecast that it might end up in tears—had never once admonished her or said I told you so. Instead she'd arrived with chocolate or wine, rattled on about the wedding reception, moaned about their mother and, despite organising her wedding, had done everything and anything to be there for her sister.

And now, on the eve of her wedding rehearsal, Kathy had again put everything on hold. Even though Meg and Flynn had been over for weeks now, Kathy wasn't insensitive enough not to realise that the wedding would only serve to ram home her sister's loss, nor that, given the fact that today Meg had said goodbye to eight years of emergency nursing, a well earned post mortem was entirely called for.

'I know I was out of order,' Meg said for the umpteenth time. 'I know I was too needy, too suspicious. But I would have changed.'

Kathy shook her head. 'You didn't need to change, Meg,' she said resolutely. 'You just needed a bit of time to find your feet and get back to the old Meg. You're the least suspicious person I know—at least you were until you found out about Vince. How else would he have managed to fool you for so long otherwise?'

Leaning over, Kathy topped up their glasses. Wine and watching slushy films on Meg's couch was an all too familiar routine at the moment.

'Will you be all right—tomorrow, I mean? I can come round and pick you up if you don't want to arrive on your own.'

'Please.'

Even though she had seen him every day at work, the thought of seeing him at such an intimate occasion, seeing Flynn surrounded by her family, had Meg in a spin. The whole wedding did, actually.

From the church service at one right through till they waved off the happy couple she and Flynn would be together, part of the glossy bridal party, smiling, toasting Kathy and Jake and dancing the mandatory slow dances. Meg closed her eyes. How was she going to do it? How was she supposed to get through this and come out with her pride intact? How could she dance with him and expect to somehow conceal the simple fact that she loved him?

Always would.

'Maybe we should have done that?' Kathy's voice seemed to be coming from far away.

'Done what?'

Kathy gestured to the television, but the film might just as well have been in Chinese for all the attention Meg was paying. 'Elope. Are you even trying to watch it, Meg?'

'No.' Meg admitted. 'I'm having a major panic attack about Saturday. Even the rehearsal tomorrow is sending me into a spin.'

'I feel awful,' Kathy groaned. 'I've honestly tried with Mum.'

Meg knew that to be true. Kathy had done her best with Mary—tried to persuade her to relax the rules, bend the occasion to fit in with the uncomfortable circumstances. But Mary O'Sullivan had waited a long time to see one of her daughters walk down the aisle, and there was no leeway in her newly purchased book of etiquette for the sisters to argue the point. Jake and Kathy would walk through the reception hall to the cheers and toasts of the crowd, followed by the best man and the bridesmaid, and bringing up the rear would be the bridal party's parents. That was what the book said and that was what was going to happen.

And that was only the start.

Meg hesitated, unsure whether or not to ask the question that was bothering her. 'Has Flynn ever said anything to Jake? About me and him, I mean.'

Kathy didn't answer.

'Come on, Kathy, I'm not going to let on to him. Surely you can tell me what he's been saying. I need to know.'

Meg was ready for anything—had braced herself to hear the worst, prepared herself for just about any eventuality, even if it involved a nineteen-year-old called Carla. The only thing she had never anticipated was the stab of pain she would feel when she heard Kathy's hesitant answer.

'He hasn't mentioned it.'

Meg sat there for a moment, digesting the news, her mind searching for comfort. But there was none. 'Nothing?'

Kathy sat there uneasily as Meg pushed harder. 'You mean he hasn't said a single thing about me?'

'I'm so sorry, Meg.'

She crumpled then, right there in front of Kathy. She just seemed to disintegrate. Kathy let her cry a while peeling off tissues and topping up her glass, before she gave up being the brave one and joined in too. The sight of Kathy's tears was enough to stop Meg. 'I'm sorry too. You've got the rehearsal tomorrow and the wedding on Saturday. You don't need this right now.'

'Don't worry about me,' Kathy said, giving Meg a big hug. 'You know how much I love a drama. If I can cry at films why not real life? Anyway, just because he hasn't spoken to Jake it doesn't mean he doesn't care. It's what he did with Lucy—just carried on like nothing had happened.'

'But something did happen, Kathy. Something big

and beautiful. We fell in love and he's just walked away without a second glance.'

'That's Flynn for you.' Picking up her glass, Kathy turned back to the film. 'That's Flynn.'

The rest of the film they spent munching chocolate, with one sister or the other occasionally coming up with a scheme that might just save the day.

'You could always sprain an ankle,' Kathy suggested as the final credits rolled. 'At least then you wouldn't have to dance with him.'

Meg snorted. 'Mum would just make him shuffle me around in a wheelchair. I can't get out of it, Kathy. You know what Mum's like.'

'You don't think she's got ulterior motives?' Kathy said suddenly. 'She's not trying to play matchmaker, is she?'

Meg gave a scornful laugh. 'Who? Mum? She hasn't got a romantic bone in her body.'

'Speaking of romance, Meg, can I ring Mum and pretend I'm crashing here tonight? Please,' Kathy begged when Meg rolled her eyes. 'She's guarding me with her life.'

'She'll kill you if she finds out.'

Kathy laughed as she picked up the phone and dialled. 'No, she won't, Meg. She'll kill *you* for encouraging me.'

'That would be right,' Meg muttered taking the phone from a grinning Kathy. 'Yes, Mum, she is really here.' Taking an affectionate swipe at Kathy, she held the phone from her ear as Mary read the riot act.

'What did she say?' Kathy asked as Meg replaced the receiver.

'Plenty. "You do realise you're not his bride until Saturday?"' She was mimicking her mother's voice. '"That you're wearing white for a reason and Jake might think less of you?"'

'Bit late for that.' Kathy laughed, grabbing her bag and planting a quick kiss on her sister's cheek. 'Thanks so much, Meg.'

It was nice how they'd become close again, Meg reflected once Kathy had gone. Now that Meg had accepted Jake—accepted Kathy too, for that matter, as a woman not a little sister—their relationship had flourished. And, despite all the emotion over Flynn, and the pain she had been through, Meg really was looking forward to the wedding, to seeing her little sister say 'I do'.

Turning off the lights, Meg went to bed. Tonight she wasn't going to cry. Tonight she would think about Kathy, think about her dress and her shoes and all the pomp that came with a good old-fashioned wedding instead of dwelling on what might have been.

Her intentions were good, of course, but it was a red-eyed Meg who awoke the next morning. Yes, Meg decided, flicking on the kettle and shivering in her flimsy nightie, she might well be happy for Kathy, and, yes, she would enjoy the wedding. But other people's joy didn't soothe your own pain, only exacerbated your loss.

At least she didn't have to go to work today and smile politely at him. She was off now until after the wedding, and then all she had to do was serve her notice. So she filled her day buying all the things she would usually have organised ages ago—like stockings and a new eyeliner pen. Well, that was what she'd meant to buy, but, staggering back into the flat laden down with carrier bags, Meg decided that shopping really was the best cure for a broken heart—albeit a temporary one. But she'd take whatever she could get at the moment.

It was only when the clock edged to ten to six that Meg started to worry. Kathy had definitely said that she'd pick her up; Meg was sure of it. She had been ready for ages, changing her outfit umpteen times before putting back what she'd had on in the first place: a simple rust silk wraparound skirt with a small black top and some very new, very gorgeous Indian-looking sandals.

As was seemingly always the case, Kathy's mobile was turned off. In a spur-of-the-moment choice Meg decided she'd take Kathy's wrath any day of the week rather than her mother's if she was late, so scribbled an apologetic note telling Kathy she'd meet her at the church, pinned it to the door and clattered her way down the stairs in her new sandals—which were already starting to rub.

'Where have you been, Megan?' Mary demanded. One look at her sister's guilt-ridden face and Meg realised that Kathy had only now remembered that she was supposed to be picking her up

'Sorry, the traffic was terrible.'

'Which is why you should have left earlier. Now, come on, we've only got the church for half an hour.'

They might have only had the church for half an

hour, but that didn't stop them from being put through their paces.

'You're supposed to be smiling as you walk up the aisle.'

'I will be, Mum, on Saturday.' Meg's sandals were really hurting now, and following a giggling Kathy for the tenth time really wasn't helping matters. Neither did the fact that Flynn, dressed in jeans and a T-shirt and looking absolutely delicious, was smothering a smile as Mary told her off.

'Okay, just one more time. Not you, Meg,' she barked. 'Just Kathy and Dad. I want to see them from the church doors and check how they look from behind. Flynn, you stand next to Jake like the book says.'

'She's not going to hum the "Bridal March" again, is she?' Flynn asked as the trio disappeared, and even Meg giggled.

But the smile soon vanished when Kathy came running through the church doors, an anguished look on her face. 'Meg, you'd better come,' she said breathlessly. 'Mum's having palpitations.'

'I'll get my bag from the car,' Flynn said, moving like lightning down the aisle. But Kathy put up her hand to stop him. 'Not those sort, Flynn.' Her eyes turned to Meg. 'Vince just turned up.'

'Vince!' Meg's shocked voice seemed amplified in the hallowed silence of the church. 'But how did he even know that I was here?'

'That was Mum's question, actually.' Kathy was trying desperately to keep the mood light, but she gave up when she realised no one else was even attempting a smile. 'He went to the flat and found your note for me on the door. He wants to see you.'

'Well, I don't want to see him,' Meg said firmly. 'You can tell him that from me.'

Kathy shook her head. 'There's something else. Apparently he's left his wife. Meg, I really think you need to talk to him.'

'There's nothing left to say. Just get rid of him, please, Kathy,' she urged.

'Your sister's got enough to contend with, without doing your dirty work.' Mary marched towards them, her face contorted with rage. *'Bloody Vince.'*

If it hadn't been such an awful moment Meg would have registered that it was the first time she had actually heard her mother swear. Mary clapped her hands over her mouth as soon as the mild expletive escaped her lips. 'Now look what you've made me do—and in God's house too. I mean it, Megan, go and sort things out once and for all.'

For a second she looked over to Flynn—hoping for what, she didn't know—but he looked as relaxed and carefree as ever, and Meg realised there and then that she was on her own. Vince was her problem and it was up to her deal with it.

'Meg,' Vince started as she marched angrily out of the church towards him, 'I'm sorry if I upset your mum.'

'No, you're not,' Meg retorted angrily. 'Just what on earth made you think you could come here?'

'I needed to see you…'

'Now?' Her voice was rising. 'You decide you need

to see me and that's it? Doesn't it matter to you that I might be in the middle of something?' She gave a cynical snort before continuing. 'But then what does a wedding mean to you? Not much, obviously.'

'Meg, I've left Rhonda. My marriage is over.'

'So?' Meg shouted. 'Tell someone who cares.'

'Please, Meg.' He was pleading with her, and, looking up, she saw how tired and utterly awful he looked. 'Please. I just want five minutes. If you still don't want me then I'll walk away.'

'I don't want you, Vince.' Her voice was definite. 'Nothing you can say will change that.'

'Five minutes. Please,' he added desperately.

She didn't owe him anything, not a single thing, but maybe Meg was curious as to what he had to say, or hopeful that hearing him out might bring her some finality. They simply couldn't go on like this. With a small shrug she nodded.

'Can we go to your flat?'

'No. There's a café down the road; you can speak to me there.'

Meg declined his offer of something to eat, in fact she chose iced coffee in the hope that she could drink it quickly and get out of there.

'I'm sorry for lying to you,' Vince began. 'And if it's any consolation I really did love you. I just didn't want to hurt Rhonda.'

'You hurt us both.' The waitress brought over their drinks and Meg fiddled with the teaspoon, dunking it in and out of her drink—anything other than look at him.

'I know that,' Vince said sadly. 'When we broke up, I really tried hard to make my marriage work, but all I could think about was you. I've left her for you, Meg.'

'No, you haven't,' Meg said slowly. 'You've left Rhonda because your marriage wasn't working—it hasn't been since the day you asked me out, and probably not for a while before that.'

'But it's over now. Can't we try again? Wipe the slate clean? I know you don't trust me, but, given a chance, in time I could show you how I've changed—earn back your trust.'

Meg gave him an incredulous look. 'You shouldn't have to earn back my trust, Vince. You had it, every last piece of it, and you ripped it up and threw it away. It's gone. I don't know how to say it any clearer: I'm never going to trust you and I'm never going to love you.'

He sat there, staring into the disintegrating froth on his cappuccino, and with a start Meg realised his eyes were brimming with tears.

'So it's over?'

Hallelujah, Meg almost said, but stopped herself. His pain, his desolation, gave her no surge of triumph, no sense of vengeance. It was all just a sorry mess.

'It's over,' she said softly. Reaching across the table, she patted his arm. 'But you'll survive, and so will Rhonda. I'm living proof. Look, Vince, I really have to go. I'm in the middle of a wedding rehearsal.'

It was an utterly innocent gesture, a compassionate final touch before she got up and walked away, and had she glanced out of the window Meg would probably have thought twice about it. But she didn't look up. She didn't see Flynn standing on the pavement rummaging in his jeans for his car keys, or the pain in his eyes as he drove away.

'Can I call you?' Vince asked. 'Not yet—in a few weeks, maybe. We could try and be friends.'

Meg shook her head. 'No, Vince, we can never be friends. I mean that. I don't want you calling me, not ever.'

Placing some money on the table, she didn't even say goodbye, and she walked out of the café with her head held high, knowing in her heart that she'd done nothing wrong and wondering just why, then, did she feel so guilty?

CHAPTER TEN

MEG actually awoke not with a smile on her face, but for the first time in weeks with a sense of peace.

She was going to be all right.

Better than all right, she was going to be fine. Who needed a man? Okay, maybe years down the track it might possibly happen, but she wasn't going to die waiting. There was simply too much to do—the world was her oyster, so to speak. The surgical day ward would just have to wait. She had enough in the bank to take a dream cruise and banish all the horrible memories once and for all. And, Meg decided, lying staring at the ceiling, if she was going to be a spinster why not go the whole hog and get a cat?

But who would look after the cat when she went on her cruise?

There were a million and one things to be done today—from important things, like picking up various relatives from the airport or train station, right down to necessary basics, like washing her hair today so it wasn't too slippery when the hairdresser put it up, and tweezing her eyebrows to match the photo of Audrey Hepburn that Meg had faithfully cut out of a glossy magazine and stuck on the mantelpiece.

Meg was sleeping at the family home tonight—heaven only knew how, as practically every O'Sullivan in the phone book had been offered a bed for the night, much to Kathy's horror. Meg had been assigned a sleeping bag on the floor of her sister's room. And, despite the prospect of a hard floor and Kathy's grinding teeth, Meg was looking forward to it in a mawkish kind of way. Looking forward to sharing a room with her sister for probably the last time. No doubt in a couple of years when the families converged, Kathy's room would be overflowing with travel cots and squeaky toys. But not tonight. Tonight it was just the two of them.

Flynn.

He popped into her mind, as he always did, but Meg couldn't deal with it today—simply couldn't go there and be expected to keep on smiling. Throwing back the sheets, she forced his image from her mind, flicking on the coffee machine and darting down the communal stairs. Her neighbours bade her g'day with barely a glance; Meg in her heart-patterned pyjama shorts and skimpy crop top, rushing to collect her newspaper, was an all too familiar sight.

What wasn't a familiar sight, Meg realised, as she picked up the paper the newspaper boy had tossed onto the grass, was the huge silver car parked on the street. Correction, it *was* familiar—very familiar. And so was the six-foot, dark-haired, delicious package climbing out of it and walking towards her.

'We need to talk.'

Meg nodded dumbly, suddenly acutely aware of her lack of attire. 'How long have you been there?'

Flynn shrugged. 'All night. Is he still here?'

On closer inspection, Meg figured he was speaking the truth. Though still looking delicious, his T-shirt was crumpled like an old dishcloth and his chin certainly hadn't met a razor for a while. 'Who?'

'Who do you think?' He sounded irritated. 'Vince, of course.'

'Vince isn't here,' Meg said, confused. 'He never has been. Honestly,' she insisted when he gave her an unbelieving look. 'Why on earth would you be sitting outside?'

Flynn completely ignored her question; he obviously had other things on his mind. 'So what was that little tête-à-tête I saw you both engaging in?'

'Flynn, I've no idea what you're talking about.' For once it was Meg sounding rational, Meg who sounded in control. It was Flynn who was obviously struggling to hold it together. 'Look, do you want to come inside?'

He nodded and walking back to the flat, held the door open for her. Meg hesitated before going inside. Oh, she wasn't nervous of Flynn—not for a second—she was more worried about going first up the stairs in a skimpy pair of shorts, which seemed a stupid thing to be getting worked up about, given the turn of events.

But she found it easier to focus on trivialities, too scared to let her mind leap ahead and ask the bigger questions—scared, so scared, of building up her hopes only to have them cruelly dashed again.

'Do you want coffee?'

He shook his head impatiently. 'I didn't come for breakfast, Meg, I want to talk.'

'Fine,' Meg replied curtly, stalling for time, not sure whether or not she wanted to hear what he had to say to her. 'I'll have a coffee while you do the talking.' She held up the jug. 'Last chance.'

The aroma of the fresh brew got Flynn down from his moral high ground a touch, and grudgingly he nodded. An uncomfortable night in a parked car, however luxurious the model, wasn't the best prelude to what he had to say, and strong, sweet black coffee was just too tempting an offer to refuse.

She carried the drinks through to the lounge and sat down, determined not to let him see how flustered she was feeling, determined not to be the one to break the uncomfortable silence.

'He'll only hurt you,' Flynn blurted out. 'He might say he loves you, that he's left his wife, but he's cheated before and he'll do it again.'

Meg just sat there, sipping her coffee, refusing point-blank to look at him.

'And even if he doesn't cheat you're going to spend your life wondering. Every time he says he's going to be late, every time there's a wrong number on the telephone you'll work yourself up into a frenzy wondering if this is it.'

'And you sat outside all night to tell me this?'

'Yes,' Flynn said simply. 'After the church I went around to your parents'. They were all a bit upset. Your mum wanted to march around and talk some sense into you, but I said I'd do it. I've been up to your door countless times in the night—half of me wanted to break it down, to give Vince what he deserves, while the other half of me knew it would be pointless, that you have to make up your own mind, see what a loser he is for yourself.'

'But I have already. I did the day I found out he was married.' Her voice was starting to rise, a smouldering anger in her starting to ignite. 'For months now I've been telling everyone it's over—you, Mum, Kathy—yet none of you would listen. Why? Do you all think I'm so weak, so desperate that I'd take him back?'

'No.' He rose to his feet, running an exasperated hand through his hair before sitting back down again. 'No one thinks that, Meg.'

'Then why didn't anyone believe me when I said it was over?'

He stared at her for the longest time before answering. 'I guess we were all just scared.'

'Scared?' She gave a questioning, cynical laugh.

'Your mum and Kathy love you. I guess they were scared of seeing you get hurt.'

'And what about you, Flynn? Why were you scared?'

'Because I love you too.'

And though the words were sweet and beautiful Meg had heard them before.

Before he'd promptly turned around and broken her heart.

'You've already told me that, Flynn, but it didn't stop you ending it. It didn't stop you telling me that I was too suspicious and needy to merit you putting in what a relationship needs.'

'Yes,' he admitted. 'But, hell, Meg, I've never had a jealous bone in my body until now. Seeing you and Vince together, sitting in my car, thinking you were up here making love to him, I finally understood where you were coming from.'

She stared at him, unblinking. The fact that they loved each other wasn't in question here; it was how they dealt with their pasts that was tearing them apart.

'Not good enough, Flynn,' Meg finally answered, her voice unmoved. 'So you were jealous; so you finally got a taste of how I was feeling. Just what's that supposed to prove? Jealousy isn't our only problem, but you refuse to acknowledge that.'

'No, I don't.' His voice was a pale whisper. 'You were right. I'm not over Lucy. All that bull about celebrating her life, not mourning her death—all the big speeches about better to have loved and lost…' His voice trailed off and he cleared his throat before turning his eyes back to Meg. 'None of it was true, but I wasn't lying when I said it. I truly believed I was coping, that I was over her.'

Meg felt the tears well in her eyes—tears for his pain and tears for herself too. He wasn't over Lucy, she had known it in her heart, but hearing it confirmed, knowing he wasn't ready to move on, felt like the final twist of the knife.

'I'm so tired, Meg, so torn and tired. All I want to do, all I can do, is get away for a while. I rang Dr Campbell from the car this morning; he's going to give me some unpaid leave.' He gave a half-laugh but there was no humour in it. 'Somehow I doubt even he could get compassionate leave approved by Personnel two years after the event.'

'Well, they should. There's no blueprint.' Her voice was strangely high. 'People deal with these things in their own way. I know you need time, Flynn, but I don't know what you expect me to say here.' She swallowed nervously, scared of saying the wrong thing, scared of putting on too much pressure that might send him scuttling away. But if she couldn't be honest, couldn't even tell him this, then there wasn't much point.

No point at all.

'I'll wait for you.'

'Meg, you don't…' He took a step towards her but she put up her hand.

'Let me finish, Flynn.' Tears were pouring down her cheeks, but there was no hysteria in her voice, just calm tones mingled with a quiet dignity. 'I was mortified when I found out about Vince. Mortified that I could have been so fooled, so used, and mortified for what I'd done to his wife and my own family.'

'It wasn't your fault.'

'I know,' she admitted. 'But it was how I felt. And, rightly or wrongly, I was embarrassed, humiliated. But the tears I cried, the pain I felt, they weren't about Vince.

Any love I had died there and then when I found out. Do you understand that?'

There was something in her voice that told him it was imperative he did, and he nodded.

'But when you and I broke up I was devastated. Not for anyone else, not over what people might think—I was devastated for us. For you and for me. And if you can understand that, then you'll know why I'm prepared to wait. Maybe you'll come back a different person—maybe I won't fit into your picture any more. And if that's the case then all you have to do is say so. I'll survive. I'll just carry right on. But if you do come back, and if you do still love me, then I'll be right here waiting.'

'Can I talk now?' Flynn's voice had all of its usual flip assurance, but the tears in his eyes told her he was moved. She sat down, the emotion of her speech having left her drained, almost numb. Nothing more could hurt her now.

'You don't have to wait for me, Meg. You don't have to wait for me because I'm not going anywhere without you.' He sat beside her and took her trembling hand as hope flickered on her face. 'I *can't* go anywhere without you. We've both been to hell and back, and we're both coming out of it, but we're coming out of it together. We're going to disappear for a month and lie on a beach in the day and hold each other at night. I want to grieve for Lucy, and I'm ready to do it now, but I want you beside me, Meg.' He took her in his arms then. 'I can't do this without you. Does that sound strange?'

She didn't answer with words. The tiny shake of her head against his chest told him she understood.

'When you were in my office, when you asked me why I came back to Emergency, it made me realise that I didn't even know what the hell I was doing there. What it was I was trying to prove.'

'You're not going to leave too?' She half-laughed, half-sobbed.

'No,' Flynn said slowly. 'Because even though it hurts like hell, even though it's sometimes the last place I want to be, it's still the best job in the world. And I know that deep down in there…' He tapped gently at her chest as he kissed the top of her head. 'Deep down in there, you love it too. Don't hand in your notice, Meg,' he whispered. 'Not yet. You need a break, a rest, and then, if you're still feeling the same when we come back, go for it—move on without a backward glance. But don't throw your career away just yet. You're tired and you're burnt out, but you're still a wonderful nurse.'

'I don't really want to leave,' Meg admitted. 'But I can't go on doing it feeling like this.'

'Those days are gone now, Meg,' Flynn said, his voice trembling with emotion. 'You're never going to be crying in the car on your way home from work again because there'll be no need. You'll be coming home to me.'

She closed her eyes, revelling in the soft caress of his words, the glimpse of the future with Flynn beside her.

'We can't promise each other that we're going to make everything all right, can't promise that we're going to take away all the pain. But we can be there for each other, and surely that can only make things better?'

Her kiss was his answer, and hot salty tears were

mingling, uniting, as they held each other close. 'I'd marry you tomorrow if it wouldn't steal Kathy's thunder.'

Meg laughed, but he noticed she was chewing her lip nervously.

'What? Come on, Meg, you can't not tell me.'

Meg pulled away. 'Flynn, about going on holiday… There's nothing I want more than to go away with you, but I don't think I can. I know you'll think I'm silly. It's just…'

'Just what?'

Meg swallowed. 'Mum would have a fit if I told her I was going on holiday with you—with any man, come to that.'

'But you're twenty-eight, for heaven's sake.' There was a humorous glint in his eye but Meg was too worked up to notice.

'I know, but it's just the way she is. I wouldn't expect you to understand. I just can't hurt her like that.'

'I think you underestimate your mum.'

'Believe me, I don't,' Meg muttered.

'Oh, yes, you do.' He popped a kiss on her nose. 'I've already asked her, and she's fine with it.'

Meg's jaw dropped to the floor. 'You never did?'

'I did.' Flynn grinned, then winced dramatically. 'A slight exaggeration—she wasn't exactly fine, but she soon came around.'

'How?'

'Are you busy today?'

'Impossibly,' Meg said, bemused. 'I've got to pick up Aunt Morag, my cousins, do some shopping…' she glanced up at Audrey, smiling demurely from the mantelpiece '…pluck my eyebrows.'

'Well, add "Buy an engagement ring" to your list,' Flynn said blithely, but there was a small muscle flickering in his cheek. 'Because if there's not a ring on your finger by the wedding tomorrow then the deal's off. According to your mother it had better be a ring that can be seen from the back rows of the church.'

'She never said that.' Meg laughed.

'And plenty more besides.' Taking her hands, he stood her up. 'Come on, we'd better get a move on.'

Though Meg couldn't wipe the smile off her face, she wondered how Flynn could even think about shopping at a time like this! 'I'd better get dressed first.'

His fingers were toying with her crop top. 'You'd better, hadn't you?' He gave a dramatic sigh. 'And if we're going to have any hope of getting things done today I guess I'll just have to give you a hand.'

Aunt Morag, her hair, her eyebrows—they didn't even merit a thought as he slithered the top over Meg's head.

Flynn was beside her now.

They'd get there in the end.

[illegible] from the [illegible]
[illegible]

[illegible]

[illegible]

[illegible] from the [illegible]

[illegible]

[illegible]

Though [illegible] the [illegible]

[illegible] this. [illegible]

[illegible] You [illegible] And it [illegible]

[illegible]

[illegible] was beside her now.

[illegible] in the end.

Celebrating Our Authors

MORE ABOUT THE BOOKS

MORE ABOUT THE AUTHOR

WE RECOMMEND

INSPIRATION FOR WRITING
Carol Marinelli on *One Magical Christmas* and *Emergency at Bayside*

I also write for Mills & Boon® Modern™ and the inspiration for *One Magical Christmas* came from one of the secondary characters in a Modern™ romance, *Hired: the Italian's Convenient Mistress* – while writing that I always had a loose idea that one of the sub-characters would appear in a later book. I met with my editor when I came over to the UK and we discussed writing a Christmassy story for Medical™ romance and I instantly knew I wanted to use that character for this book.

I definitely felt the germ of an idea taking place. There was a big tragedy in *Hired: the Italian's Convenient Mistress* (I am trying not to spoil the story for you all!) and I wondered if I could take that tragedy and visit it from the doctors' and nurses' point of view…

The day I started to write it, I immediately conjured up Imogen. She had fine red hair, pale blue eyes, was a little overweight and painfully shy. But she was also the wisest, nicest person – *so* lovely deep down. I had to chop a lot of my writing (long before it saw an editor) because, as I tried to control this story, it wrote itself and my big arguments and dramas, that I usually do readily, just didn't work for her character. She was gentle and nice (the opposite of me!) and at one point I can remember staring at my computer because at that moment the hero should have been so angry with her and I wanted them to have a huge stonk-

"... I get tired of hearing about that "formula" by which Mills & Boon® romances are written. I'd kill for a formula, it would mean that I'd be in bed a lot earlier!"

ing row, and yet he just held her. He pulled her in his arms and cuddled her. I paced up and down for about half an hour before I realised that that was exactly what Imogen needed!

I get tired of hearing about that "formula" by which Mills & Boon® romances are written. I'd kill for a formula, it would mean that I'd be in bed a lot earlier! I chewed my nails for Imogen and I felt sick when I sent the manuscript in – I just wanted my editor to love Imogen as much as I did.

I'm thrilled *Emergency at Bayside* is out there again. I loved this story. Initially I had written the heroine's sister as the main character – except it didn't work, she just fell in love. There was no conflict, she was just blissfully happy! So it sat in my slush pile for years. Later, her sister's story emerged in my mind – and Meg was born. We enter Meg's life when everything is falling apart and no matter how fast she juggles something eventually has to give. I think this story had been sitting in my head for years, because when I actually sat down and typed, it just flew – I had no idea what would happen next, but I knew I needed to find Meg her happy ever after!

AUTHOR BIOGRAPHY

My mum and dad were from Scotland. My dad joined the Metropolitan Police and moved to Islington in London where I was born. Then we moved to Middlesex – now Greater London – I'm already confused so you can be too. I was the middle one of three girls and the song *Our House* by Madness can reduce me to tears at the intro – it was our house and it was loud and fun and busy. I did my nursing training, then moved up to the Midlands. I loved my job, loved the guys and gals, but never settled. I went to Australia for a year and am still here – fifteen years and three children later.

My dad's sudden death stunned me – it changed me, not overnight, but it changed every cell of me. At some level I realised how precious life is, that, as the saying goes, it isn't a dress rehearsal. It wasn't a rapid awakening; I still haven't properly worked it out. I concentrated on my writing in the year after his death and was accepted by Mills & Boon. This might sound like an ending but really it was just the beginning – I have found acceptance, as well as so many friends, through my writing. Despite a dream to earn a living solely from writing, recently I have found myself back nursing, doing a job I love and, I am proud to say, a job I am very good at.

I have my own "Our House" now. Every morning I wake the kids, or they wake me and we grin, or moan, or try to find a pen…every day they make me laugh, they just infuse me with their energy, ideas and humour and I never want to put a damper on it. The reason for having kids, I have decided, is that they get your jokes – with one look, with one smirk, my daughter can reduce me to tears of laughter. My mum comes over to visit me in Australia regularly, my older sister is coming in September and I just spoke to my little sister for an hour on the phone. I was back in the UK last year and am hoping to be back again soon.

"…The reason for having kids, I have decided, is that they get your jokes – with one look, with one smirk, my daughter can reduce me to tears of laughter…."

CAROL MARINELLI ON WRITING

What do you love most about being a writer?

Something I wasn't counting on when I signed my first contract – the friendship. I can remember talking to an editor about revisions and just starting to laugh (not too manically I hope) because for the first time ever I was able to discuss the plots and characters with someone who understood. From there it grew. Lunches, annual conferences, cyber friends, and just the relief of finally, for the first time, fitting in – with a group of people who accepted me – neuroses and all – as I accept them.

Where do you go for inspiration?

It varies. The airport, a café, anywhere really – I was in England in September and since then all my books have either been based there or had an English hero. When I really need to get away and concentrate, I go to a guest house – it is about a fifteen-minute drive from me, but it is like another world. The lady who runs it is lovely and it is a real labour of love for her. I rang around to find my ideal place and I was lucky enough to find her. She has this little loft in her fabulous garden and I am never disturbed. There is a card welcoming me, wishing me productive writing time, then I lock myself away for two or three days and eat all the lovely food she has left me. It is normally used for honeymooners – just this utter retreat! I have to pinch myself sometimes, I'm so lucky to have found it.

Where do your characters come from and do they ever surprise you as you write?

My characters just appear and they always surprise me as I write. I don't plot at all, the best way I can describe it is like watching a movie and trying to type up what I see. Sometimes I have a very clear picture (bliss), other times it's grainy and not quite ready to be written.

Do you have a favourite character that you've created and what is it that you like about that character?

There are two, no, three. Levander Kolovsky, my Russian hero, and then his brother Iosef – they were just so sexy, so, so sexy it's almost criminal I won't meet them in real life. And, even though you will think I am just saying it, Imogen, my heroine in *One Magical Christmas,* was so special. I could see her so closely, especially when she was standing in the car park and there was snow on her eyelashes… I was terrified about getting revisions because I didn't know how to change her. I didn't want to change her. When my editor rang and said she loved the book, I actually burst out crying, I really wanted someone to love Imogen as much as I did.

"…My characters just appear and they always surprise me as I write…"

When did you start writing?

I started trying to write my first Medical™ romance when I was training, so around nineteen years old. It was a hobby really, something I did to relax some evenings, and it sort of grew from there.

What one piece of advice would you give to a writer wanting to start a career?

Write.

It is so hard to justify the time when life is busy, especially when you don't know if your work will ever be published, but that is the nature of the job. Even when you have been published there are no guarantees, so finding time to write, even a little bit each day, is important. I used to get up very early to write before I was published and I also put my kids into crèche one morning a week and used it as my writing time. It felt selfish, but I knew I had to make the time.

What are you currently working on?

I have just finished the first draft of what I hope will be my next Modern™ romance.

Could you tell us about your future projects?

I am hoping to go back to my "Russians" and explore the Kolovsky family some more. I really enjoyed writing them. I am also working on a different type of book – I have no idea if it will ever see the light of day. I am writing it in longhand in bed at night – and it's starting to get to the stage where I might just have to sit down at the computer, type it up and see if it's got legs!

A DAY IN THE LIFE OF CAROL MARINELLI

I don't have a typical day. Having a typical day is one of my ambitions. I try to go to the library to write for four hours a day, Monday to Friday. There I am free from e-mails and a pulsating laundry basket and gorgeous friends who drop in for coffee (please don't stop).

Today is typically non-typical. I am very near the end of a Modern™ – there is something missing from the plot and I can't see it, but I know it's almost there. I couldn't sleep at all last night as I know I am meeting writing friends for lunch tomorrow and, as they would understand, I really feel I ought to cancel and spend that time writing. So I got up very early, reading through my draft and still not able to make sense. It was a rather distracted mum who took the kids to school this morning (I probably mixed up their sandwiches and forgot to wave to people). I hid my car in the garage and tried for a couple of hours to make it work. In the meantime the postman arrived with some proofs that need to be checked and corrected.

"...I try to go to the library to write for four hours a day, Monday to Friday. There I am free from e-mails and a pulsating laundry basket..."

With a bit of a headache I drove to lunch, sat down and then remembered the reason I don't miss our monthly lunches. It is just so nice to relax, to dress up, to get out and meet your friends – and to talk! To just pause for a moment and love the life you've got. I drove home smiling, spoke to myself all the way, sorted out my plot and picked up the children from school. Teeny bit of road rage from an angry dad in the playground because I refused to reverse when he was going the wrong way in a one-way system and, where once I would have burst into tears, instead

I looked him in the eye and said something good romance writers don't say!

OK, homework, signing forms, dinner, final of *Big Brother*, bed, and now can I please get to my resolved plot. Not yet – once I've written this and done my proofs, tomorrow I will be lining up before the library opens and hopefully my next Modern™ will be born.

I love my job.

Every mad minute of it!

If you enjoyed *One Magical Christmas* we know you'll love…

The Greek Doctor's New-Year Baby
by Kate Hardy

New year, new father

Madison Gregory's temporary new boss, obstetric consultant Theo Petrakis, has everything – gorgeous body, gorgeous mind, gorgeous heart. He's a great doctor and he can cook! She knows he's the one, even if she won't admit it. There is just one problem – he has vowed never to marry or have children. However much he wants Madison, he knows it wouldn't be right to have a relationship with her when he can't fulfil her dreams.

Yet Theo's behaviour just doesn't add up. He behaves as if he loves her, he just doesn't say it, and he adores kids, so why doesn't he want any of his own? Then, just as Madison discovers the reason, she also discovers she is pregnant with his child…

THE LONDON VICTORIA
These city doctors are ready to wed!

Coming next month from Mills & Boon® Medical™ romance

English Doctor, Italian Bride
by Carol Marinelli

Honourable English doctor, fiery Italian nurse

Six years ago English consultant Hugh Armstrong was welcomed into the Azetti family when he was far from home – and unwittingly stole the heart of their youngest daughter, Bonny. Their passion culminated in one earth-shattering kiss. Hugh, realising that taking her was no way to repay the family's kindness, retreated quickly back to England.

Now Hugh has returned to Australia, and not only is he the heart-throb of the emergency department, he is also nurse Bonny's boss. She seems more out of bounds than ever, but his desire to help Bonny through her father's illness only makes their bond and their passion stronger. It also gives Hugh the courage to step out of line for the beautiful woman who has captured his heart – and finally make her his, once and for all!

Coming from Mills & Boon® Medical™ romance in March 2009

100th Birthday Prize Draw!

£500 worth of prizes to be won every month. Now that's worth celebrating!

To enter, simply visit **www.millsandboon.co.uk**, click through to the prize draw entry page and quote promotional code **CEN08DC12**

Alternatively, complete the entry form below and send to:
Mills & Boon® 100th Birthday Prize Draw
PO Box 676, Richmond, Surrey, TW9 1WU

Mills & Boon® 100th Birthday Prize Draw (CEN08DC12)

Name: ______________________________

Address: ______________________________

Post Code: ______________________________

Daytime Telephone No: ______________________________

E-mail Address: ______________________________

❑ I have read the terms and conditions (please tick this box before entering).

❑ Please tick here if you do not wish to receive special offers from Harlequin Mills & Boon Ltd.

Closing date for entries is 15th January 2009

Terms & Conditions

1. Draw open to UK and Eire residents aged 18 and over. No purchase necessary. One entry per household per prize draw only. 2. Prizes are non-transferable and no cash alternatives will be offered. 3. All prizes are subject to availability. Should any prize be unavailable, a prize of similar value will be substituted. 4. Employees and immediate family members of Harlequin Mills & Boon Ltd are not eligible to enter. 5. Prize winners will be randomly selected from the eligible entries received. No correspondence will be entered into and no entry returned. 6. To be eligible, all entries must be received by 15th January 2009. 7. Prize winner notification will be made by e-mail or letter no later than 15 days after the deadline for entry. 8. No responsibility can be accepted for entries that are lost, delayed or damaged. Proof of postage cannot be accepted as proof of delivery. 9. If any winner notification or prize is returned as undeliverable, an alternative winner will be drawn from eligible entries. 10. Names of competition winners are available on request. 11. See www.millsandboon.co.uk for full terms and conditions.

0109/10/MB190

A mistress should be at his command… At his pleasure… And in his bed!

But these tempting beauties will make these three tycoons break *all* their rules!

Available 19th December 2008

Wedded at his decree… Pleasured in his bed… Taken for his revenge!

But these three commanding Mediterranean billionaires may just have met their match!

Available 2nd January 2009

www.millsandboon.co.uk

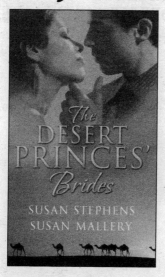